WINE KILLER

William Edgerton

For Red
Enjoy good wine in
good health!
Bill Edgerton

This book is a work of fiction. Names, places, characters, and incidents either are products of the author's imagination or are used fictitiously, except that all towns and cities mentioned do exist in Connecticut, and the two restaurants mentioned do exist and have given permission for their inclusion.

Copyright © 2011 by William Edgerton

ISBN: 978-0-9834938-0-8

Published by:

Halsey Press
PO Box 1007
Darien, CT 06820

Cover art: SandyGarnett.com

Visit us at www.halseypress.com

For Ann and Annie

"There are two ways of spreading light;
to be the candle, or the mirror that reflects it."

Andreas Vesalius, Flemish anatomist (1514-1564)

CHAPTER ONE

Greenwich, Connecticut, October 20, 2003

The cellar was vast, stretching more than 150 feet beneath the length of the house. Its two aisles were carpeted in plush crimson broadloom, above which towered multiple rows of beautifully crafted mahogany wine racks softly illuminated by state-of-the-art heatless lighting. These racks held sixteen thousand single bottles of wine perfectly aligned in individual bins, as well as thousands of other bottles in unopened wooden cases stacked along one wall.

A body lay face down in the aisle at the end of the room farthest from the entrance. Its splayed limbs were cocked at angles that would have been painful for a living man. The expression in the still-open eyes underscored the impression that the last moments of life had come as a surprise.

An opened bottle of wine lay on its side on the floor next to the man's outstretched right hand. More than half of the bottle's contents had been spilled out and wicked away, absorbed by the carpet to form a dark, irregular stain. Wine also discolored the dead man's bright white Hathaway shirt and navy repeating-pattern tie. An unbroken glass lay on its side about six inches from the left hand. The label showed the wine to be a 1990 Vin Santo produced by Giovelli, a respected Tuscan grower. It was a luscious, sweet dessert wine, and its fragrance of raisins and almonds permeated the cellar, overpowering even the vision of death.

Mitchell Livingston III had spent years developing a palate on which few subtleties were lost. The sensitivity of that palate was both deep and broad, even legendary, among local wine lovers. Friends and acquaintances around Greenwich had often described Livingston as a *bon vivant*,

1

and all who knew him well meant it as a compliment. He was an exceptionally generous man, hosting special tastings for friends, and could always be counted on to provide one or more valuable bottles for any local charity auction. All of his good friends and a surprising number of acquaintances could credit Livingston with introducing them to unusual wines and vintages they had come to treasure.

Now he was spectacularly and unexpectedly dead. The police and other experts who came to this house after Livingston's death would have a hard time finding signs that such an event was imminent. Livingston had spent the day at his Manhattan-based investment banking business, worked out at his midtown gym, and returned home to Connecticut in the evening to host a dinner for six friends. The friends were waiting upstairs with Darleen Livingston, Mitchell's second wife, an attractive blonde with traces of East Tennessee in her accent.

It was a TV crime drama set-up—the wealthy sixty-something man dies, leaving an ornamental younger wife behind to grieve and spend his money. This was not lost on Greenwich Chief of Detectives David Riley, but he'd kept his imagination in check as he interviewed the widow and her friends. Although he knew of both Mr. and Mrs. Livingston, his cynicism was pushed into the background, as he had been impressed with both her beauty and her expression of raw incomprehension when she realized that her husband would never return from his trip to the wine cellar.

At present, Riley was standing silently in the Livingston's cellar, just outside the entrance to the carpeted wine room, watching associates perform a series of tasks he could never view as routine. He was unhappy with the circumstances of this nascent investigation, as was evident in the glare he directed at rookie detective Chris Kavanagh.

Riley was dark-haired, with intense blue eyes, thick, straight eyebrows, and the compact musculature of a bull mastiff. This made even his abstract frowns seem menacing. The expression on his face now was far from abstract as he confronted the junior officer who had carried a Styrofoam cup of coffee into the cellar.

"Take that goddamn coffee outside, dump it and put the empty cup in your car," he growled. "Haven't you figured out yet that this may be a crime scene?"

Detective Kavanagh flinched. Before Riley finished the sentence, he was already on his way to dispose of the evidence of his ineptitude. Though he was unhappy with the reprimand, he knew damn well he deserved it. The chief had joined the force long after the much-publicized 1975 murder of teenager Martha Moxley, when the Greenwich Police Department had received strong criticism for mishandling the ensuing investigation.

Some twenty-nine years later, the entire department was still smarting from criticism about their treatment of the Moxley investigation. It had made them acutely sensitive about procedural matters and was referred to in every training class. Kavanagh mentally kicked himself for the rookie mistake.

He was on his way up the stairs when Riley spoke again. "Kavanagh, wait a minute. You just got here. The scene has already been photographed and the paramedics and medical examiner have come and gone. I'm expecting an expert consultant, who is en route. When he gets here, bring him straight down. Got it?"

"Yes, sir. Got it." He hesitated. "A consultant?"

Riley's expressive brows shot upward. "Jake Halsey. You have an opinion about that?"

Kavanagh did have an opinion, as it happened, but didn't hang around to express it. He took the stairs two at a time and hustled out of the house as fast as he could without spilling the coffee. He was heading for his unit near the garage when a uniformed patrolman stationed in the driveway saw him and flashed him an eye-roll.

"Hey, Kav, check this out."

He turned to see a distinctive car come up the driveway. It was obviously an antique—large and round-backed and painted in the dark, iridescent shades of a beetle's shell. A series of ornamental oval portholes along the edge of the long hood identified it as a Buick.

"What the hell is that?" Kavanagh asked. "The Buick Cockroach?"

The uniform chuckled. "God knows. Can't figure what Sherlock Halsey sees in those buckets he collects." He glanced sideways at Kavanagh. "Don't tell him I called him. . . ."

"Wouldn't think of it." Kavanagh hurried to get rid of the offensive coffee cup as the Buick pulled in among the various blue-and-whites and unmarked police vehicles. By the time he'd returned to the driveway a tall man had unfolded himself from the driver's seat.

The patrolman watched, shaking his head. "Good luck, kid," he said to Kavanagh. "Thought this time they'd leave detecting to the pros."

The patrolman looked to Kavanagh for some affirmation of his skepticism, but Kavanagh did not seem to share the sentiment. Rookie or not, he'd been with the force long enough to see Jake Halsey deliver the goods on more than one occasion, and he'd heard stories about Halsey's success from a number of career detectives, though, oddly none came from Riley, the man who knew Halsey best.

Several years before, Riley had asked the chief if he could use a civilian to help solve a crime. The answer was short and sweet, "If he screws up, it's your ass on the line."

Jake Halsey walked past the patrolman and Kavanagh at a crisp pace. He offered a subtle but perceptible nod of recognition to Kavanagh. Halsey was, among other things, a wine lover. His father had been in the wine business, and Jake had collected eight thousand bottles, as well as retaining a small interest in a Napa winery he'd acquired a few years before. Riley had called Jake because he thought his friend might be able to provide useful information about the wine found near Livingston's body and also assess whether anything about the wine or the cellar might have contributed to the man's death.

Riley looked up as Jake strode toward him up one of the maroon aisles. Halsey had on a pair of old jeans and a black nylon windbreaker and stood out from the police personnel. He was a lean six-foot two, with dirty blond hair and an outdoorsman's focused, unflinching gaze.

Ellen Green, a plainclothes detective from Riley's team, was kneeling down to check the carpet edge. On Halsey's approach, she stood to make room for him in the narrow space, offering a restrained smile as she placed her evidence in a bag and sealed it, completing the evidence collection phase around the body.

"Hey, Dave, Ellen," said Halsey, by way of greeting. Then, taking in the body on the floor, his face grew more serious. "What happened?" he asked. "I could smell the wine all the way down the stairs."

Riley shook his head. "We don't know yet. It's doubtful that it was natural causes, so we're treating it as a possible homicide. This was Mitchell Livingston III. Successful businessman . . . had his own investment firm down in midtown. Know him at all?"

"I've heard his name around town. Might have run across him at a wine tasting, but I'm sure we've never spoken."

"Straight shooter, by all accounts. His wife tells us he was given a clean bill of health when he had a physical two weeks ago. Problem is, there's no wound or any other indication of violence. Since he came down here to get a bottle of wine and since you know a lot about wine, I thought you might come up with something we missed."

"Tell me what happened," Jake said.

"Livingston and his wife, Darleen, were entertaining six friends for dinner," Riley responded. "When it was time for the pecan tart, he headed down here for a bottle of dessert wine. I gather the discussion upstairs was pretty animated, and they went on talking for quite a while until somebody realized twenty minutes had gone by. Mrs. Livingston came down to look for her husband and found him." He gestured at the awkwardly arranged corpse.

"Apparently, she let out a scream, and one of the guests came down to see what was wrong. The guest"—here Riley referred to his notes—"Stanton Walsh, called 911, more for Darleen than for Mitchell, who seemed to be beyond help. The EMTs gave Mrs. Livingston a mild sedative. She was already pretty groggy when our guys arrived, but she did tell us that her husband was in the habit of opening and tasting his wine before serving it to weed out any bad bottles. That's the only thing we've got to go on.

"Our first man on the scene found nothing suspicious and thought this looked like a natural death. But, wanting to play it safe, he called me and I called in the chief. We agreed it looked like a heart attack, but we'll keep the house sealed off until we know for sure. The medical examiner also thought it looked natural, but wants an autopsy. Right now our guys are interviewing the family and friends and checking for any past calls about domestic violence."

Jake winced at this reference. Rapidly enough, he hoped, that nobody had noticed. *That's one more reason I could never be on the force for real,* he thought. *Look a killer in the eye and stay calm? I'd be OK with that, I'm pretty sure. But who knows until the time comes.*

He refocused his thoughts and stepped over to the body to give the area a closer look. A cork lay in a tray on the wine rack next to a squeeze-action corkscrew of a type that withdrew the cork by grabbing its sides without puncturing it. He examined these items as closely as he could without touching them, then knelt to check the body, bottle, and glass.

"Uniforms manage to keep from drop-kicking anything here?" Jake was looking toward Detective Green as he said this, but Riley knew it was meant for him.

"Kavanagh seemed to mistake the place for a Starbucks. Otherwise, complete professionalism all around."

After a moment, Jake stood. "At first glance the label, cork, and capsule look just as they should. I'm familiar enough with that wine to tell you that it smells like it ought to, and the brownish-yellow color of what's left in the glass is right. So, if something in the wine is what caused Livingston's death, you'll have to find that out from a lab." His gaze on Riley's face, he added, "Which is not to say there's nothing there. Just that it's not immediately evident."

"There is a smell of almonds," commented Green.

"Yeah, but that's part and parcel of this particular variety. Which, I guess, would make it a good candidate for hiding cyanide."

Green grimaced. "If only it could be that easy."

"Notice anything about the body itself?" Riley asked.

Halsey glanced at the deceased, frowning. "The light in here isn't great, but his skin seems almost gray."

"Yes," Riley said. "That was our impression, too. When we're finished here, we'll pack up the bottle with what's left of the wine, along with the cork and glass, and take that and the remaining five bottles of this stuff for the lab. We'll also be looking at what's left of everybody's dinner. If Livingston used a cocktail glass before the meal, we'll pick that up as well."

"Take the capsule, too," said Jake, indicating the piece of metal that had been slit away from the top of the bottle.

"Will do," said Riley. "I'll give you a call as soon as I see the lab report."

Jake Halsey returned to his car unescorted. Dave had said nothing to him in parting, but he understood his friend's expression.

Responding to sudden death was the most burdensome job Jake could imagine, and he had enormous respect for anyone who had to take it on. Unlike the mythical English detective to whom a few cops clumsily compared him, Jake felt no anticipation, no sense that "the game is afoot." Nothing about this was a game.

Jake concluded that the only possible consolation for

Dave Riley was that, in this instance, no one would have to deliver the news to Livingston's widow.

CHAPTER TWO

Jake Halsey and Dave Riley had grown up together in Greenwich—Riley in the partially blue-collar Byram section on the western end of town, Halsey in a wealthier neighborhood bordering Cos Cob. They had both been three-letter athletes in high school: Halsey in baseball, basketball, and soccer; Riley in baseball, wrestling, and football. Each spring their paths crossed on the diamond, where the lanky Halsey, who reached base surprisingly often for a pitcher, was accorded a non-traditional lineup position. Riley, Greenwich High's feisty shortstop and cleanup hitter, had batted his teammate in more times than either could count.

In those days, a regimen of daily laps around the school track and longer mandated runs through the city's parks was bearable only with a running partner. Jake and Dave had soon discovered that they were ideal workout companions—both serious about staying in shape, both comfortable with long periods of silence. When they did chat, they discovered, to their mutual surprise, that they had a great deal in common. Both were interested in machinery and in discovering what made things work. Both were inordinately fond of detective fiction. And both were fascinated by—and immensely successful with—the opposite sex.

They shared adventures and they shared dreams, cementing a friendship they knew neither years nor distance would alter.

After graduating from Yale, Jake finally answered the call of the West, pursuing an MBA at Stanford, then working in a startup technology firm in San Francisco. This had led, through a logic Dave had yet to decode, to a reserve enlistment in the Air Force. It took a pretty long leap of imagination to see his old friend wearing olive drab, but

9

seeing Jake learn to fly was no stretch at all. Planes had long been the only thing that could draw his attention away from girls.

He resumed civilian life after a couple of years, newly knowledgeable about aircraft, avionics, and several other things, his own resistance to military discipline among them. He found a more natural home in the Silicon Valley amid the information technology boom of the 1990s. Riley heard from him less frequently during those days, but they made a handful of enjoyable pilgrimages to each other's coasts, including a wedding each.

And then, for a time, Riley didn't hear from Jake at all.

Jake had returned to live in Greenwich only the previous year under difficult conditions. Riley had been the first friend Jake had looked up on his return, and the detective had observed an unusual gravitas in his old friend's bearing. Jake described the circumstances surrounding his return in less than a dozen words, and Riley was too good a friend to press for more.

Their friendship had taken on a professional dimension when a sports bar conversation uncovered an area of expertise Riley hadn't been aware Halsey possessed. Halsey's San Francisco-based software firm, he'd discovered, had developed and marketed software to aid in police investigations; software that the Greenwich PD had put to occasional use. More than that, Dave Riley quickly found his friend's expertise and knowledge of police investigatory procedure, combined with his native intelligence and problem-solving skills, made him an asset to the department.

Jake's first case as a consultant had involved the death of a popular operatic soprano, a death initially regarded as an accidental electrocution during a performance in a private home. Halsey understood enough about electronics to know how unlikely the woman's exposure to lethal voltage would have been in that setting. His reconstruction of the incident, coupled with some patient documentation work by Riley's Criminal Investigations staff, had married method to motive and led to a conviction. Halsey had found the work intriguing, and Riley was impressed with the particular skill set his friend brought to solving problems.

The chief of police had surprised Riley—and others in the department—by approving an arrangement to involve Halsey as a civilian expert in certain investigations, unpaid and not uniformed. Suspicious deaths were rare in Greenwich, maybe one every other year or so, but the small Violent Crimes Division was glad to have occasional help.

No one on the Greenwich force had worked with anyone like Halsey before, either. Detached from departmental procedures and politics, he could analyze patterns of evidence as if they were black box systems. No matter how disorderly the inputs, Jake had been indispensable in helping the department secure several convictions and several more unexpected exonerations.

His unofficial and unpaid status rankled some officers, particularly a few in the Uniformed Services Division who trusted no one wearing anything but blue, the long-timers who used "civilian" and "potential suspect" as interchangeable terms. Still, begrudgingly or otherwise, Jake got points from both beat cops and brass for getting results. The detectives under Riley's supervision had come to regard him as one of the team. This didn't mean that any of them, except for Chief Riley himself, would claim to know him well.

Detective Green had a nickname for Halsey that she never spoke out loud. Like other female officers, and nearly every other woman who came in contact with him, she had wondered about his personal life—not checking him out on her own behalf, she was quick to remind herself, but out of habitual curiosity. Green was the department's psychological profiling specialist, accustomed to speculating about everyone. A direct question to Riley, however, had elicited nothing but the blankest of stares. She knew the chief well enough not to ask again.

With a teenage daughter going through an extended comic book phase, and a few vintage issues of *Batman* consequently strewn around her living room, Green couldn't help but think of Halsey as *The Somewhat Darker Knight.*

CHAPTER THREE

Jake's phone rang early Monday morning, three days after Livingston's death.

"Jake," Dave Riley said without preamble, "we just got the Livingston lab report. The wine in that open bottle was riddled with cyanide. I'd appreciate it if you could come down to police headquarters."

Jake looked at his watch—a little after seven. "Now? I'm not through my first cup of coffee."

Dave chuckled. "I'll put you on retainer if you can suck down that caffeine fix and be here in fifteen minutes."

"A retainer? I come cheap."

Dave laughed outright at that. "See you in fifteen?"

"Hey, with an incentive like that, you bet."

Two minutes later, Jake pulled his dark metallic blue Renault Laguna out of the driveway and balanced his freshly topped-off travel mug of coffee on the passenger seat. On his way downtown he started running through his mental files for some facts on how cyanide killed people.

Biologically, the stuff worked at a fundamental level: it kept cells from using oxygen, hitting oxygen-hungry organs like the brain and heart hard and fast. Cyanide in his wine meant that, for a short while, Livingston would have had a nasty time of it. There is no pleasant way to die, but finding yourself unable to breathe is one of the worst. With cyanide, the only mercy is that a fatal coma, heart attack, or both come quickly.

There must have been a lot of the stuff, Jake reasoned, and it had to have been administered in one dose. Gradual poisonings did happen, sometimes pulled off by someone close to the victim, but more often, cyanide poisoning was accidental and involved people who worked around hydrogen cyanide gas. In those cases, the body and breath would evidence the famous bitter almond aroma. Jake hadn't picked that up from Livingston's body when he was at the crime scene. All he'd smelled was the spilled Giovelli Vin Santo, the cellar mustiness, and early-stage decomposition. Livingston, a wine connoisseur, undoubtedly had a strong sense of taste and smell. Whoever wanted to kill him, Jake figured, probably knew that Vin Santo had an almond component.

One acute dose, in a wine with just the right characteristics to hide the distinctive odor associated with the poison. A wine of which there were six bottles in the cellar.

Even so, it seemed a bit random—even in the event all six bottles were laced with cyanide. Did the killer have some idea which wine Livingston would choose for dessert? Did one of the dinner guests ask for the Giovelli specifically? If so, was the request coincidental or intentional—how did you prove it one way or another? Come to think of it, how could the murderer be certain that Livingston would ever imbibe the poisoned wine? Or that someone else wouldn't drink it instead?

Heading south on North Street—now that was a metaphor for something—Jake noticed the thickening commuter traffic. Some morning haze was still visible among the multimillion-dollar homes. Jake sipped more coffee and directed his attention back to the subject of cyanide compounds and the possibility of an accidental exposure.

At a few degrees above room temperature, liquid cyanide, HCN, easily mixed with air and formed a gas, the same stuff the Nazis had used in their gas chambers. Accidental cyanide deaths were usually caused by exposure to that gas. Not everybody could smell it, which was why industrial exposures were hard to prevent. There was supposed to be a genetic aspect to that talent.

Jake was at the point of making a mental note to find out whether there was a test for it and ask the ME about tissue samples from Livingston, when the wine expert living in his head spoke up: *No, scratch that. There couldn't have been any gaseous HCN in the wine cellar. Too cool down there. So it had to be liquid. And intentional.*

Don't go building too many alternative scenarios on this one, Jake told himself. Remember Occam's Razor: slice away the unnecessary entities and the answer with the fewest assumptions is usually correct. Occam's Razor just about always worked. There was damn little chance this was anything but a murder.

Jake pulled into the parking lot of the Greenwich Police station, turned the engine off and glanced down at the battered watch on his wrist. This morning, his trusty Breguet indicated that it was barely eight o'clock, far too early for a man who'd been tinkering in his workshop until nearly two a.m. Nevertheless, he'd made the trip in less than ten minutes. He smiled wryly—that retainer was looking good.

Jake crossed the parking lot to the limestone-faced edifice, enjoying the crispness of a morning breeze that tossed hair into his eyes. Despite the early hour, the fall day promised to be one of a handful each year that were truly perfect: sunny, warm, and breezy, with low humidity and scattered clouds.

In Riley's office, the atmosphere was considerably darker. Riley had assembled his crime analysis team: Brian Allen, a young computer whiz who still sported the once-inevitable, now old fashioned plastic pocket protector; Ellen Green, whose brilliant smile somewhat offset her ungainly appearance; and Anthony Pezzi, a short, dark, young man with a bulldog face and receding hairline. Pezzi and Green were a true Mutt and Jeff team who had worked the good cop/bad cop routine many times.

Jake took the lone empty seat at the small conference table and afforded it a raised eyebrow. It was already littered with coffee cups and a half-filled ashtray—in defiance of local ordinances—indications of a much earlier start to the meeting.

"And I was feeling like the early bird," he said.

"Morning, Jake," Riley said, and then, indicating the carafe on his credenza, added, "Grab a coffee. You look like you need it."

"How kind."

Tony Pezzi chuckled. "Ain't he always?"

Jake had worked with Allen, Green, and Pezzi on a prior case, and although his involvement in police matters continued to be questioned by the rank and file, this group was a mutual admiration society. Even the chief of police, although nervous about Halsey's amateur status, was well aware of the contributions the civilian had made to his department. Better yet, especially considering the department budget, Halsey was willing to volunteer his time, despite the joke about a retainer.

Jake doffed his leather jacket, and deposited himself into a chair, "Okay. Fill me in."

"To start with," Riley said, "I suspected from the beginning that cyanide was involved. As you know from prior experience, a body's complexion—lividity—can be a clue to the cause of death."

Jake nodded. "Right—cherry red can mean carbon monoxide poisoning."

"But Livingston wasn't red. Blue usually indicates a coronary or other heart malfunction, and Livingston wasn't blue either. However, as you noted, he *was* ash gray, which can be an indicator of cyanide. So we set up a 'to do' list: who had access to the wine, check the wife's phone records to see if there was a boyfriend or any affairs, troublesome business deals, was this an accident and, if not, where's a motive?"

"Brian checked Livingston's wine purchase records and found an invoice for six bottles of the Giovelli Vin Santo. It was purchased at a small Manhattan wine shop, which we'll have to drop in on. Tony took statements from the Livingston guests and everybody checks out. No one went anywhere near the wine cellar that night. And no one put in a special request for Vin Santo."

"Unless it was a conspiracy," said Tony, deadpan. "You know, if he cheesed all of 'em off. Served rosé straight out of the box or something."

Riley ignored him. "Mrs. Livingston was too sedated to be much use last night so we're going to question her again today."

"Was everything normal at dinner?" Jake asked.

"Yeah, so normal it was almost boring. They talked about kids, family plans, that sort of thing. They were good friends and had plenty to talk about.

"We confirmed that it was Livingston's habit to visit the cellar when he wanted a dessert wine and to taste it first. As a matter of fact, as far as we can tell, Livingston was the only one who'd been in the cellar for more than a month, and the Giovelli Vin Santo was purchased about three weeks ago. As you know, my guys took the other bottles of the wine to the lab. I guess this case lit a fire under them. They've already determined that only the one bottle had any trace of cyanide."

Jake sat up a bit straighter. "Only one?"

Riley nodded. "Yeah. Weird, huh? If the odds were bad if only six bottles were poisoned—"

"In this case, the odds against would be astronomical," said Brian. "Livingston could have gone years without opening that particular bottle."

Ellen Green leaned back in her chair and tapped the eraser of her pencil on the table. "Unless he was a man of particular and abiding habit and someone knew it."

Riley gave her a sideways glance. "Care to enlarge on that, Ms. Profiler?"

"Some people—especially meticulous people—develop little . . . rituals, I guess you'd call them, that go with repeated activities or behaviors. Suppose he goes into the cellar every night and, to keep the game fresh, he takes tonight's wine from a particular section of a shelf so that he never grabs the same wine two times in a row. Or, he and his wife often serve pecan tarts to guests and he always chooses Vin Santo to go with them. Or, he doesn't open more than X number of bottles in a given period, or whatever. His wine rack was divided into sections, so let's say on Monday evening he goes to section one and he chooses the bottle in bin nine."

"Why nine?" asked Tony.

Ellen shot him a look. "I'm hypothesizing, Tony. Maybe, he chose... ."

"Five," said Jake.

Everybody turned to look at him.

"I noticed that the fifth slot in the section where he kept the dessert wines was empty."

Riley nodded. "Okay, let's say the murderer was someone who knew Livingston well enough to know his particular ritual, whatever that was."

"The wife might have some idea about it," Riley continued, "if wine collecting was something they did together. Tony, check that during your interview today. Has she ever seen him use any sort of methodology to choose a wine—eenie-meenie, flip a coin, whatever? Next question, gang: What are the possible points of contamination? Who could possibly have had access to this bottle, and when?"

"There are a number of possible points of contamination," said Jake. "The winery, the distribution center, the shipping firm, the retailer, and the home."

Riley thought about this for a moment, and then said, "Brian, clear your desk and get started on a list of people who had access to that lot of wine from the source to the final destination. Ellen and Tony, you have an appointment with Mrs. Livingston."

Turning back to Jake, he said, "Jake, the cork and capsule are still up at the lab. They've done the chemical sweep, but I'd appreciate it if you could go up there and look into the mechanical aspect of this. Specifically, see if you and the lab tech can discover how the lethal dose was inserted into the bottle. I'm hoping any method you discover will help us eliminate some of these possible contamination points."

Jake left immediately for the crime lab, wondering if his findings might not raise more questions than they answered. Part of him was impatient to become immersed in the physical details of the incident, to get a clearer view of Mitchell Livingston's last moments through the prism of the bottle. Part of him, a part he wouldn't overtly recognize, was relieved to have a new obsession to fill his hours, to crowd out what inevitably filled them when they lay empty too long.

CHAPTER FOUR

Upon his return, Jake reported.

"When the lab tech and I examined the capsule, I noticed it had a tiny hole in it, just visible to the naked eye."

In the soundproof silence of Dave Riley's office, Jake was hyper-aware of the four detectives hanging on his words. Even Brian had stopped taking notes, and his mouth was open as he gazed at the photographs Jake had brought back from the lab.

"If you look at this microscopic enlargement," Jake continued, "you can see that the edges of the hole are pressed downwards, which means that something was pushed in from the top of the bottle. When we flattened out the tiny flaps of metal at the edges of the hole, it appeared that the hole was made by something with a chisel point, immediately followed by a circular cross-section. Working on a hunch, I asked the lab to find a range of syringe needle sizes. Allowing for the wiggling that probably took place, the hole could easily have been made by a number eighteen needle. Luckily, since Livingston used a squeeze-action corkscrew. . . ."

"I really enjoy a little squeeze action," said Tony.

Ellen rolled her eyes.

"The cork was compressed slightly, but otherwise intact," Jake continued, affording the younger man a wry glance, "except for a vertical crease on each side from the metal prongs. The cork also had a tiny hole in it. When we twisted the cork and capsule around just so, the holes in them lined up. The number eighteen needle slid easily into the cork at a very slight angle, which probably indicates that the needle was inserted by hand and not by machine. That tells us the insertion of the poison happened post-production."

"How so?" asked Riley.

"Someone with access to the production line might have administered the poison secretly, during the random quality testing. Certain wineries occasionally test by machine to preclude contamination of a particular lot."

"It also means," Riley surmised, "that if the poison was put into the storage tanks or casks, it would have been detected during testing."

Jake nodded.

The sense of relief in the room was palpable. Jake was sure the idea that this poisoning was the random act of a rogue winery employee, who might have poisoned dozens or hundreds of other bottles, had occurred to everyone. It was something none of them had been willing to voice.

Brian Allen made a show of checking something off his list. "That excludes the winery. Mr. Giovelli can relax."

"Wow," said Tony wryly, "that narrows it down a lot. Just the distributor, the shipper, the retailer, the deceased's friends and family, dogs and cats, disgruntled parakeets . . . ."

"It's still murder," Riley said, which quieted Pezzi.

Ellen added, "And the question still remains: Was it random, or targeted?"

Riley shook his head. "Damned if I can figure out why anybody would have chosen this way to murder someone. Assuming this was an intentional act, the killer couldn't know exactly when the bottle would be opened or even who might drink it. So the timing of the resulting death couldn't have been important to the killer, which seems strange to me. He could have waited forever. And, the fact that someone besides Livingston might have been killed doesn't seem to have mattered either." Riley raked a hand through his hair. "So, who did this and why? What's the motive?"

"Depends on who the target was," said Ellen. "In this case it's not 'follow the money.' It's 'look at the wine trail.' Is there anybody on it who'd have reason to kill Mitchell Livingston or someone close to him?"

"All right," said Riley. "Let's look at the trail. Darleen Livingston said her husband was very friendly with the retailer who sold him the Giovelli, and that he had bought a lot of wine from him over the past few years." He looked to Brian, who'd researched the provenance of the wine.

"Their reputation is impeccable and they've been in business for more than twenty years," Brian told him.

"New employees?" asked Riley.

Brian shook his head. "Not in the past two years."

"The importer?"

"Same deal. Longtime business. Impeccable reputation. The owner told me that his firm had handled the last dozen vintages of this wine without any sign of tampering. All along the line, I got the same story—never any sign of tampering. Which doesn't rule it out. It just means it hasn't been noticed up until now."

Jake broke his ruminative silence. "Why did this death happen at this time? A specific reason—hatred of an individual or a type of individual—or a random act of mayhem?"

Riley's gaze was hard. "Are you relating this to the Tylenol cyanide scare from the '80s?"

"This is a bit more than a scare, but yes. So far we're assuming that only one bottle of the entire production run was tampered with. We could be wrong: Even if it happened further along the line, there could be more than one bottle involved."

"Do you think that's likely?"

"I don't know. We *do* know that none of the other bottles of Vin Santo in Livingston's cellar were poisoned. Plus none of the other grape varieties, or types of wine, would sustain a dose of cyanide without telegraphing it to a wine lover with a sensitive sense of smell. But, if Livingston was the target, how likely is it the killer would have been so casual about when he'd be killed? Or even whether?" He looked across the table at Ellen, who was shaking her head.

"Not very likely," she said. "Poisoning is usually very personal. The killer has a vested interest in making sure his victim is dead. He wants revenge; he wants closure; he wants safety. Which means, gentlemen, that we're not dealing with a. . . ." She stopped and smiled wryly. "I was going to say a normal murderer, if there is such a thing. We're not dealing with a *typical* murderer. We might be dealing with a sociopathic personality. Far from personalizing the victim, that type of murderer *de*personalizes them. They aren't people; they're ciphers, pieces on a game board."

"Pieces," repeated Jake softly.

Riley pushed himself away from the table. "Brian, start a check for any crimes—*any*—that involve tampering with wine in any way. Go back a year—no five years."

"What's my scope?" Brian asked.

"The entire state, plus other major New England or New York cities within a two-hundred-mile radius, but also check the VICAP nationwide database."

Brian cocked an eyebrow. "There are 169 towns in Connecticut alone."

"If Ellen is right about the type of personality we're dealing with, he might have struck just about anywhere."

"Or," offered Ellen, "it could be his first and only crime."

"Let's hope so," Riley said, but Jake could tell from the expression on his face he didn't think so.

Dave Riley's hope ebbed even further when Brian Allen stuck his head into his office that evening. It was late and Dave knew he should go home, but he couldn't make himself get up, put on his jacket and walk out the door. So he told himself he was waiting for just this eventuality.

Brian dropped a single printed page on his boss's desk and jammed his hands deep into his pockets. "The VICAP database wasn't much help except for a few homicides caused by wine bottles used as weapons. Out of about two dozen responses we've netted in New England, we've already got three hits. All in Connecticut."

"Three hits?" Dave repeated, picking up the page.

"Three wine-related crimes. I haven't had time to explore the motives and victims."

Dave gave the information a quick once-over and frowned. "No poisonings?"

"Nope. But it's odd, don't you think, to find even three crimes related specifically to wine in the same small area?"

Dave stabbed a finger at an item on the list. "This one is arson."

Brian scratched behind his ear and looked intrigued. Brian always looked intrigued, Dave realized, when data of any kind was involved. Crimes, to the younger detective, were mental puzzles that could be worked out by sorting and sifting data in new and clever ways.

"Yeah," Brian said, "it is. So, along with asking why someone would poison a random bottle of wine, we can be asking why someone would burn down a random wine store—and, as the police report concludes, without stealing anything in the process."

CHAPTER FIVE

At eight the following morning Jake climbed into Dave
Riley's unmarked police car and they headed for Danbury, the
scene of the wine store arson. It was a gray and overcast day,
with rain expected before nightfall. Riley drove from
downtown Greenwich up North Street and headed east on the
Merritt Parkway, then turned north onto the winding, two-lane
Route 7. Traffic was reasonably light going north, but there
was a steady stream of cars heading south during the morning
rush hour.

Watching the line of cars snaking past them, Jake thought
that not everyone was as fortunate as he had been. Most
people, he reminded himself, worked for someone else, doing
something that was far from either a calling or a dream job. He
hadn't worked for anyone else since just before his brief tour
of duty in the Air Force.

"I asked if you thought the Sox had another World Series
in 'em." Riley had brought the car to a stop at one of the
innumerable red lights along the busy road to Danbury. He
was poker-faced, except for the slight furrowing of his brows.

Lifted out of the past, Jake smiled. "Was I wool
gathering? Sorry. With all due respect to the Sox, I'd rather
get an idea of what we're going to see when we get to the
site."

"A burnt-out shell, basically. The fire happened this past
winter. Bob's Fine Wines had one of the best inventories in
the city, until a fire of suspicious origin began in the cellar and
consumed most of the building. The Fire Department report
called it arson. The building's owner, Bob Daniels, reported
that there were a lot of valuable wines in that cellar, and he
provided an inventory he'd taken home on his laptop the night
before the fire to back up his assertion. All of the wine was

destroyed by either the heat of the fire or the attempt to put it out."

"Not an insurance scam, then."

"That's unlikely. I think you'd want to empty out your valuables before you torched your shop if an insurance claim was the goal. Otherwise, what's the point? Daniels lost a lot of money, apparently. Couldn't afford to insure it all. When the cops interviewed Daniels and his employees at length they found nothing."

Jake said. "I wouldn't have thought that good wine would be found in Danbury."

"Why not?" Riley asked.

"Hat City is still pretty much on the skids, right?" Jake said. "I always thought of Danbury as one of those jinxed manufacturing cities straight out of a Springsteen song. Not to be a snob, but doesn't the place have a lot more beer drinkers than wine connoisseurs?"

"You've got your history right," Dave told him, "but things have changed since you left the East Coast. The hat factories that employed thousands are now distribution or electronics businesses employing hundreds. Over the last twenty years, the population has changed—the factory workers left, the housing prices dropped, and the commuters to Stamford or Manhattan swept in like locusts." He nodded out the driver's side window at the traffic bustling past them in the southbound lane. "Demand for upscale products like wine has skyrocketed."

"Guess I need to get out more," Jake said, flashing him a quick grin.

Riley's grin turned to a grimace as he changed the subject. "Since you bring it up, I don't want to intrude on your personal life, but . . . I sort of promised Barbara. . . ."

Here it comes, Jake thought. For the past year or so, well-intentioned friends—especially, it seemed, well-intentioned female friends—had been trying to convince him that it was time to have a new woman in his life. As if it were as simple as shopping for one. Hell, maybe with Internet dating it was. He looked at his friend knowing that, as always, he would listen with a deaf ear. He wasn't ready for another woman—and maybe never would be.

"With whom does Barbara want to fix me up?" he asked.

"Am I that obvious?" the detective countered.

"Let's just say you're that obviously uncomfortable. How about if you tell Barbara you did your duty and we leave it at that?"

"Look, it's not just Barb who wonders when you're going to—to get on with life."

"Who says I haven't?"

Dave ignored the question. "I only met Melinda a couple of times when you brought her back here, but I can tell you that it made her happy to see *you* happy. This hermit thing sure as hell wouldn't be her choice for you."

"Noted." Jake turned to look out the window. Dave Riley's concerned glance failed to connect.

Ten minutes later, Riley took the first exit and, after a few turns, pulled up in front of a burned-out building whose roof had fallen in. Even though the fire had occurred months ago, faded yellow police tape still cordoned off the building entrance, and the air of abandonment was still as strong as the smell of charred wood and smoke when Riley and Halsey approached. As prearranged, the Danbury fire chief and a local detective were waiting for them. The four men shook hands.

After introductions, Riley got to the point. "Chief, have your guys reconstructed what happened here?"

The fire chief nodded, gesturing at the gutted shop. "As you can see, this was a wood-frame building. As far as we can tell, the fire started in the basement near the electric service panel. The flames spread to the wood racking and wine cases, and from there got up into the cellar ceiling and ran through the building very rapidly. The alarm came in at 11:45 pm. By 11:55, when the first engine arrived, the building was pretty well engulfed. Naturally, with a fire that voracious, we suspected arson. The state lab tested some of the debris and found hydrocarbons." He glanced at Jake and added, "Traces of an accelerant—probably gasoline, but we're not sure. We failed to find any ignition device—probably never will find it, given the mess the fire caused. But, because of the probable use of an accelerant, we're treating this as arson. Bob Daniels, the owner, was devastated, economically and psychologically. He lost about $220,000 in wine alone and only part of that was insured, so we pretty much ruled out insurance fraud. He doesn't plan to re-open."

"We've considered this a crime scene from the time it happened," the detective added, "but without any more evidence, or motive, or any clue as to who the arsonist might have been, it's become a cold case. To be frank, more important crimes have taken up our time."

Jake nodded, understanding the logic. He walked around the burnt-out shell. When he returned to the front of the building, he faced the other men and asked, "So where *is* the motive? The real estate's not all that desirable and the loss wasn't fully insured. Assuming this fire was set, who stood to gain? This doesn't look like the work of a couple of kids playing with matches. If it is arson, someone has to have benefited in some way."

"You can see why we didn't get very far," the detective responded. "The owner is a quiet guy: pillar of the community, two kids, school-teacher wife, supports the local chamber of commerce, not an enemy in the world that we could find. A real gentleman. I'd love to help you guys, but there just isn't anything more the chief or I can tell you. Beside the fact that this was a wine store, what could possibly connect it to your murder?"

"Good question," Jake murmured, conscious of a twinge in his gut and shivering a bit as he pulled his coat closer around him against the increasing wind. He and Riley thanked the men for their time and climbed back into the police car just as the first drops of rain began to fall.

CHAPTER SIX

Fairfield, Connecticut, July 2003
     *A nondescript Chevy four-door sedan moved slowly down
Fairfield Beach Road, which paralleled the shore. The car
coasted to a stop in front of number 2021.*
     *In the 1940s and 1950s, Fairfield Beach had been lined
by simple wood-frame cottages with very few amenities, more
glorified cabanas than houses. Even the word "cottage" was
too elegant for most of them. But as waterfront property
increased in desirability and value over the rest of the century,
the tiny cottages on the beach were torn down, one by one, to
make way for larger, more stylish year-round dwellings. By
2000, few of the cottages remained and Fairfield Beach was
unremittingly upscale.*
     *The house at 2021 was no exception. It was a structure
that looked less like a beach house than a random jumble of
large wooden crates. Even the green-stained wooden siding
seemed out of place in this New England village. The few
street-facing windows were dark and there were no vehicles in
the granite paving-block driveway.*
     *A man dressed entirely in black got out of the parked
Chevy and donned a workman's orange reflective vest and a
baseball cap with an indistinct logo on the front. He carried
two pieces of electronic equipment, each in a leatherette case.
He walked around the house to the beach behind and strode
purposefully down to the water's edge. The tide was exactly
halfway in. The man knelt on the sand and from one of the
cases removed a portable altimeter that, when set to the local
atmospheric pressure, showed the number of feet above mean
sea level. Bending down to the water level, he calibrated the
barometric level of the altimeter with a precise adjustment of
its black knob. Then he walked back up the beach to the house.*

He moved to a spot below the seaward deck and made a show of opening the cover of the gas meter there. He noted that the altimeter showed the first floor approximately twelve feet above sea level. He put the altimeter back in its case, opened the other case, and removed a hand-held, global positioning system receiver. He made note of the latitude and longitude coordinates of the spot upon which he stood, then pushed a button, storing the data as a navigation waypoint. He then used the instrument's keypad to type in a name for it: target.

After closing the gas meter's metal cover, he walked casually back to the street, climbed into his car, and slowly drove off, blending at once into the beach traffic.

Three hours later, with the sun nearly set, the man in black drove down a dirt road past a private waterfront airfield about ten miles east of Port Jefferson, on the north shore of Long Island. Just out of sight of the cluster of deserted buildings and hangars, he backed into the surrounding woods near the village of Wildwood and parked his car. Opening the trunk, he peeled off his outer layer of clothing, revealing a pair of black shorts beneath. He dumped the discarded clothing into the trunk of the car, then removed a seven-cell canopy parachute and a small canvas tool bag. Hefting these, he moved to the edge of the woods and looked out across the airstrip.

Practically at the edge of the tarmac was a solitary airplane, blocked from the sight-line of the main hangar by a row of small metal storage buildings. The man in black watched the airstrip and buildings for a full minute, making sure that he was alone. Satisfied, he approached the plane as the sun disappeared below the horizon.

It was a Cessna Skylane four-seater, powered by a 230 horsepower engine and capable of flying at 155 miles per hour. The N-number identification painted on its fuselage assured him that this was the plane he'd identified in his research and expected to find. A glance through the window confirmed that the plane had not only an autopilot but also a

Garmin GNS 480 navigator. The 480 was a highly accurate digital device, capable of instructing the autopilot to fly the airplane to any pre-entered waypoint. It was accurate to within a few meters.

Using the fuselage of the plane to hide his activities, the man opened the bag and removed a selection of tools. Working methodically but with no lost motion, he removed the left door of the aircraft, placed it inside the cabin in front of the rear seats, and climbed into the cockpit. Once inside, he bent down, reached behind the instrument panel on the left side, and located the back of magneto switch, a key part of the plane's ignition system. He made the engine's two magnetos "hot" by cutting wires behind the switch. Next, he clipped two wires to the switch and let them hang down. These would permit the engine to be started without a key. He carefully set the throttle and mixture control and checked the fuel valve.

He sat back, and glanced at his watch, pleased with the speed with which he'd readied the plane for starting. He then removed a package of explosives from his canvas bag and wired its blasting cap to the inertial switch in the airplane's emergency locator transmitter, already in the plane. He momentarily smiled, knowing that, should the plane come to an abrupt stop, the ELT would send an electrical signal to the explosive device instead of the transmitter. . . with spectacular results.

The man stowed the explosive device in the glove compartment, stroked the engine primer three times, turned on the master switch, and held the ends of the two wires dangling from the ignition switch together. The engine cranked, coughed to life, and then settled smoothly into its normal idle mode. The man released the two wires, donned the parachute, tightened its straps, and belted himself into the seat.

Dusk had passed; it was nearly dark. Working by the instrument panel lights, the man set the altimeter to the field elevation and entered into the GPS the coordinates he'd recorded for the house in Fairfield. The airfield was too small to require takeoff clearance by radio, a common requirement at larger fields. Revving the engine, he taxied to the runway, ran up the engine to check its performance, and took off to the south. He climbed to 1,000 feet under radio silence and reversed direction, pointing the plane's nose toward the Fairfield shoreline twenty-three miles away. An adjustment to the plane's pitch trim, power setting, and ten degrees of flaps brought the airspeed down to 63 miles per hour, about as slow as possible without causing the plane to be unstable and a comfortable speed at which to bail out. On the instrument panel, he set the autopilot to select the GPS as its navigation data source. The plane turned slightly, responding to the setting.

When he neared Long Island's north coast at a point almost directly above where he took off, the man un-strapped his seatbelt, pre-selected an altitude of twenty-five feet into the autopilot, and set it. As the plane began its descent, he turned in his seat and placed his heels on the doorsill, waiting patiently. At the moment the plane crossed the coastline and headed out over Long Island Sound, he jumped.

Less than a minute later he was floating in the Sound, not more than twenty yards from shore. He jettisoned the parachute harness, swam to shore, and trudged up the beach to the high-water line. In the unlimited visibility of the cloudless evening, he traced the course of the plane's nav lights. It had leveled out at twenty-five feet on a compass course of 314 degrees and was headed across the dark water for Fairfield. About twenty minutes later, the plane crashed into the house at 2021 Fairfield Beach Road.

The house and plane exploded into a massive fireball that consumed, not only the dwelling, but also the irreplaceable million-dollar collection of red Burgundy kept in the wine storage room on the main floor.

Watching the fire across the water, the man in black let a small, crooked smile play momentarily at the edges of his mouth, then turned and headed back to his car.

CHAPTER SEVEN

A drink at The Ginger Man was Riley's idea. Allen, Pezzi, and Green had all politely declined: Allen because he was searching online records and would be glued to his monitor until well past midnight; Pezzi because he rarely drank and usually felt like a fifth wheel in bars; Green because she'd promised her daughter she'd be at her basketball game that evening. Jake, on the other hand, had perked up at the suggestion. He got into the Renault and followed Riley's Honda.

They found an open booth and ordered drinks. Riley, with a lifelong cop's reflexes and peripheral vision, took in the room quickly without appearing to. Jake tried to see the room the way Riley saw it: largely an unremarkable after-work crowd in their twenties and thirties, more men than women, and with a smattering of slightly broken-looking older gents. Nobody looked too likely to start trouble, although a cluster of boisterous young men gathered at the front end of the bar. They were focused on a ball game, and one was particularly noisy.

After ordering, Riley settled in the booth across from Jake. "Whatever he's on, it's probably not Giovelli Vin Santo," he said, exaggerating the pronunciation theatrically. Both men chuckled as the waitress brought their drinks: Glenfiddich single-malt for Jake, neat, and a pint of Guinness for Dave.

"What do we know about the rest of that shipment from the shop in Tribeca?" Jake asked.

"Ellen followed up on the receipts. Out of the other six bottles in the one case of Vin Santo the store had, four were credit card purchases. She talked to three of those customers, and nobody's had trouble with it. Two guys were a little hot about having their purchases traced, but Ellen's pretty good at defusing folks who get their backs up. Eventually she got 'em to understand this wasn't about them. Anyway, there was one left in the shop: no cyanide, no holes. Assuming the one that went for cash was just as clean, it all says isolated incident and puts the tampering somewhere between the time Livingston bought it and the night he opened it."

Jake considered the implications. "So . . . the car or the cellar? More likely somebody got into his cellar than his car. What's coming up on the wife?"

"Got Brian on that. She's wife number two, the former Darleen McGonigle, Miss Teenage Tennessee 1987. Not the ditz a lot of people assume, though. They met through a business connection shortly *after* his divorce in the mid-'90s. As far as Brian can reconstruct the records, she was a rising young broker in a real estate firm in Atlanta that Livingston was handling some accounts for. He was flying down there for a lot of meetings. Bodies in motion tend to collide."

"So they do." Jake's gaze drifted for a moment; he fell silent, his eyes on the TV at the head of the bar.

"You saw her briefly the night of the killing," Dave observed, pulling him back. "Get any gut feelings about her?"

"Nah, but you've seen more distraught widows than I have. She looked completely shattered—which is to say, completely normal. Everything she was going through? Let's just say it's a look that's hard to fake. What did *you* think?"

Riley paused and knocked back more of his beer. "No alarms going off with me either. She was named in the will and stood to do pretty well, but so were his kids from his first marriage. When Ellen and Tony talked with them, they didn't sound like they had any more beefs than the standard step-mom gripes. Liked her okay, actually, especially the daughter. Apparently the first Mrs. L was a real piece of work: multiple DUIs, big shopping binges in the city, nasty to the help, nasty to the kids. Bipolar, as it turned out, but refused to be medicated. Probably busted old Mitch's balls for twenty years until he'd had enough. He's the one who filed and around Livingston's crowd that's unusual. The son didn't talk a lot about this stuff, but our guys got the daughter to open up a little. She had some *Mommie Dearest* stories that would have curled Tony's hair. If he still had any."

"Have you located the ex-wife?"

"Not yet. Brian dug up a track or two, and it looks like she's out of the country. Milked Livingston for enough alimony to become an international woman of leisure." Riley put a spin on the phrase as he signaled the waitress for a second pint. "Not my business, but I'd have thought Livingston would be too sharp to marry the likes of her in the first place. Even if she's on a cruise ship entertaining diplomats in her stateroom while the killer's knocking around her ex's cellar, I'm inclined to keep her on the short list."

Jake looked thoughtfully at his drink. "She might have already used up her motivation, though. What's left to gain from having him killed? Or his wife and friends, come to think of it."

"Good point. If she's rational—strike that—if her *lawyer's* rational, she knows she's not going to be in the will. Still, I wouldn't rule out sheer venom. Seen it before. Plus, she's got two estranged adult kids, so the maternal instinct factor might be twisted up in there too. Maybe she thinks speeding up their inheritance a little might give her some traction. Or she has it in for Livingston Family Version Two enough to want to bitch it up nicely by setting the kids against the wife."

"I don't know—all this psych stuff sounds like voodoo from my side of the aisle. I'm happy to leave that to Ellen. I'm more interested in working from the tech end, like how somebody got into that cellar."

Riley shifted to one side to make room for the waitress to set down his next beer. He thanked her profusely, asked her to relay his compliments to the bartender for the shamrock skillfully drawn in its head with the last flow from the tap, and watched the foam settle for a few seconds before lifting the glass. He tipped it slightly in Halsey's direction before he drank. "Yeah, I probably ought to slow down on that part. The old chief used to tell me, 'Never let speculation get too far ahead of the forensics.'" He took another drink, a deeper one. "And I may be inclined to think the worst of *wives* these days, anyway."

"Oh?" Jake looked squarely at his old friend. "Fire when ready."

Riley shook his head. "Nah, I shouldn't burden you. . . ."

"Dave?"

"Okay, okay." He chewed his lower lip for a moment. "A couple of months ago I would have figured it was a whole lotta not much. Lately?" He paused and fumbled for words. "Lately, I can't keep telling myself that. Either Barbara's not herself these days, or she's herself and I never really knew who that was. Whatever it is, my paychecks ought to be on direct deposit to Interstate Lumber, 'cause I'm building myself a new doghouse about every other day."

Jake had met Barbara Riley only a handful of times and had found her likable and easygoing. She was a bubbly redhead with an infectious laugh and a galaxy of freckles. It was hard to imagine her morphing into the Wicked Witch of the West, but he stayed quiet and gave Dave ample time to dredge up whatever he was about to dredge up.

"You know how some people are pretty much the same before and after they get married? Some just relax a little and some pull the old Jekyll and Hyde on you. Maybe I see the worst in everybody because of my work. Hell, around here we get mostly domestic disputes. I've heard a lot more nasty marital stuff than I want to know about. That wedding ring is like a light switch for some people: it goes on and, a little while later, the good times just go off. And you never figure it's gonna happen to you."

"Nobody'd ever take the walk if they expected that."

"Right. Anyway, meet the guy who went to bed with Miss Jekyll and woke up with Mrs. Hyde. Yeah, one more."

At first Jake thought Dave was referring to his home situation; then he noticed the waitress and realized Dave was ordering another beer. He hadn't seen Riley throw them down so quickly since high school.

"Coffee for me, please," Jake said.

Two more rounds for Riley and another coffee for Jake, and by that time the situation was laid out. Riley hadn't stopped caring for the hometown girl he'd married some two decades before, but he'd spent several months on the cold side of a bed that grew steadily wider. The past three weeks he'd been on a foldout sofa in the guest room. There had been no single incident, no unpardonable offense or bloodcurdling argument, just the maddening attrition of incessant complaint and a futile inability to bridge the gap.

Three nights earlier Barbara had walked in on Riley in his basement workroom cleaning his revolver—a routine operation, but something he always did behind closed doors. Knowing how unsettling firearms were to Barbara, Riley was as careful about keeping the pistol out of sight as he was about the procedure.

Even with an exhaust fan set on max, the smell of solvent and gun oil in the room was powerful. The fan whirred loudly enough so that her footsteps on the carpeted concrete were essentially silent. Barbara had opened the door and stood unnoticed behind Dave for nearly a minute before speaking.

"If I've driven you to this, couldn't you at least do it somewhere where your children and I wouldn't find the body?" Her tone was pure ice. Riley hardly recognized his wife's voice.

He flipped around on his stool, revealing the disassembled revolver. "Barb, that's just nuts. You know I keep ammo out of the room where I clean and lube this thing. And you know damn well I'm not capable of—or you *ought* to know. You know me a lot better than. . . ." He stopped before his voice sputtered into rage. What Barb knew, or believed, was no longer something he could speak of. That she could imagine him harming himself, and abandoning her, was beyond comprehension.

A strange memory had resurfaced from his schooldays and lodged in his head: The literal meaning of Barbara in Greek was *stranger*.

"The hell of it is that she beefs about things I supposedly never do," he said, "while she's standing right there watching me do them. Or she yells about some problem that's been taken care of. And when I point that out, the yelling turns to what a monster I am for pointing that out. Or she wants things that she always knew a public servant's family wasn't likely to have, things she never had or wanted or even took seriously. I'm damned if I do, damned if I don't, and damned if I split the difference."

"You think she's going through, well . . . ."

"If you're thinking menopause, stop. Saw her ob/gyn. That's not the case."

"So, she is aware that. . . ." How to put it? "that something's not quite right."

Riley blinked as if that hadn't occurred to him. "Well, yeah. I guess."

"What if she's spooked by your work? I'm sure you don't consciously bring it home, but think about what you have to try to *avoid* bringing home."

Barbara had known Dave Riley first as a teenager with a dream of being a detective; then as a young cop on his way to plainclothes rank faster than anyone in the GPD had ever moved up. Somewhere in there she had married him, and somewhere on the way to his becoming chief of detectives, they had to have talked about what he did. If something about being married to a cop was going to take her by surprise, Jake supposed, she'd had ample time to discover it. Still . . . .

"She talk to the other wives much?"

"Yeah, she always has. She's always looked at the blue community as a sort of extended family. What of it?"

"Could they be telling her stuff that puts a different spin on being a cop's wife? Things going on in your work now that might have changed the way she looks at it?"

"What sort of things?"

"For a detective, you're being damn dense here. Are there any new widows? Close calls? Divorces? Crooked cops being exposed? Maybe something she's heard or seen lately might have changed the way she feels about police work?"

Dave looked confused. "Why wouldn't she just say so?"

"Oh, for God's sake, Dave! Law enforcement is your life.

You think she'd just blurt out something that would screw that up for you? Look, you remember when I tried the Air Force on for size?"

"If ever there was a square peg in a round hole."

"And I knew it. And when we were married, Melinda knew it. But neither of us said a damn thing until it was the biggest elephant in the room. She thought I really wanted it and didn't want to interrupt my career; I thought she really wanted her teaching job and didn't want to take her away from that. Could something like that be going on here?"

"I don't know. Maybe I'm afraid to know. Hell, maybe I should just let nature—or whatever—take its course. I'm not good at this. . . ."

Jake pressed his fists into the table top and leaned forward, pitching his voice low. "Then *get* good at it. Letting this take its course is the last thing you should do. What you should do is go home, sober up, then take Barbara aside and ask her what's wrong. Beg, grovel, threaten, whatever it takes. And refuse to let her out of your sight until she answers you in a way that makes sense to both of you."

Riley looked at him as if he'd suddenly started to speak Swahili.

"Dammit, Riley, listen to me. Neither of you knows how much time you have left in this life. Imagine getting home tonight and finding Barbara gone. I don't mean walked out gone or divorced gone, I mean *gone* gone."

Riley drained the last of his beer and gave Jake an uneasy look before his gaze flickered back to the TV.

"How about . . . that cellar door? Are we sure nobody but Livingston got his hands on the key?"

Jake sighed. *Dodgeball. Okay, we'll go with that. I'm an expert at it, after all.* He switched to the new subject. "We'll soon find out. In the meantime, I'm driving you home. We can't have a detective in the tank overnight."

Riley shook his head. "It's only a few blocks."

"Dave." Jake's voice was sharper than he'd intended. "It's either me or a citizen's arrest. Your choice."

Riley looked up at him through eyes that were barely

tracking, a red stain of shame blossoming from his collar to the tips of his ears. "Jesus, I'm sorry. What the hell was I thinking?"

"You're pretty hammered. You *weren't* thinking."

"I'm sorry."

"Stop apologizing. Just go home and talk to Barbara."

Riley gave him a long, bleary look. "I'll think about it."

"Do more than think about it," Jake murmured to himself as he dropped Riley off ten minutes later.

Dave Riley felt like shit. It wasn't the hangover that hit him like a bulldozer when he awoke in his lonely guest room at 2:00 am. It was knowing that everything he had said and done that evening had reminded Jake Halsey of the hole in his own life.

Barbara would say the wounds had had time to heal . . . wouldn't she? It suddenly dawned on him that he had no idea what Barbara might say.

He'd watched from a distance as Jake went through his abortive, but transformative stint as an Air Force pilot, connecting him with one thing he found joyful, a thousand things he had no patience for, and one person he intended never to encounter again. Jake had spoken only indirectly of that. There had apparently been trouble with a Captain Wallace, a hard case from the Deep South who had had it in for him personally. Dave figured that particular story would emerge when Jake was good and ready for it to emerge.

If nothing else, the Air Force had motivated Jake to focus on essentials. His return to California, just as the software industry was on the verge of exploding, was the central one. Jake had started his own technology company to organize the results of searches through technical literature, then showing university laboratory chiefs how his program could help everyone—from undergraduate technicians to tenured colleagues—sift through the world's torrent of published work and make quick sense of overlapping fields of expertise.

Many programs could hunt for keywords, but Jake's

included a network of associations and probabilities based on what the technical terms actually meant, plus an algorithm that could "learn" from new search results, basically upgrading itself on the fly.

During those years, the two men's lives had intersected only at intervals over the phone or during Jake's rare visits to Connecticut. But when Jake's firm modified its basic program to aid criminal investigations, manipulating the data they generated in ways previously impossible, their worlds had begun to overlap more frequently.

Within three years, the Halsey System had become an industry standard for legal, academic, and corporate researchers and their libraries. Then, with a foresight that colleagues would first misunderstand and later come to envy, Jake had sold his firm to a Silicon Valley conglomerate at the peak of the NASDAQ boom in January 2000. At the age of thirty-nine, two years after the birth of his first child, Jake Halsey had retired as a billionaire and bought a four-bedroom Victorian in Pacific Heights.

Parenthood seemed to suit both Halseys well, something Jake had imparted to Riley with undisguised and ingenuous astonishment. Watching his daughter, Courtney, take in more and more of the world was an education in itself, he'd said; both he and Melinda found it even more compelling than research or inventions.

The Halseys had a joyful home life and a lively circle of friends, and something few of their peers could claim: time to enjoy them. Riley couldn't help but be a little envious of both his friend's wealth and his idyllic existence, until he realized that wealth could not provide everything.

A few months into his new life—retirement hardly seemed the right term—Jake Halsey was spending a Sunday evening in his basement lab while his wife and daughter enjoyed a play date across the Bay. Mesmerized by the work, Jake was startled from his concentration by the realization that it was 9:00 pm. Still no sign of Melinda and Courtney.

He'd called Melinda's cell only to receive a recorded explanation that she was outside the service area. He contacted the number Melinda had left, spoke with a woman on a kitchen speakerphone above a tired child's squeals, and learned that his wife and daughter had left Oakland about 6:30, as planned. He tried Melinda again and listened to the cell phone company's recording a second time.

Uncertain in a way he'd never experienced, Jake was eating a cold slice of leftover pizza when two highway patrol officers arrived at his front door.

Paulie Ponick—that was the name. Paulie was 23, with four prior moving violations, a suspended driver's license, an explosive recent breakup with a girlfriend, a head full of primitive unfocused wrath, and a blood alcohol level of 0.17%. He had taken his souped-up Camaro the wrong way up Folsom through two red lights. The second of these was Fifth Street, where Melinda Black-Halsey had just come off a crowded I-80 below the bridge. At 7:30 pm, Ponick had entered the intersection at forty-five miles per hour with a black-and-white in hot pursuit and broadsided Melinda's Camry. There were no survivors.

Jake's father had died of a heart attack the year before, and his mother was in a Greenwich hospice in poor condition. Jake never had the opportunity to tell her; she died a month later, not knowing.

In a heartbeat, Jake Halsey had gone from son and family man to orphan and widower. He had no brothers or sisters. He did have his oldest friend, who heard him move slowly through levels of grief no counselor, no matter how well intentioned, could ever fathom. Jake had told him haltingly of having to identify the shattered remains of his wife and little girl. For the first and only time in his life, Riley heard Jake Halsey weep.

Lying awake in the predawn gloom, Riley tried to imagine visiting the ME's lab as a civilian. Tried to imagine having to identify Barbara or Denny or Drew. He couldn't—or wouldn't.

Dave Riley swallowed his confusion and ambivalence, left his fold-out sofa, and returned to the master bedroom.

I'm not waking up one more morning thinking I've married a stranger.

CHAPTER EIGHT

Jake met Riley in the police station parking lot the next morning. The rain had ended and it was another lovely fall day, with a gentle breeze from the south sending leaves of many colors skittering across the pavement.

Riley looked exhausted. Dark circles framed his eyes, which were suspiciously red.

"Hangover?" Jake asked. "Maybe you should take the day off."

Dave snorted. "In the middle of a murder investigation? Right. I'm fine. And no, I'm not hung over." He shook his head and smiled ruefully. "Barb and I had a long talk starting at about two this morning. I got maybe two hours of sleep."

Jake rubbed absently at his abdomen, which had chosen an inopportune moment to go into spasm. "Is this good news?"

Dave shrugged but he was smiling. "Who knows? Too close to call at this point. But maybe we cleared the air a bit."

Jake smiled.

"Don't look so smug. As it happens, though, you were right. Turns out her best friend among the law enforcement wives has a brother who's a plainclothes detective in Omaha. He's been in a coma for six weeks because an informant in a vice investigation confessed his police connections to the wrong individual. Barb said it got her thinking what life would be like for her and the boys if something like that happened to me."

"I'm glad to hear that," Jake said sincerely, then winced as his gut spasmed again.

Riley's gaze sharpened. "What's wrong?"

"I don't. . . ." A sudden, overwhelming urge caused Jake to turn away and vomit into the bushes.

Dave Riley was right behind him when Jake finally

straightened up and caught his breath. He felt a solid hand on his shoulder.

"Are you okay?"

Jake shook himself. "Boy, that came on suddenly. You know, I tried to ignore it but I've had a pain in my gut for a few days."

"You seemed a little off during the drive back from Danbury. And in the bar last night." Riley glanced across the parking lot at the station house. "Look, I'm gonna flag down a police cruiser and get you to the hospital."

"No, I. . . ."

"Wrong answer. Get checked out. If you're okay, you can come back. Come back sick and I'll fire your ass off this team. You hear me?"

Jake smiled weakly. "I hear you."

Half an hour later Jake was in the emergency room at Greenwich Hospital, trying to distract himself from the pain in his side, and the annoyance of having waited unattended for more than twenty minutes.

He sat, paced, read outdated news magazines and one unreadable entertainment magazine, and gritted his teeth for nearly an hour. Finally a doctor appeared, spent five minutes prodding and questioning, and bluntly announced, "Mr. Halsey, you've got the clearest case of appendicitis I've seen in a long time. I'd guess that if it hasn't already burst it's about to, and that's one thing you don't want to have happen. If you'll change into this gown, I want to perform a quick sonogram to confirm the diagnosis."

Jake felt like a cartoon figure in the flimsy hospital gown, which certainly hadn't been designed for a man with his broad shoulders and long legs. He hoped he'd not meet anyone he knew. The doctor performed the sonogram in the exam room, however, and quickly settled any doubts as to his diagnosis. Even Jake, squinting sideways at the grainy sonographic image, could tell his appendix was inflamed.

The ER doctor scheduled him for emergency surgery. "Luckily, our on call surgeon is already here doing a post-op on another patient. Don't worry, Mr. Halsey, an appendectomy is the most common abdominal surgical procedure in the western world. We use a laparoscopic technique, which is a lot less invasive than traditional surgery, and the recovery time is a lot faster. In a few hours you'll feel a lot better, and you won't have much scarring. You just wait here. A nurse will be in to prep you soon." The doctor patted his shoulder as if he were a frightened child, then left the room.

At least he didn't offer me a lollipop, Jake thought, but he had to admit he was anxious about any type of surgery. He didn't like the idea of being drugged into unconsciousness. It was too much like being bound and gagged . . . and out of control.

And I've seen just enough of what people can do to each other, he reflected, *when one of them is out of control.*

Stupid, he told himself. The doctor was right. He had an uncomplicated problem for which there was an uncomplicated surgery. He should be relieved.

He wasn't.

When Jake came swimming up out of the haze of anesthesia, hours later, the first thing he saw was a pair of shockingly blue eyes framed by a surgical mask and a pale green cap. As he blinked back to awareness, feeling quite fine, really, the surgeon pulled off the mask and cap to reveal a blonde ponytail and the face of a Botticelli angel. An angel in green scrubs.

The angel smiled. "Welcome back, Mr. Halsey. I'm Dr. Taylor. How're you feeling?"

Her husky voice startled him—it wasn't the voice one would expect from a Botticelli—but it conveyed the confidence of a woman who knew the intimidating power of both her profession and her beauty.

Jake made appropriate noises, his tongue still a bit thick. "Great," he said at last. "Really great."

Her smile deepened. "That's the sodium pentothal

talking. Good stuff, isn't it? Better than a stiff drink.

"Okay, Mr. Halsey, here's the bad news: your appendix burst just about the time we were rolling you into the OR. The good news is we were able to clean everything up. You'll be sore for about a week or so but ultimately you'll be just fine. I'm going to have you stay overnight just to be sure, but you'll be discharged tomorrow. I'll prescribe Vicodin for the residual pain."

Jake shook his head. Or thought he did. For all he could tell, his head might have been floating in a bucket of molasses. Whatever he did, it was enough to stop her.

"No . . . Vicodin," he whispered.

"Ah, macho man, are we? Okay, take ibuprofen then. Two instead of one."

He started to protest but she forestalled him with a ferocious look.

"Please don't be one of those patients who insists they know best, or can handle the pain, or never take medication. *I'm* the doctor. You *will* heed my instructions. *Two* ibuprofen every four to six hours. Short term it won't harm your kidneys." She raised her right hand in a Girl Scout pledge. "Promise."

He nodded contritely.

"Good. Please make an appointment in ten days so we can take a look and check on the healing. We used melt-away stitches in there, but sometimes they don't melt away as planned. Call my office if you have any redness or swelling, and. . . ."

She was interrupted by a hesitant knock at the door of the recovery room. Dave Riley stuck his head through the door, smiling as he saw Dr. Taylor.

"Hi, Catherine," he said, nodding toward Jake. "How's my buddy?"

"Chief Riley," the surgeon said warmly, answering the detective's smile with one of her own. "I had no idea Mr. Halsey was a friend of yours. He's fine, but if he's as active as you are—and as stubborn—perhaps I'd better recommend tying him down for a few days." She turned a narrow blue gaze on her patient. "The incisions need time to mend."

Turning on her heel, she started for the door, untying her surgical mask from around her neck as she went. "An orderly will be along shortly to take you to your room, Mr. Halsey. Remember, when you're in pain, take a painkiller. It's the smart thing to do. Don't tough it out." She flashed him a grin, then disappeared.

"You refused to take painkillers?" Riley asked.

"Vicodin," Jake said, and cleared his throat. "I didn't want Vicodin. I'll take ibuprofen."

Riley grinned. "Rebel. You'd better do it, too, or Catherine will know. I swear that woman has ESP."

Jake didn't doubt it. But ESP, he decided, was not all that woman had.

Jake dozed on and off in his hospital bed. His longest stretch of sleep was not a peaceful one. Only intermittently aware he was dreaming, and hoping at those moments that he could trust that odd sensation of standing outside his own mind, he found himself back in Alabama for basic training.

Jake walked around the corner of a nondescript concrete-block building to find some half-dozen men in fatigues squirming and shuffling above a broken figure on the ground, jockeying for position. Someone—Jake couldn't quite see him, but he was fairly sure who it was—was mangled beyond recognition, bleeding heavily, in extremis, begging to be finished off. Whatever had happened here had been nothing close to a fair fight. It had also been over before Jake arrived.

Laughter arose from the heap, mirthless and deafening, assaulting his ears. There were more than six men in the scrum now, he could see. He couldn't tell where they were coming from, but their numbers appeared to be expanding. He saw repeated vicious kicks and heard the sickly percussion of knuckles on unprotected flesh. The man on the ground was in no position to escape or offer resistance; the kicks and blows were beyond all purpose except to vent tribal rage. Without a target, these men looked feral enough to turn on each other.

Jake tried to get close enough to understand what was going on, but by the time he realized he didn't really want to know, he was surrounded. Their attention turned from the broken man to him.

Every soldier in the crowd had the same face. They were all Captain Wallace, the squad leader. The real Wallace, in full regalia, stood just outside the others, egging them on. He recognized Jake.

"Cadet Halsey!" Wallace got the contemptuous look he always got when addressing Jake. "Look at something I bet you never saw in Green Witch, Conneck-ti-cut." He deliberately mispronounced every syllable and spat out the consonants. "We've set up a little show for you, college boy. Airman McLean here has finally figured out a way to serve his country."

Stanley McLean was the man on the ground. A true eight-ball, a magnet for abuse. Every unit had one, even if they had to create one, but pudgy McLean was the real thing—equally unskilled at pull-ups, personal hygiene, and maintaining his weapon. The squadron had a betting pool on McLean's washout date. No one had wagered that he would actually finish basic.

McLean was making a high muffled sound like a kicked dog. The herd instinct to hold in all sounds of complaint, never strong in him, was close to complete breakdown. Jake tried to get closer, but there was nothing he could do to stop this.

"This is why the good Lord created losers, Halsey. They ever explain that to you at your college up in Connecticut? After convincing you a gorilla's your second cousin, did they get around to the part where the unfit never survive?"

The faces on the hovering men were moving in and out of focus. Jake tried to remind himself he was not part of this, not one of them, that home and the airbase and reality were elsewhere. Some of the faces no longer resembled Wallace, and others no longer entirely resembled people.

The scrum containing McLean was becoming a single throbbing organism. Jake saw unrecognizable things, unnamable parts; he couldn't be sure that some weren't tentacles or hooves.

"America needs fighting men, Airman Halsey, and a fighting man needs the taste of blood. That is the one and only thing a loser like McLean is for. These men get it, and no matter how high you fly, you candy-assed little preppy prince, you never will." He grinned, knowing Jake wouldn't correct him about the difference between Greenwich High and private schools. That had happened once in Jake's first week at Maxwell, resulting in brig time for insubordination.

McLean's breath became a death rattle. Jake struggled to get closer through the herd, knowing the best he could be, the only thing he could be, was a witness. What he saw on the ground was no longer McLean.

The broken body was female now. Fortyish, in a torn denim knee-length skirt, no longer slim, but showing signs she had once been more than attractive. Jake had seen this woman only two or three times, but once had been enough.

The broken body was Valerie Wallace, the captain's wife.

Wallace was in the center of the scrum now, flushed with rage and joy. The final pummelings were his, in time with the accents of his voice.

"A fighting man needs the taste of blood. Have you ever tasted blood, Halsey?"

You are the Lord of the Flies, Wallace. You disgrace your uniform.

But Jake held his tongue. Whatever he saw, whatever he had heard about life in the off-base apartments, he had to remember that he was outranked.

Waking up to hospital sheets, soaked with sweat but not with blood, was one of the better recent sensations Jake could recall.

In his moments of wakefulness, he considered the brief meeting with his beautiful surgeon and reflected on his experiences with the opposite sex. He'd discovered in high school that girls seemed to flirt with him almost as a reflex. He hadn't, to his embarrassment, noticed it himself, as Dave Riley had had to tell him.

"You're a chick magnet, Jake," he'd said.

"I am not!" Jake had protested. He was gangly, awkward everywhere but on the field of play. Still, Dave's observation had intrigued him, and he'd gradually come to realize his friend was right. The fact that he chose to ignore flirtatious gestures only increased his attractiveness to the ladies. As a result, he'd been no wallflower his junior and senior years in high school. In his years at college before Melinda, he'd had no difficulty attracting women and had had his share of relationships, short and long.

Now, however, though Barbara Riley had assured him he was one of Greenwich's most eligible single men, the idea of dating held little appeal. He'd been celibate since Melinda's death and had almost no social life. Yet, despite the discomfort of his appendectomy, Catherine Taylor had awakened his attention for the first time in a very long while.

Maybe that was the sodium pentothal talking, maybe not. He had nearly two weeks, he realized, to figure it out. Who knew—he might meet Dr. Taylor for his checkup and find her utterly unappealing.

Somehow, he doubted that.

Dave Riley returned the following morning to check on his friend. "Feel up to some conversation?" he asked.

"Bored silly by some nonsense talk show," Jake responded, gratefully switching off the TV. "If I ever start to show any interest in mindless daytime TV, or anything similar, please take me out and have me shot."

Riley unbuttoned his suit coat and plopped himself comfortably into a side chair. "In that case, my friend, let me fill you in."

The detective looked relaxed, Jake thought, if not rested. Jake hoped that meant more good news in the marital department.

"Late yesterday," Riley said, "I had a long chat with a Detective Adams of the Bridgeport Police. It seems that a little over a year ago, a wine lover named Brad Perkins, who lives in the Black Rock section of town, came home after a week in Florida and discovered his house alarm system was off. He and his wife both reported that they had turned it on when leaving—that, in fact, they never left the house without engaging it. Perkins checked the house and found nothing missing or out of place. When he got to his wine cellar, he discovered what I think you'd have to call a pretty damned gruesome sight."

Jake waited as the detective shook his head, looking suddenly gray.

"This fellow turns on the light, and there in front of him—on his tasting table, for God's sake—tied down and spread-eagled, is a naked, dead woman. I have the details in my office, but the most interesting fact is that the ME said she had been embalmed—presumably by her killer—with cabernet sauvignon."

"Embalmed," Jake repeated, considering the sudden images in his head. "But that requires special equipment, doesn't it?"

Riley was nodding. "For arterial embalming, yeah. In this case, the embalmer, whoever it was, injected wine under the skin. No blood pumps needed. Takes longer, but assuming the perp knew that Perkins was on vacation, he had plenty of time."

"He? You know the perp was a man?"

Riley's face stilled. "No, but I'd bet money on it, given the brutality of the crime."

Jake slumped against his pillows. "If that's our guy, whoever he is, he's a monster. A certifiable monster."

"You got that right," said Riley, and stood. "Get better fast. I want this guy bad. This is not happening again on my watch."

CHAPTER NINE

Jake rejoined Riley's task force three days after he got out of the hospital, limping into his friend's office on a cane.

Normally, in Connecticut, the officer in charge of detectives would be a lieutenant detective or detective sergeant. Although the title chief of detectives was usually found in large cities and came with largely managerial responsibilities, the title had been given to Riley somewhat affectionately. He both managed and investigated, and no one in the chief of police's memory had ever been so adept at either task.

Jake's need to play catch-up was minor; Riley had kept him well apprised of developments. The newest information Riley brought to the group related to the gruesome Bridgeport murder. He sat at the head of the conference table, the case file in front of him.

"On Sunday, September 15, 2002," Riley said, referring to the file, "a retired insurance executive named Brad Perkins went down to his wine cellar and discovered a dead woman spread-eagled on his wine-tasting table—that part you know. Perkins dialed 911. He told the homicide detective who took the call that he and his wife had been in Florida for a week. We confirmed that alibi. Apparently, when they'd gotten home from the airport, the house alarm had been shut off— and both distinctly remembered setting it. That is, Perkins setting it and Mrs. Perkins watching him do it. But neither Perkins nor his wife found anything wrong until he went into the wine cellar. No doors or windows were forced or broken. Nothing seemed to be missing. The cellar, by the way, connects to a hallway that leads to an outside door. That was also intact, and that door and the others were properly locked, although he did admit that the cellar door lock was not a dead bolt."

Riley paused to flip to the forensics report. "The ME identified the woman as Rachel Charleson, a 24-year-old graduate student at Fairfield U who'd been reported missing the week before. She had been viciously beaten, but with no evidence of sexual assault. The ME determined that the cause of death was suffocation. From the lack of evidence at the scene, he postulated that she was killed somewhere else and brought to the Perkins house post-mortem."

Dave Riley scanned the file for a moment. "Perkins kept his wine cellar at fifty degrees."

Jake reacted at once. "Hold on a sec—*fifty* degrees?"

Riley quirked an eyebrow at him. "That's what it says here. Isn't that. . . ?"

"Unusually low. Most wine cellars are kept at fifty-five or a few degrees higher. Maybe the killer turned the thermostat down."

"That would help explain why the body was so well preserved. It was estimated to have been there for about four days. The kicker, of course," Riley continued, raising his eyes to the group at the table, "is that, in what the ME termed a reasonably professional job, the corpse had been hypodermically embalmed with red wine."

"Jesus." Tony Pezzi's soft exclamation eloquently expressed the group's sentiments.

Ellen grimaced and rubbed her arms as if she were suddenly cold. "That's a whole new level of aberrant psychology."

Brian shook his head. "Who'd even do something like that?"

"Someone who thinks he does good work and wants it to be admired, no matter how deviant that work was," Ellen suggested.

Her grim assessment fell into a thick silence that ended when her boss cleared his throat and riffled the papers in the file.

"Ms. Charleson's roommate said she didn't come home one Friday evening," he read, turning to the missing person report. "Since she frequently went to see her folks in New York on the spur of the moment, the roommate wasn't particularly worried until Monday passed with no word. She called the girl's parents, found she hadn't been home that weekend—never even called. That's when the police were brought in."

"Was there *any* physical evidence?" asked Brian.

"There's no indication of where she was abducted, so obviously we've only got the scene of the—hell, I was gonna say the scene of the murder, but it's not even that. The Perkins cellar was clean. Too clean. No fibers, fingerprints, or other similar evidence to be found. It's as if the guy wore surgical scrubs and plastic booties."

"Doctor Death," murmured Pezzi.

"A canvass of the street determined the neighbors had seen nothing," Riley continued. "It's not clear how the murderer gained access to the house, though the outside basement door is the most likely route he'd take to leave."

Jake stirred. "Anything on the wine he used to do the embalming?"

Riley nodded. "A sample was sent to a California laboratory specializing in wine analysis. Their technician identified it as a cabernet sauvignon, but couldn't offer any other clues. He did make a point of saying that this was the first—and he hoped the last—time he'd be asked to analyze a wine used in this manner. Bottom line is that after a few months of work, without any clues and with not one bit of success, the Bridgeport Police gave up on the case. If they'd had idea one about where she was picked up . . . ."

"Didn't she have a class schedule?" asked Ellen. "Surely someone knew where she was supposed to be."

"She had no classes on Friday afternoon. No one knew her plans. She just dropped off the face of the earth and turned up in Perkins's wine cellar." Riley paused and looked around the room. "Any thoughts?"

"Besides that this guy is a card-carrying member of Monsters 'R Us?" asked Pezzi.

"I think there's an interesting similarity to the Livingston murder," Jake offered, "primarily with respect to timing. With Livingston, there was no way for the killer to know when the bottle would be consumed. With Perkins, there was no way to know exactly when the body would be discovered. Hard to believe the killer or killers wouldn't be sensitive to these issues."

"Unless the perp knew of their plans," said Ellen. "He may have even chosen the Perkins house because—in addition to having a wine collection—they wouldn't be there to get in the way. I mean, consider how much planning must have gone into this one. He had to be outfitted to embalm the girl before he took her into that cellar."

Pezzi snorted. "Maybe he just carries an embalming kit around for kicks."

"Tony," Riley warned.

"We have three wine-related events—a poisoning, the fire in Danbury, and a murder," Brian Allen chimed in. "All occurred in Connecticut and all happened over a six-month period. Any chance they're unrelated?"

"I've been in police work for more than two decades and I don't remember any wine-related crimes," said Riley. "And I agree: three such events in such a short period are pretty unusual. Ellen, how does this look from your profiler's seat?"

Ellen grimaced. "Honestly, when the Perkins case turned up, I lost any doubts I had as to whether the crimes were unrelated. The arson was downright mundane in comparison to the Livingston murder, but this? *This* takes the cake, as my granny used to say."

"Wait a minute," Pezzi interrupted, slapping his hand on the table. "Didn't that plane crash in Fairfield last summer wipe out some guy's wine stash?" He snapped his fingers several times as he tried to recall the case. "Uh . . . uh . . . started with a J. Jennings, Jeffries—no, *Johnson*. That's it—Johnson. Private plane took out the guy's beach house."

Jake's heart rate kicked up a bit. "I read about that," he said. "I remember the case because it was so weird. They never found the pilot's body."

Pezzi snapped his fingers again and pointed at Jake.

"Right! Hey, maybe our perp is the Invisible Man."

Riley pointed at Pezzi. "You called the case, you get to dig up the dirt. Talk to Chief Ritchie, Fairfield PD."

Pezzi nodded. "Sure, boss."

"*Now*, Tony." Riley's tone was sharp.

"Yes, sir." Pezzi launched himself from the table and disappeared into the hall.

Riley shook his head. "Sometimes I wonder why he joined the force."

The expression on Ellen Green's face suggested she'd heard this before. "Tony's okay," she said.

"Yeah, but he's gotta be joking all the time. Mostly, I can just ignore him, but sometimes it's really inappropriate. Irks me."

"You know why he does it," Ellen said, doggedly. "We all have different ways of coping."

Riley sighed. "I get that, I do. I just wish his way of coping wasn't so damned annoying."

Jake hid a smile and repositioned his cane against the edge of the table. "That was a good piece of information he just came up with."

"Potentially," Riley said. "We'll see how good it turns out to be. Anybody else got anything?"

Brian Allen raised his hand. "A question for Jake. You're a wine expert. Does the fact that all three incidents—okay, potentially four—involve wine suggest anything to you?"

"I wish it did. Let me think out loud here for a minute. First, the people involved in these crimes aren't just wine *drinkers*, they're wine *collectors*, or in the Danbury case, a fine wine merchant. Wine as a collectible, or even as a beverage, has only been prominent in America since the 1960s even though Prohibition ended in 1933. Even today, about ninety-nine percent of wine is consumed the day it's purchased. That makes people who collect on the scale of Livingston and Perkins—or who maintain an inventory like that at Bob's—pretty unusual."

Brian raised ruddy eyebrows. "I hadn't realized it was that specialized a collectible. Then this Fairfield case. . . ."

". . .comes under the heading of 'what-are-the-odds,'" Jake finished for him. "The sixty-four-thousand-dollar question is, Who would have something to gain from crimes involving collections of wine?"

Ellen's gaze was focused. "As opposed to the collectors themselves, right?" On Brian and Riley's puzzled looks, she added, "The arson involved no injury to the collector. Neither did the Bridgeport case, even though it resulted in a death. And, if we're right about Fairfield being part of this, the owner there wasn't hurt either."

"What does that suggest to you?" Riley asked her.

"It's odd, that's for sure. It's almost as if whoever's doing this is hiding behind the wine. He's not striking directly at the collectors, though they may be his real target. He's striking at them *indirectly* by destroying their collections, or their pleasure in owning or consuming them. I'll bet poor Mr. Perkins can't walk into his wine cellar or look at his tasting table without thinking about Rachel Charleson."

"But how about Livingston? He won't be contemplating much of anything again," suggested Brian.

Riley nodded. "Back to the sixty-four-thousand-dollar question—who stands to gain? Jake, you were saying?"

Jake shifted uncomfortably in his seat. His incisions were itching, but that wasn't the problem; he was trying not to imagine the scene that had met Brad Perkins in his cellar. "Since the end of Prohibition," he said, "the Mob seems to have ignored alcoholic beverages, wine included. No way to corner the market. So I'd probably rule out organized crime. As far as there being a scheme involving the wine itself, stories about counterfeit bottles or adulteration are pretty rare, although there was one large Austrian scandal where wine was sweetened with antifreeze."

"Jeez," Brian interjected, "I'm glad Pezzi didn't hear that. We'd be up to our radiator caps in antifreeze jokes." The others smiled knowingly.

"And, if it *were* an attempt to manipulate a market, it would have to be more specific," Jake went on, ignoring the aside. "Conceivably, a speculator could affect values by reducing the supply of one grape variety, but the wines involved in these crimes are all over the place—everything from a sweet Italian dessert wine to a dry West Coast cab. Our monster seems to have pretty broad tastes. At the moment, I've got to confess that the reason for wine being involved stumps me."

The phone on Riley's desk beeped and he rose to answer it. After a clipped conversation, he hung up and met the three curious gazes from the conference table.

"Pezzi was right," he said.

"I was right," the younger detective announced ten minutes later when he rejoined them. As proof, he submitted a folder with a hard copy of his download from the Fairfield police chief. "Chief Ritchie confirmed that last July a small plane crashed into a house on Fairfield Beach, blowing up the house and a large collection of red Burgundy. Fortunately, the resulting fire didn't spread to any other residences. Looks like somebody *is* out to get wine lovers, and it's happening in our backyard."

"Try not to sound so enthusiastic," said Ellen wryly. "These are violent crimes."

"Sorry. It's just nice not to be laughed at once in a while."

Jake didn't miss the swift glance he shifted toward Riley.

"Anyway, it's another absent owner situation. The Fairfield house was unoccupied at the time of the explosion" he added, with a nod at Ellen. "Whoever engineered that plane crash did some meticulous planning, and it had to have cost some money. The plane was stolen, but the lack of a body anywhere in or near the house suggests the pilot bailed out before the crash. There must've been a good GPS system involved, explosives, possibly some sort of homing beacon. Even with the best navigational equipment, it's highly unlikely somebody could use remote control to get a plane to take off—or guide one once it's already airborne—so odds are the perp started in the pilot's seat and parachuted out. It's got to be somebody with skydiving skills and a foolproof escape plan. Who would go to all that trouble, and why? And is the fact that nobody was home significant? If so, how would the perp have known that?"

"Fits the profile so far," said Ellen. "The murderer who doesn't want to get involved with his victims. Except for Livingston and the Charleson girl. They were the only ones who were directly harmed. Everything else is an indirect slap at the collectors."

"She wasn't related to the Perkins in any way, was she?" Jake asked.

Riley shook his head. "No connection, or none that could be found."

"Then why? Why Mitchell Livingston? Why Rachel Charleson? And why depart from the impersonal approach?" Jake asked.

"Overload?" Ellen suggested. "Maybe the indirect injury isn't enough, so he occasionally explodes." She shrugged. "It's certainly worth looking into. There just isn't enough to go on yet."

Jake turned to Riley. "May I suggest that we get a flipchart and markers and organize what information we have?"

Riley nodded at Brian, who took three brisk steps to the corner of Riley's office and manhandled a large easel into place at the end of the table.

Forsaking his cane, Jake limped over to the easel, took a marker, and read as he wrote:

1. Greenwich—10/2003—Poison
   Owner and Victim: Mitchell Livingston
2. Danbury—2/2003—Arson
   Owner: Bob Daniels of Bob's Fine Wines
3. Bridgeport—9/2002—Murder
   Owner: Brad Perkins/Victim: Rachel Charleson
4. Fairfield—7/2003—Plane crash & explosion
   Owner: Harry Johnson

"That's what we've got, so far," he said, putting down the

marker. "Except for Bridgeport, all the incidents occurred in 2003. Danbury and Fairfield were separated by five months, as were Bridgeport and Danbury. The shortest time lapse is three months, Fairfield to Greenwich. We've got four distinctly different types of events: poison, fire by arson, murder, and a plane crash and explosion. Also, technically an arson, I guess, but radically different from the Danbury fire."

"Plus three of the cities are along the coastline and one is inland," Ellen said. "If there's a pattern, what is it?"

"All these events have been in the southwest section of the state," Riley noted. "I wonder if that's important."

Jake studied what he had written. "What if we put them in chronological. . . ."

His thoughts were interrupted by the appearance of a department secretary with a multiple-page fax, which she handed to Riley. The rest of the team watched as he read through it. After a moment of intense study, he looked up, his expression quizzical. "Another hit from our initial query. This one in Ansonia. The Ansonia police report that a truck belonging to the Bailey Brothers wine and liquor wholesale firm crashed into the side of a building in June 2002. The crash killed the driver, a Dennis Cox, and destroyed most of the cargo, which, according to the Bailey Brothers manifest, included forty cases of fine wine."

"A bit tardy, aren't they?" asked Brian. "That query went out last week."

Riley held up the top sheet of the report. "The summary refers to a delivery truck. There's a little note here from the police chief that says he'd forgotten it was a *wine* delivery truck. One of the officers who worked on the case saw our dispatch and brought it to his attention yesterday."

He returned his glance to the report. "And the mystery deepens. The driver's route didn't include any stops in Ansonia. Neither the police nor the folks at Bailey Brothers have any idea what the truck was doing there. The crash site's in an old industrial section near the center of Ansonia, not exactly a neighborhood where you'll find a lot of wine retailers. Apparently Cox was coming into the city from the

East, on State Street, and lost his brakes on a twenty-degree downgrade in front of the Armory. He crashed into a chain-link fence at the bottom of the hill, then hit an industrial building beyond that, killing himself and smashing all the bottles in the back of the truck."

"Is the truck still around?" asked Jake.

Dave nodded, looking once more at the fax. "Yes, since an insurance claim is pending and Cox's death hasn't been resolved. It's at a garage on Main Street."

"I'd like to run up next week and take a look at it, if you've no objection," said Jake. "Can you alert the Ansonia police and have them tell the garage I'll be coming?"

"Consider it done," Riley answered.

"What were you saying before this came in? Something about the order of the cases?"

Jake nodded. "Right now they're arranged as we found out about them. I was thinking that if we arranged them in other ways, maybe chronologically or geographically, we might see some sort of pattern emerge." He turned to the flip chart. "So, um, Bridgeport is the earliest."

"Not any more," Dave said. "Ansonia. Ansonia happened in June of 2002—roughly three months before Bridgeport."

Jake stepped back to the easel and rewrote the list on the bottom of the page:

1. Ansonia—6/2002—Truck crash & fatality
   Victim: Dennis Cox
2. Bridgeport—9/2002—Murder
   Owner: Brad Perkins/Victim: Rachel Charleson
3. Danbury—2/2003—Arson
   Owner: Bob's Fine Wines
4. Fairfield—7/2003—Plane crash & explosion
   Owner: Harry Johnson
5. Greenwich—10/2003—Poison
   Owner and Victim: Mitchell Livingston

"My God. Now that you've done it that way. . . ." Brian left the sentence unfinished.

"Well, whaddaya know about that?" Pezzi murmured.

"The Alphabet Murders."

Riley looked at him sharply. "You whisper that phrase outside this room and I'll chain you to a desk for the duration of this investigation."

"Wouldn't think of it, sir," Pezzi said. "But what are the odds our guy has filled in the blanks?"

"As horrible as it is to think about. . . ." All heads in the room swiveled toward Ellen. She spoke slowly, looking at a blank section of the wall, as if any stimuli outside her own mind would interfere with her concentration. "We just might learn more about him if he has."

Riley made an effort to refocus. "Go on."

"If he's making a deliberate allusion to a book or a film, that might be a message. To somebody, at least." Ellen, as she often did when she lowered her voice, now had her colleagues' rapt attention. "Maybe to us, maybe to the world at large, maybe to some party we haven't identified yet, maybe just to himself. But a pattern as obvious as the alphabet has to be a coded signal on some level."

Pezzi looked at her with the eager eyes of a front row student. Allen produced a pad and started taking notes.

"We already know he's a careful planner; maybe he's got a bookworm side, too. Possibly he's a pretentious bastard who wants people to see his work in a literary context.

"Come to think of it," she continued, "He could be toying with the whole idea of patterning in serial murder; if you've read the book"—she looked quickly at Pezzi—"you'll remember the killer actually set up his arbitrary alphabetical series to try to draw Poirot's attention away from one particular murder, with a very personal motive. Or, maybe it has nothing to do with Dame Agatha. It still implies something about our monster's attitude."

"And that implication would be?" Riley's words were skeptical, but his tone told Ellen it was a constructive skepticism, that of someone who took her speculation seriously and respected it. He had never known her to waste an idea.

"He's attracted to order for order's sake, and he insists on being the one who defines what counts as order. We should expect a control freak, but also somebody who acts on whims. He's cavalier about death; he's showing off; he's flexing a muscle in the mirror like a teenager. He's certain he's too smart to get caught." Her eyes narrowed. "And if we're on the ball reading his signals, that's exactly how we're going to catch him. Sooner or later he'll get smug enough to screw up."

Riley gave Green a look of cautious professional approval. "You're damned right about that last part. We need to watch the line between inferences and assumptions, but you could be right about all of it." He took a slow sip from a mug of room-temperature coffee. "In my bones, this makes sense."

"I imagine we'd all agree," Jake offered, and the silent nods around the room backed him up. "But as much as we do—for the moment, the killer's absolutely right. He's been appallingly good at this."

In the silence that followed this observation, Riley grabbed a zip code directory from his bookcase, flipping to the Connecticut listings.

"There are twenty-six towns beginning with the letter C." he noted. "None stand out, and most are small. The Es account for twenty-eight towns. Again, small and unremarkable. We're going to have to spend time narrowing down the possibilities, but we've got to do it."

He held the directory out to Detective Allen. "Please send an urgent message to the chief of police in each of these towns, explaining what we've discovered and requesting them to check their case files for any crime that's even vaguely wine-related. It would be between September 2002 and February 2003 for the Cs and between February and July 2003 for the Es."

Brian nodded, scribbled a quick note, grabbed the directory and headed out of the room.

Jake met his friend's eyes. Urgent didn't even begin to cover what he was thinking. "The time period between Fairfield and Greenwich was three months," he said. "If we're right about this . . . ?"

Riley responded in a low voice, "If we're right about this,

we've got to move fast. As much as I hate to say it, the clock is ticking for towns beginning with H."

CHAPTER TEN

The morning he was scheduled to have his incisions checked, Jake made a concentrated effort to mentally set aside the police investigation and focus on other matters. Specifically, his beautiful and intriguing surgeon.

His first sight of her standing in her office doorway had confirmed what he'd already suspected—the tingle of attraction he'd felt post-op was not the effect of anesthesia. She was every bit as compelling to him now that his head had cleared—on second thought, distinctly more so.

As she ushered him into the examination room, he noted that she wore no rings on her left hand. A few questions disguised as small talk confirmed that Catherine Taylor, MD, FACS, was single and unattached.

Jake was surprised at his nervousness around her, but reasoned that it had been a very long time since he had even considered courting such a stunning woman—or any woman other than his late wife.

Courting? What had made him think that? He shook his head. Courtship, if that's what this was leading up to, was not at all like remembering how to ride a bike. He glanced up from his internal dialogue to see the doctor looking at him expectantly.

"I asked you to please remove your shirt and unbutton your trousers. If you're uncomfortable with that, I can get one of my male partners to examine you."

"Oh . . . uh . . . no, I . . . ." He smiled, and then tested the waters. "It's been quite a while since a beautiful woman asked me to undress."

"That, Mr. Halsey, may be more than I need to know," she responded, her blue eyes filled with laughter.

As he unbuttoned and removed his shirt, he read her face,

but saw nothing but good humor. His confidence returned. "My apologies, Dr. Taylor." She responded with a fleeting grin and a gentle, even quicker roll of her eyes. He caught her glance for a split-second longer than she might have expected, nodded imperceptibly in return, then looked aside at an anatomic diagram on the wall.

She performed a few preliminary examinations, taking his temperature, blood pressure, and pulse. Asking Jake to inhale and exhale deeply, she watched his expression as his torso expanded and contracted, her steady professional hand positioning a stethoscope at various points. He made sure to suppress a momentary impulse to grimace while taking in air.

His next impulse he decided not to suppress. "Perhaps I can make up for my entirely unwarranted revelation by inviting you to accompany me on a sedate outing this Saturday."

Her eyes met his for a moment before she turned her attention to his stitches, checking for bleeding, redness, or swelling. "Sedate? That's a word I haven't heard for a while. What do you have in mind?"

"If the weather cooperates I thought you'd enjoy an informal picnic on the beach."

"Would I need a chaperone?"

"Alas, the vehicle I have in mind won't allow it," he replied in mock seriousness, then gasped as she hit a sore spot on his abdomen. "But if you'll give me your address, I would be pleased to call for you at 11:00 am."

She raised her head to glance at his face. She didn't respond directly, instead asking, "You and Dave Riley go back a ways, don't you? You can button your shirt," she added.

He nodded, pulling the front of his shirt together. "High school. We played sports together."

She seemed bemused. "Really. Somehow I got the feeling you two were both in law enforcement and became friends that way."

"Not me. But I contribute to that cause in other ways."

"I could swear I caught something about an investigation you were on together. During one of his visits."

Jake smiled, perversely pleased that she'd eavesdropped. "I sort of freelance."

"Ah." Dr. Taylor moved to the counter and scribbled something on a prescription pad. "Your incisions look fine. They're healing very nicely." She turned and handed him the paper.

He reached for it, puzzled. "Then why the prescription?"

"That's my address and unlisted phone number. You won't need a return visit, so I'm not officially your physician as soon as you walk out of the office. There's no ethical problem with my seeing you socially." She smiled. "May I ask where our sedate outing will take us?"

Jake returned the smile, pocketing the slip of paper. "I'd like it to be a surprise. Dress casually and bring something warm. You should probably reserve the entire day and, while you're at it, tomorrow evening, too."

Dr. Taylor leaned back against the counter and folded her arms. "The whole day?"

Jake wondered if he was pressing too hard. "A day trip, out of state," he said tentatively. "And—if you'd be willing— dinner Tuesday? Both related."

She hesitated for only a moment, then nodded. "Okay, Mr. Mysterious. But remember, Detective Riley and *I* go way back, too."

CHAPTER ELEVEN

Jake rang Catherine Taylor's doorbell on Saturday, precisely at eleven. When she came to the door in jeans and an old leather jacket, the appreciative expression in his eyes verified that she was attractively and appropriately dressed.

"This casual enough?" she asked, and then stared wide-eyed at the vehicle parked at the curb.

"What in heaven's name is that?" she asked.

Jake smiled, glancing back over his shoulder at the car. "It's a 1910 Model 19 Buick Touring Car. That's an authentic paint job: Buick green with ivory wheels. I started to restore it myself, but it was a bigger job than I wanted to handle at the time, so I had it restored to better than original condition a couple of years ago."

Catherine shook her head in amazement. "Are we actually going to travel in that?"

"Absolutely. You're welcome to drive, assuming you can use a stick shift."

Catherine put her hands on her hips and gave him a scowl.

"And, of course, she does take a lot of muscle-power to steer," he added, grinning at her expression. "Power steering hadn't been invented when this car was made."

She flexed her biceps. "I'm a surgeon, Mr. Halsey. I occasionally have to lift people twice my size on and off gurneys. I could probably heft you, if I had to. Thank you very much—I would love to drive your mechanical lady friend."

"Okay, but only if you deep-six the Mr. Halsey bit. I'm Jake."

She smiled and held out her hand. "And I'm Catherine. Now lemme at 'er."

Jake's warning about the manual steering

notwithstanding, Catherine found the lovely old car easy to manage. By the time they left her neighborhood, she was driving confidently.

"Where to, navigator?" she asked as they approached a major cross street.

"All in good time, all in good time," Jake replied. "Just turn left on North Street."

They drove in silence, attracting waves and smiles from other vehicles. From time to time, Jake stole a glance at Catherine. She pretended not to notice for a while, then said, "What?"

'I was just admiring the way you handle the Buick—and the way your hair shines in the sun. Turn right at the next drive."

Catherine turned into a compound made up of several wooden buildings whose architecture suggested haphazard construction in different decades. Jake directed her down a tree-lined drive to a large, two-story structure on the edge of a grassy, flat field. As the car came to a stop, he stepped out, grabbed an insulated bag from the back seat, and walked around to open Catherine's door.

Although the building looked like a New England antiquity with Colonial windows and wooden shutters, inside it was a huge, one-story hangar that housed an array of machines. As she stepped through the door Catherine spotted a helicopter, two airplanes, and several antique automobiles. On one side of the hangar, behind a glass wall, there seemed to be a gallery of sorts with a couple of large, antique wooden cases along the perimeter. On the opposite side she recognized a Wurlitzer jukebox with colorful tubes resembling neon lights on each side. She turned to Jake, who was watching her reaction. "What is this, a museum?"

"In a manner of speaking, yes—a private one. I spend a lot of my spare time here. I happen to like tinkering with antique machinery—cars, planes, music machines—anything mechanical. Everything in here is at least forty years old."

Catherine did a slow 360, marveling at the diverse and unusual contents of the building. "This is where you live?"

Jake nodded. "Just across the driveway. Returning to my roots, I guess. I've got forty acres here—straddles the New York State border."

"Isn't that unusual?"

Jake gave her an almost sheepish smile. "This is going to sound odd, but I've got a private airstrip." He gestured at the hangar doors. "Greenwich restricts takeoffs and landings. New York is more lenient, so I can taxi across the Connecticut border and take off legally in New Castle, New York."

She laughed. "You wily *dog*."

He laughed with her, seeming to relax just a bit more. "I'll show you around the place another time," Jake said, "but the tide won't wait, so we'd better get under way."

"The tide?" Catherine echoed.

Jake directed her to a large yellow airplane trimmed in glossy black. Perched on amphibious floats, its belly was at the level of Catherine's head. On each side of the engine cowling the name was lettered in bold script: *SHADY LADY*.

A lady to be reckoned with, Catherine thought.

"How old is she?"

"Hey, it's not polite to inquire about a lady's age," Jake teased. "And before you worry that her age makes her unsafe, let me assure you that she has a chrome-molybdenum steel cage around her cockpit and that her fuel tanks are rubber bladders guaranteed not to rupture on impact. She can fly quite slowly, maneuver well, and operate safely with very short takeoffs and landings. Trust me, she's safe."

"I never supposed otherwise," Catherine replied wryly. "What is she?"

Jake smiled and ran a caressing hand along the underside of the plane's fuselage. "A Helio H-295 Super Courier, manufactured in 1968 and at your service. Please just step back a bit, I've just got to pull her outside."

Outside the hangar on the well-maintained airstrip, Jake did a pre-flight walk-around. With that completed, he ushered Catherine to the plane and said, "Hop in," boosting her to the top of one float.

Catherine ducked into the cockpit, running her hand

appreciatively over the sleek, old side panel.

Jake stowed his bag, climbed into the pilot's seat and snugged up both seat belts. He handed Catherine a headset. "*Shady Lady* is a genteel but noisy old girl. These headsets will cancel out some of the noise and allow us to talk."

As Jake started the engine, Catherine looked around, wide-eyed. She was at home in many unusual places, including an operating room, but this experience was completely new to her. She'd flown in small planes before, but never one that was part of a seemingly vast collection of miscellaneous machinery. And, unlike the low-wing planes she was used to, the Helio's wings were mounted atop the fuselage and braced with solid-looking fittings. Catherine could see the ground as they moved out onto the field.

He, on the other hand, seems right at home in this machine. Among all these reconstructed things, she thought. *What are they all for, and would he be at home without them surrounding him?*

Jake revved the engine, accelerated to the north, and took off. At about 1,500 feet, he leveled off and headed east.

Catherine could see Long Island Sound in the distance. "Where are we going?" she asked.

"There are two points of land over the horizon," Jake replied, gesturing ahead. "They're the North and South Forks of Long Island. In the middle is Gardiner's Island. It's about eighty miles away, and we'll be there in about thirty minutes. I know a member of the family that owns it and have been given *carte blanche* to land on the northwest side." He grinned. "We're going to have a picnic lunch on a truly deserted beach."

As the plane droned on Catherine said nothing, but looked around her—the experience was so very different from the commercial jets in which she'd traveled, like being whisked through the air on a noisy kite. Being with Jake, she guessed, would seldom be an ordinary ride.

"Is there cell phone service up here?" She un-pocketed her phone and held it up. "I'm not on call, but emergencies do happen."

Jake grimaced. "Sorry. I didn't mean this outing to seem so much like an abduction. Yes, there's cell coverage, but it could cause a problem with the plane's systems—just as it might with a commercial jet. Your service shouldn't have any trouble reaching you once we've landed."

"Don't apologize. I'm just not used to being whisked away to parts unknown." She turned off her phone.

Jake returned his attention to flying while Catherine watched the choppy waves below. She returned to earth both figuratively and literally as Jake descended to within a few dozen feet of the water's surface. A moment of trepidation made her sit up straighter in her seat.

"*You* may walk on water," she said, as the plane dropped toward the waves, "but it's a talent that eludes me. I trust you'll forgive me for mentioning that we seem to be missing the island."

"Not to worry," said Jake. "She's got floats, remember? She'll walk on water for us."

He set the craft down on the water, slowed, and headed toward the beach. The tide was halfway out. Jake taxied to the edge of the water and right up onto the hard-packed sand where the four wheels, hidden from view inside the floats until Jake had extended the landing gear, took over.

"Doesn't the salt water damage her paint job?" Catherine asked, looking back at their wake.

Jake shrugged. "Yeah. Salt water's pretty corrosive, which is why most seaplane pilots try to avoid salt-water landings. But I've got a first-rate maintenance guy to worry about things like that; he washes the plane in fresh water after every salt-water landing. We've got two hours before the tide is out so far that the sand turns mushy. Think we can manage a picnic lunch in two hours?"

Catherine nodded, realizing that she was famished.

Jake picked up the insulated bag he'd brought and grabbed a folded blanket from behind the seat. They walked up to the dunes above high-tide level. He spread the blanket and began to lay out assorted dishes.

"Let's see, we've got a shrimp and garlic appetizer,

ravioli with duck *confit* and *hoisin* sauce hidden inside, and strawberries for dessert. And, for you, a half bottle of Krug multi-vintage Champagne, appropriately chilled. Since I'm flying I can't drink, so. . . ." He held up a plastic bottle of spring water.

Catherine pointed at the bottle of champagne with one finger and gave him a solemn look. "You assume that I drink? Many doctors don't, you know."

He shook his head. "I *did* make that assumption, didn't I?"

She smiled. "It's okay. I was only teasing. I do enjoy a glass of good wine occasionally and, since I'm told you're an expert, I'll assume I'm in for a treat."

"In my opinion, Krug is the best non-vintage-dated Champagne made."

Jake poured, they toasted, they ate, and they shared bits and pieces of their life stories. Catherine told Jake of her childhood in a family of doctors and the predetermined career established for her. Jake told her about his early interest in law enforcement and his stint learning to fly, courtesy of the American taxpayer. He then talked about his subsequent work with computers, the search software he'd pioneered, and his adaptation of it to help with criminal investigations. He downplayed the success he'd achieved in the business world.

"And what about women?" Catherine teased. "Is *Shady Lady* named after some notorious dame from your past?" She was surprised to see Jake tense. "I'm sorry," she said quickly, reaching out to touch his arm. "I didn't mean to pry." She paused. Then looking him squarely in the eye, she added, "Frankly, I wouldn't expect a man like you to be unattached."

"One could say the same of a woman like you."

Catherine shrugged. "Bad timing, other priorities. Something like that."

"Actually, *Shady Lady* was her name and already painted on her side when I bought her. I thought enough of the name to continue using it."

"You *do* know that wasn't really my question."

Jake studied the waves lapping the shore for so long

Catherine thought he wasn't going to respond. She'd opened her mouth to apologize again when he said, "I was married."

She waited.

"I was married and I had a little girl. My wife and daughter died in an automobile accident."

"Oh, my God," Catherine responded, tears suddenly filling her eyes. "I am so sorry."

He stumbled through a brief account of his courtship of Melinda, of their time together, of the miraculous birth of their baby girl—and of the accident that had claimed their lives. He spared her all but the barest details of that, relieved to spare himself as well.

Listening quietly, Catherine was moved. This chink in his urbane, suave façade was attractive. She liked this softer side of Jake Halsey.

But he carried a lot of baggage, too. Maybe too much baggage.

Not that I'm flying without a few checked items of my own, she reflected. "That must have been horrible for you," she said and touched his hand. "But how lucky you are to have known that kind of love. I don't think many people are blessed that way."

"Maybe not." Jake took her hand in his and glanced at it, then looked up into her eyes. "Now, tell me about the many loves of Dr. Catherine Taylor."

"Many likes might be a better way to put it," she said. She spoke quickly, and Jake silently noted that the subject brought out an unusually emphatic tone in her voice. If he were listening to a witness in an investigation . . . but he immediately cut short that line of thinking. *This isn't an investigation.*

"I've never been married and though it rather embarrasses me to confess it, never had a truly serious relationship. My career has been my sole focus for more years than I can count."

What she didn't say was that, approaching forty, she questioned whether she had followed her path too exclusively and might be looking at spending her entire life alone. She forced a smile and, pulling her hand free, reached down to offer Jake the last of the strawberries. "I could get used to this," she said, sipping her champagne.

"I hope so," Jake murmured.

A few green strawberry stems were all that was left of the lunch when Jake looked at his watch. "We'd better make tracks or we'll be stuck here in a sea of mud for another four hours."

They stood, putting away the odds and ends of their meal and shaking the sand from the blanket. Jake helped Catherine across the wet sand and up into *Shady Lady*, stowed the blanket and the insulated bag, and climbed in. He watched as Catherine expertly strapped herself in and shook back her hair to put on the headset.

"Ready to go?" he asked.

"Affirmative, Captain," she responded with a nod.

Smiling, he rolled the plane down the beach and into the water. Once the wheels lifted off the bottom, Jake retracted the landing gear, and they took off into the wind. The mid-afternoon sun was ahead of them on the return, and they flew in companionable silence.

Looking down on Jake's private airstrip, Catherine smiled. *Straddling the state line*, she thought. How logical—and how typical of the man she was getting to know. She had the feeling that Jake was someone who would always know the right answer, in business or in a relationship. She wasn't sure whether the thought pleased her or not. At the same time she realized, glancing at her watch, the afternoon seemed to have gone by in minutes.

Jake took the wheel of the Buick for the return trip to Catherine's house. As she alighted from the car in her driveway, he reminded her that she'd agreed to have dinner with him on Tuesday.

"Oh, did I promise that?" she teased. "Well, if I did. . . ."

"I'll pick you up at 6:45. It'll be dressy." He smiled. "We won't be sitting on a beach."

Catherine ran up the steps, unlocked the door, and waved to Jake as she stepped inside. She watched him drive away, giving herself a mental shake. What a confusing man. There was much about him she liked, much that fascinated and intrigued her. Yet, there were things that made her hesitate, too.

She slipped inside and went to survey her wardrobe for just the right outfit. All things considered, she imagined that their dinner would surprise her in ways that had nothing to do with airplanes.

CHAPTER TWELVE

On Monday Jake headed to Ansonia to take a look at the Bailey's delivery truck that had crashed, killing Dennis Cox. He drove east on the Merritt Parkway and turned north on Route 8, an expressway that wound through the wooded foothills of southern Connecticut. The Ansonia exit led to an area on the outskirts of the city that was cluttered with strip malls and fast-food restaurants. It was a weekday, and the traffic was congested. Jake crossed a short bridge into downtown Ansonia and drove up Main Street. Despite the bustle on its western perimeter, Ansonia seemed passed over by progress. Even in the middle of a business day, downtown traffic was sparse.

Evidence of the town's factory roots was still visible. Main Street was lined with late-nineteenth-century brick buildings, some with granite quoins and window ledges. They were imposing architectural examples and carried their age well.

There were no businesses of size or consequence. Instead, the visitor saw pizza parlors, hair salons, a pawn shop, an armed forces recruiting center, and a dozen or so vacant storefronts with "For Sale or Lease" signs prominently displayed. Many New England towns with similar industrial pasts had met the challenge of change, but Jake could see that Ansonia had yet to experience its renaissance.

Consulting his dashboard GPS system, Jake turned left and drove to State Street at the north end of the city. He didn't have to look very hard to locate the scene of the accident. It was immediately clear which building the truck had hit. The damage had been repaired with new red bricks and mortar that stood out in stark contrast to the color and texture of the old surrounding wall. The shine of a new chain-link fence protecting the property had not been dulled with time or weather, either. He drove slowly up State Street and back down to the accident site, but there was nothing on the pavement indicating that a truck had crashed and killed a man there—no skid marks, no oil stains, no scarred asphalt. He reasoned that the accident had occurred over eighteen months previously. Time had erased any specific evidence on the pavement, if it had ever been there.

He reversed course and drove to the southern end of town, where gas stations and garages abounded. Jake soon spotted Andy's Towing and Gas on the west side of the street and noticed a couple of trucks in the yard. One had a completely smashed-in front end and the typical cargo box used by liquor distributors. The truck was covered with dust and dirt, evidence it had been there a while. The words "Bailey Bros." and Bailey's city name were painted on the side panels, but there was no mention of either liquor or wine—typical of such vehicles, which might otherwise attract the unwanted attention of potential hijackers or thieves.

Jake grabbed a bag from his back seat and made a stop in the office to alert the owners to his presence.

"Oh, yes, Mr. Halsey, we've been expecting you," said the woman behind the counter. "The truck is in the back lot, up against the fence. It's been there a long time."

"Why isn't it in a police impound lot?" asked Jake.

"The Ansonia police don't actually have one. We don't get many vehicles that have to be impounded, but when there is one, the police send it over here. We've been told to permit inspections of impounded vehicles only by authorized persons, so there is some kind of control."

"Do you have a record of who has been here to inspect the truck, other than the police?"

"There were several insurance investigators who nosed around a few days after the crash. But the damage to the truck was clear, and the Ansonia police eventually determined the crash had been an accident." That answer seemed to satisfy Jake, who went outside to examine the truck.

He pulled a pair of dark blue coveralls and a flashlight

from his bag, donned the work clothes and a pair of latex gloves, and headed for the rear parking lot.

Jake took his time with the inspection. First, he walked entirely around the truck, finding no damage other than the mangled front end. Looking in through the driver's-side window, he noted dried bloodstains on the dash, wheel, and seat. The truck hadn't been cleaned since the accident. Jake's nostrils confirmed that the instant he opened the door. For a moment, he was back in San Francisco, looking at Melinda's mangled Camry, the smashed baby seat still strapped crookedly in place. Quickly, he pushed the thought aside and closed the door with a shudder. Whatever he needed to learn about this vehicle was unlikely to be in the passenger compartment.

Crawling underneath the chassis, he slowly ran his light over the truck's undercarriage. From his brief inspection, the rear brakes, shocks, drive shaft, exhaust pipe, mufflers, and wiring to the rear lights looked normal. He then singled out the brake lines and followed them forward, noting where they joined a proportioning valve. The main lines ran upward toward the master brake cylinder under the smashed-in hood. They looked normal—uncut, unblemished.

Jake craned his neck and shone the flashlight in a spot just above a piece of the structural frame. Something caught his eye. A thin wire protruded from a small space above. In order to see clearly, he had to put his head almost up into a small void in the truck's interior. He repositioned the light, shining it as directly as possible into the small space. There, wired to the brake lines, Jake identified two radio-signal receiving modules from garage door openers, each with a four-inch wire hanging down. The wire he had seen wasn't a wire at all: it was the antenna of one of the modules.

Looking more closely, he could just make out another small rust-colored wire running to the vehicle's electrical system. *The 12-volt power source for the modules and the attached electrical solenoid coils*, Jake thought. The intent was obvious: When triggered by an ordinary garage door opener set to the right radio frequency, this rudimentary but lethal system would activate the solenoid valves, opening a hole in the brake line and causing the truck to spill most of its brake fluid on the ground . . . and lose its brakes. Whoever operated that opener would have to be within about a hundred feet, which meant one of two things: Either he had been following Bailey's delivery truck or he knew where the truck was going to be and was waiting for it.

Jake thought for a moment, but all he could come up with were questions. How could the equipment have been installed in the truck? How could it have been triggered at just the right time to cause the crash? Why hadn't a previous inspection revealed the compromised brakes? He took a couple of photos to take back to Greenwich.

Jake pulled himself out of the engine compartment and lay back on the ground, his eyes no longer seeing the smashed engine. After a moment he realized he was breathing unnaturally heavily.

It wasn't an accident that had killed the truck driver. The presence of this specialized mechanism confirmed Jake's worst fears. Dennis Cox had been murdered. Something about the unknown man behind this steering wheel—or the employer he drove for, or the cargo he carried, or someone or someplace he was carrying it to—had motivated a clever tinkerer to develop an ingenious, insidious way of ending a life.

CHAPTER THIRTEEN

At home, Jake checked his phone messages, torn between hope and dread that something new had come in on the wine crimes. There was one message from Riley to let him know they were checking up on Dennis Cox, the driver of the wrecked Bailey's delivery truck. Nothing significant yet. Other than that, there were two annoyance calls from marketers—how *did* they get unlisted numbers?—and two hang-ups. Jake erased the messages and picked up the phone to place a call of his own.

At 6:45 on the dot Jake stepped from the back seat of a vintage, chauffeur-driven 1929 Rolls Royce 20/25 Saloon touring car onto the sidewalk in front of Catherine's restored Victorian house. Before he'd reached the front porch, she came to the door in a pale blue cocktail dress with a plunging neckline. The double strand of pearls at her throat perfectly matched her bracelet and earrings. Her hair was arranged in a French braid pinned up in the back, a strand of tiny freshwater pearls woven into the gold.

As Jake climbed up the front steps, his breath caught in his throat. The deep blue of her eyes was a match for the evening sky.

"You look lovely," he managed to say. The words were inadequate, he knew, but Catherine's answering smile made him hope she'd read between them.

"Where's my Buick?" she asked, looking over his shoulder at the Rolls Royce.

He turned to follow her gaze. Burgundy and black, the car had a look of elegance and raw power.

"The Buick is in the garage, unfortunately," Jake told her. "Something I'm not comfortable about with the brakes. Besides, tonight I want to enjoy all the wines myself and there will be several of them."

The chauffeur drove down Greenwich Avenue, the town's main shopping street, turned left on Lewis Street, and stopped halfway down the block across from Restaurant Jean-Louis.

"Have you been here before?" Jake asked, helping Catherine from the car.

"I've heard a lot about it and read some reviews, but I've never had the opportunity to eat here."

"You're in for a real treat."

As they entered the restaurant, Jake told Catherine that Jean-Louis Gerin and his charming wife Linda had run the restaurant—which many considered the best in New England—for more than twenty years.

Appearing from the rear of the dining room, Linda Gerin greeted Jake warmly with a kiss on each cheek. He introduced Catherine just as Jean-Louis, always aware of the presence of an attractive woman, hurried out of his kitchen.

"*Bon soir*! Welcome to our restaurant." The restaurateur hugged Catherine as if he'd known her for many years.

After Linda had seated them, Catherine remarked, "I haven't known the Gerins for five minutes. . . ."

"But you feel like you've known them for years?" Jake finished. "I'll guarantee that by the end of the evening you'll feel as if you've dined in their home."

When he'd made the reservation, Jake had pre-ordered the tasting menu. He'd also made special arrangements about the wines.

The courses began to arrive almost immediately: turtle soup, perfectly matched with a glass of Leacock's Sercial Madeira, vintage 1910. Then an herbed *loupe de mer*, a Mediterranean fish so fresh Catherine remarked that it must still have been alive that morning. It was accompanied by a 2000 Drouhin Corton-Charlemagne.

"Are these courses going to keep coming?" asked Catherine, smiling. "I guess I'll have to start watching my waistline."

"I don't believe that's necessary," Jake offered.

Jean-Louis then sent out a *poussin*, a tiny bird served with equally tiny vegetables on a bed of mesclun lettuce with a hint of raspberry vinaigrette. Jake had matched it to a 1990 Musigny, Vieilles Vignes from the Burgundy producer Comte Georges de Vogue that echoed the raspberry flavor of the vinaigrette. Finally, Jean-Louis produced a fillet of ostrich in a Port reduction sauce.

"I'm really impressed with the ostrich," Catherine said. "It tastes more like lean sirloin than fowl."

"I'm not sure, but that's possibly because the ostrich doesn't fly. It's certainly become a popular meat in the U.S. over the last ten years or so."

"Especially with nutritionists," Catherine observed. "Low in fat. My waistline thanks you."

"You're joking, right? You're not one of those women who worries incessantly about her weight?"

"Worries, no. I do try to be careful. And healthy. But there's always room for a good splurge." She grinned at him and took another bite.

For this course Jake did splurge—on a bottle of 1982 Chateau Mouton-Rothschild, slightly over twenty years old and at its peak, an excellent match for the ostrich.

After her first sip, Catherine leaned back in her chair, closed her eyes, and murmured, "It tastes like liquid velvet."

Jake applauded her description and was pleased that he'd chosen something she enjoyed. During dinner he decided to ask a serious question.

"All right," he said, "I want to hear all about *Doctor* Catherine Taylor. You're a surgeon from a family of surgeons—that I know. But somehow I get the feeling it wasn't just genealogy and fate that put you in the operating room. Am I right?"

Catherine nodded. "Every time I go into the OR, I get a rush. You suit up, you scrub, your adrenaline kicks in. It's like . . . ." She paused to think, her eyes unfocused on the table. Then she smiled. "It's like flying that airplane of yours. Like the moment the plane leaves the runway and becomes airborne. And then, when it's over, there's this feeling that goes with that last stitch—a fine sense of satisfaction. You know you've saved an organ, a limb . . . a life."

"Okay, so what makes Catherine Taylor light up?"

Her answer was immediate this time. "Music. Roses. I have a garden in my back yard that is, if I do say so myself, quite something."

"Roses," repeated Jake. "Somehow I picture you with irises or tulips, maybe."

"Nope. Roses. Tea roses. I love the miniature ones. Cecil Brunner, Gingersnap. Oh, and when it's too dark to garden, I do embroidery."

Jake laughed. "Now you're pulling my leg."

Catherine wiggled her fingers. "I just love to stitch things up."

He bowed his head, "For which I am most grateful. Um, you don't embroider roses, do you?"

"No, I just grow them." She leaned over the table as if she were about to divulge a secret. "I'm experimenting and trying to grow a blue rose."

"Blue?"

She nodded. "It's the Holy Grail of the rose world, now that black ones have been grown successfully."

"So, let me guess—you enjoy reading about . . . roses?"

She laughed at his expression. "Sometimes. I enjoy history. The history of rose breeding is fascinating stuff. To some of us," she added when he smiled wryly.

"I also like historical fiction."

"It's the wine. Too much *veritas*." She smiled. "But what about you? You've got to be a reader. I mean, how else would you find out about all these wines or all those machines you collect?"

"Guilty, I guess. I do read a lot of technical stuff. But I like fiction, too. Crime fiction, mostly."

"You're kidding. I'd think with your interest in real criminology you might run the other way."

"No, I enjoy it. It's a real hoot when someone gets it wrong—finds prints on a piece of sandpaper, for example, or gets lab results in minutes instead of days or weeks. And it's gratifying when someone gets it right."

"What else? What makes your blood pound?"

You, he thought, but didn't say it. "Criminology. Music. Wine."

"There, you see? We do have something in common. We both like music."

Jake laughed ruefully. "It does rather sound like opposites attracting, doesn't it? I'm all machines and hard edges, and you're all nature and soft. . . ."

She held up her glass. "Wine," she said. "That's natural. Wine and roses. They go together."

He lifted his own glass and met her gaze. He was certainly beginning to hope they went together. "To wine and roses, then."

As if she read his thoughts, Catherine dropped her gaze and sipped. "So you're involved with law enforcement."

"Some years ago it used to be software for police use. I'm now working with Dave Riley on a murder case."

"That's worth a shiver or two. What's the case?"

Jake shook his head. "I really can't talk about an ongoing investigation."

She smiled. "Ah, more mysteries. I'm afraid I'll bore you. I'm mostly an open book."

"Well, you're a new book to me. Unique and intriguing."

He watched her as she went back to her dinner. *You could never bore me*, he thought. *When was the last time I thought that about anyone?*

He nearly stopped breathing at the implicit answer to his own question.

At the end of the meal, Jake waved off Linda's suggestion of anything but Jean-Louis' signature green apple tart, so light and thin one could almost see through it. Jake ordered two glasses of the 1983 Chateau d'Yquem, a luscious Sauternes. It was a sweet, powerful wine, tasting of butterscotch, apricots, honey, and botrytis, the noble rot that perforated the grapes and helped concentrate the juice.

Sated, Jake and Catherine lingered over the Yquem. Jean-Louis personally delivered a plate of tiny confections to conclude the meal, then stayed to chat.

Later, as they faced each other across the welcome mat on Catherine's small front porch, she looked up at him and said, "Not only was Saturday one of the most adventurous days of my life, but this was absolutely the best meal I've ever had. And you were right—I felt as if I were in the home of old friends. It was wonderful. Thank you. And you can thank Linda and Jean-Louis for me, too. It was very flattering for him to take time away from his other customers to chat with us."

"Jean-Louis appreciates a beautiful woman almost as much as I do," Jake said, with an admiring glance.

He was caught off balance by a sudden flicker of reserve in Catherine's eyes. Melinda would have glowed at a compliment like that. But Catherine, he reminded himself, was not Melinda. He shook his head. "I'm sorry, Catherine. That didn't come out as I meant it to. It was supposed to be a compliment."

Her gaze warmed. "Then that's the way I'll take it—from you *and* Jean-Louis."

"As a matter of fact, Jean-Louis took me aside as we were leaving and said to be sure to bring you back often."

"I think I'd like that."

Then, in a move that seemed absolutely natural, Jake tenderly drew her into his arms and kissed her. She hesitated, momentarily, then returned the kiss.

Catherine broke away just as the embrace became passionate. Turning for her door, she said, "I'm going to take that as a compliment, too, Jake Halsey. Good night." With an unreadable backward glance, she unlocked her door and disappeared inside.

Jake was driven home, feeling pleasantly uncertain of his future with Catherine. For the moment, he decided, he would be happy just to fall into bed and dream of her. He had every expectation of doing just that. But when the lights went out, the image behind his closed eyelids wasn't Catherine's lovely face. It was a flip-chart page with a haunting list of Connecticut towns and cities.

CHAPTER FOURTEEN

At the end of the conference table, Dave Riley steepled his fingers and pressed the tips against his forehead. He was a man in conflict. He said under his breath, "Tell me this was a simple traffic accident."

"The killer had to be within thirty or forty feet of the truck to trigger the device," Jake concluded. "Maybe he was following the truck; maybe he was lying in wait. Either way, this was a setup."

Pezzi yawned broadly and took a sip of his coffee. "A pretty extreme way to bust up some wine bottles," he said. "If that's what was going on."

Ellen noticed Jake eyeing the coffee carafe and silently passed it to him for a refill.

"All these incidents are extreme," Riley said, raising his head. "The only involvement Dennis Cox had with wine was that he made his living driving it around the countryside. Bob Daniels, in Danbury, sold it, and Mitchell Livingston, right here in town, collected it. And now?" He leaned back in his chair, nodding at the file folder that lay on the table before him. "I've got another likely event to add to the list."

All eyes widened. Pezzi's posture snapped to attention in military fashion.

Riley continued. "Over the weekend we heard from the police in Essex. Back in April, one Raymond DiVito—the recently retired CEO of a major consumer products company—was using a work boat to place his thirty-foot sailboat's summer mooring. He was out on the water in front of his house, which sits on the edge of the Connecticut River. The mooring was a large, 100-pound mushroom anchor with about twenty feet of heavy galvanized chain attached to it with a big shackle and a heavy manila line to run up to the surface. Somehow, DiVito's foot got tangled in the chain, and when he pushed the anchor over the side, he went with it. The water there was about twenty-five feet deep. He drowned trying to extricate himself."

"I assume it was ruled an accidental death?" Jake set down the carafe and took a seat at the table.

Riley nodded. "And as such, it would be meaningless to our investigation. However, DiVito had a wine cellar with some seven thousand bottles in it about 250 feet from where he lost his life."

Pezzi whistled.

"Is there any evidence our perp was involved?" asked Jake. "Wine cellar aside, wasn't DiVito's death just an unfortunate boating accident?"

Pezzi was nodding. "If our killer was involved, how'd he make *this* accident happen?

"Good question," said Riley. "I don't have the answer, but I had Brian run an online check of the Essex newspapers, the *Main Street News* and the *Valley Courier*. The DiVito death showed up when we searched on the words wine and accident. But there was nothing else. The death was reported in both papers, but neither suggested there was anything suspicious about it."

"And the local police?" Jake asked.

"Accident, pure and simple."

"Which means we've got a lot of questions and no answers," Brian Allen noted.

Jake stood and moved to the easel to update the chart. It was no longer in his hasty handwriting; a department secretary had prepared another version, larger and more legible. The orderly columns and wide spaces for new entries struck him as a sign that some strange and irreversible process was under way. Private vision was now public fact—the pattern of crimes that had first appeared in his head was past the point where he could doubt its reality. He grimaced. There was nothing comfortable about this observation.

1. Ansonia—June, 2002—Truck Crash & Fatality
Victim: Dennis Cox
2. Bridgeport—September, 2002—Murder
Owner: Brad Perkins/Victim: Rachel Charleson
3. C?
4. Danbury—February, 2003—Arson
Owner: Bob Daniels of Bob's Fine Wines
5. Essex—April, 2003—Drowning
Victim: Raymond DiVito
6. Fairfield—July, 2003—Plane Crash & Explosion
Owner: Harry Johnson
7. Greenwich—October, 2003—Poison
Owner and Victim: Mitchell Livingston
8. H?

"Pardon me while I add another wrinkle," said Brian. "With six confirmed events already on our list, we've got to consider that there may have been crimes in cities past the letter H that we don't know about yet."

Riley felt his stomach turn over. "That would mean he's accelerating his timetable. Or that we estimated the timetable incorrectly in the first place."

Brian nodded. "There might have also been other attempts that failed for some reason."

"You're right. But we've got so much on our plate right now, we don't have the time or the manpower to go looking for the dog that *didn't* bark. A more productive approach would be to just concentrate on adding the missing C to our list, so we can figure what the hell is going on before this guy strikes again.

"There are twenty-eight possibilities. I'm going to grab every extra man and woman we've got around here and get them calling local PDs. I'll bet something will turn up in the next couple of hours."

"Phone records," said Jake.

Riley glanced over at him and saw the distracted expression in his eyes. "Phone records?"

"Cox's visit to Ansonia wasn't business related. Maybe

he was meeting someone. If he did, maybe his phone records will suggest why he was off his route that day. I mean, think about it. This was an intentional hit—either on Cox or on the wines he was carrying. Either way, how would the perp know he'd be in Ansonia, where he wasn't supposed to be?"

Tony Pezzi snorted. "Maybe he was just following him around hoping he'd go to a town that started with the letter A."

Riley bit back a tart comment and said, "Maybe he was a regular visitor."

Jake met his gaze. "A check of his phone records, land-line or cell, might turn up something. It's a long-shot, but. . . ."

Riley pointed at Allen. "Brian, you're on it."

Two hours later there was a shout from the squad room. Riley stuck his head out the door of his office to see Officer Arlene Bianchini grinning as if she'd hit the lottery.

"Hey, Arlene, calm down," he said, moving quickly to her desk with the rest of the task force on his heels. "What have you got?"

"Clinton PD. Their chief told me that last October, Edward Plessy, a doctor at the Yale–New Haven Hospital, came home from spending an afternoon at the beach with his family, kicked off his shoes, and went down to his basement to get a bottle of wine for a pre-dinner drink with his wife. Seems he had a small collection of about 700 bottles. His wine cellar was in a separate room, an older part of the cellar two steps down from the rest of the basement.

"The wall switch for the wine-cellar lights was inside the door. Plessy entered in the dark and stepped down into about a half-an-inch of water on the floor. Naturally, he reached for the light switch to find out why." She paused, then dropped the bomb. "He was electrocuted."

Riley and Jake exchanged glances.

"Wow," Pezzi interjected, "that's a lot more original than a hairdryer in the bathtub, huh?"

Riley bit his lip. "Accident?"

"Down, boy," Arlene told Tony, then continued her

report, speaking directly to Riley. "Not according to the Clinton PD. They found a heavy-duty extension cord plugged into a duplex outlet intended for a winter heating unit the Plessys used to keep the cellar temperature even. It was connected to the switched circuit and the bare ends of the cord were lying on the floor, so the water was energized. Plessy's wife said she'd never seen that cord before and there never had been water on the wine-cellar floor in the twenty or so years they'd been in the house." She shivered, grimacing. "What an awful way to die."

Minutes later, in Riley's office, Jake stepped back from the flip chart, capped his marker, and took a deep breath, feeling the rest of the team breathe with him. No more blanks to fill in except the last—H.

1. Ansonia—June, 2002—Truck Crash & Fatality
   Victim: Dennis Cox
2. Bridgeport—September, 2002—Strangulation
   Owner: Brad Perkins
   Victim: Rachel Charleson
3. Clinton—October, 2002—Electrocution
   Owner and Victim: Edward Plessy, MD
4. Danbury—February, 2003—Arson Fire
   Owner: Bob Daniels of Bob's Fine Wines
5. Essex—April, 2003—Drowning
   Victim: Raymond DiVito
6. Fairfield—July, 2003—Plane Crash & Explosion
   Owner: Harry Johnson
7. Greenwich—October, 2003—Poison
   Owner and Victim: Mitchell Livingston
8. H?

"Now that we've filled in the blanks," Jake mused, "there's another characteristic we haven't yet considered that really stands out. The different methods the perp used. Look. Each of the seven incidents had a different MO: truck crash, strangulation, electrocution, arson, drowning, plane crash, explosion, and poison. No repeats. With this many data points, that's too unlikely to be coincidence. It's *got* to be by design."

Riley moved from the doorway to resume his seat at the conference table. "Since so little time has passed since the Livingston murder, I hope we can assume the killer hasn't struck again."

Ellen Green looked over at her boss with a sharp glint of eagerness in her eyes. "If this pattern is what it seems to be— an alpha-listing—we can actually predict a range of possible locations for the killer's next strike."

"That's something a detective doesn't see every day," said Tony.

Jake glanced at Riley and caught him fighting a smile. Sometimes Tony's comments were right on the dime.

Brian Allen entered the room just then to drop a file folder onto the table top in front of his boss. "Bingo," he said, sliding into his chair. "Dennis Cox had both a land line and a cell phone. Over the course of the last several months he called one number in Ansonia twice each week, on Tuesday and Thursday mornings—always using the cell. The timing suggests that he made the calls while on the road in his delivery truck. The number belongs to a Madeleine Norette— widowed, age forty-eight, lives alone. Zero calls to her number in his land-line records. I'll bet my next paycheck she's the reason Cox was driving to Ansonia."

Tony Pezzi shook his head. "Man, they say you shouldn't mix. . . ." He glanced at Riley and stopped. "Uh. . . ." He cleared his throat. "I guess you'll want me and Ellen to trot on up to Ansonia and interview the widow Norette?"

Riley smiled tightly. "You read my mind."

CHAPTER FIFTEEN

Jake extended his hand to the tall, angular woman who'd opened the door hesitantly in response to his knock. "Mrs. DiVito? I'm Jake Halsey. I'm working with the Greenwich police to solve a series of crimes they suspect might have some relation to your husband's death."

She opened the door a bit wider. "Yes. They called. A civilian consultant, they called you. Please . . . come in." She stepped back, allowing him into the foyer of the renovated Cape Cod.

The DiVito home, Jake noted, was a good deal less ornate than its Colonial and Victorian neighbors. Situated five miles upstream from the mouth of the Connecticut River, the streets of Essex were lined with fine examples of historical residential architecture, including a number of houses with the requisite ornamentation. One outrageously ornate example he'd passed at the top of the street was so proud of its gee-gaws that it sported a sign reading "The Gingerbread House." Mrs. DiVito herself reminded Jake of an injured flamingo. She wore a bright pink dress that had once fit more closely than it did today. The weight loss had to be recent. She appeared to be struggling to meet his gaze.

"I spoke with the police many times last spring when the accident happened," she told him as she led the way into an airy parlor at the rear of the house. "I was surprised when I got the call yesterday. But I'm willing to help in any way I can."

She gestured Jake to a wicker armchair and seated herself in its mate across a wicker and glass coffee table. She offered coffee, and he noticed a visible hand tremor as she poured a cup and handed it to him. Sunlight from a row of French doors overlooking a whitewashed rear deck reflected off the tabletop. Beyond the deck, Jake could see a private pier and a

93

mooring at which a medium-sized sloop was tied up.

Placid place, thought Jake. *The river; a better than average home library down the hall; comfortable unpretentious furniture. Their life here must have been pretty peaceful. Now she's about as relaxed as a cornered rat.*

He considered his words carefully, then said, "Mrs. DiVito, I am truly sorry to be opening barely healed wounds, but there is a possibility that your husband's death was not an accident."

He'd expected her to be shocked. To protest that, of course, her husband's death couldn't have been anything but an accident. He was braced for the worst and prepared to handle it like a gentleman.

She surprised him.

"I'll tell you frankly, Mr. Halsey," she said, "I've had trouble accepting the accidental nature of Ray's death from the beginning. The police were very kind, but I could tell they thought I was overwrought and paranoid." She leaned toward him, her elbows on her knees. "Ray was a seasoned yachtsman. I've just never accepted the logic of the police explanation of his death. I find it hard to believe that a man who learned to sail when he was ten could drown in such an unlikely way. If you have an alternate explanation, I'd like very much to hear it."

She gestured through the French doors to the magnificent view of the Connecticut River and the sunny dock. "That's where it happened. Right out there. He was all alone that day, putting the mooring in to get the boat ready for the summer. He went out just after breakfast and didn't return." She stopped, her eyes brimming with tears. "I never got to say goodbye."

Jake gave her a moment to regain her composure and then said gently, "I know you've gone over the details many times already, but has anything new about that day come to mind in the intervening six months? Something in particular that makes you think your husband's death wasn't accidental?"

She continued to gaze out at the dock. "I've thought

about that day a thousand times and so has our daughter, Hannah. She's an actress and lives in New York now, but she was here when the accident occurred. I remember vividly, it was a beautiful spring day. It was so nice, in fact, that Hannah was taking pictures of everything, hoping to get a few photos to enlarge to decorate her new apartment. She was using an old camera we'd given her for her fifteenth birthday—an Olympus OM-2. A film camera." She smiled. "Ray teased her about it. Called her an antique. He told her real photographers now use pixels, not film. But she was quite the traditionalist about this. She took some pictures of Ray and the boat."

"How did the photos come out?" asked Jake when she hesitated, struggling with her grief.

"I don't know. I . . . we forgot about them at first, Hannah and I. But later . . . I couldn't bring myself to . . . ." She paused, took a deep breath.

"Mrs. DiVito, did you ever consider that those photos might provide some insight into. . . ." He didn't know what to call it. Not the accident certainly. Not now.

She looked at him with tears still sparkling in her lashes. Her expression was sober, her eyes direct. She shook her head.

That explained why the detailed police report of Raymond DiVito's death had failed to mention the photographs.

"Do you still have the film?"

She nodded, rose, and moved to a Shaker-style cabinet with glass doors. There were several cameras in it, Jake noted, including an old Box Brownie, a Polaroid Land Camera, and the Olympus OM-2. She removed the Olympus from the shelf and brought it to him.

"I don't know how to get the film out safely without finishing the roll," she said, handing it to him. Her smile was on the edge of breaking up. "My present camera's digital."

He accepted the camera and checked the roll. There were five shots left. He carefully rewound the film to the beginning, opened the camera, and removed the roll. He looked up at Helen DiVito. "Are you sure you're willing to. . . ."

"Please take it, Mr. Halsey. All I ask is that you let me

know if you find anything, and . . . and I'd like copies of the prints."

He nodded. "Of course."

She took a deep breath and let it out. She was letting go of more than a roll of film. "Now, I suppose you'll want to see the dock."

He did. She showed him the exact spot where her husband had died six months earlier, pointing to it as she stood on the pier above the floating dock. He looked at the sloop and the small work boat DiVito had been using, but saw nothing unusual. Except for Helen DiVito's expression: this was her home, but she was watching the river as a caged songbird would eye the family cat.

She looked away, with effort, and returned her attention to Jake. "Have you ever loved a place, Mr. Halsey, and then fallen out of love with it? I haven't stopped coming down here, but I don't know whether I can ever feel comfortable near this river again." Jake nodded in silent assent.

Pocketing the film, he said goodbye and headed for the police lab near Hartford where he dropped the film off to maintain a proper chain of custody. The lab tech said to come back in an hour for the results.

Just over an hour later, he was sitting in a nearby Starbucks looking through the developed prints. There were thirty-one in all, mostly of the river, the shoreline, spring flowers in the family garden, and the house itself: the sort of things one might enlarge and frame. The shots of her father were the last ones Hannah DiVito had taken. There were four, all shot from the rear deck of the house above the dock.

Jake gave each a cursory look. He started to set one aside because the target of the shot was a speedboat going upriver, not DiVito's boat, but something about the picture made him stop for a closer look. Though the speedboat was centered in the shot, in the foreground he could just make out the bow and part of the port side of Ray DiVito's workboat, with the mushroom anchor clearly visible on its deck. Ray DiVito's head and shoulders made a blurred appearance in the photo. So did the head and shoulders of a second man—a man who seemed to be standing in a second boat on the riverward side. Both men had their heads turned away from the camera toward the speedboat. The stranger was gesturing to something out in the current.

A chill ran up Jake's spine. If Ray DiVito was alone that day, as his wife had said, who was the second man?

Jake realized he might be looking at a photograph of Ray DiVito's killer.

CHAPTER SIXTEEN

During the ride back to Greenwich the clouds had cleared and, for a change, the traffic was very light on Route 95. The adrenaline rush caused by the photo had diminished and Jake started to daydream. Photos taken by his parents on a 1961 trip to Hong Kong surfaced in his mind, as did the story of their trip that had been referred to frequently when he was young.

Kowloon, Hong Kong, December 1, 1961
The tall, elegantly dressed couple stepped out of the main lobby door of the Peninsula Hotel, made their way through the hotel parking area, glanced at the houses on cloud-shrouded Victoria Peak, and turned left up the slight incline of Nathan Road.

Both wore the uniform of the Western tourist—she was in tailored slacks, a jacket and scarf; he in a blazer over a shirt and ascot.

It was a lovely winter day. The blue sky and fleecy clouds were reminiscent of fall days back at the couple's home in Connecticut and the temperature was in the low sixties. It was, in fact, a perfect day for a leisurely walk prior to the thirteen-course Chinese banquet they would attend later in the evening. They had planned their day carefully to include enough time for the luxury of a bath, for even in the highly regarded Peninsula Hotel, water was turned on only one hour a day due to an extreme shortage.

As the couple walked along the heavily traveled road, they noted frenzied construction activity all around. Many of the buildings had an outer grid of bouncy bamboo scaffolding that writhed like interwoven snakes as scurrying workers moved on it with agility. The latticework itself encroached on the already-crowded sidewalk and lent an Old World character to the scene. To the left and right, down cross streets and alleyways, laundry hung like colored pennants, strung on lines between buildings in anticipation of the few moments of sun the narrow streets allowed.

On both sides of the road, the trade of each business occupant was spelled out in both Chinese characters and English letters. Since many American and European visitors frequented this section of Kowloon, there were an inordinate number of tailor shops. Signs offering custom-made shirts for $12, suits for $55, and shoes for $20 were frequent. Even chinchilla stoles and coats were offered. Food was for sale everywhere, hawked by street vendors and tourist-trap eateries at street level and served with studied elegance in second floor restaurants with thick menus and headwaiters dressed in tuxedos.

Traffic was both intense and slow. Throngs of pedestrians crossed the road haphazardly, and Chinese taxi-men with broad, flat hats ferried their human cargo in frail-looking rickshaws.

As they walked, the American woman occasionally made absent attempts to pull her jacket down over her hips and belly. The jacket had fit her well before the birth of her son two months earlier, and she looked forward to the day when it would fit her again. Her son, born three weeks premature, had been put on formula immediately; perhaps she should have tried harder to breastfeed once she had left the hospital. Her mother had assured her breastfeeding was nature's way of taking care of what she wryly called "baby fat." She gave a fond moment's thought to her son, now sleeping peacefully back at the hotel in the care of their live-in nanny. An occasional abdominal cramp was dismissed as the uterus reducing in size

The couple, well-traveled in Europe, had never been to the Far East. The man felt that a change of scene and a trip to the Orient would hasten his wife's recovery from her difficult pregnancy. In a week, the couple would be returning to their home in Greenwich. She'd start a new exercise regimen then, she decided, and try to catch up on some long-delayed reading whenever the routine of infant care allowed the time. She was lucky, she thought, that her son was such a sound sleeper.

The pain in her abdomen was sudden and sharp. She groaned and doubled over, stopped in her tracks by the unexpectedness of it. A wave of nausea followed, drawing another groan. Her husband grabbed her arm and tried to help her straighten, but she couldn't.

Frantic, he glanced around for help. An urchin who'd been watching the couple's progress from the shadows ran up and tugged at his sleeve.

"Want doctor, mistair?" he asked, his dark eyes wide.

"Yes, yes!" cried the man, in a panic.

The boy turned and hurried down a side street, beckoning the couple to follow. He passed several tiny markets, then turned in and climbed a flight of narrow stairs, calling ahead at the top of his lungs in Chinese.

By the time they'd reached the second floor, an elderly Chinese gentleman with a drooping white Fu Manchu mustache was awaiting them. His facial hair stood in stark contrast to his Western garb, which included a pale green smock.

"Do you speak English?" the American panted. "It's my wife. I don't know what's wrong. Maybe it's something she ate."

The Chinese gentleman nodded. "Your wife is pregnant?" he asked in musically accented English.

"Not any more. She gave birth—uh, had a baby—two months ago.

The man gently took custody of the ill woman and directed the man to a black-lacquered armchair in the small anteroom. "I examine. You wait." He then led the woman through a bead-curtained doorway and down a long hall.

More than an hour passed, and the man grew increasingly nervous. As he was pacing the worn silk carpet the Chinese man reappeared and said, "No worry. She is fine—resting. Was retained piece of placenta I remove with instruments. You see her one or two more hours only."

The man sighed with relief, and sat back in his chair. Glancing at his watch, he realized that his bath would have to wait—the hours of water operation had passed.

CHAPTER SEVENTEEN

Jake pulled the Renault into the police parking lot and turned down the Rolling Stones CD blasting from his custom speakers. His mood called for something far more upbeat than a classical orchestra. Ever since seeing Hannah DiVito's photograph of her dad and the tall stranger, Jake had felt a rush like a hundred cups of coffee.

Maybe, just maybe, they'd stumbled on their first break in the case. Maybe, despite the Stones warning, they *were* about to get some satisfaction. He jogged more than walked to Riley's office, anxious to share his find.

When Jake entered, the others were seated around the table.

"What?" Riley asked. "You look like the cat after it polished off the canary."

"I've got a photo that may show the killer." The reaction in the room was electric. "Hannah DiVito, the daughter, took some pictures the day her Dad drowned. One of them just happens to show a guy in another boat alongside DiVito. The question is, is this the guy, or just some random fellow with a boat?" He held up his enlarged copy of the photo of Ray DiVito and his anonymous visitor and put several additional copies on the table.

The mood in the room had quieted.

Riley moved back to his seat and reached down to snag a copy of the print.

"That's clearly a very tall man," Ellen said, her eyes on the print in front of her. "I'd say over six feet. Jake, did you show this to Mrs. DiVito?"

Jake nodded. "I took a run up there the other day for just that reason. She couldn't identify the guy. But you're right about the height. Helen DiVito told me her husband was

102

nearly six feet tall, and the man in the photograph is taller. No one, including the DiVitos' daughter, remembers seeing anyone else or any other boat."

"Weird," muttered Tony. "She takes a picture, but doesn't see what's in it."

"Happens all the time," Ellen said. "Haven't you ever shot a picture of something while you were on vacation and been surprised at what was in the background?"

Tony grinned. "What's a vacation?"

The detectives chuckled; even Dave Riley smiled briefly.

Jake said, "Based on this photo, I'd be willing to bet a few bucks that DiVito didn't drown accidentally. He was murdered, and you're looking at a picture of his killer."

The room was quiet for a moment, as the detectives pored over the photographs, all wondering, Jake guessed, what tiny, telling detail they might have missed.

Jake rubbed his eyes and found that, even with them closed, he still saw the flip-chart image with its dire record of the case. "Including Greenwich," he said, "we've got six towns or cities involved in this case. Pardon me for asking, but I've only been involved with you in local cases before. Since five of the other towns aren't in your jurisdiction, aren't the State Police going to want to be involved in this thing sooner or later?"

"You need to know a little about procedure," Riley replied from his place at the head of the table. "In Connecticut, the state's Major Crimes Squad will process a crime scene and collect evidence, but it doesn't have the manpower to handle the actual investigation. That's left up to the local gang. Any evidence that's actually collected later in any investigation is sent to the state labs for analysis.

"Each of the other five towns where these crimes occurred has—at least up until now—been treating them as routine, according to the reports we've gathered. As an example, our own investigation of the Livingston death was a routine operation for us, if you can call any violent crime in Greenwich routine, and our initial report reflects that. What makes this case extraordinary is the probable connection with the other crimes. Just because they've occurred in different jurisdictions won't necessarily attract the attention of the State Police, except for investigatory activities by the Major Crimes Squad. Even they will want to see just cause for their involvement. So, if the dots are going to be connected. . . ."

"We're going to have to do the connecting," Jake summarized.

Riley rose and began a restless circuit of the room, rubbing at his eyes. He didn't look like a man who'd had a quiet night, and his next words confirmed that. "Couldn't sleep last night. The sheep were out to pasture and all I could count were. . . ." He gestured at the growing list of towns. "Here's the bottom line: No matter how connected this looks to us, all we have here is a jumble of unconnected information about scattered crimes that *seem* to form a pattern. But we're going to need to have a nice little package all set when the time comes to bring in the DA or the State Police."

"*Package?*" repeated Tony Pezzi. "We need a damned *perpetrator*. Right now, we've got nothing on this guy but a fuzzy picture that may or may not be him."

Riley shot the younger detective a glance, but said only, "No killer, no motive, weapons that keep changing, not even a whole lot of concern who his victim is gonna be."

Jake leaned against the credenza next to the flip chart. "But we do have three of the weapons in hand: the poisoned bottle of wine, the garage door openers from the Bailey's truck, and the wreckage from the plane crash. Okay, so no fingerprints, no DNA, no connective tissue *except* that these are all unusual ways—*theatrical* ways—of committing a crime."

Ellen lifted her head and followed her boss's progress around the room. "Jake's right. It's possible that the extraordinary nature of the MO is enough to reasonably connect the crimes."

"Yeah, that's how it looks to us, but are we going to get a prosecutor to bite on that idea? Right now we've got a lot of unanswered questions and some big holes in our data. Those questions need to get answered and those holes plugged. One example of our problem is Rachel Charleson, the murder victim in Bridgeport. Yes, she was embalmed with wine. Yes, she was found in a wine cellar. But how was she chosen? Why was she killed?"

Nobody spoke for a moment, then Pezzi said, "We did find out what Dennis Cox was doing in Ansonia, but, unfortunately, it doesn't look like his trysts with Ms. Norette had anything to do with what happened to him. If this were isolated, we'd be thinking about a jealous significant other on either side." He glanced around the table at the others and shrugged. "There's a heck of a lot we don't know about that truck crash. Were they after Cox specifically? If so, why? Were they after Bailey Brothers? Why? And what about the Clinton electrocution? We also need to know if Johnson, the house owner in the Fairfield plane crash, was involved in any way except as an innocent bystander. Was he supposed to have been killed, but just wasn't home at the right time?

"And then there's this DiVito photograph. Who is this, and how does he fit in?

"Okay," Riley said, tossing his copy of the print onto the table, "let's get busy. Tony, see what you can find out about the Fairfield Beach house that got blown up by the plane. We've got to figure out why it was chosen by our killer. Yeah, yeah," he said, as Tony's mouth popped open, "it had wine in it. But why? *Why wine?* Why not beer or model trains or stamps or any of a hundred other things people collect? Jake, if you would, go up to Bridgeport and dig around to find out how our guy could have gotten into the Perkins place, how he might have brought in his victim without setting off the alarm. We also need to know more about why he chose Rachel Charleson and where he killed her. Ellen, maybe you can do some brainstorming around the 'whys.' Brian, you work out some way of ensuring thorough coverage of all 'H' towns."

Riley glanced down at the DiVito photo and pursed his lips. "Also, if you've got any extra time on your hands, see if you can digitally enhance this image."

Brian raised his sandy-colored brows. "Great. I love a challenge."

Riley pinched the bridge of his nose, looking like a man fighting off a headache. "Okay, gang, let's scramble. Next time I see you, I want an angle on this guy. Something. *Anything*."

CHAPTER EIGHTEEN

"You're not a police detective, are you?" Brad Perkins asked as he ushered Jake into his Bridgeport home.

The unusual bluntness of the question surprised a chuckle out of Jake. "No. As unusual as it might seem, I'm a retired software developer with a knack for sorting through evidence."

That explanation didn't seem to satisfy Perkins. "Mr. Halsey, even though the police clerk called me to set up this appointment, I must say I'm reluctant to go over this again with someone without credentials. Care to tell me why I should?"

"A number of years ago my software company created a program to help police departments assemble and collate evidence from crime scenes and share it with other investigative bodies. The Greenwich police don't use my software very often, but they do have me. I've studied forensics, and I have a background in electronics that complements the skills of the Greenwich Police. In fact, I've helped them solve several crimes. Also, since it pertains to this case and some others we've got under review right now, I know a lot about wine."

"Just what I need on top of a dead body in my basement. A goddamned amateur."

Just what I need, too, thought Jake. *A guy who watches TV police procedurals and thinks that makes him an insider. Brace yourself: bumpy ride ahead.*

Perkins studied him a moment longer, then said, "I suppose if I send you away, they'll just send someone else."

"Most likely."

"Fine. How can I help you?" Perkins's voice wasn't quite dripping with sarcasm, but it was damp.

"I'd like to see your wine cellar and the alarm panel, if you don't mind. I'm particularly curious to discover how the alarm system might have been compromised."

Perkins nodded curtly, then led the way through the house and down the cellar stairs. He was middle-aged and heavyset, with a brushy mustache and a brusque manner. He reminded Halsey of several men he'd run across in the Air Force. All were career officers; most were competent; one or two were more than competent. Jake had disliked them all in varying degrees, but he had found ways of respecting the ones who did their work well.

"There's the door the police think the intruder used," Perkins said, pointing to an external exit. It was pure colonial, with mullioned panes that looked out into an alley. "On that wall is the central alarm box and right over here is the entrance to the wine cellar."

He moved to open an unlocked wooden panel door, switched on the light, and stood aside to let Jake enter the room.

Jake quickly took in the wine racks and the long, obviously antique tasting table that ran lengthwise in front of them. Over the table hung the room's sole illumination, a pendant light of the type usually found over pool tables.

"That poor girl was lying on this table." Perkins gestured at it. "Top is still stained. I want it out of here. I'm trying to work something out with your law-enforcement buddies. Have them take it off our hands."

"You didn't know the girl?" Jake asked, though he already knew the answer.

"We'd never seen her before." Perkins cleared his throat, then looked up at Jake through thick bifocal lenses. "We have granddaughters, Mr. Halsey. Just about that girl's age. I can only hope they're more responsible about keeping their parents informed as to their whereabouts."

"With all due respect, Mr. Perkins, Rachel Charleson did nothing irresponsible to bring on this crime." Jake was liking Perkins less with each remark.

"Ah, of course. She was simply out in the world

unsupervised, doing whatever she wanted to do, with no one in a position to defend her from a sociopath. At best, I'd say she was fatally naive. I can't comment on whether she was dressed as a walking invitation to assault, like so many of her peers, because by the time I found her on my property she wasn't dressed at all. And before I have to listen to a lot of liberal rhetoric about the independence of young women, I suppose I'll leave you to your work, whatever you believe that is."

Jake nodded through clenched teeth and suppressed several possible responses. "I'd just like to poke around down here a bit, if you don't mind," he said.

"Certainly," responded Perkins. "Just come upstairs and holler when you're finished."

"One more thing—you haven't had the alarm repaired since the murder, have you?"

"Didn't need repair," Perkins said. "Just turned it back on." He went back upstairs, leaving Jake to his own devices.

Jake turned out the wine cellar light and closed the door, relieved to be away from Perkins.

I'm a guest in this man's house, Jake thought, *here for professional purposes. No good can come from rising to his provocations. So what's with this adrenaline surge? I feel like I could cold-cock a buffalo.*

He exited through the outside door, leaving it unlocked so he could re-enter. It opened onto a narrow alleyway with a concrete sidewalk that followed the side of the house, running toward the street. The Perkinses lived in a fairly urban residential area and there was a utility pole close to the door, set out a bit from the house, presumably on the property line.

Jake raised his eyes and followed the main electrical wires, a telephone line, and a TV cable from the pole across and down the side of the house. He found what he was looking for. It was becoming a common utility practice to make a small coil at each end of any wire being installed, adjacent to the point where the wire was attached. In the event of a storm or other unexpected pulling of the wire, the coil would straighten out like a shock absorber, saving a detached wire and a service call. The telephone wire serving the Perkins house was neatly coiled in a few circles just below a locked cabinet right at the spot where it entered the building.

Jake reached into his kit for a pair of surgical rubber gloves, tweezers, and a plastic bag, then crouched down. He examined the coil closely, brushing the alley dirt from the rubber coating. The wire was gritty, as might be expected. Then something caught his eye. Using the small high-intensity flashlight on his keychain, he illuminated the wire. Damn! He *had* seen it, a short blond hair caught in a three-inch cut in the wire's coating.

He gingerly opened up the cut with one hand, grabbed the hair with his tweezers, and sealed it in the plastic bag. He then exposed the conductors. They had been snipped, spliced back together, and then soldered very professionally, probably with a battery-operated soldering gun. Jake now realized why the central station had not received an alarm signal. With all the time in the world, the perpetrator had simply covered his tracks.

Returning inside, Jake opened the unlocked alarm panel in the hallway. It was well marked as to which terminals represented the incoming wires from the three key pads reported to be in the house. The alarm system appeared to be an older model that had been in place for some years. Since the house was not too far from Long Island Sound, the exposed brass screws of the wire terminals were heavily tarnished from the salt air. That made the scratch marks on the dull surface stand out with burnished brilliance.

Alligator clips. The murderer had used alligator clips to connect a device of some kind to the screws, most likely a battery-operated decoding machine or similar device. Upon entry, and in less time than the usual forty-five-second alarm delay, such an attached electronic device could try thousands of combinations for the Perkins alarm code and find the correct one. For a burglar with the tools and knowledge, overcoming the alarm system and getting into the Perkins house would have been child's play.

Jake went upstairs to find Brad Perkins sitting at his

kitchen table nursing a faraway look and a cup of black coffee.

"I'm finished," Jake said.

Perkins took a conspicuous look at his watch. "Already? Did you find something or has this all been a waste of my time?"

"It's been worth both your time and mine. There was some pretty clear evidence outside, and I think I know what happened. The killer defeated your alarm system with a couple of electronic tricks."

Perkins's mouth opened in astonishment. "Goddammit, if you knew what I spent on this system, young man, you wouldn't be so cavalier about it. I suppose he used some high tech stuff?"

"One part high tech, one not so high tech. He must have cut the telephone line temporarily, in the event that the alarm sounded before the decoding device he used sorted through all the permutations and figured out your pass code. If his decoder hadn't worked, there could have been a local alarm sounded, but at least there would have been no signal to the central station. The police report confirms that no neighbor heard any alarm go off while you were away, so apparently his decoder worked perfectly."

"But the alarm wasn't disabled when we came home, just off. Don't insinuate I don't pay close attention to my home's security."

"I'm not implying anything of the kind, Mr. Perkins. Before he left, he patched it up. Very professional job, too. Nice, clean, shiny solder joints."

Perkins stiffened. "Then the police were more right than they knew. This wasn't some nut case committing a crime of passion. He planned it—planned killing that poor girl. But why? Why this house—*our* house? Why that girl?"

Jake shook his head. "I was hoping you could enlighten me on that point."

"I don't know how I can, Halsey, and I resent the inference that I'd know anything about this."

Implication, you goon. Not that it matters, but if I'd said anything you had a reason to object to, you'd resent something I implied, not something I inferred. He let it pass without comment; Perkins's command of English wasn't the thing Jake found objectionable about him.

"Did the Bridgeport police ever figure out where Rachel Charleson came from or why she was here? The report I've seen was prepared before the Greenwich PD pointed out a possible connection to other cases."

Perkins shook his head slowly. "All they told me was that she was a student, one of those rich kids from Fairfield University. She was from New York. Family probably thought she'd be less likely to come to harm up here among the Jesuits than at NYU or some such place, around the fast-living crowd. Money came from a grandfather. Pretty horrible irony to find her in a wine cellar that way. The old guy must have turned over in his grave."

He had Jake's full attention. "Why would you say that?"

"Charleson family business is wine. They import and distribute wines out of a storefront in Manhattan. Coincidentally, I've ordered a few bottles from them over the years."

Jake's pulse was racing. "Recently?"

"It's been years. Probably since before that girl was born."

Jake paused before speaking.

"Do you remember what you ordered from them? Is there anything else you can tell me about their business?"

"No. What the hell else do you want? I've been a customer off and on. I saw their ad in a magazine and requested a catalogue and ordered some things. I haven't bothered keeping track of which vintages in my cellar come from which suppliers, and don't ask me what magazine the ad was in; I never had a photographic memory, and it's not getting any better. Maybe *Gourmet*; my wife reads that. Maybe *Food and Wine*, *Wine Spectator*, I don't know—hell, *Guns and Ammo*, for all I know. That's the only one I've always kept a subscription to."

Noted.

"Thanks, but I think we may be getting a little off track. I was thinking more of. . . ."

"I'm beginning to think I don't care all that much about what you're thinking. Do you bastards have any leads about this dead woman, or don't you?"

Jake felt his pulse accelerating. Perkins was clearly close to the end of his patience. He wasn't alone in that.

"Sir," Jake said, "we have certain information, and I'm here to gather anything more that might help. I'll tell you in complete honesty that anything beyond my physical examinations is a fishing expedition, but a purposeful one. If there's some aspect of the Charleson firm that might have made them a target for a killer, I'm interested, and it may not be anything that looks special to you. If there's really nothing you recall about them, we're probably done here."

"You gonna tell me why any of this makes a difference? Or is this something it takes a wet-behind-the-ears, ex-software developer to figure out?" Perkins was standing more stiffly now, forearm muscles tense, looking Jake directly in the eye. "Don't try to tell me the city's head detective counts on amateur talent to interpret his forensic evidence as well as collect it. My tax dollars at work, as usual. I wonder how much of your input he actually listens to."

Jake took deliberate control of his breathing and his words. "Mr. Perkins, you've been helpful opening your home for this examination, and I don't want to take up much more of your day. You've had something happen downstairs that you didn't ask for. I appreciate your cooperation." He extended his right hand to Perkins, formally, unsmiling. Perkins did not shake it.

"You appreciate jack shit. You come in here and play cop and tell me I've invested four figures in a system that some murderous freak can defeat with a gadget from Radio Shack. Exactly what qualifies you to poke around my house and troubleshoot my alarm rig, anyway?"

"Let's just say that's on a need-to-know basis and I'm done with the troubleshooting."

Perkins glared and took a sudden swing at Jake, a right roundhouse. He put his shoulder into it, and he had plenty of force, but he lacked deception, and Jake dodged the blow without trouble. He seized Perkins's right wrist and quickly stepped around behind him, grabbing the left elbow and flipping both arms into a tight double hammerlock.

"Would you mind explaining what that was about?"

"What, am I a suspect now?"

He held Perkins firmly immobile but took care not to do serious injury. *Even after throwing a punch, this jerk would sue.*

"No, Perkins," said Jake, struggling to rein in his anger, "you're just a loose cannon and a mouthy minor nuisance. The department already checked out your whereabouts and cleared you of any connection to the crime. I came here expecting a routine encounter with a citizen who's gone through something disturbing. I treated you and your property respectfully. And you act like this investigation is the biggest imposition since the Brits burned Madison's White House. What's with you, you cowboy? You flunk anger management class?"

"Congratulations, big shot. What are you, 35, 40? You got the drop on a guy old enough that half my mail's from AARP. If I were about a decade younger, you'd be flat on that floor."

"If you were a decade younger, I doubt I'd have stopped with a hammerlock. Count yourself lucky I'm not in a mood to press charges—and also that I don't carry a badge myself. I'm sure a phone call from jail would be just the thing for your wife's peace of mind." Jake released Perkins's arms slowly, maintaining enough force to prevent a surprise move, and walked to the door. Peripheral vision gave him enough of an angle view of Perkins that he could avoid paying the implicit compliment of looking back.

There's no need to waste more energy here. Got what I came for. Dave finally has something for the lab. Miracle it was there after this long.

"You're a big nothing, Halsey," Perkins yelled. "Software guy. I'll bet my left nut you never served and saw action. I was in the 24th Infantry at Taejon when the Commies took General Dean, but you wouldn't know or care about that. Where I come from, a man wouldn't pull that tricky Jap wrestling crap. You ever really go *mano a mano* with anybody, with your life at stake? You ever find out what you're made of?"

Class act all the way, Jake thought, saying nothing as he got in the Renault. *Shows he's read a little Hemingway in school and misunderstood what* mano a mano *meant, and that he knows even less about jujitsu—and that he'll make an assumption about a guy he knows absolutely zilch about, and that he's at least a borderline racist, all within a few seconds.*

He wondered what Riley and his team went through in daily dealings with the public. Full-time investigators must see people at their worst moments, and not just suspects, and not just when they had a reason. How many were as belligerent as this clown? *Forget him.* He poked through the glove compartment for something cathartic and put a dissonant, furious Mingus album in the slot. Wrathful rhythms accompanied him home. Not every implication was easy to forget.

Mano a mano. A fighting man needs the taste of blood. Right, Airman Halsey?

What you're made of. These men get it. You never will.

CHAPTER NINETEEN

Catherine put the finishing touches on her makeup, wondering what an invitation to a "casual home-cooked meal" meant from a man who owned an airplane hangar full of exotic antique machinery—and kept it in running order. Despite her protest that she was perfectly capable of driving to his house, Jake had insisted on picking her up. She could only imagine what vehicle might appear at the curb this time.

Following their picnic and dinner, they had met twice for lunch during unexpected lulls in her OR schedule. One other evening, Jake had called on the spur of the moment, and they had spent an enjoyable two hours at a movie. These impromptu dates had been very casual, and their conversations had been wide-ranging and enlightening. She now had a clearer idea of where their tastes in composers and directors overlapped (Stravinsky and Bartok, Bergman and Hitchcock) and how Jake had acquired a local reputation as a monkish eccentric. She sensed that he was making an intensive study of her in turn.

Jake was the first man in a long time to cause Catherine to think "relationship." She'd dated too many men whose favorite topics were themselves and their own passions and interests, but Jake seemed interested in discussing her profession and passions, as well as his own. He had a strong personality, but she'd come to realize it was habitual rather than conscious. He was an entrepreneur, after all. He'd had to take charge in his business just as she took charge in the operating room. And, if he was assertive, he was also flexible. They'd yet to have a serious conflict caused by mutual stubbornness.

"Yet," Catherine reminded herself, was the operative term. Their mutual confidences had progressed only so far.

Other things had progressed only so far, too, and she wondered whether she was sending the signals she wanted to send. *Assuming I know*, she added to herself, *what signals those would be.*

Much to her surprise, Jake arrived for the date in the Renault.

"I was expecting another antique," Catherine told him.

"I hate to admit it, but the antiques stay in the garage most of the time. They're too hard to keep clean, if you want the unvarnished truth. I drove the Buick the first time because I wanted to impress you."

He had, she assured him, succeeded.

Back at Jake's compound, he helped Catherine off with her coat and ushered her into the spacious kitchen of his colonial home. Jake already had several pots sitting atop the professional-quality Viking range.

He motioned Catherine to one of the stools at his serving island and popped the cork on a chilled bottle of non-vintage Krug. He poured two glasses, handing one to Catherine and inviting her to make herself comfortable. As she sipped the Champagne, he busied himself in the kitchen.

Pulling two Dover soles from their place on ice in the fridge, Jake expertly skinned them, put some asparagus on the stove to steam, sautéed some potatoes, and put some butter in a pan for the sole.

"Ready for a bit more Champagne?"

She nodded.

He refilled Catherine's glass, whipped up some hollandaise, cut a lemon, and chopped some dill for the fish.

Catherine raised her glass. "You gave me some of this several weeks ago, but the previous time I had Krug was at the Deux Magots in Paris. Luckily, we were staying close by and were able to stagger home."

We. Hmm. OK. Jake sensed this wasn't the time for any exploring in that direction. *If it's important to unpack that "we," she'll get around to it.*

"I don't really know the Latin Quarter," Jake said. "When I was a kid, my parents took me to Paris, but they were Right

Bank folks."

"The George V?" Catherine guessed.

"As a matter of fact, yes. But please don't hold it against me. Later, Melinda preferred Italy to France, so that's where we went the few times the two of us were able to get away. If I go to Paris again, I think I'll need a special, personal guide. Know anyone familiar with, say, the Rive Gauche?"

"Mr. Halsey," Catherine smiled, "don't promise a girl Paris. Don't even hint at promising a girl Paris, unless you are in dead earnest." She sipped her drink. "To change the subject, if I may, you sure are at home in a kitchen. A gal could get pretty spoiled."

"I like to eat well," Jake responded, "and if you do it yourself, you know exactly how it will turn out. I can immodestly say that a decade ago *Gourmet* magazine published a recipe of mine involving sole and artichokes." He raised his glass to Catherine in a toast. "Maybe we can try that another time."

"Has anyone ever told you that if you weren't so charming, you would be impossibly arrogant?" Catherine said, laughing.

"Once or twice," Jake answered with an understated grin as he placed the fish in a sizzling pan. He stirred the potatoes, checked the asparagus, and asked Catherine to set the table in the kitchen's bay window,

When the fish was done, Jake expertly de-boned it and served the plates with a "Voila!" He poured two glasses of a William Fèvre Chablis, Valmur, and held Catherine's chair out for her.

Once seated, he raised a glass to Catherine in a toast. "I think, Dr. Taylor, you deserve to be spoiled, and I'm trying my best."

"*Doctor* Taylor," she said, "sounds a bit formal for a fourth date, don't you think?"

"Fifth," he corrected.

"Well, there you go." She hesitated momentarily, then added, "My family and close friends call me Cat."

Jake shot her a boyish grin. "I hope that's an invitation?

I'd like to think of myself as a close friend."

She returned the smile. "Me too."

They ate in companionable silence for a while, then Catherine picked up her wine glass and toasted Jake across the table. "This is a wonderful meal. I was making fun of you before, but I must admit that every time we're together you show me new skills. What can possibly be next?"

"I whipped up a pear and lemon crème tart this afternoon for our dessert," Jake offered, grinning.

Catherine laughed. "Did you grow the pears yourself?"

"Ah, no. As much as I'd like to take credit, one thing I don't have is a green thumb. Anything green you see around here is either a product of Nature or of my very talented landscaping contractor."

"Ha!" She raised her wine glass triumphantly. "Finally, something I can do that you can't."

He raised an eyebrow. "*Doctor* Cat—I'd say there were a great many things you can do that I can't. Perform complicated surgeries, for one. Understand the complex workings of the human body for another. Mine included. I don't think I'll ever understand human beings as well as I understand machines."

"Or like them as much?" Catherine guessed.

He angled his head in thought. "Like may be too broad. Trust, maybe. People often do things that are incomprehensible or unpredictable. Most machines never do. There's always a reason for what machines do; you can find a cause for a machine's behavior. With people . . . ." He shrugged.

"Which is why," she suggested, "you're drawn to the technical side of investigative work?"

He looked at her as though the idea were novel. "I think you may be right. Take the case I'm working on with Dave right now, for example. *What* the perpetrator is doing, and *why*, are completely beyond me. But *how* he does it—that's something I can grasp. Sink my teeth into. Analyze."

"And you do, don't you?" she asked solemnly. "I'd say you . . . have a passion for detective work. And yet. . . ." She paused, suddenly unsure of the ground she was treading.

"And yet?" he prompted.

"When I mentioned to one of my colleagues that we've been . . . seeing each other, he said, 'Good grief, Catherine, you'd be the last person I'd imagine would be interested in a dilettante like Jake Halsey.'"

Jake looked up sharply in mid-bite. He lowered his fork. "Dilettante? Did he say why he used that particular word?"

Uncomfortable under his gaze, Catherine shrugged. "Actually, I asked. He cited your expensive collections, dabbling in amateur detective work, your occasional extravagant behavior."

"Extravagant behavior?"

"*Flying* a woman to an island on a first date? Hiring a chauffeur to drive us a few blocks?"

Jake thought for a moment, his unfocused gaze going to the lit fountain beyond the window.

"Fair observations," he finally said. "First, all of what I collect has risen in value, and I consider my collections to be investments. So, you'll have to tell your colleague that there are practical aspects to that. They're not just toys. Second, and more important—to me, at least—is that I can guarantee no stock certificate is going to make anybody's eyes light up as yours did when you first saw my Buick. Am I right?"

She nodded, smiling. "Right."

"Third, I suppose I'm an amateur detective but only in the sense that I'm not paid, not because I'm amateurish. I've taken academy-level law enforcement forensics classes to write the evidence collection and analysis software my company marketed. Software that is widely accepted and universally acclaimed, I might add. I've consulted with Riley and his crew on several difficult cases in the last couple of years. I like to think my contributions have been valuable—at least Riley *tells* me they've been valuable." He smiled. "I hope not too much of my ego is showing."

Catherine nodded in acknowledgement. "Riley told me the same thing, and my ego shows occasionally."

"Fourth, I think the dictionary definition of dilettante is—

as your colleague suggested—a dabbler. Someone who does something for amusement, someone whose interest is superficial. I feel . . . *know* . . . I do lots of things well despite this being an age of specialists. My interest in law enforcement—in *justice*—is anything but superficial."

He lifted his wine glass, peering through the liquid at the fountain. "Finally, I'm financially able to enjoy myself doing these things—working for the intrinsic value of the work rather than working in the traditional sense, that is, for somebody else's money—so I do. Why not?" He aimed a toast at the view beyond the window, then sipped the wine.

"And that's why you brought an antique airplane on a first date?"

Jake chuckled, shaking his head, as he topped off their wine glasses. "I told you—I was hoping to impress you with my extravagance."

Catherine sobered. "That wasn't what impressed me. What impressed me were your abilities, your problem solving, your knowledge of many subjects. You care about things. You're not wrapped up in yourself. And that," she added, "is what I told my colleague. Right after I told him to mind his own damned business."

They relaxed after that, discussing subjects from the genetics of roses to favorite holidays to forensics. She told him about her love of carnivals and how her parents had taken her to one that was in town every year on her birthday. He told her about his childhood tinkering with household machinery and how his dad had been at once proud and exasperated when eight-year-old Jake had dismantled his alarm clock, causing him to stand up an important client.

Once he'd cleared away the dishes, Jake served slices of his tart and poured small glasses of a 1959 Anjou Moulin Touchais, a nutty and lusciously sweet dessert wine from the Loire region of Western France.

"You," Catherine told him, "missed your calling. You could have been a five-star chef or a *sommelier*."

Jake laughed. "Actually, my parents would've loved that. Almost as much as they'd have loved my taking over the family wine business."

"Why didn't you? Take over the family business, I mean?"

He shrugged. "I've often wondered that myself. I enjoy wine. I *am* an amateur in that arena, in the truest sense of the word."

Catherine nodded. "A wine *lover*."

"Exactly. And maybe because I enjoyed it, loved it, I didn't want it to be my career. So I sold my interest in the vineyard to someone who enjoyed the business as much as she enjoyed the wine itself."

After dinner, Jake turned down Catherine's offer of help with the dishes, telling her they could wait. He helped her on with her jacket, then took her arm and steered her across the driveway to a plain one-story structure in the shadow of the hangar she had visited her first time there. Jake unlocked the door and ushered her in. Triggered by their presence, fluorescent lights flickered on.

Catherine gasped. She was in a huge workshop, perhaps forty by eighty feet, with tools and equipment everywhere.

"A milling machine!"

Standing right before her was a numerically controlled Bridgeport, the Rolls Royce of such tools. She nearly laughed aloud at the priceless expression of amazement on Jake's face.

"My grandfather was a machinist. I know what a milling machine looks like."

Catherine reached toward Jake, touched his arm warmly and naturally, then hesitated and pulled back. He made a decent effort at pretending not to notice.

She couldn't help rebuking herself for checking the spontaneous gesture. *Old habits die hard, girl*, she thought. *But maybe it's time to let that one die.*

She turned slowly, spotting many other machines clearly designed for metalworking. Farther away, behind a glass partition, was woodworking equipment and a massive dust-collection system.

Her gaze left the machinery, traveling down the wide center aisle of the room.

She rolled her eyes heavenward. "All this, *and* he can cook."

Jake showed Catherine around the workshop, including an electronics bench behind yet another glass wall, with an array of test equipment and a digital oscilloscope.

"I confess I haven't been in many industrial shops," said Catherine, "but even so, I've never seen a room with such a variety of equipment, unless it was an operating room in a large teaching hospital."

"I like crafting things, problem-solving. I enjoy being able to make or fix anything electronic. I enjoy wood and metal work. A lot of collectors of mechanical things hire specialists to make repairs or to do restorations for them, but most of the time, I like to do the work myself. But just wait until you see what I've got next door."

He's like a kid showing off a new train set, Catherine thought, as Jake turned out the shop lights and directed her down the drive to the hangar. The urbane man of the world was supplanted by the ingenious enthusiast, excited at being able to share his interests. She found it oddly endearing.

In the hangar, Catherine made a point of taking in her surroundings. In addition to *Shady Lady* there was a biplane and a Bell Jet Ranger helicopter, the two-seat model with an almost-spherical plastic canopy. There were several other vehicles, including one that looked like a motorized sleigh.

"What in God's name is that?" asked Catherine.

"It's a 1904 Oldsmobile. All I could locate of an original was the one-cylinder engine, one wheel, and a few other miscellaneous parts, so I had no other choice than to build the rest." He shook his head at the recollection. "Building the wooden body entirely myself severely tested my woodworking skills; it has almost no right angles. I'd offer to take you for a ride, but it sometimes takes ten minutes to get the engine started."

"That's all right, though I would love to see her in action," Catherine said.

Her attention was drawn to a glass wall. "What's on the other side of that glass?"

Again, the boyish smile and backlit eyes. "Let me show you."

Jake escorted Catherine into a large temperature- and humidity-controlled space with palace-sized Oriental carpets on the floor. The shapes of the machines that ranged along the walls were at once familiar and alien.

"Are these jukeboxes?"

"Everything in here," Jake said, making a sweeping gesture at the room, "is a self-playing music machine. Most play from rolls or punched cardboard books, much like early computer punch cards connected and folded together."

"Early software," Catherine said. "Right? Like they used to use with Jacquard production looms."

He smiled. "Exactly. And like the looms, they were exceedingly sophisticated for their day." He opened the front of one of the machines.

"Are those organ pipes?"

Jake nodded. "This is an orchestrion. It was built by Gebruder Weber in 1928 in Germany. It plays a piano, xylophone, drums, and organ pipes of various voices. It's the musical equivalent of a ten-piece orchestra, built to play dance music in the style of the period."

Catherine laughed. "Old World disco! The bane of live musicians."

Jake laughed with her as he flipped the On switch; a lively "Twelfth Street Rag" filled the air.

As the music played, Catherine tapped her foot and swayed back and forth. "I can imagine something like this playing in an old mansion," she said. "I can just see the bathtub gin flowing while Scott and Zelda Fitzgerald danced to this music."

"You've got the right setting," Jake agreed.

He moved over to a large, finely detailed oak cabinet featuring a colored glass panel. "For example, this is a 1927 Seeburg model KT Special. It plays ten instruments but only takes up about two-thirds of the space of an upright piano. Most home parlors didn't have room even for something like this, but bars and taverns did. These machines made millionaires out of a lot of guys in the 1920s from the endless stream of nickels they consumed."

Jake took a coin from a brass bowl atop the orchestrion and inserted it into the slot. The machine lit up and started to play.

Catherine tapped her fingers in time with the lively melody. "So they were status symbols, then. Like having a grand piano in your conservatory in Victorian times."

"Not a bad comparison."

Before the tune ended, Catherine's gaze had moved to a jukebox with multicolored tubes running up each side. "What's this one? It's *beautiful*."

"That's a Wurlitzer model 1015 jukebox, made in 1944." Jake put in a nickel and the 1950s hit tune "I'd Like to Get You on a Slow Boat to China" thumped out.

"I remember that tune," Catherine said, delighted. "Mom sang it sometimes when I was a little girl."

Jake glanced at the machine. "I could swear I had this set to play 'It Had to Be You.'"

"You prepared it for our date?"

"Well, yes, I did, actually."

Catherine shook her head. "You don't leave anything to chance, do you?"

"Sometimes I do. This next one is different." Smiling, Jake steered Catherine to a very large organ with an ornate façade that featured two carved cherubs playing drums. "I bet you can guess where this came from."

Catherine stood back and studied the colorful, intricate machine. "A carousel!"

Jake started the organ, which played a complex version of an obscure European waltz. "It's a Style 38 Ruth fairground organ, also originally from Germany," he said, raising his voice over the music.

"This one spent much of its life in a large, forty-eight-horse Belgian carousel."

"What an unbelievable sound that has," Catherine commented, dreamily. She could almost see the horses—all forty-eight of them—rising and falling like brightly painted waves. "Too bad you don't have the whole carousel."

Jake put his arm around her. "I might be able to track it down." His eyes lit up. "Or, better yet. . . ."

"Build it," they said in unison.

Catherine laughed. "You would, too, wouldn't you?"

The music stopped. In the sudden silence, Jake gazed at her, his arm still lying loosely around her shoulders. "If you asked me to, I would."

She lowered her eyes. "That's a big job."

He turned her to face him. "For the woman who mended my battered frame, anything."

"It was hardly battered, just. . . ." She looked up and met his eyes. They were serious, questioning. She felt herself swaying toward him.

He framed her face with his hands and kissed her. The kiss was gentle, undemanding. She accepted the kiss and kissed him back. Enthusiastically, at first.

When Jake noticed the barest change in her enthusiasm, as if she were assisting a flame with a bellows rather than letting it burn on its own, he gradually and gently released her cheeks from his fingers. She looked at him directly, with something he hoped he was right to interpret as trust, and time moved extremely slowly for both of them.

She spoke first. "Don't worry about anything. You have nothing to worry about here. I'm—I'm on a timetable I'm going to have a little trouble explaining. Things aren't—not everything is easy for me, even when it naturally ought to be."

He said nothing. It seemed clear, for reasons he wouldn't be able to articulate, that this wasn't a time for him to do much of the talking.

"Before things go anywhere further with us, I need to tell you something. Something happened to me long ago. You've told me some important things about the past, about Melinda, and it's only fair you know what I've gone through as well. Promise me you'll keep an open mind about this."

"Of course. Whatever it is."

Catherine's words came with great effort, but her eyes never left his. Not even when they began misting up.

"I was assaulted by an uncle from age twelve to about fifteen. Sexually. I guess using the word assault isn't quite right, and it didn't seem like an assault at the time, but that's what society calls it today. It took me a while to call it that. I don't really want to call it anything. I never want to think about it enough to find the exact words for it.

"My father's brother stayed with us sometimes when he was without a job, which was frequently, and he used to babysit. He called himself a poet and styled himself as a handsome rogue. Part of that was accurate, I suppose. I listened to him talk about poets and writers. It was always long stories about how he'd drunk whisky with Dylan Thomas or studied with this one or that one, 'me and J. C. Ransom,' 'me and Bob Penn Warren'—but I never saw anything he wrote. I definitely never saw anything he published. I was too young and too damn dumb to ask.

"In the beginning, he'd come into my room and tell me I was so pretty, and then just rub himself, but it quickly became more than that. He'd ask me to undress, and he'd remove his clothes and—and masturbate. I didn't know what to think; I guess I was more flattered than anything else.

"But it then became still more. He'd get me to laugh somehow and start tickling me, then touch me, then rub me, and then, ultimately . . . enter me. At first, that hurt. A lot. I was terrified. But as I got used to it, I'd enjoy it. Thinking about it these many years later, I recall that I was excited: both by what was happening and that it made me feel so grown-up. But at the same time I was troubled, knowing that it was wrong but not understanding what would happen if we were ever discovered together.

"It ended badly, of course—as if anything like that could end otherwise." She looked up at Jake with an expression he couldn't have imagined ever seeing in her eyes. "Please, *please* promise me this stays right here."

"Of course. It goes without saying, but I'll say it without hesitation."

"My father must have found out. I don't know how. Maybe my uncle—I can't even speak his name; it's an

127

obscenity to me—maybe he let something slip while in his cups. Maybe it was just parental radar. Dad never uttered word one about it, but my uncle just disappeared one day, and nobody in the family ever mentioned him. Dad took a business trip for about a week and said almost nothing in my direction for about a month after that; I could tell something was bothering him, but silence was always his way of dealing with troubles. I asked my mother once what had happened to my uncle and got a look that made sure I never brought it up again.

"I was devastated for the next year or two, but I did what I already sensed was what Taylors were expected to do under stress: I lost myself in my work. And I didn't let a guy near me until I was a senior in college. If you ever see my old high school yearbook, you'll see where my best friend Sarah signed it 'to the Crystal Cat.' That was her nickname for me, and the Crystal part meant iceberg.

"I think I'm over it by now, as much as anyone could be. It has colored my relationships with men right up to the present, but you're the only one I've ever told."

Jake weighed his words and parceled them out very slowly.

"You were so young. You know you're completely without blame in all of this, don't you?"

"In my mind I know. In other places I'm not so sure."

"Is there any way of knowing whether your uncle," Jake asked even more slowly, "might still be alive?" He found it impossible to suppress an upwelling of unfathomable wrath at this thought. After a moment's reflection he knew it would be unwise and unfair to try to suppress it. Directing it was a different matter. He silently told himself he could make it to his grave without either meeting this man or finding that six feet of earth already kept him safely away from Catherine. He wasn't at all sure he believed it.

"I don't know. I don't want to know."

"You shouldn't have to. You got through all that and became Catherine Taylor—that's the only thing that matters. It's pretty much a miracle." He looked steadily into her eyes.

"*You're* a miracle."

"I have a history in some people's eyes."

"Not in mine," Jake said. "Never in mine. And not in the eyes of anybody worth a goddamn. What kind of man would I be if—?" He saw the relief in her expression, and he didn't need to finish the question.

"It has affected my entire life. Not my work, I'm pretty sure, but this part of my life." She took his hand in hers. "I wanted you to know—but I never want to refer to it again." She was sobbing quietly.

"And what kind of person would I be," Jake said, "if I ever brought it up again?" He drew away, his lips still near hers, and cast a look back across the room. She followed his gaze and dried her tears with a movement of her hand that struck Jake as the most graceful gesture he had seen in years. "Shall I build it?"

"If you want to."

"I want to."

After a moment, Jake spoke. "It's been a long time since I've felt this way about anyone. A long time since I've *let* myself feel . . . anything. I said you'd mended my body. I think you've mended much more than that."

She met his gaze.

"Build it," she said. "Build me a carousel."

Jake's master suite was large, carpeted in white, and heavily draped, with a king-size bed and an intricately carved headboard. It was an elegant, masculine room, as was the green marble master bath, just visible through a door to the right.

As he led her across the threshold, Catherine stopped, a half-full glass of Port in her free hand. Jake had given her a taste of 1963 Warre.

He turned to look at her, frowning. "If you're not sure about this . . . if you're not sure about us . . . ."

"Us, I'm sure about." Then, with an impish smile, she added, "What I'm not sure about is walking across your white carpet carrying a glass of Port."

Jake was relieved. Chuckling, he took Catherine's glass and moved across the room to set it down on a table near the gas fireplace, which he turned on. Then he returned to the door, pulled Catherine smoothly into the room, and took her in his arms for a long, lingering kiss.

By the time he raised his head, he was certain he wasn't imagining the kiss had affected them both equally. He inhaled her exotic scent and felt it go straight to his heart.

"You're sure about that carousel?" Jake murmured.

"Well, you know what they say: 'If you build it. . . .'" She pressed closer, lifting her face for another kiss.

In a slow erotic waltz, they undressed each other, moving toward the bed in a series of lazy movements. It was neither as fluid nor as graceful as it was made to look in the movies; ardor overcame coordination. They failed to reach the bed, ending up instead on the carpet in front of the hearth. The carpet was soft; the flames warmed their naked flesh and echoed their mutual arousal.

Jake was aware, as they moved in harmony, that whatever the future held, this act forever changed the relationship of a man and woman. For him, personally, it brought a level of pleasure he hadn't experienced in so long he'd forgotten what it was like—just as he'd forgotten how good it felt to share his bed with someone. It was like stepping from a long, cold hallway into a warm, welcoming room.

"I don't think," Jake told Catherine much later, as they lay in his bed holding hands, "that you'll be able to adequately oversee the building of your carousel from your place."

She knew what he was asking, and this time he sensed her hesitation was real.

CHAPTER TWENTY

"Jewett City? Where the hell is that?"

The reproach in Arlene Bianchini's eyes was enough to make Dave Riley regret his outburst. He was stressed, surely; he had too many open cases on his desk, woven together in a clear but maddening pattern, and he was in no mood for interruptions. He wasn't at all happy knowing that the homeowner in Black Rock had been enough of a hothead to get into an altercation with Halsey. Or vice versa, though he doubted Jake had done much to provoke him. But none of that, he told himself, should crack his cool.

"You don't have to yell," Arlene told him. "I just wanted to tell you we just got word of another wine-related incident."

That got Riley's complete attention. "So tell me, damn it." He shook himself. "Sorry. Tell me, please."

Rolling her eyes, Bianchini said, "Jewett City—population about three thousand—is about seven miles northeast of Norwich on route I-395, not far from the Rhode Island border. As the result of our inquiries, the Jewett City police chief came up with a fresh robbery-murder that may fit our profile."

"How fresh?"

"The Jewett Wine Shop was held up yesterday. The robber pistol-whipped the owner and then, when he attempted to pull a shotgun from behind the counter, the perp shot him and a male customer dead. The customer was a wealthy financial guy from Norwich named Benjamin Shepherd, who frequently bought wine there." She paused as if for effect, then added, "By the case."

"Jewett City," Riley repeated. Then the implications of that hit him. "Jesus. It could be his J. If this shooting belongs on our list, we've been blindsided. Oh, shit. This could mean

131

that our killer has already committed crimes in both H and I towns that we don't know anything about." He jumped up. "*Tony!*"

Pezzi practically skidded through the door, a cup of coffee sloshing its contents onto his hand. "Boss?"

"Go up to Jewett City, ASAP, siren on all the way, and pick up whatever you can about the liquor store holdup that happened yesterday. If this crime is one of ours, our alphabetic schedule may be way off. I'll call the chief up there and tell him you're on your way."

Riley nearly jumped out of his skin three hours later when Pezzi rang his cell phone. It vibrated in his pocket, causing him to spill lukewarm coffee onto a case file.

"You getting even for the coffee this morning?" he asked Pezzi. "Why didn't you use the radio?"

"Out of range. Listen, boss, here's what I've got."

Riley heard the riffling of paper as the detective flipped through his notes. "This looks like a typical liquor store holdup. And I mean that literally; the killer was caught by a security camera. He may have been on drugs or something, because on the tape he was hyper and nervous, bouncing around like a jumping jack. He asked for money and apparently the owner behind the counter didn't respond fast enough, so the robber hit him on the side of the head with the pistol. When the owner went for a weapon he had beneath the counter, the robber shot him, then turned to the store's only customer and shot him, too. The chief figures it was because the customer could ID him." He paused. "Poor guy was just there to pick up his wine order. Talk about being in the wrong place at the wrong time. Anyway, the killer ran out of the store and took off in a beat-up car. Nobody got the plate."

"Arlene told me most of that. Was the perp alone? Any accomplices?"

"The tape doesn't show anyone else. I watched it a couple of times. It was kind of grainy, so there's really nothing on it anybody can use. Ever wonder about that, Chief? Why is it that security-cam pictures are so damned grainy?"

"It's the lighting and film speed," growled Riley. "Focus, Tony."

"Sorry. Anyway, the robber wasn't wearing a mask or even a hat, so there's one pretty good image of him. A black-and-white print copy of his face is already in circulation, and I asked the chief to email one to you. I also had a copy of the DiVito picture in the car and checked it against this shot, but neither shot was good enough to tell for sure if there was a match.

"The guy wasn't in the store long enough to leave any evidence. The local cops scoured the parking lot, also with no luck. The chief thinks the robbery attempt was a spur-of-the-moment drive-by, and the killer had an itchy trigger finger. I picked up the names and addresses of the victims, but there's not much more I can do here."

"Head back. We'll add this one to our list. Check it out further."

"Yes, sir. See you in about ninety minutes."

Riley had no sooner hung up with Pezzi than he called Jake.

"We have a robbery-murder at a liquor store in Jewett City that may be part of our sequence."

After a moment of silence, Jake repeated, "Robbery? Did the perp actually *take* something?"

"No. But he left his face print on a security video. If you're not in the middle of something important. . . ."

"I'm just around the corner buying a couple of shirts. I'll be there in a few minutes."

Five minutes later, the two men were studying the flip chart, which Jake had hauled over to Riley's desk.

"Okay," Jake said, "so we've got a robbery in which the thief didn't actually take anything and a double murder that was caught on security tape. How soon will we have photos?"

"Arlene is downloading and printing still images from the tape even as we speak," Riley said. He flicked a finger at the flip chart. "What do you think of this?"

1. Ansonia—June, 2002—Truck Crash & Fatality
   Victim: Dennis Cox
2. Bridgeport   September, 2002   Murder
              Owner: Brad Perkins
              Victim: Rachel Charleson
3. Clinton—October, 2002—Electrocution
   Owner and Victim: Edward Plessy, MD
4. Danbury—February, 2003—Arson
              Owner: Bob's Fine Wines
5. Essex—April, 2003—Drowning
   Victim: Raymond DiVito
6. Fairfield—July, 2003—Plane Crash & Explosion
              Owner: Harry Johnson
7. Greenwich—October, 2003 —Poison
              Owner and Victim: Mitchell Livingston
8. H?
9. I?
10. Jewett City—November, 2003—Robbery Attempt &
    Double Murder

"I think," Jake said, "that we've got a series of events we're pretty certain are related, in towns and cities from A to G. We have no wine-related incidents in the H and I cities and we've had feelers out for weeks. There's only one I in the state, luckily—that narrows things down, assuming he stays in the state. Under H, there are a slew of small towns and one big city keeping us hopping, but we've been on it and there's been zilch. Now, suddenly, we have a J. Do you really think it's related?"

Riley felt a knot of frustration somewhere in the pit of his stomach. "Jesus, look at it. It's wine-related but the MO is different—we've yet to catalogue a robbery or a shooting."

"Have you shown this to Ellen?"

Riley shook his head. "She's home with her daughter, who sprained her wrist falling out of a tree." He chuckled suddenly at the perplexity in Ellen Green's voice as she'd described the events. "Kid was trying to pin a bird killing on the neighbor's cat and was in the tree collecting evidence."

Jake grinned. "Takes after her mom, does she?"

Riley took a deep breath. "Yeah. You're right, we need to run this past her. And we need to see what Brian can do with the security shots." He glanced at his watch. "Tony'll be back in about an hour. Can you. . . ."

"Stick around? Sure thing."

Riley cleared his throat. "You positive? You don't have a lunch date or something?"

Jake turned to look at him, eyes narrowed. "You've been talking to Catherine. What's she been telling you?"

Riley shook his head. "Not a lot. Except that she spends more time at your place than she does at her own. This is serious, I guess."

Jake smiled and dropped his gaze. "Yes. It's serious. Tell Barbara she can stop worrying about me. I think I'm officially taken."

Riley grinned. "Finally, something I can tell Barb that she actually wants to hear! That'll make her day." *And mine.*

"I'll tell you what would make mine," Jake said, changing the subject. "If we've heard anything from the state lab about that hair I found at the Perkins home."

Riley shook his head. "Nothing yet. And, again, sorry you had to deal with that idiot."

"Little unexpected workout, that's all. I guess not everybody handles it too well when something reminds him his home's more like a sieve than a castle. It looks like Perkins is already choking on enough extra testosterone to put a dozen endocrinologists' kids through school. Anyway, we've already learned a thing or two about our guy from the place, and maybe if you called. . . ."

"It's the state lab. They've got bigger stuff coming in than a single hair from the Greenwich PD. Why make them mad by nagging?"

While Brian Allen worked at enhancing the digital images they'd collected, the rest of the task force listened to Tony Pezzi report on his interview with the woman responsible for Dennis Cox's presence in Ansonia. Ellen was on the speaker phone.

"I spent a productive hour with Ms. Madeleine Norette," Tony told them. "I can see why Cox didn't mind the drive. She's a pretty sexy little number."

"A *number*?" asked Ellen, her voice piping through the phone in the middle of the conference table. "I'm pretty sure she's not a number."

"Hey, it's just an expression! I meant she's a very attractive middle-aged widow."

Tony looked down at his notes. "Her husband died suddenly about three years ago. Seems she and Cox go back a ways. Their families knew each other as the result of a couple of Atlantic City trips when they were teenagers. When Mrs. Cox died the year before last after a long illness, the two renewed their acquaintance at her funeral and, to quote Ms. Norette, 'things just blossomed from there.' Cox didn't live near Ansonia, but when his daily delivery route brought him anywhere in Madeleine's vicinity, he'd stop and visit, if you know what I mean."

"We know what you mean," grumbled Riley.

"Madeleine, is it?" said Ellen.

Tony cleared his throat. "So, uh, that's why Dennis Cox was in Ansonia that afternoon. Although it's none of our business, I don't think there were any, you know, significant others around to, uh, care if they . . . you know."

Riley's were not the only raised brows in the room; the normally imperturbable Pezzi was flustered. Ms. Madeleine Norette had apparently made quite an impression.

"I hope your visit was entirely professional," challenged Riley.

"What?" Tony paused, recovering his equilibrium. "Hey, Chief, she was hot, but even *I* have to have at least one date before I make any moves!"

"So, Tony, assuming you can forget your new crush for a moment and move this whole conversation past the junior-high-school level, they'd been seeing each other since around the time his wife died?" Riley asked.

"Yeah. About a year and a half, two years. Cox tried to get over to see her at least once a week. The way I figure it is that if we're right, and Ansonia is the first in a series of cities our guy wanted to hit, he may have decided to follow one of Bailey's vans to see where it went. Considering that Bailey Brothers doesn't label its vehicles, it just underscores that the guy we seek is pretty knowledgeable about wine and who deals in it."

"Yeah," Ellen agreed. "This is not a guy who's afraid of a little research. I'm going to assume he's pretty technically savvy, too. He'd have to be to get some of the info he's obviously tracked down."

"And to pull off some of these scenarios," added Jake. "Hijacking a plane, decrypting an alarm system, someone like me. . . . " Jake chuckled at his own logical conclusion.

"Embalming someone with wine," Tony said.

At the head of the table, Riley stirred restively. "Let's assume for the moment that he was looking for some opportunity in his chosen A town, saw the truck, knew or figured out what its contents were, and followed it. That still leaves the question as to how and where he sabotaged the vehicle."

"I looked into that," Tony said. "The distributor's lot wasn't particularly secure since the trucks parked there were empty. Cox used the same truck every day. It would have been easy for the perp to get into the lot at night and install his device."

"Cox drove it every day," repeated Jake, "Did he ever take it home?"

Tony nodded. "As a matter of fact, yeah. I interviewed his neighbors across the street and on each side. They all commented that he'd sometimes bring the truck home and park it in his driveway. His boss said the same thing: If a driver has a late afternoon run or an early morning one, he'll often take the truck home so he doesn't end up working overtime. The boss's decision, of course, not the driver's. Still, I'd put my money on the distributor's lot as the scene of the sabotage; Cox's neighbors are a fairly nosy bunch, and the ones on both sides had barky, over-zealous dogs." His expression said he had good reason to know this. "I think they'd've noticed if someone was messing with the van."

"Makes sense." Riley turned to Jake. "What have you got for us, other than implicating yourself as a suspect?"

Jake ignored the wisecrack. "Rachel Charleson's father was a New York wine distributor, which seems to explain how she fits in. I suppose it could be a random coincidence. . . . "

"I don't think our perp believes in either randomness or coincidence," Ellen offered. "He likes to be in control."

Jake nodded. "A coincidence that big would be *too* big."

"You talked to the parents?" Riley asked.

Jake lowered his gaze. "After their daughter's death, her parents came very close to selling the business and moving away. Her mother just lost interest in . . . everything, really. And her father's had to invest a lot of time nursing his wife back to health and reason. He told me he kept the company to preserve his own sanity. Immersed himself in his work."

Jake raked long fingers through his hair. "Whoever is committing these crimes is spreading pain and havoc. He's destroying careers, lives, families. Is that part of his motive or just a side effect?" He looked sharply at the speaker phone as if Ellen might provide an answer. She didn't.

He waved aside his own question with an emphatic gesture. "It doesn't matter. Whatever his motive, the DiVito and Charleson families have been devastated. And I don't think Brad Perkins and his wife are comfortable in their own skins anymore—let alone the house they've lived in for over twenty years. Madeleine Norette is essentially a widow all over again, and Darleen Livingston is getting to experience that for the first time."

"The state lab will get us a DNA profile," Riley said. "The hair you found up in Bridgeport was from the guy's arm, and the follicle was still attached. There was enough to get a healthy sample." On Jake's questioning look, he added, "I phoned just before we convened to see if I could light a fire under them." He shrugged in response to Jake's obvious bemusement. "I figured, what the hell. The worst they can do is tell me to go away and stop bothering them. Instead, they said they should have the profile completed by this evening and will run it against the various state public safety databases beginning tomorrow morning. We'll be getting reports back from that as evidence comes up." He paused. "*If* it comes up."

"FBI, too?" Ellen asked.

Riley nodded, then remembered she couldn't see him. "FBI, too. Even if we don't get any hits, we'll have his profile to compare against any new evidence that turns up in future cases."

No one said anything, but Riley knew they were sharing the same thought: We don't *want* future cases. We want to stop this SOB *now.*

Riley changed the subject. "While I've got the floor, I wanted to confirm that the homeowner in Fairfield, Harold Johnson, is clean. His alibi is tight; he and his family were out to dinner when their house was hit. They were not over-insured, and replacing the house and wine will take a lot of money and time. He's still shaken at how lucky they were."

"They weren't lucky," said Ellen. "This guy doesn't trust to luck. I'd bet dollars to donuts that family has a pattern of nights they're out."

"You're right, as it happens—I noted they keep a schedule for dinners out and a bridge club—but I didn't feel the need to emphasize that to Mr. Johnson. I think knowing that someone was watching his family that closely would just add a whole new level of worry to an already stressful situation. Jake, I thought I'd turn this one over to you. Your technical savvy might shed some light on how our guy engineered this explosion. Would you mind going to Fairfield and nosing around? If we can squeeze out a few more drops of information about where that plane came from. . . ."

"I'll take care of it tomorrow," Jake replied.

Brian Allen entered the room carrying a thin sheaf of prints. "Did what I could, which wasn't much. The security cam photos are pretty sharp, but the DiVito picture?" He shook his head as he handed the prints to Riley. "No way to focus an out of focus camera shot, really. Hey, Ellen, yours are coming your way by email."

Brian seated himself as Riley passed out the prints. Three

were from the security camera at the Jewett City liquor store, and one was the DiVito enlargement.

"We did better with towns in the alphabetical profile," Brian told Riley. "You want that now or. . . ?" He gestured at the photos.

"Good news first."

"Sure thing, Chief. There are eight towns or cities we can consider primary that begin with the letter H, and twenty-five other townships or villages or areas within towns beginning with H. I spoke with a contact in each of them and communicated the urgency of figuring out where this guy is going to strike next. We'll be called immediately on any crime that seems to fit our mold: wine involvement of any kind, any MO imaginable. We finally seem to have enough background and profile information that the cops in those towns are paying attention."

Riley looked down at the photographs in front of him—Jewett City shots on the left, Hannah DiVito's photo on the right. He could count the positives on the fingers of one hand. Caucasian, same hair color. That was it. The height was a question mark because of the angle of the security camera, and the guy's build—who knew? One man's body was hidden from view by DiVito's boat, the other disguised by a long brown trench coat.

"Ellen, you got these images?" Riley asked the profiler.

"Yeah, looking at 'em. If this was just a visual ID, I'd have to say it *could* be our guy."

"I hear a huge 'but' at the end of that sentence."

"But this crime doesn't fit the pattern for a number of reasons. First, except for Rachel Charleson, our guy keeps his distance from the victims. And she wasn't so much a target as a means of targeting Perkins's wine collection. Second, our guy has shown a lot of technical savvy. Too much not to have known there was a security camera in that store. Up till now, he hasn't shown his face. He's Autopilot Guy. Remote Control Guy. And third, this is a brute force crime. There's no mystery, no finesse, no attempt to misdirect. He walks in, he pulls out a gun, he seems to panic, he shoots."

"In other words," Jake murmured, "he didn't show off."

"Exactly. He didn't strut his stuff in front of the camera. Just judging from the report you forwarded, and these photos, I'd say this is not one of ours," Ellen commented.

"Wishful thinking," muttered Tony.

Riley shook his head. "I think Ellen's right. Look at the expression on this guy's face in this liquor store shooting. His eyes are probably red and certainly bleary, his skin is sweaty and pasty. He looks like he's just woken up from a bad dream, or some bad drugs. This is not a man with a clear head and a sharp wit."

Jake was nodding. "Then there's the target. Look at these shelves." He indicated one shot that showed the length of an aisle. Hard liquor, mostly cheaper domestic wines. "The target doesn't really even fit the profile. This is a liquor store with delusions of wine shop, although any licensee can secure wine by the case for a good customer. I think. . . ." He paused and weighed his words. "I really think Jewett City is a false alarm. And not just because I want it to be one."

Riley pushed the photos away from him on the table, locked his fingers behind his head, and gazed up at the ceiling. "Okay, we have a decision to make. We disregard this one and focus our attention on the I and H towns, *or* we say it's part of the pattern and move on to include the letter K as well. Our killer's going to make a mistake. I can feel it. No criminal alive can pull off this many different killings without making a mistake. But this isn't it. I can't reconcile these shots with the quality of the alarm disabling that Jake found at the Perkins house, or the fancy-schmancy wiring that blew up the Johnson house. Showing his face on a security camera is not the kind of mistake we have any reason to expect from this joker." He lowered his gaze to the group at the table and shook his head. "We proceed without Jewett City in the data set. And when our perp does make that mistake, we're going to land on it like a ton of bricks."

"This is more and more not a local case," Jake pointed out. "I don't want to rain on our parade, and I know we've discussed this already, but are you sure the State Police won't want to take this thing over?"

"Maybe," responded Riley, "but probably not. They tend to collect and analyze evidence and leave the beating of the bushes to the locals. Besides, we've done all the work, and we're not going to give up this case without a fight. If we crack it, if we bust the guy, all the Connecticut DAs in the alphabet can stand in line to take a whack at him. Until then, he's ours."

"Unless," said Tony, "he commits a crime across the state line. Then we'll have the FBI camped on our doorstep."

Riley stood, preferring to ignore that possibility. "Let's clear the decks, guys. We get any leads we need to be ready to pounce on them—hopefully before an officer in Hamden or Huntington finds a guy lying face down in a bathtub full of lukewarm Pinot Grigio."

CHAPTER TWENTY-ONE

As Riley had already interviewed the Johnson family, Jake made an appointment with the Fairfield chief of police to discuss the explosion at the Johnson house. The March day was overcast, with a palette of colors limited to shades of gray, but its unseasonable warmth held a distinct promise of spring. Connecticut was known for its riot of springtime flowering shrubs, especially along its parkways, but all Jake could see was an occasional green leaf or two of skunk cabbage.

His thoughts about his mission were as gray as the landscape. The one mitigating factor was that, in this case, no one had died.

Chief Ritchie's office was warm and comfortable, with leather armchairs, many framed citations, the obligatory family picture, and the equally obligatory U.S. and Connecticut flags. After cordial greetings, the two men got down to business.

"Ideally," Ritchie said, "I'd take you out to the crime scene, but as you might expect, the Johnsons were eager to rebuild their house. They've already got the roof on the new structure. But I do have these."

He laid out a series of color and black-and-white photographs along the edge of his desk. They showed a scene of utter destruction. Only a few charred bits of frame and a crumbled flight of steps leading to the beach gave any hint that the blackened hole in the ground had once been a family home. Also among the photos were close-up shots of the twisted metal scrap that had once been a small airplane.

"After the fire department put out the fire and the house had cooled down," Ritchie continued, as Jake looked over the photos, "we went over the premises with a fine-toothed comb. There wasn't enough evidence to put in a kid's lunch box.

Certainly nothing to indicate why someone would target the Johnsons. Harry Johnson is pretty much a regular guy. Owns a marina and rents pleasure craft to tourists. No enemies that he knows of—least of all any that would rig something like this."

Jake glanced up at the chief. "Dave Riley said you theorized the plane was on autopilot when it crashed. I'm assuming that was in part because no body was found in the wreckage."

Chief Ritchie nodded. "We entertained the idea that the explosion was so hot it just vaporized the pilot's body, but the forensics team ruled that out. We would have found teeth, bone fragments, something. But there was nothing to find. We also contemplated the possibility that it was a bizarre accident. We knew the plane was stolen, so we looked at a scenario in which the pilot lost control while out on a joy ride and ditched it."

"That would be extraordinary."

"You're telling me? He ditches the plane, it just happens to take out a single house, he disappears, or maybe drowns in the Sound, but no body is ever recovered? Oh, and the Johnsons just happen to be out to dinner, so the house was empty. That's a lot of serendipity."

"From our seat over in Greenwich, it's even more unlikely," Jake told him. "On top of all the other coincidences, the crash just happens to destroy a valuable wine collection, which fits in a series of crimes we're investigating. *And* it just happens to fit in by chronology and location with those same crimes."

Ritchie rocked back in his chair and folded his hands over his trim waist. "Riley mentioned that. So, you've got a serial killer who plans elaborate crimes, but doesn't care if he gets his target?"

"He cares. He got his target—the wine."

Ritchie frowned. "Riley said there were murders."

Jake nodded. "Yes. There have been several, but the victims weren't necessarily or directly the targets. The wine collections *and* their owners seem to have been the targets. Some of the victims were collateral damage."

Except for Rachel Charleson and Ray DiVito and Mitchell Livingston. Was Ellen right? Were these the lethal explosions of pent-up rage? Were the explosions going to escalate?

"The house was certainly totaled," the chief said. "What the crash and the explosion didn't damage, the fire did. As you can see, all that's left of the place is some charred chunks of its frame and a couple of two-by-ten rafters. The house was not far above the waterline on the beach, so there was no basement. That was fortunate, because if the house had a basement all the debris would have fallen into the lower level, which would have made the investigation much more difficult. As it was, I'd have to say we were pretty lucky. There was enough of the plane left to indicate the presence of an explosive." He lifted a couple of pages from the file folder in front of him and passed them to Jake.

"What about the wine cellar?" Jake asked, glancing at the document. It was a report from the state crime lab.

"The wine cellar took up a good portion of the first floor. All the wines were damaged beyond salvage by either the explosion, water, or heat. Johnson could only save two bottles." Here he referred to his notes. "Both 1990 Leroy Vosne-Romané Beaux Monts. He took a taste from a third bottle of the same wine and found it had been spoiled by the heat, so the two salvaged bottles are really only souvenirs."

"C-4." Jake tapped the lab report thoughtfully.

Ritchie nodded. "Good choice for arson. Widely available on the gray market and, in this case, it left no source markers. The guy must know some pretty well-connected suppliers."

"If you were to re-cast this as one of a series of crimes targeting wine collectors or collections, can you think of anything in the debris that might look different in that context?"

The chief paged through the report on his desk, then closed his eyes in thought. After a moment, he shook his head. "Nothing leaps to mind, though it does reinforce the idea that this was the intended target. We poked through the debris for several days and canvassed the neighborhood for any other clues. We kept the site pristine as long as possible, but by now, whatever remained of the building has been removed."

Jake gestured at the photos of the plane wreckage. "What about the plane? I know the New York Tracon system keeps its tapes for a period of time after any accident involving an aircraft."

"That's right. In fact, the explosion fixed the event in time. Riley mentioned that you're a pilot. So you know that at most small airfields it's legal to fly under Visual Flight Rules without clearance or communication with an air traffic controller. However, Tracon tapes show a small and faint radar return signal from the plane. We were able to trace its track from start to finish. It took off from a private Long Island field, flew south, turned 180 degrees, and then flew north directly above its starting point. It crossed the New York coastline and flew right toward the house on Fairfield Beach. Looks pretty damned intentional from where I sit."

"Radar only? Then he was flying with the transponder off."

Ritchie shrugged. "Makes sense, if his intent was to destroy that house. It's illegal to fly with the transponder off, but rules are irrelevant to a criminal. Anyway, a plane flying under VFR and not in communication is still of only passing interest to the air traffic control system unless it violates restricted airspace."

"I assume that the pilot didn't do that."

"Not according to the FAA. We checked the airfield. Determined that the plane was owned by a Stanley Weiskopff of Port Jefferson, New York, who was in Texas visiting family at the time of the crash. Imagine his surprise when he was told his plane was involved in an explosion."

"More collateral damage," murmured Jake. "And the airfield?"

"A whole lot of nothing. Well, not exactly nothing. Someone had parked a car in the woods at the edge of the tarmac, but they did a dandy job of obliterating their tracks. There wasn't one tire print left intact to lift a cast from."

Jake shook his head. "My God, this guy literally covers his tracks. He seems to think of everything."

"No kidding. I tell you, I'd give my eyeteeth to know how he pulled off the targeting and the crash. He had to have been in the plane at some point and bailed. But no one reported seeing a parachute."

"This happened around dusk?"

"Just. Sure, I guess even something as big as a parachute would be hard to see at that time of day, but you'd think. . . ." The chief shrugged. "I suppose he might have drowned."

Jake smiled wryly. "No, Chief, that's something we're dead certain of. He didn't drown."

CHAPTER TWENTY-TWO

The man in black eased his dark-colored Chevy onto busy Interstate 95, heading east toward New Haven. The day was overcast, with intermittent rain, and the traffic was heavy. At New Haven, he turned north on Interstate 91. As the highway increased in elevation, the clouds brushed the ground, shedding water droplets on everything they touched. The traffic had thinned, but he maintained his speed at no more than sixty to avoid drawing attention.

At Hartford, the man bore left on Interstate 84, traveling west for several exits until he turned off onto local streets in West Hartford. Within a few blocks, he was deep in an upscale neighborhood. He passed a country club, deserted in the gray wetness. Not long after, he slowed, then parked on the street near a small, empty commercial building that seemed out of place in its surroundings.

The man grabbed a bulky umbrella from the back seat, pulled on a black windbreaker and a pair of fine-grained leather gloves, and started up the street as the afternoon eased into night. He moved at an unhurried pace, looking like a local resident out for a pre-dinner stroll. The rain had stopped; he used the umbrella as a walking stick. Anyone watching him closely would notice that this was strictly an affectation—he put no actual weight on it and treated it quite gingerly—but he was doing nothing to give passersby a reason to watch him closely.

Turning a corner onto a block lined with expensive colonial homes, he strolled to the third house on the right, then walked briskly up a natural alleyway of plantings separating it from the home next door. With two slender picks and a few deft movements of his gloved hands, he released the spring-loaded lock on the cellar door and disappeared inside, pleased with the efficiency of his effort. Anyone watching would assume he'd had a key.

Inside the door he listened for a moment, then hurried down the cellar hallway with its sheetrock walls and garish overhead lights and through a dark-stained oak door, which he closed silently before flipping the light switch. A row of track lights illuminated the small, cluttered wine cellar. Open wooden and cardboard boxes lay scattered about, and wooden planks stacked on concrete blocks passed for wine racks. The dividers from wooden cases were piled in one corner.

The man's lips curled in disgust at the sloppy, haphazard work. Clearly the owner of this cellar grabbed something to drink without much thought of organization.

Other people's desires and deficiencies were frequently useful to him. He had known that since Boston.

He went to work quickly, piling several unopened wooden Bordeaux cases in a single stack about eight feet inside the wine cellar door. He then partially opened the umbrella and withdrew a rolled-up sheet of thin, ribbed metal. He unrolled the sheet, placed it atop the pile of cases, and attached it with clips, which he tucked under the corners of the top case of wine to hold the sheet metal firmly in place.

He then dismantled the center shaft of the umbrella, peeling away the struts and fabric to reveal a single-barrel, break-action shotgun with no stock. He withdrew a shotgun shell from the pocket of his windbreaker, pushed it into the chamber, and closed the breech. He sighted along the barrel to line it up on the center of the wine cellar door at approximately chest height.

He checked his watch—6:50 PM. Plenty of time to set the triggering mechanism. He smiled, enjoying this work.

He pulled off his leather gloves and held them in his teeth while he withdrew a pair of latex surgical gloves from his pocket. He was partway through the process of pulling on the second glove when he heard the unmistakable sound of the basement door opening and a man's heavy footsteps on the wooden treads.

He tensed, glancing again at his watch. It was 6:52—the

target was early, as he had never been during the entire time the gunman had monitored his habits.

The man in black was trapped in the cellar.

Well then, he thought, another smile touching his lips. Abandoning his struggle with the latex glove, he stuffed it and the leather gloves into his pocket and knelt behind the makeshift gun stand. And none too soon—in the hall outside the wine cellar, footfalls approached the door.

The gunman placed his finger on the trigger. The door swung open, and a hand made a swipe at the light switch, which was already in the ON position.

The gunman didn't wait to see the look of surprise and confusion on the homeowner's face at the sight of an intruder. He pulled the trigger, blowing the man against the sheetrock wall of the corridor and decorating it with splashes of vivid red.

Immediately there were sounds of activity from upstairs— a woman's voice calling inarticulately. The man in black abandoned the shotgun and bolted from the room, stepping carefully around the fallen body in its widening pool of blood. He walked briskly to the cellar door and melted away into the darkness outside.

He didn't check his pockets until he reached his car, realizing only then that one of the leather gloves was missing. Momentarily, he considered going back for it, but he was already hearing the sounds of sirens on the fringes of the neighborhood.

No matter. He had left no fingerprints at the scene. Since he had no criminal record, it wouldn't have mattered if he had. Any DNA that might be extracted from the glove would be meaningless within the patchwork law enforcement system.

He started the car, pulled away from the curb, and left the neighborhood at a sedate pace, pulling over once to allow an ambulance moving in the opposite direction to pass.

CHAPTER TWENTY-THREE

A ringing bell crept into Jake's dreams just before he crawled upward to wakefulness.

He had been driving the 1910 Buick at breakneck speed through deserted roads, passing wreck after wreck, some vehicles resting on the shoulder, some abandoned right in the middle of a lane. Each car was mangled in a different way, and each scene was too horrific to gaze at for long. Still, he couldn't simply pass by. As he slowed to a stop and drew close to one twisted hulk that had once been a bright lime-green Volkswagen van, he saw that its driver—dead in the driver's seat like all the others—saddened him more than he could have imagined. He tried to back away, but couldn't move. What could be weighing down his legs?

Groggy, he realized that the bell he was hearing was not a car alarm. but the phone. He picked up, noting that it was 1:15 a.m. On the other side of the bed, Catherine stirred sleepily.

"We caught a break; get up and get dressed," Dave Riley said without preamble. "I'll pick you up in fifteen minutes."

Jake wrenched himself out of bed, staggered over to the bathroom, splashed some water on his face, and told Catherine's inert body that Riley was picking him up. He dressed hastily in jeans and a shirt and headed to the kitchen to make a cup of instant coffee.

The microwave dinged just as Riley's headlights swept across the front of the house. Jake grabbed his coffee and headed out the door to the detective's unmarked car. Riley's tires squealed as he left the driveway.

Jake fought to keep his coffee in the cup where it belonged. "In a hurry, are we?"

Riley merely shot him a sideways glance from beneath thick brows. After a few moments, he turned east on the

Merritt Parkway, snapped on his roof light, and pushed his speed up to about eighty, despite the patchy mist.

"Our boy just struck again," Riley said once they were on the Parkway. "And this time we're only a few hours behind him." He grimaced and shrugged his shoulders. "Well, a few in forensic terms, anyway."

"H?" Jake asked.

Riley nodded. "The western part of Hartford, to be exact. And evidence suggests he was there at the time of death—pulled the trigger himself. He's ratcheting up the intensity of his crimes—and the intimacy. Which means he's increasing his chances of getting caught."

"Tell me what you know."

"The victim is Michael Whitney, a respected Hartford businessman. He was killed in his home wine cellar by a shotgun in a stationary mount on a sheet-metal platform. It was secured to a stack of wooden wine crates."

Jake jerked sharply, burning his lips on the coffee. "Booby trap?"

"Sure looks like one. Whitney left work at 6:30 every night, arrived home just after seven and, pretty much like clockwork, went down to his wine cellar to bring up a bottle for the evening meal. But last night, Mr. Whitney left work early and stopped by a jewelry store to pick up an anniversary present for his wife, Sara. He got home roughly ten minutes earlier than usual. From what we can tell, the killer was still in the wine cellar when Whitney went down for his Bordeaux. Whitney's wife heard the shot. She was sure the water heater had exploded. She ran downstairs and found her husband's body in the doorway to the wine cellar."

Jake let out a sharp breath. *Happy anniversary.* "How'd the killer get himself and his shotgun into the house unobserved?"

"He cut the stock off the damn thing and disguised it as an umbrella—a perfect disguise, considering the weather last night." He thought for a moment, then added, "Although the umbrella had to be bulky as a result, I doubt anyone who saw him would have thought much of it. He left the fabric and frame behind. The Hartford boys believe he jimmied the cellar door, though there's no scratching around the lock mechanism, so he might've had a key. If he picked it, he did a damn fine job."

The coffee had done its work, and Jake was fully awake. "So he left something behind? Sounds as if our boy might have panicked. He leave anything else?"

Riley smiled grimly. "He dropped a glove."

Yes! Fallible at last!

"In the cellar?"

"In the little alley that runs down the property line between the Whitney house and the neighbor on the east side."

"You're sure it belongs to the perp?"

"Odds are good. It was within seven feet of the cellar door. There was no indication that it had been exposed to the elements and it doesn't look like he left fingerprints in the house."

Jake nodded, drinking the last of his coffee. "Gloved hands."

"Based on what we know," Riley continued, "it's pretty clear that our killer was banking on Whitney's adherence to his predictable schedule. According to Sara Whitney, her husband's punctuality is—*was*—legendary. The killer must have been watching them for some time, long enough to be sure of the schedule, and he thought he'd arrived there early enough to slip inside before Whitney got home. And then, presumably, to get back out."

"I wonder how he picks his victims?" Jake mused. "He must spend a lot of time preparing for each of these things. I mean, you don't invent an event-triggered shotgun stand on a whim. Nor can you come into a community like this one cold, waltz into the local wine shop, and ask a bunch of questions about the habits of one of its customers. That in itself may explain why there are sometimes months between the killings."

"The guy's as slick as he is deadly. We'll interview the neighbors and the folks at Whitney's favorite wine shop—find out if anyone's been asking questions."

Riley stayed quiet for most of the rest of the drive. As they left the Merritt for local roads, he turned toward Jake with a look that his old friend recognized as unusually complex. Jake had seen several times how Riley's expression could acquire a feral tinge while he was on a suspect's trail, but this was a haunted Riley, a Riley losing even more sleep than was normal for him. The whites of his eyes looked like a highway map.

"Hey, do me one favor over the next few days, OK?" Riley turned to Jake.

"You got it. What is it?"

"Any chance you pick up a phone and it's Barb, for any reason, or you run across her in town somewhere—not a word about this guy or about these killings. I'd really appreciate it. You remember the guy in Omaha, in the coma?"

Jake nodded.

"The coma turned permanent a couple of days ago. Of course, her friend couldn't resist sharing a little more than a healthy level of detail about the funeral and everything that led to it. Since then, Barb's been asking some mighty nervous questions. Doesn't matter what I say or don't say about work, though I'm trying not to say much. Last thing in the world I need right now is her getting a picture in her head about the sort of son of a bitch we're chasing."

"Done. That is, not done." Jake reflected for a moment. "You ever think Barb might benefit from a social circle that isn't quite so well-stocked with blue?"

"Only about thirty or forty times a day."

Riley pulled up in front of a Cape Cod Colonial in a prosperous-looking West Hartford neighborhood and showed his badge to the officer at the bottom of the driveway behind yellow crime scene tape. There were several law enforcement vehicles parked along the block. There were even a few neighbors about, though it was about 2:30 in the morning, seven hours after the killing.

With a respectful, but decisive nod to indicate that he did not intend to break his stride, Riley flashed his badge to the other officer stationed at the door of the house, then headed for the cellar. He stepped around the chalk outline that showed where Michael Whitney had died.

Jake stopped and stared at it. He took in the floor and the sheetrock wall, both of which were thickly stained with blood. He shuddered and tore his attention away just as Riley was shaking hands with the detective in charge, a lean, wiry young man named Kennedy.

"This is Jake Halsey, a forensics consultant." Riley indicated Jake with a nod of his head. "Do me a favor, Detective—go over the evidence for him. Wouldn't hurt me to hear it again, either," he added.

The detective flipped back through his casebook, returning to his first page of notes. "The victim is Michael Whitney. Age forty-three. Married. No kids at home. According to Mrs. Whitney, he came down here every night at about 7:00 p.m. to choose a bottle of wine for dinner. Tonight, he arrived home early and came down for a bottle of Champagne to celebrate their wedding anniversary. A few minutes later, Mrs. Whitney heard the gunshot, came downstairs, and found her husband's body.

"Point of entry seems to be the external cellar door. It was unlocked and shouldn't have been. No broken windows. Chances are he picked the lock—a clean job. We're pretty sure he did the whole setup this evening. Mrs. Whitney was down here yesterday afternoon and says that these cases were definitely not piled like this or she would have asked her husband about it." He gestured at the neat stack of wine crates with their peculiar cargo.

"Mind if I take a look at that?" Jake asked, his eyes on the shotgun barrel.

"Go to it."

Jake moved to examine the shotgun mount, careful not to touch anything. Kennedy and Riley came up behind him to watch over his shoulder.

"The body's been taken to the morgue," Kennedy said. "Whitney was badly shot up around the face and chest. You can see the blood and pellet overspray there on the walls and door frame." He pointed to several areas near the wine cellar door.

Jake flicked a glance in that direction, then asked, "Where's the main entrance door from the outside?"

"Just down the hall to the left," said the detective. "We're not *absolutely* sure he came in that way—though it's most likely—but he definitely exited that way."

"Does the house have an alarm system?" asked Riley.

"Negative," said the detective. "I guess Whitney didn't think one was necessary. There are no special antiques or anything like that upstairs to protect with an alarm. Still, it's a bit unusual in a neighborhood this upscale."

Riley shrugged. "In this case, an alarm probably wouldn't have helped anyway. If this is our guy, he knows how to defeat an alarm system." Kennedy's eyebrows twitched at this, but he said nothing.

Jake turned his attention to the wine on the cellar racks. "The wine here is nothing special, either. These bottles are mainly California large-production bottlings in the twenty- to forty-dollar range. Some of the vintages are older and not currently available, but none of these bottles are worth very much. Certainly not hundreds or thousands."

"That significant?" Riley asked.

Jake turned to look at him. "I don't know. But this cellar isn't in the same class as the others we've been in lately. This guy had a great cellar for everyday drinking, but it's certainly not investment grade. Not so much a collection as a stash."

He turned his attention back to the weapon on its homemade mount. "Nothing special about this, either. Single-barrel, 12-gauge, break-action shotgun, with the stock removed. Probably a competition model used for skeet shooting. The way it's attached is very clever, though; it uses the weight of the full cases to anchor it in place. These projections here—" he pointed at a pair of guides along the back of the metal sheet, "are probably intended to hold the wire he was going to use to fire the gun. They would have given him a lot of flexibility in setting up the trigger wire."

Kennedy blinked at him. "Flexibility?"

Jake gestured at the door. "Unless our guy had already

been in the house, he'd have no way of knowing which way the door opened—out, in, left, right. He could've set this thing up for any eventuality."

"Yeah," said Riley. "If he'd had the time."

Jake chewed his lower lip, thoughtfully, his eyes still on the gun. "If this is our guy—and I'll bet it is—he keeps showing us new skills. Picks locks, builds murder machines, flies planes, parachutes to safety."

"Jeez," said Kennedy. "*Our* guy? I take it he's pulled some stunts in your jurisdiction too, then."

Riley nodded. "You could say that." Riley then summarized for him the seven incidents they'd uncovered so far, beginning with the Greenwich murder. As Riley spoke, the detective's eyes got progressively wider.

"So this clown's left victims all over the state. Damn. Well, you'll be interested to know that there appear to be at least partial prints on that glove we found outside. If they're his, you might have a shot at ID-ing this bozo."

"We believe this murder is connected to the series of crimes we have under investigation," Riley responded. "But it's the first time he's come this close to getting caught. I'll be interested to get the results on those prints. And any DNA evidence you pick up. We've got a hair sample from another crime scene. I wouldn't be surprised if we made a match."

Kennedy's radio squawked. As he stepped away to answer it, Riley turned to Jake. "I've got a funny feeling about this," Riley said quietly. "We might locate the killer before we figure out what his motive is, which is backwards from the usual." He paused. "You bring a different perspective to these incidents. What do you think of this one?"

Jake thought for a moment. "First, I'm sure it's the same guy. The alphabetic city order is consistent with his MO. Despite his leaving the glove and gun behind, the cleverness of the crime, particularly the mounting of the gun, certainly fits the mold. What I'm wondering is, *why* the cleverness? Why didn't he just hold the gun and shoot, then take it with him when he left? Mounting it like this just about guaranteed that he'd have to jettison it if something went wrong."

"What's your hunch?"

"Maybe it's like Ellen says—maybe he's literally showing off. Maybe he wants you to realize how clever he is. He can kill someone without being in the same room. He can kill in a variety of ways. Then there's the fact that we're looking at low value wines here. That looks like an anomaly until you add in the truck crash in Ansonia, which also involved cheaper wines. I don't think the kind, quality, quantity, or value of the wines are factors in his choice of victims. Nonetheless, wine is central to each of the murders and to the fire, so I think we'd better try to figure out what it is the killer doesn't like about wine. Or wine lovers."

"I almost hope you're right about the guy being a showoff. In my experience, that could very well make him overreach. It's happened before."

Jake nodded. "He may already have done that. He's also upping the ante by being here so close to the arrival of his victim. He may not have planned to pull the trigger himself, but considering the timeline, he did plan on cutting it close."

"A daredevil?" suggested Riley. "Wouldn't be the first time."

"I don't know if he intended to raise the stakes, but he just did. And I'm worried about how he could raise them any higher without killing several people at one time. Even the possibility that he might do that. . . ." Jake thought of the victim's wife, herself now a patient at a local hospital. Of Hannah DiVito, now fatherless. Of the Charlesons, who'd had to bury their only child.

And of other families.

"We've got to get closer to him, soon."

Jake suspected Riley's thoughts had taken a similar tack; his expression was grim. "Maybe the glove will help us do that."

"Something else," Jake said. "We're coming up on a ready-made, one-time-only opportunity to be there when he strikes next."

"How do you figure that?" responded Riley.

"When I first looked through the Connecticut

alphabetical list of towns in the zip code directory, I noticed there are three entries under the letter I, but two of them don't have post offices and are parts of larger towns. That leaves Ivoryton as the only I town he could choose, assuming he continues with the alphabet. He'll know that too, so if he's playing games with us the way it appears he is, he's going to plan a real hot dog performance for the place. I think we have to be there first. Check out all the wine stores, wine clubs, restaurants, or inns with regular tasting events. Make inquiries about their customers' and members' high profile collections."

"Right," Riley said. "Let's do it. Get the locals and take that town apart, building by building." He was already on his way out the door.

CHAPTER TWENTY-FOUR

"Cat, tell me what you know about DNA." With those words Jake completely changed the tenor of their casual Sunday breakfast.

Catherine looked up from the English muffin she was buttering. "You've got DNA?"

Jake grinned. "Me personally? Yeah, I'm pretty sure I do."

She swatted at him with her napkin. "Not what I meant. I meant your case. You've got DNA evidence?"

He nodded. "Yes, as a matter of fact, we do. A hair and some skin cells, which will probably do us no good in the short term if the guy doesn't have a criminal record. Anyway, can you give me the simplified version?"

Catherine nodded. "This was my favorite subject in school, so it's sort of like asking you about how jukeboxes work, but I'll just give you Genetics 101. Stop me if you've heard any of this before. DNA is a genetic blueprint. It's made up of four different nucleotides—which are simple proteins— in pairs. There are enough of those pairs in every molecule to form the whole complicated code that spells out the structure and functions of every living thing, including us. With the exception of identical twins—those from a single egg— everyone's DNA is unique. If you have a complete enough sample, you should be able to identify a unique individual." She paused. "Too basic?"

"No, go on," said Jake. "I'm just trying to get some ideas to gel in my head."

"OK, then. A person's DNA can be used for prognosis and diagnosis, but if you can't locate the individual it came from, it's moot whether having the DNA information would be helpful. However, once a report is ready, a geneticist could be of help in analyzing what the report shows."

Jake frowned. "Look, I'm going to trust you with some confidential information. We've got DNA from two crime scenes that we're pretty sure is from the guy who's doing these killings. Even though we have it, we can't do much with it. It doesn't match anything in the law enforcement databases. That means either the murderer has no criminal record or he's been so careful he's never left evidence until now. So we've got this great scientific tool, but it doesn't add one iota to our practical knowledge of the killer. No address, background, or physical description. Nothing to help us find out who or where he is. It's as if we had the world's most powerful processing computer and no code to run on it."

"Maddening, I'm sure," Catherine said sympathetically. "For forensic purposes, DNA is 100 per cent effective in matching two samples from the same person. But having the information doesn't help at all in locating that person unless they're leaving a trail of DNA evidence. I gather your guy isn't doing that."

"As I said, he's been very careful. He got caught by surprise on his last caper and dropped a piece of evidence with saliva, skin cells, and prints." Jake pushed his breakfast plate away and sat back in his chair. "Listen to me: caper, like this was a Keystone Kops movie. When I close my eyes, I can still see the last victim's blood."

Catherine put her hand over his, exerting gentle pressure. "Stop it, *please*. You can't do anything to change what's happened."

He shook his head. "I'm not doing a hell of a lot to stop what's *going* to happen, either. He's getting careless, but we can't count on him staying that way. This last murder might just have been a wake-up call for him. He may react by being more careful, or even dropping out of sight for a while, hoping the police will slack off."

Catherine commented, "Dave Riley doesn't slack off."

"Thank God for that."

Jake's cell phone rang, pulling him out of his ruminative mood. *Just as well*, he thought, taking it out of his shirt pocket to answer it; he'd been bordering on morbid.

"Jake Halsey," he said.

"Hey, good news," Dave Riley's voice came through briskly with no hint of the fatigue he should have been feeling.

"Speak of the devil," Jake said, smiling. "Catherine and I were just talking about you."

"Ouch. That's what that was, huh? Thought it might be sciatica. Listen, I just got a detailed report back from the state lab on the hair, the skin cells, and the saliva."

"That was fast. You just submitted those."

"Apparently when they saw the new evidence kit come through on the same case file, they expedited the whole thing. The cases are linked. The Charleson and Whitney murders were committed by the same guy."

Catching the excitement and vindication in Riley's voice, Jake glanced at Catherine, who was watching him intently. "So we're dealing with a serial criminal. What else do we have on the guy?"

"The detailed DNA profile probably wouldn't mean all that much to you, but here's a significant fact: the guy's blood type is AB negative. Do you have any idea how rare that is?"

Jake moved the cell phone to his other ear. "AB negative? Yeah. I do have some idea." A very good one, in fact.

Across the table, Catherine was frowning at him, making him realize his face had given away his sudden discomfort.

"Less than one percent of the global population is all," Riley was saying. "So now we've got some material that will open up a whole new area of investigation—unsolved cases where unmatched DNA or blood evidence was collected. This is coming together, man. It's finally coming together."

Jake hung up, feeling slightly stung. He shook himself. The sense of familiarity mixed with vague unease was hard to keep at bay.

Catherine was still watching him. "AB negative? Your killer's blood type is AB negative?"

He met her eyes, realizing that he'd repeated the information aloud. "I'm sorry, I should have taken the call in the other. . . ."

"*Your* blood type is AB negative."

He nodded, remembering that they'd had to ensure the blood bank had enough of the rare blood to cover potential problems during his appendectomy.

Catherine leaned forward, still holding his gaze. "What are you thinking?"

"That it's a creepy coincidence." He shook his head. "What are the odds?"

She studied him a moment longer then said, "This is going to eat at you, isn't it?"

"I've never been real big on cosmic coincidences."

"But they happen."

"I know. But just to be sure this is really a coincidence, maybe I ought to have my own DNA tested."

"Jake, that's nuts. Just because you have the same blood type it doesn't mean that you might be related to this—this killer."

"No, that's not what I . . . well, now that you mention it, actually, technically, I suppose it's possible. I didn't have any siblings, but there might be branches of the family I'm not aware of. Cousins, that sort of thing."

"Do you have any cousins?"

"Not that I know of."

"Well then?"

"Come on, Cat. Humor me. I'm a bit eccentric, remember?"

She stared at him. After a silence they both recognized as the least comfortable moment they had yet shared, she spoke first. "You really are thorough about all this Hercule Poirot business, aren't you? You know, they don't have a genetic marker for OCD yet."

Jake silently flashed through a few familiar phrases.

"Obsessive Compulsive Disorder," Cat supplied

"Ah. Okay. Don't worry. I've never spent an evening rearranging my sock drawer, or counted the fence posts when I'm walking down the sidewalk. What I'm really thinking is I want to know what's in my own blueprint. Mom and Dad both died younger than they should have. Maybe if I find some biological bomb that's ticking away, I can do something to defuse it. And as I'm thinking about this, it also makes sense to establish some DNA records on me in case any question ever comes up about forensic samples found around crime scenes. God forbid there'll be any more crime scenes. They're not supposed to be chaotic places, but sometimes they get that way. If the lab has to deal with anything that might include material from the killer, from me, from Dave, from Pezzi, from anybody else who might be working around there, it's best the techs can find out what my DNA looks like and sort it out."

"This sounds more like the Jake I know." She reached for his hand.

"Thanks. To tell the truth, I'm glad you can tell something's giving me the willies. You know, it'd be a relief if we could just . . . not that I'm in a big hurry, but . . . ."

"Now?"

"Sure. Soon would be good. Now would be great."

Catherine sighed and rose from the table. "Let's go down to my office. I'll need a sterile swab kit."

Jake grinned, trying to break the tension. "You don't carry one in your purse?"

"Used that one Tuesday, sorry." She fixed him with a calm gaze. "You're sure you want to do this?"

"What's the worst thing that can happen?" He shrugged. "We find out I'm carrying the genes for something horrible and incurable, or we find out I'm a schizophrenic homicidal maniac?"

Catherine didn't laugh. "That's not even remotely funny," she told him. "What are you going to do with this information once you have it?"

"If I'm carrying some sort of genetic dynamite, I'll talk to the best docs I can find about how to defuse it, even if that means I have to take meds or change how I live. I have some pretty huge incentives to stay alive as long as possible." He gave Catherine a warm look. "If by some remote chance it turns out the killer is my fourth cousin five times removed, I'll turn the information over to Dave—little good that will do him. As far as I know, I don't have any family now that Mom and Dad are gone. I wouldn't even be able to help him locate the guy."

"All right, Mr. Eccentric," Catherine said wryly. "Let's get this over with."

A few days later Catherine was in her office reviewing patient records when the day's mail landed on her desk. Included in the pile was a thick envelope with Jake's DNA test results. She laid the envelope on her desk and stared at it.

This was stupid. What did she expect was going to happen? Logically, even Jake's half-joking, fourth-cousin-five-times-removed scenario was stretching credulity. Still, the serious possibilities could be grim enough. She had always wanted to know her own biology inside and out. She could still smile at how relieved she had been a few years earlier when she learned that she didn't share the marker for the fearsome neurological condition that had unexpectedly claimed her aunt. She admired Jake's willingness to face similar risks armed with knowledge.

She hesitated a moment, then unlocked her desk file drawer and eased out a thin envelope that had been delivered to her by special courier the day before. It was a lab report. *The* lab report. Unlike Jake's, this one was for forensic purposes, stamped "Top Priority" and not entrusted to the postal system.

She had called Jake the moment it had landed on her desk, asking if Dave Riley knew it was coming. Jake had said only, "If he needs to know, he'll know. Otherwise, why distract him from the case?"

"But, Jake, this is police business," she had objected. "You're. . . ."

"I'm a consultant," he'd told her. "And right now, the consultant needs a consultant with your expertise, Dr. Taylor."

She opened the envelope and removed Jake's DNA profile, laying it atop her desk. A summary prepared by the lab technician informed her she'd be able to give Jake good news about twenty-seven major hereditary disorders. Considering the nature of his activities, she might always worry about him perishing in an airplane crash or at the hands of some vengeful sociopath. But if she ever began thinking about a long range future with Jake—*and is this any time to let myself start speculating along those lines?* she asked herself, and quickly answered *No!*—she needn't worry about Parkinson's disease, Huntington's chorea, Alzheimer's disease, or adult-onset muscular dystrophy. The list went on: negative, negative, negative.

Pretty sturdy genes you've got there, she mused. *The things that took your parents were awful, but they don't show up here. Nature apparently builds Halseys to last.*

Then she looked further at the detailed profile and set it side by side with the killer's profile from her drawer. She made herself look at them twice, three times, point by point by point. She checked the raw data behind the written conclusions.

She had to remind herself to breathe.

After five minutes of study, she put the profiles back into their envelopes, then sat and stared at the featureless manila for what seemed like another five. Then she dialed police headquarters and asked for Jake. He wasn't there. He was in Ivoryton with Dave Riley, Arlene Bianchini told her.

She thanked Arlene for the information and got out her cell phone. She pulled up Jake's number on her speed dial, and paused with her thumb over the SEND button.

Finally, she put it away and called the Greenwich PD again. This wasn't the sort of news you delivered over the phone.

"Arlene, when do you expect Dave and Jake back?"

"In a couple of hours. Two at the latest. They've got a task force meeting."

"Will you call me and let me know when Jake's back?" Catherine asked quietly.

"I can have him call you, if you want."

"No. Just . . . just let me know when he's back."

166

Arlene was silent for a moment, then asked, "Dr. Taylor, is something wrong? You sound funny."

I don't feel funny, Catherine thought irrelevantly. "I'm fine," she said aloud. "I just need to talk to Jake."

CHAPTER TWENTY-FIVE

Ivoryton, Connecticut, is adjacent to the town of Essex and lies about five miles north of Route I-95 on the west side of the Connecticut River. Just off Route 9, the principal thoroughfare from Old Saybrook at the south to Hartford in the north, it is a classic example of a New England town designed around a factory. As such, its colonial architecture, with occasional Victorian examples, is attractive in the eyes of most observers, but no match for the classic houses of nearby Essex.

The village of Ivoryton was named for the ivory used in the mid-nineteenth-century manufacture of piano keys by the Samuel Comstock Company. As the company grew, so did the village, but by any measure, it remained small. Comstock's son Archibald inherited the company on the death of his father and expanded its product line, making billiard balls, dominoes, and combs, and the company became one of the largest producers of ivory products in the world. In 1890, Archibald built an estate on the edge of the village. The building survived into the twenty-first century as a distinguished inn and restaurant.

The Great Depression, the Endangered Species Act, and the banning of ivory products made the Comstock Company itself an endangered species. It merged with another firm in 1936 and eventually closed its doors in the late twentieth century. Ivoryton's present-day population of 2,800, for the most part, commutes to other nearby cities and towns for its livelihood. Except for the occasional visitor to its Fife and Drum Museum and to the Ivoryton Playhouse, America's oldest professional summer theater, the town attracts few outsiders.

On that delightful March day, the warm weather a

precursor of spring, Jake and Dave drove to Ivoryton. Riley, apparently feeling pretty chipper, dominated the conversation during their drive.

"So, as our wine expert, what can you tell me about our two possible Ivoryton targets, Phillips and Miller?" asked Dave, after a five-minute rundown on the state lab report.

"What?"

Riley laughed. "Earth to Jake. You were a million miles away."

"No, not quite that many." He gathered his scattered thoughts and applied himself to Riley's question. "Ian Phillips owns the Copper Beech Inn."

"Ah," said Riley. "That's the restaurant in Archibald Comstock's old estate. I took Barbara there for our fifteenth anniversary. Very nice."

Jake nodded. "Ian—and he will insist you call him Ian— told me the inn is open seven days a week, and somebody is in the kitchen from 6:00 AM to midnight, daily. I would think that those hours would rule it out for our suspect, especially since the liquor and wine are locked up at night. Despite having booze on the premises, there is no alarm system."

"Alarm systems haven't stopped him before," Riley reminded him.

"True. I think we should keep our options open and assume that he might go to the inn."

"I've got to figure that whatever we've doped out about these places, we should assume he's aware of too," said Riley. "As you've mentioned before, it probably hasn't escaped his notice that there's only one I-town, that it's logical we'll expect him there, and that it's only got the two big collections, so it's the place to try to trap him. He may not know who we are yet—GPD, Hartford PD, the half-dozen others—but he's bound to know *somebody's* paying attention."

"That's what Ellen figures floats his boat, right: attention?"

"In part. Floats his showboat, you might say. I doubt that's all there is to it, but we have every reason to expect a command performance up ahead. Not just another new MO—

they always have been new; he's not one to repeat himself—but something really off the wall. I don't know . . . what's the weirdest way you can think of for a guy to kill people?"

"Something specific for this town?" Jake gazed out the passenger-side window, for a moment in contemplation. "A stampede of ticked-off elephants, trying to get their tusks back, remembering where they all wound up."

"Not bad," Dave replied. "A little tough to set up, though. Hard to hide 'em, for one thing.

"Anyway, I didn't let you finish before; what about the other guy, the collector?"

"The second target, Harry Miller, is a retired Wall Street executive who moved up here a couple of years ago with his family. He bought an old Ivoryton house and remodeled it extensively. By all accounts he also built a fantastic wine cellar for his 25,000 bottles."

Riley whistled in disbelief. "Is that possible? He really has 25,000?"

"He sure does. And, just so you know, there are many larger collections around. For thirty years, Miller has bought only the best wines at auctions here and in London, and he's built one of the finest collections in the country. I haven't met him, but he's a legend in the collecting fraternity. By all reports, he's a nice guy as well."

"He's our second stop," said Riley. "We're scheduled to see Phillips first."

"As I see it," Jake continued, "our goal is get to the killer's targets before he does, and I think we can do that. Miller has a very sophisticated alarm system, but as you noted, we know that our perp can handle those. We'll have to rely on technology that's both silent and secret. Something he won't expect."

Riley glanced at him sharply. "You sound like you have a plan to catch him. Care to share?"

Jake shrugged. "I did a little tinkering the other night and managed to get a miniature black-and-white video camera into an empty wine bottle. I opened up both ends of the bottle: first, by cutting the capsule and putting the camera in place of the cork, and also by grinding a small hole in the center of the punt."

"The what? As in 'when in doubt. . .'?"

Jake chuckled. "Punt. That's the indentation in the bottom of most wine bottles. In both cases, the power and video wires lead out the back end of the bottle so they won't be visible from the front of the rack. The video recording and transmitting equipment can be located wherever space is available, even forty or fifty feet away. We can put a bunch of these bottle cameras in both the Copper Beech Inn and Miller's cellar, assuming I can build them in bulk, and after the first one I think I've got the hang of it. Finally, we set up a website and broadcast the output from the video server to the website showing images from all those bottles. We can access that website from anywhere we want and keep an eye on both cellars twenty-four hours a day."

Riley cleared his throat. "That sounds as if it might be kind of pricey."

"It is, and given the probable state of your budget, I'd be happy to underwrite the cost of the gear. I'll find some other use for it afterward."

"Now, that's the kind of consultant I like to deal with. I'll have to negotiate you a raise."

"Once we're set up, the ball's in your court. We'll need a control room—someplace we can monitor the surveillance equipment. But when we alert the local or state police. . . ."

Riley didn't seem to have heard him. He chuckled. "We're gonna catch this son of a bitch. I can feel it."

Jake was feeling much less confident. "Based on his timetables with the other crimes, we may be watching video monitors for a few months."

He felt more than saw Riley's gaze shift to his face. "You don't think we're close on this one?"

Jake sighed. "I don't know. But, yeah, my gut says this is where he'll come next, and we'll be waiting for him. I just hope we can spring the trap."

"You were clever in school, and you still are. I knew making you my best buddy was a good idea." He swung the car into a left-hand turn and slowed. "There's the Copper Beech."

Jake looked up as they pulled into the parking lot before a lovely old Victorian mansion. Inside, they met with owner Ian Phillips and his wine buyer and sommelier, Ed Dublinski.

"Dublinski," Riley said, shaking hands with that gentleman in the Inn's cozy entrance. "That's an unusual name."

"Ah, well," Dublinski replied, affecting a thick brogue, "You see, me father was an Irishman from Dublin and me mother was Polish. Her family was a bit down on the match, ya might say. One night after work, Father dear got drunk and had his name legally changed to Dublinski to appease the powers that be. We've had to live with it ever since."

"And did it?" Jake asked. "Appease the powers?"

"Oh, aye," laughed Dublinski. "We're in like Flynn."

"Which was. . . ."

"Our previous surname," the sommelier told him. Jake smiled.

"You don't serve lunch, I gather," Riley said, changing the subject as he eyed the empty dining rooms.

Ian shook his head. "Dinner only. But rest assured we have whipped you up some ample sustenance."

"You've put a lot of time and effort into this place," Jake observed, as they moved through the building to Phillips's small private dining room.

"And money. After a few lackluster years under its former owner, I bought the place and made a few changes."

"I'll say," Ed said. "The *Zagat Guide* recently referred to the inn as 'a Grand Dame of fine dining.' Got a hot review from the *Times*, too."

The lunch of *crocques-messieurs*, the simple French ham and cheese sandwiches, and a small mesclun salad, together with a glass of a Cru Beaujolais, told Jake that the *Zagat Guide* and *Times* weren't kidding. The food and wine, though simple, were both wonderful and Jake regretted that his friend's sense of duty forced him to decline the alcohol.

During the course of the meal, Halsey and Riley spelled

out the background of their mission and their reason for being there.

After lunch, Phillips led the men to the cellar. A recently installed sprinkler system required by Connecticut regulations was an incongruous contrast to the thick floor joists above it, which was original structure dating to the nineteenth century. The window next to the rear outside door was protected by horizontal steel bars fastened to the inside and each of the two wine cellars had a padlocked door. Jake did not see any evidence of an alarm system, but he did see several spots where the video-equipped wine bottles could be placed to obtain a good viewing angle. One of the wine cellars had a concrete ceiling and masonry walls that would prove virtually impenetrable to all but the most determined intruder.

Phillips confirmed that the inn had no intrusion alarm system; the only alarm occurred if the fire-suppression system was triggered. Registered guests who intended to be out for the evening were given keys to the front door. The door to the cellar stairs was locked at the main level when the kitchen was not operating.

"Installing video equipment in this cellar will be a piece of cake," Jake offered. "There are so many pipes and wires running through the space that it would take a very determined individual to see any new ones, once they're installed."

Ascending from the cellar, the men parted company, with Jake promising to return in the next several days to install the surveillance equipment.

Once in the car, Riley let loose a smile he'd been holding back since before lunch. "How many times," he asked Jake, "have you heard Ed's story about his family name?"

"Four," Jake answered. "Still, a good bit o' the blarney the fourth time around, too."

The next stop was Harry Miller's private residence. The town was so small that their trip took only moments.

The Miller property was ringed by a wall of dense evergreens, but was not fenced. Riley and Halsey drove through a pair of stone gateposts, up a long winding drive, and into a turnaround in front of a large and elegant New England

Colonial. The house was more what Jake would have expected to find among the ornate houses of Essex rather than the simpler architecture of Ivoryton.

Harry Miller himself answered the door and invited them in. He was a wiry and compact man in his fifties, graying at the temples. He carried himself with an air of success and confidence, exactly what Jake expected of a man who had the wherewithal to amass a cellar of 25,000 bottles. Miller ushered his visitors into a comfortable and well-appointed library and offered coffee, which both men declined.

Riley got right to the point. "We're on the trail of a serial criminal, Mr. Miller."

Miller's brows rose toward his graying hair. "A murderer?"

"He has committed murders. But his chief aim seems to be to destroy wine collections, whether in private homes or businesses. Evidence indicates he's been working in the state for some time, committing a crime, then waiting several months before committing another one. We've detected a pattern to his crimes that lead us to believe he may strike in Ivoryton next. Your wine collection would almost certainly attract his attention."

Miller sat up straighter in his chair and set down his coffee cup. "How . . . what sort of methods does he use?"

"So far we know he's skilled with electronic devices, explosives, chemicals, poisons, airplanes, and guns." Miller's eyebrows rose further.

Riley continued. "To a certain extent, time is on our side, because with a serial or pattern killer, presumably there will always be another crime. And, as I said, the pattern we've observed leads us here. We've also met with the owner of the Copper Beech Inn who has a prodigious collection to protect. I'll be perfectly straight with you, Mr. Miller: we want to make absolutely certain that nothing will happen to you or your family, to anyone else in Ivoryton, or to your wine. We'd like your help."

"What sort of help?"

"Here's the plan," Jake said, on cue. "This guy is very

adept at circumventing alarm systems and gaining access to his targets. The Essex PD covers Ivoryton, and they'll make extra patrols and will be watching for any suspicious activity, but we want to add to that.

"We'd like to install several wine bottles, modified to hide video cameras, in your wine cellar. We'll also install an on-premises video server and record our surveillance to hard disk. In the event our suspect gets clever and cuts power, we've got plans for battery backup, good for about three hours. We'll also send the output of the equipment in your house to a static IP address via a business-level Internet service. The server will upload images from your wine cellar to a website. That site can be monitored 24/7 and, if anything happens, the police can be alerted immediately. You will even be able to monitor those images from any computer here in your house or your office, just by logging on to that site. If the power should go off for any reason, the system will immediately alert us or the police. We intend to install the same equipment in the Copper Beech Inn."

Miller was silent for a moment, then asked, "How great is the danger to my family?"

"We honestly don't know," Riley said. "Our perpetrator has both timed his hits to coincide with his victims' absences, and lain in wait to target someone. In all good conscience, I should advise you that the coming month would be a very good time for a vacation."

"You said your suspect has a pattern. How has that led you to conclude that I might be a target?"

"The nature of the pattern is subject to police confidentiality, Mr. Miller. But I can tell you that we've researched possible Ivoryton wine collections both private and commercial. The only two that amount to anything more than a few dozen bottles are yours and that of the Copper Beech Inn, although modest collections have been hit, too. This guy may not come to Ivoryton at all, but we're pretty certain he will. If he does, we don't know which collection he might choose, so we've covering both bases."

Miller nodded, then said, "Let me show you the wine

cellar."

They descended a right-angle staircase. Side-by-side varnished wooden wine case ends made a natural wall decoration. At the bottom of the stairs was a massive dark oak door. To the left was a small period table holding a hand-held barcode scanner.

Jake paused to give the device a bemused look.

Miller caught the look and smiled wryly. "Yeah, I know, it's out of place down here. I had a lot of trouble keeping track of what was in my cellar when we first moved in and set it up, so I hired a fellow to barcode all the bottles. Now, when I take out a bottle, I just swipe it past this reader, and the inventory is automatically updated on the computer."

Jake appreciated the situation, especially now that Catherine was sometimes the one to remove a bottle from his own cellar, and was pleased at the simplicity of Miller's solution. He made a mental note to consider adopting it himself.

Miller's cellar had both bins and individual slots for bottles and identifying tags were screwed on the front of each bin or slot, simplifying choice of a specific wine. The space stretched for perhaps fifty feet and had a high, flat ceiling, from which designer track lighting was suspended on slender filaments.

In the distance, Jake noticed a bluish light emanating from a wine bin and asked Miller about it.

Miller grinned, pleased to be able to show off his prize. "That's my very rare bottle of 1847 Chateau Lafite. The light you see is several feet away and conducted over to the bin by fiber optics for illumination, avoiding unnecessary heat. You probably think that's overkill."

"Not for something that is more than 150 years old," Jake told him.

"Is it still drinkable?" asked Riley.

"Probably not, but we'll never know for sure, at least in my lifetime. The bottle is too valuable to open, and it's a piece of history."

Though he longed to closely examine the Lafite, Jake

kept his attention on the layout of the cellar, judging the best places to put surveillance points. At last, he knew he'd seen enough. After allowing himself one last look at the Lafite, he let Harry Miller lead them back upstairs.

"I have to admit," commented Riley, as they started their drive back to Greenwich, "both those places seem likely targets for our killer. I can't see how he could possibly resist them."

"Yeah, but which one?" Jake stared out at the passing scenery.

"Doesn't matter. We'll set up the surveillance system in both places. I just want to see his face when we catch him red-handed!"

Jake didn't comment. He only hoped this was one crime the killer would decide to pull off in person. After the close call in Hartford, he might opt for a more indirect method. And if he did, all their careful planning would be worthless. No surveillance cameras made could have averted the plane crash that destroyed Harry Johnson's family home.

CHAPTER TWENTY-SIX

Intent on her work, Arlene Bianchini only just registered the sound of Dave Riley's voice in the muted hubbub of the squad room. She glanced up in time to see him and Jake Halsey heading across the crowded bullpen area toward Riley's office-cum-conference room. She watched them, wondering if she should say anything to Jake about Catherine Taylor's odd call. Dr. Taylor hadn't exactly asked her not to—at least not in so many words—and she'd sounded so deadly serious. Was it fair to Halsey not to give him a heads-up?

As if he could feel her scrutiny, Jake looked her way. He waved at her and mouthed, "Hi," but the expression on his face showed nothing else.

No wonder, Arlene thought, putting on a bright smile and returning the wave. *I probably looked like I was about to tell him his dog had died.*

The two men turned the corner into Riley's office, and Arlene bit her lip. She glanced down at her In basket. There was a closed-case file there that needed to go to the chief for his signature. She picked it up and headed to Riley's office.

"Closed case for you to sign off on," she told Riley, pulling him out of a conversation with Halsey. She handed him the file, then let her gaze glide to the other man.

Should I? Shouldn't I? She mentally flipped a coin that came up on edge.

"Dr. Taylor was looking for you," she said.

"For me?" Halsey asked.

Riley snorted, not glancing up from his paperwork. "Well, she'd hardly be looking for *me*, now, would she?" Arlene picked up on her boss's amusement. For her part, she was curious why Catherine had called the department instead of just phoning Jake's cell directly.

Halsey was still looking over at Arlene. "Did she say what she wanted?"

"Nope."

"Did she want me to call her?"

"No, no. Just wondering where you were. Probably at loose ends for lunch or something."

Halsey nodded. "Probably." He glanced at Riley. "I doubt I'm going to be free for lunch today, though."

"Not a chance," Riley said, handing the case file back to Arlene. She tried discreetly to read his expression and got a distinct sense that he was doing the same to her. "We'll order in."

"I'll tell her that if she calls back," Arlene said. She took the file, hustled back to her desk, and called Dr. Taylor's office.

"We've got a lot to tell you guys," Riley told his assembled task force ten minutes later. "First, the bad news. The state lab returned their complete report. The DNA matches nothing in the FBI databases; the fingerprints match nothing in Integrated AFIS. We more or less expected that, so it's not devastating news. The good news is that there's a match on two of the crimes. The alarm system at the Perkins residence was disarmed by the same individual who murdered the Hartford victim, Whitney."

"The ambiguous news," added Jake, "is that he got careless—for him. His quarry departed from his routine the day of the murder and came home early, while our fella was still setting up his booby trap."

Tony Pezzi, scanning the crime scene photos from the Hartford murder that Riley had passed out, emitted a low whistle. "And quite a booby trap it was. Look at that jury-rigged gun mount. Elegant. He's something of an artist, don't you think?"

Ellen made a loud raspberry. "Come on, Tony, a man's *dead* because of that elegant mount. "

"Actually," Jake corrected, "he's dead regardless of it. It didn't figure in the murder. Our killer got pressed for time and had to pull the trigger himself."

Ellen sat back on a loud exhalation. "Unexpectedly, huh? But he improvised . . . or he panicked. I sure wish we knew which."

"It makes a difference?" asked Brian.

"Yes, it makes a difference," said Ellen, shooting Brian a wry smile. "It could affect how he plans and executes his next crime."

Jake nodded. "That's something I wondered about too. We've scoped out two locations in Ivoryton that match this guy's pattern, but there's no way of telling what kind of attack he might stage. In fact, that's what I was hoping we could brainstorm today. Scenarios for the next crime."

Riley looked to his profiler. "Ellen, can you toss out some general ideas about how a rude awakening like Hartford might affect our killer?"

"Well, first of all, it might not be a rude awakening, as you called it. He might choose to take it as a challenge. He might have gotten a real adrenaline high from not only pulling off his hit, but escaping unscathed. That may incline him to riskier behavior. Intentionally or subconsciously *planning* his next hit to be a close call or a hands-on affair. Conversely, it might scare him into backing off. Waiting longer, planning better, and making sure he can effectively keep his distance from the victim."

"So a lot could depend on whether he's more of a risk junkie or a control freak," replied Riley, "and there are reasons to identify him as both."

Ellen got to her feet and circled the table to the flip chart. "If you look at our progression of crimes here, you can see that the attacks get personal on occasion." She pointed out the pattern within the pattern. "The Charleson murder, the DiVito drowning, now the gunshot."

"He did intend the guy to be shot, but it may not have been planned for that moment, while he was still there," reminded Tony.

"No. Although, he was certainly cutting it pretty close. I guess the question is, has he fed his ego for killing up close and personal, or has he merely been excited? Of course, there may be no pattern to this at all. His methods may be chosen simply because they vary from what he's done before."

"Which is exactly what I'd like to explore," said Jake.

Ellen relinquished the floor as Jake walked to the chart. He flipped to a new page and quickly created a fresh list. It contained only the methods the killer had used. When he'd finished, he stood back from the chart to give the group a good look.

- truck crash and fatality
- suffocation
- electrocution
- arson
- drowning (boating "accident")
- plane crash and explosion
- poison
- gunshot
- next???

Tony shook his head. "He doesn't like to repeat himself, does he?"

"No, he doesn't. And, assuming the next town is Ivoryton, what methods might he use? It would seem that indirect methods outnumber the hands-on kind. He hasn't stabbed anybody yet or bludgeoned them with a blunt object."

"Harder to get away with," Ellen observed. "Messy, bloody, noisy. Our guy doesn't like to make noise. At least not when he's around to hear it. The shotgun blast in Hartford was, to all appearances, a fluke. He's a quiet killer. He relies on stealth."

Jake nodded eagerly. "Thank you, Ellen, that's just the sort of observation we need. So we're most likely looking for hands-on crimes, as you call them, that are stealthy. Any ideas? Just let your imaginations run wild, and I'll make a list. We can whittle it down later when we've thought about it and have more time. Just give me anything."

Tony Pezzi immediately suggested, "Another poison? He used cyanide this time. Maybe he'll try arsenic or maybe peanut butter."

"Peanut butter?" repeated Brian.

"Hey, some folks are deathly allergic," Tony defended the idea. "He does his homework, maybe he finds a potential victim with a peanut allergy."

Jake wrote "another poison" and "allergy—anaphylaxis" below the initial list.

"Here's one out of left field," said Ellen. "Weather. Since he's such a nut for timing, he might try to synch a hit to a weather pattern. The U.S. Weather Service would give him a week's notice on—oh, I dunno, electrical storms, maybe? Hail?"

Jake interjected. "This guy's done some pretty unlikely things already. Let's not rule it out."

"For all we know, he's got the whole alphabet mapped out and every MO pre-selected."

"Let's look at what appears to be the real target here," Riley suggested. "The wine. What if he freezes a cellar or heats it up so the wine spoils?"

Jake nodded. "That's good. He might also be able to arrange water damage. Flood a cellar." He continued to add items to the chart.

"I've got one," said Jake. "Biological or chemical alteration of the wine. Something that would make it unfit for use."

"That's not unlikely," Ellen agreed. "He seems to like ambiguity. Who gets killed or on what timetable doesn't seem to be of paramount importance to him. Maybe he even finds it titillating, the idea of someone opening their Pinot Noir at a big do and having it taste like vinegar, or worse."

"I thought it *all* tasted that way," said Tony, a beer drinker.

"Philistine," Ellen said, then suggested "What about manipulating the assets of the victim so he loses his collection that way? Has to sell it or has it liquidated to pay debts?"

"That's back to computer crime or some other sort of financial fraud," said Brian.

"Suffocation, asphyxiation, or burial alive?" suggested

Riley.

Tony shivered. "Spooky. Burying some poor wine connoisseur with his collection? Works for me."

"Those aren't too bad," commented Jake. "Anybody got any others?"

The room was quiet.

"All right," Jake said. "Here's the list so far."

- a different poison
- allergy—anaphylaxis
- weather-related
- freezing
- excessive heat
- flooding
- computer crime—affecting wine directly
- biological or chemical alteration of wine
- dropping from extreme height
- simple breakage
- suffocation
- asphyxiation
- burial alive
- computer crime—affecting wine owner

"Jeez," said Tony. "How do we narrow that list down?"

"It may get worse," said Jake wryly. "He used an accelerant in the Danbury arson and C4 to cause the Fairfield fire. Arsons, but two completely different vehicles for delivery. For all we know, that could be significant."

"A different poison," Riley read from the top of the list. "He can repeat himself without repeating himself."

"Yeah, but he hasn't done that yet," observed Ellen. "Sure, there are two arsons, but the delivery methods are *way* different, not just a matter of using gasoline for one fire and kerosene for another. My gut tells me that's glass-half-empty talk. He's going to go for something different this time. The question is, will he go for the collection or the collector?"

Jake sat down on the edge of the conference table and shook his head. He looked really tired, Riley noticed, like a man who hadn't slept much for several days. There were dark circles under his eyes and little lines of strain at their corners. Riley replayed the odd little conversation between Jake and Arlene Bianchini earlier and wondered if there was some subtext there. Were things between Jake and Catherine going south? Did he dare ask?

Jake turned to look at him, and Riley was glad he had a good poker face.

"We suggested to Mr. Miller that he might want to take his family away for a month or so. Was that a mistake? Might it keep this guy from striking?"

Riley deferred to Ellen.

"I doubt it," she answered, "but it might cause him to choose a different target. Or it might fit right in with his plans. It all depends, gentlemen, on whether our guy decides to be a killer this time or merely a vandal."

Arlene Bianchini tapped at the office door just then, gesturing at Riley through the sidelight. He nodded, and she opened the door a crack and put her head in.

"Mr. Halsey? Dr. Taylor is here to see you. She says it's important."

Jake rose slowly from his chair, his gaze finally going to Riley. "I'm sorry, I need to. . . ."

"Go ahead," Riley told him. "We'll stare at the list some more. Maybe add some real wild stuff."

Jake gave him a tight smile and left the room.

What was that about? Riley thought, and wondered whether he should be concerned for his friend's health or for his heart.

CHAPTER TWENTY-SEVEN

Jake met Catherine in an unused interrogation room down the hall from Riley's office. She wore an expression he hadn't seen on her before. The beautiful, confident physician was still beautiful—she would be, he reflected, under any imaginable conditions—but she seemed strangely jittery and brittle. Hearing her begin, hearing the quaver in her voice, he thought of a twelve-year-old kid at a recital or a scholastic contest.

"There's something I need to . . . well, nothing I could talk about over the phone. Something I have to tell you right away. I know it's hard to pull you away from the case. . . ."

"Don't worry about that. They have plenty of work that doesn't depend on my being there. What's up?"

"Something I can't make any sense of. I got the results back from your DNA test."

Jake steeled himself for unwelcome news. *If I'm a walking time bomb, at least I know some damn good specialists.* He thought quickly of his father's heart attack, his mother's battle with cancer, his wife and daughter's horrific final drive. "I know you have to tell people some hard news," he said, slowly. "And that's with strangers. I'm not sure I could do it. This has to be worse, I know. If it makes it any easier, can you try to pretend for a moment that I'm someone else?"

"It's not what we thought this was about. Jake, you aren't carrying any hereditary diseases, at least not the major ones they screen for. But when I saw the profile from your test, I saw a pattern I thought I recognized. And it turned out that was the case. You're not going to believe this."

She glanced away from him toward the two-way mirror. "Wait—does anybody know we're here?"

"If they do, they'll respect our privacy," Jake replied.

"Still, just to make sure there's not some kind of mistake . . . shouldn't we look in the hall for a second?"

"Of course. I'll check." Jake rose and went to the door, opening it silently and stepping outside for a moment. His faith in the GPD remained unshaken. No one was there.

He returned to the room, this time standing imperceptibly closer to Catherine. "Nobody. Fire when ready."

"When we were talking about this the other morning," she explained, "you made a joke about having more than a rare blood group in common with the lunatic who's been committing all these crimes. Something about his being a fourth or fifth cousin. Well, you were joking, but the data is serious. I looked at your profile next to the report from the crime scene evidence and they have a lot of markers in common. They actually have so many sequences in common that he could be a lot closer to you than a cousin. He's almost certain to be family. He could be your brother." She hesitated and struggled to meet his gaze. "If—if I were somebody else entirely, and these reports were the only thing I knew about you, I'd think he could even be you."

Jake was silent and motionless. His throat felt like he'd swallowed a baseball. For several seconds they looked directly into each other's eyes without saying a word. At some point he noticed they had a firm hold on each other's arms, though he couldn't recall a specific point where he began to embrace her. They were simply locked together, both shaken by the information and instinctively resolved to keep each other as steady as possible.

Catherine was first to break the silence.

"Don't say it. You know you don't need to worry about that. I could never think that. Not in a million years. But somebody could, somebody who doesn't know you. We have to find a way to make sense of this, *before* it could reach anyone who'd want to do you harm."

"I just . . . it just doesn't make sense. I mean, it's not beyond reason that there could be some relatives I don't know about, but nobody that close. Are you sure it's not just a fluke, or a mistake in the test?"

"Both Y-chromosome and mitochondrial haplogroups match up with high probability of similar mutations and polymorphisms at all the major loci tested. The odds are astronomical against that being random."

An incongruous smile flashed across Jake's face. *"Anglais, s'il vous plait. Je ne parle pas le* genetics babble."

"Unless there's been an unbelievable foul-up, you have some sort of close relative, and he's nobody you'd want to welcome into the family."

Jake took his time replying. "I have to think there's some logical reason for the DNA match-up that doesn't make my dad a philanderer. He could have been, I know. Every happy family is actually unhappy, the writers keep telling us, and they keep on inventing new ways."

Catherine's eyes twinkled for the first time at the reference, and her expression brought Jake some relief as he continued. "But what are the alternative explanations? We've been making lists about what we think this sick freak might do next. Let's try the same strategy here. What if the shortest distance between these two reports and the truth isn't some spooky goings on in the family history, but a lab foul-up? Or a mistake I made myself in gathering some of the evidence? I found that first hair at the Perkins house in Bridgeport. Since I'm a layman, I try to be rigorous as hell about procedure, especially chain of custody. But I'm human."

Never more human than now. When I find out I may be related to a monster.

"That could explain it if there were only the one sample," said Catherine. "But the DNA profile also included the blood and skin-cell specimens the police had processed from the other scene, things you never touched." She picked up the profile documents. "These give you—give *us*—something harder to figure out."

Jake looked pensive and pained. "It just doesn't make sense. It's not that I doubt you, Cat. I don't have the background to sift through the data and verify this, hands on. I know you wouldn't make a mistake about what you see there. I just wonder how what you see actually got." He paused again and weighed his words carefully. "Having a blood relationship to this guy is so far-fetched that I can't let myself believe it until we've ruled out all the—call it the near-fetched stuff."

"I want that to be the case too," Catherine said. "I want these patterns to mean something else. We'll figure this out." She squeezed his arm, and he noticed her voice again sounding natural. "But right now, I think we have to be absolutely discreet. Can you think of anybody who would want to see you under suspicion? Anybody with a grudge? Anybody who could think you're capable of. . . ."

"Don't even say it. I can think of exactly one person who'd have it in for me, but she's no longer in this area. The one who set up that electrocution of an opera singer I worked on with Dave two years ago. She won't be out of York Correctional for another twenty-five years, if ever."

He grew momentarily lost in thought. "What about tampering a little closer to home? It'd have to be someone with access to evidence. I'm aware of people on the force, outside Dave's department, who don't think too highly of having me work on cases. Some of these cops don't care if I hear them call me an amateur. But that's not in the same ballpark with wanting to see me framed as the Wine Killer."

"What if we tell Dave about the DNA? Would that help?"

"Best ally we could possibly have. Especially if this news got loose and things turned weird around here. And I'll make sure he does know. . .as soon as we're sure the info is reliable enough to be relevant to the case. Not before, not until we've eliminated the loose ends and the glitches. Dave's got more than enough on his plate right now. I want to keep a firm hand on Occam's Razor."

"And there was never a more unnaturally multiplying entity than this."

Jake looked Catherine directly and intensely in the eyes. "I want to make sure you know how much I appreciate what you've done. You might have drawn every horrible conclusion. . . ."

"No, you don't need to say it. I couldn't have. Not

without becoming somebody completely foreign to you, and to myself."

Few words were needed between them after that.

It took Jake a moment longer than one might have expected to recall that his presence was needed back in Riley's office, among the charts and Ellen's profiles and Pezzi's desperate one-liners.

CHAPTER TWENTY-EIGHT

He had rented the house in the Riverside section of Greenwich under an assumed name three years before. Paying rent in advance and in cash had not only endeared him to his landlord, but also kept him safely anonymous. The utilities and yard care remained in the name of the owner.

The house was a nondescript 1950s split-level, which still retained its wide asbestos shingles, mostly hidden by the forlorn and overgrown yews marching around its perimeter. A single-car garage opened onto a short, straight driveway, which permitted the tenant to drive inside and close the door before getting out of his car. He drove a dark gray Chevy sedan with a single distinguishing feature, darkened window glass resembling that of a limousine. In three years, though they had seen the car coming and going, no neighbor had seen the man himself. The few who'd taken any notice of the vehicle might have assumed its driver was either a reclusive celebrity or a gangster, if his house had been large enough to encourage that kind of fantasy. As it was, no one in Greenwich gave him a thought.

He moved purposefully through the house now, heading for the cellar, which was accessible from the kitchen. He opened the cellar door and hit the switch at the top of the stairs, turning on all the lights below. Not a bit of this light escaped to the outside. He had secured plywood panels on the insides of the cellar windows and sealed the seams tightly with joint compound.

Reaching the bottom of the stairs, he unlocked a steel door and entered his workshop. It was not the type of room that term usually conjures. Overhead, double-tube, eight-foot fluorescent lights provided more than enough illumination for the work tables, which were cluttered with a motley collection of bottles, jars, electronic equipment, wire, and assorted tools and test equipment. A box of surgical gloves sat at the end of one table. The man pulled on a pair of the gloves, opened one of the cabinets, and withdrew a bottle labeled "DMSO" in large type. Beneath those letters in parentheses were the words "Dimethyl Sulfoxide."

He measured out seventy-five milliliters of the colorless commercial solvent—about the amount in a small wine glass. Then, turning to a refrigerator, he reached for a plastic bottle with a rubber stopper crudely marked "Curare." Inside the bottle was a heavy, dark, viscous liquid of the type used by South American Indians to kill game animals.

With a large syringe, he withdrew five milliliters of the liquid and added it to the first chemical. Finally, he grasped a small medicine bottle labeled with Chinese characters and, using an eyedropper, added twenty drops to the existing solution. He poured the contents into a wide-mouthed jar and screwed the cover down tightly. A plain white plastic bag containing a cheap two-inch paintbrush lay on the worktable. The witch's brew of chemicals went into the plastic bag with a blue gel ice-pack from the freezer; the source containers went back into their cabinet.

With the bag in hand, the man left the room, turned out the light, and went up the stairs to the garage where he deposited the plastic bag in the trunk of his Chevrolet, sliding the jar into a Styrofoam cup holder of the type used in swimming pools. Satisfied the package would be held upright until it fulfilled its deadly purpose, he turned out the light and closed the door to the garage.

Returning to the house, he removed his gloves and disposed of them; they went into a Ziploc plastic bag and then into the trash compactor. At the kitchen sink, he carefully washed his hands to remove any trace of the chemicals.

He spoke a single word out loud, as if reciting an incantation sacred only to himself.

"One."

He entered the basement again, went to another table, donned goggles, and examined several dozen small, concave discs cut and stamped from aluminum sheets of varying thicknesses, suspended above a long glass trough. Each disc was corroded at its center, and most were eaten through; the corrosive liquid puddled in the glass vessel below. The man measured the corroded areas of each disc precisely with a caliper and recorded the dimensions painstakingly on a yellow pad. He examined the figures silently for several minutes, correlating dimensions and durations. He had done this several times daily for the past week.

Inwardly, though not outwardly, he smiled. He had enough data now and the answer he needed. He could proceed from experiment to fabrication.

He selected appropriate thicknesses of aluminum sheeting from several orderly stacks at the opposite end of the work table. Cutting them to shape, clamping them in a vise, and bending them carefully with pliers, he built his simple instrument: a three-chamber tray resembling the compartments of a fishing tackle box. He would not fill the chambers until the day of operation, but he was now confident that the device would work: he had determined how long it would take the solution of sodium hydroxide in water to eat through the walls of the center chamber, left and right, marrying the contents of the other two chambers, consummating the reaction.

He was fond of sodium hydroxide. Sodium hydroxide ate aluminum for breakfast. Sodium hydroxide was to aluminum, he believed, as his own mind was to the minds of lesser men.

Five to six hours would suffice, given the strength of the solution and the thickness of the compartment walls on either side, to bring together the water that would occupy the left chamber and the concentrated sulfuric acid to the right. The mixture would spontaneously generate a great deal of heat, more than enough to animate the final element of the device, a small clump the size of a pencil eraser, suspended above the center chamber in a plastic package. Fulminate of mercury, highly unstable under any conditions, would go up quickly, mightily, and gloriously once the water and acid had combined and generated enough heat. So would everything *and anyone nearby.*

"Two," he intoned.

His opponents might conceivably interfere with one of his Ivoryton events, but they would not be prepared for the simultaneous Two.

His two plans conferred power, and the power was his alone. He was the master. As lesser men dissolved, his solidity would sublimate and through his power he would rise. They would know his power and respect it and pay him tribute in the coin he deserved, the awe he had earned. He could scarcely imagine the sensation that would ultimately transfigure him.

Climbing the stairs once more, he again went to the sink and washed carefully.

After satisfying himself that his touch carried none of the noxious liquids from either project, he picked up a bottle of Johnny Walker Black Label from the counter, poured three fingers' worth into a glass and sipped it as he entered the living room and dropped into a chair. As he drank, his glance fell on a bamboo-framed photo on the fireplace mantle. The photograph showed a smiling Chinese couple standing in front of a large, brick house. Barely discernible in the house's doorway was a boy of about three whose long blond hair obscured nearly half of his face.

The man in black stared at the photograph for a long time.

His parents had called him Daniel, when they bothered to call him at all. He had been obtained from a doctor, perhaps as a status symbol. But as he had grown from infant to toddler, it had been obvious that something was wrong. His adoptive parents discovered that during his birth, his facial nerves had been injured; they did not heal. As a result, there was little movement on one side of his face, one eye could not be fully closed, and his ability to taste was compromised. Honor, he had later discovered, had forbidden the couple from disposing of him, but his presence did little more than remind them of a bargain gone bad. Embarrassed and disgraced by their disfigured son, they had hidden him from their wealthy friends, treating him like an outcast.

If his handicap had dulled his sense of taste and his repertoire of facial expressions, it had done nothing to blunt his intellectual capabilities. He had grown up trilingual, speaking Cantonese and the less-encountered Mandarin, in addition to English.

Even as a boy he had been smart and athletic, but because of his disfigurement he had had trouble attracting friends. He had grown to hate the boys and girls who snubbed him, learned to despise their privileged lives and indulgent parents. As for his "parents"—the word made him cringe— their wealth was nothing more than a constant and tantalizing reminder of all he might have had, but didn't.

He fingered his glass, sipping the amber liquid. Funny how fate turned things around. He thought back on the event that, with the optimism of adolescence, he'd believed would change his life. A phone call from the United States had offered his father a dream job in Boston, prompting the family to emigrate to America.

It was during preparation for their journey that Daniel had stumbled across the evidence that led to a painful reconstruction of the circumstances surrounding his adoption. His Hong Kong parents had always painted themselves as the kind-hearted saviors of a homeless, parentless child. The reality—spelled out in documents he found in a sealed envelope in his father's desk—was far more disturbing. The doctor who had ushered him into this household had treated his birth mother while she was vacationing in Hong Kong. His so-called "real" parents had left him behind when they returned to America. From the scant medical records he found, it was unclear whether those parents even knew he existed. The doctor had briefly noted his biological mother's dazed condition during the delivery, then mentioned nothing of her afterward. His adoptive parents, reeling from a series of miscarriages, had purchased him from the doctor—as if he had been a puppy.

He had never let on that he knew. To his adoptive parents, any increase in Daniel's surliness after their move to

America was imperceptible.

How he had loved it when his father's new job hadn't worked out, when he had watched the man lose some of his pride, smugness, and certainty. But Daniel's joy had been short-lived. Trapped in a foreign world, suddenly pressed for money in the expensive house they'd purchased, his parents had increasingly resented his presence. It had quickly become clear that they saw in him the Americans they felt had misled and betrayed them.

Perhaps even more painful was the fact that, where he should have been finally at home, where he should have looked like everyone else, he was more of an outcast than ever. Before he'd come to the U. S. at least he'd been with people who were accustomed to his disfigurement; people who, in some ways, viewed it as a mark of distinction. In America, he was a stranger with a funny accent, a freak with a twisted face. God, how he'd hated the Boston suburb in which his family had lived, how he'd despised the broad streets and narrow minds.

The country of his real parents' birth would remain a foreign land to him.

As his relationship with his adoptive parents dissolved completely, he had begun to try to find the couple who'd abandoned him in Hong Kong. Until fairly recently, he'd had little luck.

There were certain organizations he did business with through a nest of contrived identities and indirect, online channels. Some of these groups performed work that didn't require elaborate recordkeeping—and certainly wouldn't subject him to any risks of attention or exposure—but still needed the services of a man with his mathematical skills.

In the business world, he had learned how to position himself at critical points in flows of complex information and to repeat impossibly detailed tasks as often as necessary. Sometimes it was just the analysis of survey data, masses of hasty and half-serious responses to inquiries about products or beliefs. He could envision these murky masses in the orderly form of statistics and transpose them into forms that carried meaning. Sometimes, it was information of a more personal nature. Every business—including the kinds that occasionally need to pack up offices late at night and set files and equipment on fire—needs its statistics crunched, its funds redirected somewhere beneficial.

He'd served some of these criminal enterprises diligently enough, and profitably enough for both parties, that he'd gained access to some of their artificial identities for his own occasional fishing expeditions. He had managed to enter a system he'd not previously gained access to, and he now learned a few things he had long wanted to know.

The noise of a car going by outside brought him back to reality, and his daydream receded, leaving only the sour residue of hate. If his Chinese parents put so much stake in honor, why hadn't they helped him? They'd had money. Why hadn't they fixed his face while he was still young enough?

Damn them, *he thought*. And damn those so-called "real" parents who abandoned me, exiled me, rejected me!

His rage was the one constant in his life and, in its chilled form, it was the atmosphere he breathed. He was fully acclimated to it, but it did not maintain a steady temperature. He could feed it in some ways, appease it for a time, and it would reliably reward him for that. But thoughts of Hong Kong or Boston or other locales could fan it into a conflagration that nothing could contain. Now, scalded by its erupting heat, he picked up his half-consumed drink with a wild look and threw it against the fireplace mantel where the heavy glass shattered into a thousand pieces.

CHAPTER TWENTY-NINE

Jake had two dozen wine bottles lined up along a table in his workshop. He had been collecting them since the Ivoryton trip, along with a small pail full of corks and some capsules. The bottles and corks were from whatever he had been drinking, but the capsules were from J. Lohr Chardonnay, an inexpensive California wine he often enjoyed in casual moments. Some months previously, he had discovered that the Lohr capsules could be carefully twisted off, more or less intact, by hand, maintaining their rounded shape. Jake had also purchased and cannibalized several glass cutters to build a crude jig that allowed him to rotate a wine bottle against the cutter's circular blades.

Under other circumstances, he would have enjoyed this problem-solving exercise, reveling in the sheer delight of cobbling together the jury-rigged surveillance system. Tonight, his enjoyment was hostage to a peculiar sense of the unknown.

What else? he thought as he carefully painted kerosene, the preferred lubricant for glass cutting, around the bottom of the first empty bottle. *What else don't I know about my family? If it's true, that is. And if it's not and the samples are from me, how in hell'd they get there?*

He rotated the lubricated bottle against the cutter and gave it a gentle tap with a rawhide mallet. The bottle bottom dropped cleanly away.

One could be accidental. I thought I handled the hair okay. Of course, nobody's perfect. But Cat's right: I had no contact with the glove from Michael Whitney's house.

Close enough to be his brother, Cat had said. Close enough to be him.

He tried to laugh at the first thought that had popped into

197

his mind: *Am I having blackouts?* Pure television, that sort of scenario. Jake wasn't much of a TV viewer, but he'd seen just enough sci-fi that stories of split personalities and alter egos struck him as the stuff of *The Outer Limits* or *The X-Files*, not of real life. But he couldn't laugh, because the alternative was just as bizarre: that his mom and dad—the people he had loved most in life until he'd met Melinda—had been living a lie. Or one of them had. He'd had a sibling.

One tap and the second bottle shattered against the cutter. *Pressed too hard, dammit.*

He tossed the broken bottle aside.

He'd gone back in his mind, trying to recall any strangeness in his childhood. Had his mother ever looked at him as if she saw someone else in his place? Was there a time of year—maybe a holiday, maybe someone's birthday—when his parents seemed particularly distant, or depressed, or edgy?

As frankly as he asked himself these questions, the answer was no. He could recall no sense of secrecy about his mother and father. They had always seemed like good people and good parents.

Hell, he thought, in a flash of anger. *They* were *good people.* The only bone of contention between them had been his refusal to take up the wine business. And even that had not distressed them unduly once they'd seen how happy he was with the career path he'd chosen.

Yet, if there was no other explanation for the DNA, then they had had another child. A hidden child—or a lost child.

Another bottle shattered. Jake swore.

Consciously calming himself, he returned to his task with extra care. When he finished, he had twenty bottles cleanly cut and ready to be fitted with surveillance gear. Earlier in the day he had driven to New York and visited an electronics store advertising miniature video cameras. He had brought several dozen back to Connecticut with him.

He picked up one of the tiny cameras to inspect it. It was little more than a small, exposed, printed-circuit board, about one and a half inches square, with a lens the size of a pencil eraser soldered to one end of the board, and terminals for a power source and video feed at the other end. Picking up a pair of small diagonal cutting pliers from the bench, Jake clipped the leads to the lens at the board end. A trip to his junk box produced several four-inch sections of insulated wire, which he soldered to the lens at one end and to the board at the other. He then attached leads for both the video feed and power wires.

Jake selected a cork to fit the bottle and drilled a hole the size of the lens in the cork. Inserting the lens without crumbling the cork took considerable patience. Next, he had to reinsert the cork. After some experimentation, he found that mounting the bottle in a vise and applying just enough pressure to hold it firmly between improvised pads of cardboard and chamois cloth provided a good working angle that freed up both hands. He selected a slender, eight-inch surgical forceps from a pegboard rack above his bench. Then he got a steady grip on the cork and carefully pushed it into the bottle neck from inside the bottle, while aligning the top of the lens with the bottle label in the uppermost position. This ensured that when the label was uppermost, the video image would be right side up.

Tamping the cork tightly up into the neck the last half-inch with a long-shafted Phillips screwdriver while guiding it with the forceps, Jake recalled a sight from his childhood, watching a Nantucket craftsman working on a model ship in a bottle. *If that old codger could glue the complex rigging into place through the neck of his bottle,* he thought, *it can't be too tricky working through the bottom of this one.* The memory helped him focus as he forced the cork into place without damaging the lens or the wires to the circuit board. After a few minutes of slow progress, the cork and lens assembly was flush with the upper lip of the bottle, and the wires led out the open bottom. Jake inserted a piece of plastic foam in the bottle beside the circuit board to keep it from moving around. He loosened the vise, removed the bottle from its chamois cradle, and examined the glass surface and label: no cracks, no chips, no scars. Finally, he cut a one-quarter-inch hole in the top of the capsule and pushed the capsule down over the bottle's top.

He sat looking at the finished "bottle-cam," reflecting on how easy it had been to both conceive and build. He even understood how the camera worked.

He just wasn't sure he still understood his own life story.

Now, following Cat's revelation, more than at any time since Melinda and Courtney's deaths, Jake felt as if the Earth on which he'd stood for forty-two years had moved out from under his feet, leaving him floating in space.

He smiled momentarily at the image that evoked and took his prototype bottle into the wine cellar, where he placed it in a slot in his wine rack. He rotated it so the label faced up, dressed the wires in the rear, and stepped back to admire his handiwork. As long as light didn't strike directly on the quarter-inch open eye in the capsule to create glare from the lens—and it didn't—the camera bottle was indistinguishable from others in the rack.

Repeating the process eleven more times resulted in a row of twelve bottle cameras, an aching neck, and a growling stomach that brought him to the realization that he had forgotten to eat lunch. He also realized that he had been listening with one ear for the phone to ring; for Cat's voice to reassure him that the good, solid earth had not sidestepped him; that some things were to be depended upon. But she hadn't called, and Jake did not want to press her.

After lunch, Jake installed his home surveillance software on two computers he'd purchased for that purpose, setting them so each would accept six video inputs and show all six video feeds on one screen. Everything worked perfectly except for one camera that showed an upside-down image; that was easily corrected.

Picking up the phone, Jake dialed Dave Riley. "I've got two sets of six video cameras masquerading as wine bottles, and they work perfectly. Interested?"

"You bet. A custom wine-cellar surveillance system! To quote my son, that's way cool. And, more to the point, it's more real-world than anything we've got on that list. Now all that's left is to go to Ivoryton and install them."

All that's left.

Somehow Jake couldn't bring himself to believe it would be that easy. He shook himself, wondering if his experiences over the past several years had put him permanently on the dark side of his own imagination. He'd have said not, but that was before he'd found himself confronting a completely bizarre question: how could I possibly have a brother? Even harder: how could I have *that* brother?

There was no one left alive to ask. Mom and Dad were both dead. He had no living grandparents, aunts, uncles, or even cousins. He had seen nothing when he'd gone over the assets of his parents' estate that indicated they'd ever supported another child. Besides, the DNA match was too close to have come from a half-brother resulting from some marital infidelity in either parent's misty past, unless the straying party strayed into an extremely similar gene pool. That, he realized, was highly unlikely. A lot of people elsewhere had the idea that southwestern Connecticut was completely homogeneous, all white bread and white picket fences. They'd paid a little too much attention to that *Stepford Wives* story. Jake had spent enough of his life here to know otherwise.

There's always laboratory error, he thought, as if trying to convince himself. Cat was following up on that. *And then there's the thing everybody tends to forget about DNA evidence: sure, it's amazingly precise, it's often definitive, and when somebody needs exculpation it's their best friend in the world. But DNA, like any other kind of evidence, can be planted.*

His thoughts stopped and eddied. *The estate lawyer.* His father and mother had retained the same legal firm for as long as he'd been aware of such things: Griffin, Stern, and Petrocelli.

He picked up the phone again and dialed information.

CHAPTER THIRTY

The next day Jake and Riley headed back to Ivoryton.

"I've set up a website to handle the video images," Jake told the detective chief en route. "We'll put six video cameras in the Miller cellar and six in the Copper Beech Inn. Those cameras will feed a computer with DSL service hidden in each cellar, and the signals will be sent to a dedicated server in Greenwich. We can log onto our website from any computer and view the images. If the computer has a twenty-one-inch screen or multiple smaller screens, all twelve images can be viewed at once. I've set the website up so that any feed can be selected, isolated, and enlarged to full screen. I tested the system at home, and you can get a good, clean image with normal wine cellar lighting."

"And if the power goes out?" Riley asked.

"They're security cams; they're battery supported and they'll go to infrared."

"I contacted both Phillips and Miller as you asked," Riley told him. "Miller already had DSL service, and Phillips had his DSL service installed yesterday. So they both should be ready for us."

"Excellent." Jake was wearing a distant expression that Riley might have called his "multitasking face," if he'd been looking in Jake's direction instead of at the road. *Right at this moment, some junior associate at Griffin, Stern could be digging up documentation that's about to turn my world inside out.*

"The crew did a little more brainstorming this morning before you arrived," Riley said. "Between the two sites, I'd definitely rather see the next incident pop up at Miller's house than at the Copper Beech Inn. Fewer people around. Fewer complications. On the other hand . . . ."

Nothing came out in probate when they settled Mom and Dad's estate, Jake thought. *No unexpected bequests, no unknown parties, no secret trust funds. Could it be possible that Dad was quietly channeling funds somewhere while he was still alive?*

". . . what's wise for the Miller family, their getting out of town for a while, may not be our best move for baiting this gentleman. Fine, if he really is primarily interested in the wine and killing is just incidental. But if Ellen's conjecture about his methods getting more personal turns out to be accurate, we may find out just how much of a taste he has for wine and how much for blood."

"True." *If he was doing something like that, he'd probably have known how to keep it off the radar screens of the probate attorneys, too. Dad was nothing if not discreet.*

"The real worst-case scenario, as Tony brought up, would be that he's growing restless and getting ready to escalate. If he decides to take out more than one victim at a time—I'm just thinking out loud here—then his target of choice would logically be the inn. But, as Ellen points out, it's rare for pattern killers to turn into mass murderers. Totally different profiles in practically every variable—motives, organization, MO, victim demographics, their own demographics. If this fellow switches categories on us, it'd be one more surprise in a long series of surprises."

This brought some of Jake's focus back. "So the bottom line is, he gives us nothing we can predict except unpredictability. Plus the one most predictable thing in the world—the goddamn alphabet."

"Right-o. Good point." Dave gripped the steering wheel so tightly his knuckles whitened. "Compadre, we are getting our chain yanked. And I do not like having my chain yanked."

And if he really does have anything to do with my family, he should have better taste than that. Halseys do not go out of their way to make people uncomfortable.

"Are you sure Pezzi isn't running a little far with the speculative stuff? Our friend seems to watch an awful lot of movies. Tony, I mean, not. . . ."

What am I thinking? Get a grip, Jake. This clown is not under any circumstances a Halsey. Being one of us takes more than genes. And I'm not yet convinced he even has the genes.

"For now, it's all intriguing, but it doesn't change what we have to do," said Dave. "Rig up your bottle-cams in both sites, make sure Phillips and Miller know what they need to know—mainly, to stay a zillion miles out of the way of all of it—and set up a monitoring detail."

"Mm-hmm. Hope that goes over okay back at the precinct. We're building the perfect modern American crime fighting force. To catch a murderer, stay inside, park your butt, and watch a hell of a lot of TV."

Both men fell silent for a few miles.

And if nothing turns up with the lawyers and the accountants, check with the doctors. Our old family GP is long dead. The pediatrician I went to as a kid is retired. Who'd they start going to when I was in college? Gotta see if that guy's still practicing. Then when they both got older, they were seeing an internist based at Greenwich Hospital. How many couples still go to the same doc? Traditionalists to the end, those two. And Dad had some specialist referrals at Yale–New Haven. Mom must have had an oncologist, though she never wanted to mention it.

That's not what this is about. Dammit. Assume nothing, as always—but anything relevant is going to be in obstetrical records.

Tracking down my mother's ob/gyn. I cringe at how that conversation is going to go.

"Ivoryton exit," Riley said.

"Back to business," said Jake, relieved. "Let's stop at the inn first. The century-old construction may give us some problems with things like dressing the wires so they can't be seen."

Ian Phillips was waiting for them at the door of the inn. "Welcome, once again, to the Copper Beech Inn." He was smiling, but above the smile his eyes were wary.

"You doing okay, Ian?" Riley asked him.

"I have to tell you, I'm nervous as a canary in a coal

mine, but also excited to be part of a sting operation. I hope this works."

"No more than we do," Riley assured him.

Ian turned his head toward the cellar door. "Shall we get started?"

Jake set up the equipment and ran a bundle of white extension cords for the cameras. Against the whitewashed walls and in the shadows behind the shelving, they were virtually invisible. He replaced real bottles with bottle-cams at intervals throughout the racks in order to give the broadest possible composite video coverage of the room. The computer was secreted on the floor of a small alcove in a corner behind the rearmost shelf. When all the equipment was set up and the computer turned on, all six images registered on the monitor.

Once he was certain the images were stable and the video controls allowed clear pictures with the room lights both on and off, Jake unplugged the monitor and removed it, leaving the unobtrusive little "pizza box" CPU on the floor, hardly visible.

Next they went upstairs to Ian's office to check the feed from the website. Jake logged onto the password-protected site and, in moments, they were looking at six real-time images of the wine cellar.

"Dave, would you go down there and sneak around a bit so we can test the system?" asked Jake.

"Glad to oblige. I don't get enough opportunities to sneak around."

He left the room and reappeared moments later in the camera eye. "Hey," he said, peering around. "I can't even tell which bottles are the spy cams, and I watched you set them up." He poked around for a few moments more, then came back upstairs.

"The bad news is," he told Ian and Jake, "you can hear the cooling fan on the CPU. The good news is, it blends into the sound of the refrigeration system. Does your cooling ever go off?"

Ian frowned. "Not for very long periods. It goes off when the wine cellar reaches the proper temperature, but turns on again whenever the temperature shifts by a degree or so. It's on pretty much constantly during the day."

Jake shrugged. "We just have to hope he doesn't notice the additional white noise in the brief periods the air conditioning is off."

"We'll be in touch tomorrow to get your schedule for cellar visits and visitors' names, so we'll know when we see someone who's supposed to be there," Riley told the innkeeper, as he and Jake were leaving. "Your staff going to have a problem with signing in every time they enter the cellar?"

Phillips smiled. "I've already briefed them without briefing them, if you know what I mean. No one knows what it's for, but I told them I needed to get a little more scientific about inventory control—what vintages are popular, what everybody's recommending to customers. I made sure to stress this isn't because I suspect anybody of personally taking the odd bottle, so nobody took it as an affront. Grumbling was minimal."

"Actually," said Jake, "the killer likes to do his homework. I think he probably prides himself on it. I wouldn't be surprised if he visits the inn during business hours."

"If he hasn't done it already," Riley added.

At the Miller home the installation went even faster, and Harry Miller was excited to see images of his wine cellar on his computer.

"So, Detective," he said to Riley when they'd completed the installation. "What's the word? Should I take my family and leave town?"

"Leave," said Jake before Riley could answer. "The worst thing that can happen if you leave is that he switches his target to the Copper Beech Inn. The worst that can happen if you stay. . . ."

". . .is something we don't want to even think about," Riley finished.

The trip back to Greenwich was silent until they were on

the open highway. After casting several sideways glances at Jake, Dave asked, "You know what bugs me the most about this idea of the perp taunting us? I mean, aside from the simple insult to all of us."

Jake stiffened.

"It's that it seems personal. He's got the whole East Coast to do what he does, and beyond. But so far he's confining himself to this state. So, within that artificial boundary, he sets up a pattern that's bone simple, a textbook puzzle right out of a nineteenth-century murder mystery. He doesn't even always appear to care who he kills. If there's a message—and any pattern implies a message—it sounds like 'I'm doing this, and doing it this way, just because I can.' Like a kid in a schoolyard saying 'I know something you don't, nyaah nyaah.' Immature, of course, and irritating as hell, but maybe more than that. Nothing else creates a linkage between the incidents, except they're around here and they involve wine. Plus, how many places do we know of where investigators employ a consultant who's a recognized oenophile?"

"I'll grant the point. Outrageous odds, I know. We got lucky with that, if you can call it luck. What are you driving at?"

"I'm wondering if the connection to an area of your expertise wasn't all luck. Maybe the personal message isn't aimed inside the department."

Jake shook his head. "I don't get you."

"Maybe he's on the case because *you're* on the case."

Jake felt the hair on his neck bristling.

What the hell? If there's one thing we Halseys absolutely refuse to do, it's assume that events revolve around us personally.

"Umm, not that the attention isn't flattering, but he's been on the case for over a year. I just came on in October."

"But what if he was committing his crimes in such away that your involvement was, if not a slam dunk, at least probable?"

"How in the name of God could he do that?"

Riley cringed visibly. "Don't shout."

He had been shouting, Jake realized. "Sorry," he conceded, as if they were playing one-on-one basketball. He took a deep, calming breath.

"I'd say," Riley continued, glancing sideways at Jake, "that entirely depends on how much he knows about you. Assume for a second he has some reason to want to get your attention. If he's been doing his homework on you as assiduously as he does for his hits. . . ."

"He knows I occasionally consult with the police," Jake finished.

"It's not widely bandied about, but we don't keep it a secret."

"Anybody who gets the *Greenwich Time* could know we've worked together."

"Yeah," said Riley. "If he was a local, it'd be that much easier for him to keep tabs on you. Anything weird going on in your life lately?"

You have no idea old friend, but you're going to know as soon as I'm sure there's something real to tell you.

Jake shook his head. "No, not really. Not anything sinister."

"Anything unsinister?"

"I don't think that's a word," said Jake.

"Well?"

Jake shook his head again. "Not that I can think of. Other than Fido running slightly amok yesterday."

Riley glanced at him sharply. "Fido? The mechanical guy you worked up in that Frankenstein's lab you call a workshop?"

"He got a little unruly over some broken glass and wouldn't hear of letting me clean it up myself. Before I could stop him, he'd taken a header onto the floor, and when I tried to help him up, he ripped my sweatshirt."

Riley's eyebrows rose. "Lucky it was just your sweatshirt."

"Yeah," said Jake, fighting off a sudden chill. "Lucky."

CHAPTER THIRTY-ONE

Jake was not prone to categorizing people by their professions. Even, he reflected, attorneys. He'd seen enough old friends go through law school, go into practice, and remain human beings—recognizable and admirable versions of their old selves, even—that he had minimal patience with lawyer jokes. Lawyers told far more of these at their own expense, he'd noticed, than people outside their profession. Maybe comparing each other to rats and snakes was how some reminded themselves what not to let themselves become, or how far they had yet to fall. But among the dozens of lawyers Jake knew reasonably well, he could think of only a handful whose professional history fit the punch lines. No more or fewer, he thought, than in any other field. No more or less human variety and complexity.

Still, when he appeared at the downtown Manhattan office of the firm his parents had retained, he had not expected anything like Mickey Stern.

Jake had heard little of Mickey, only that he was the son of a founding partner at Griffin, Stern, and Petrocelli. His father, the venerable and formidable Morton Stern, had handled Frederick and Mary Halsey's legal affairs discreetly, from an annoying business dispute in the 1950s through the probate proceedings after their deaths. In the early days, Halsey Wine Importing and Distributing, unpaid by one commercial client for nearly two years after a substantial transaction, had needed to raise the specter of embarrassing litigation to shake the payment loose. Three increasingly terrifying letters over the elder Stern's signature had brought the desired result, at minimal expense to Halsey Wine. A secondary result was that the Halseys became Stern clients for life. Jake recalled hearing his parents speak of Mort Stern in tones usually reserved for references to Mark Twain, Jackie Robinson, Walter Cronkite, or the Founding Fathers.

Entering the firm's waiting room, Jake examined an oil painting of the elder Stern and imagined the same portrait appearing in the margin of a massive unabridged dictionary, used to illustrate the definition of a term like *authoritative*.

Mickey Stern came out to the front desk immediately after the receptionist announced Jake had arrived. He was slightly over six feet, not tall in comparison to Jake, but he brought into the room a robust presence. As soon as he shook Jake's hand with a vigor that would have thrown some men off their balance, Jake realized there was not an unnecessary ounce on him. Jake had numbered several competitive athletes among his friends at Yale, but Mickey Stern was the closest thing he had ever seen to a human bear.

Stern moved at a velocity that implied enormous doses of caffeine. He spoke equally quickly, somehow managing to do this without making his listener uneasy.

"Mr. Halsey, I'm Mickey Stern. It's an honor to meet you," he began. "Come this way. My office is being renovated, so we can talk in the east conference room. I imagine you're pressed for time. Griffin, Stern has never been the sort of firm that pads out meetings to add billable hours, so I'd like to get directly to your inquiry." He led Jake down a discreetly lit curved hallway.

"My late father and your late father were fortunate in having, for the most part, the types of legal business that could be handled outside the court system," Stern explained. "Most of the documentation our associates have uncovered from the files is fairly mundane: contracts, investment records, only a few court filings in minor matters, the little civil suits or threats of suits that almost no business can avoid. Though I should add that, from everything we've been able to reconstruct, if every firm conducted itself as Halsey Wine did, there would be practically no such thing as civil litigation over torts or product liability. Your dad was an absolute straight shooter. But first, let me get you some coffee. I've assembled some associates to sit in on the meeting."

As the coffee brewed, Stern introduced the associates quickly and emphatically—Tina Chao, Jack McAllister, and George Petropoulos—and then simply pointed at the first of them. "Chao. Go."

Ms. Chao led off with a tightly organized summary of all contracts documented in the Frederick/Mary Halsey and Halsey Wine files, covering the essential history of the Halsey family's dealings in four-and-a-half minutes, with simple computer graphics indicating annual flows of cash in and out, including taxes. Her colleague McAllister followed suit with summaries of Fred and Mary's personal investments.

Petropoulos, assigned the lawsuits and probate records, had the simplest task. Few disputes, as Stern had indicated, had ever reached the point of bringing Halsey Wine officials into court as either plaintiffs or defendants, and each parent had left a simple will. Frederick had given practically everything he had to Mary and to a few nonprofits dedicated to medical, educational, and overseas development causes. Mary's will, which neither of them had expected to be executed a mere year later, had augmented these donations. Jake's own inheritance, by mutual consent, had been limited to heirlooms; he had built his own fortune.

In just under half an hour, the Griffin, Stern team delivered a succinct yet thorough elaboration of the Halseys's professional and financial life. Matters Jake had heard his parents discussing obliquely throughout his youth took on a tangible form. He felt he knew them both better now. Their lifelong habits of reticence had concealed so much of the material underpinnings of the family's well-being from him. A surge of filial loyalty quickened his pulse.

He noticed Stern's gaze discreetly directed toward him throughout most of the presentation. Neither man raised many questions for the associates, but Jake had an unmistakable sense that his reactions, such as they were, were being quietly assessed.

There was much to be proud of in what he heard. No employee had ever sued Halsey Wine for injuries, wrongful dismissal, or any other form of malfeasance. There were no trusting suppliers turned hostile creditors, no customers with justifiable grudges, no mysterious missing funds, not even any dubious expense account paperwork by middle-level managers. Halsey Wine was proof that it was not impossible for a firm and its proprietors to make a comfortable living honestly and honorably.

When Frederick Halsey had finally retired and sought a buyer for the family firm, he had resisted advice from his accountant and several armchair advisors to take the highest bid and merge the company into a major national distributor. A longer search uncovered another privately held wine importer, based in Cleveland, whose officials were willing to structure the contract to include language protecting every Halsey employee from layoffs for ten years. The sale went through at a slightly lower price than a handful of business journalists had estimated, but it was still more than enough in Frederick and Mary's eyes. Within a few years marked by consolidations in the industry, the Halsey Wine division had become the other company's most predictable asset.

By the end of the discussion, Jake was satisfied that he could rule out the dreaded discoveries he had half-expected to find. Meticulous recordkeeping on the parts of Frederick Halsey and his Greenwich accountant confirmed that his personal finances were never mingled with Halsey Wine's and that there were no unexplained income sources, disbursements, or investments.

"Mr. Stern. . .," he began.

"Mickey, please. I don't talk to *anybody* past two minutes if they don't strike me as a first-name basis person, which you do. I haven't been Mr. Stern since I taught seventh-graders, back before law school."

"Okay, Mickey—and please call me Jake—I'm impressed with your team's research, the whole presentation."

"Oh, you'd be amazed the kind of performance you can get out of some of these young punks when they're in line to make partner." Chao and Petropoulos reddened instantly and McAllister went stone-faced.

"What I wonder about, though," Jake continued, "is how

you could put this all together so fast. I only called you a couple of days ago. Things can't be so slow around here that your firm—even these all-stars you've got here—could drop everything and focus on my family."

"Jake, this is where I have to throw you a serious curveball. It's actually not something we whipped together in a couple of days or in a fragment of a couple of days. It couldn't have been, considering the complexity of what's in all these folders. As it happens, your request isn't the first inquiry we've had lately about your parents and the firm. You're getting the benefit of another party's curiosity. A few months back, I believe . . . December, was it, Tina?" She nodded yes.

Jake's blood ran a bit colder. "Oh?"

Stern shifted into a higher gear. "We received a subpoena from some overseas lawyers representing a vague-looking Swiss holding company involved in litigation over possible securities fraud, asking about any evidence of investments involving Fred Halsey or Halsey Wine. Pre-trial discovery, for a case that ended up never going to trial. We thought about getting the subpoena quashed, since we didn't have a dog in that fight and didn't want to put time into it. Attorney-client privilege outlives the client; that was settled pretty decisively some years back.

"Then our office manager ran some numbers and figured out it'd take less hassle just to comply with it than contest it, since it was likely to be a big fat zero anyway. What we ended up giving the Swiss company's guys were summaries and documents we'd redacted all the way to hell and back. Deceased or not, Frederick's finances are absolutely none of their business, but it sufficed to show them that neither Frederick nor Mary nor company employees knew these guys from the east end of a westbound horse.

"But what the exercise did apparently accomplish, besides keeping our international-law specialists busy on jurisdictional questions, was to lay the groundwork for the presentation you just saw, not that we could have known that at the time. As it turns out, your dad's personal books and the firm's records were in such good order that our outfielders over here. . . " he gestured toward the associates, "actually had some fun putting this stuff together. Then they had to watch it all go nowhere. Your request gave them the chance to put a little gift-wrap on some reports that were probably going to stay internal forever.

"The guys representing the Swiss never heard all this, of course. They got the two-and-a-half-minute cut, but as executors of the estate, we ended up doing the research and reconstructing the whole story just to be able to tell them what's *not* in it. Funny thing was, even though they came after it with a subpoena so we couldn't just turn down their request without at least an explanation and maybe a fight, they insisted on paying us for our time and trouble. That part was a minor, but very welcome professional courtesy. We didn't hesitate too long over accepting it."

"Did the other firm indicate anything of interest about their client?"

"Aside from a corporate name registered in Basel—the filings we examined involved something called Transalpinia, Ltd.—we heard *nothing*. Every question we asked ran into a wall of attorney-client privilege. Not that they respected ours with Frederick, getting the subpoena in the first place. Maybe now I see why they insisted on paying us expenses. This Russian firm, Konstantinov and Plotkin, may have thought by paying they'd become a client of ours in this matter, which would place their communications to us under privilege as well. Under U. S. law it doesn't, but as a Russian firm with a small U.S. presence, they may not have known that or grasped the concept all that clearly in the first place. Frankly, at the time, it was such a heap of nothing that we didn't give its implications a second thought."

"I can't say I'd blame you," said Jake. "I'm no lawyer, but with your original client deceased and his one living heir not among your clients, at least not so far, I doubt I would have either. I do want to check out that firm and Transalpinia, if you don't mind."

"Now that their pointless request to us begins to look like

it might have some odd point to it, I'd be delighted if yo
If they approach us again, we'll turn them down; they
some costs, not a long-term retainer. And if you l
anything, please keep us in the loop. That subpoena is start
to smell like last week's fish. Oh, it's Konstantinov with a
and a V, and they keep a rinky-dink little local branch office
Brighton Beach. Home office is in Moscow." As if on cue, th
associates quietly began packing their materials back in the
large folders and setting their laptops on hibernate.

"Will do. Mickey, I appreciate your candor about this, as
well as your exceptional efforts. I'm sure we'll be speaking
again before long. Ms. Chao, Mr. McAllister, Mr. Petropoulos,
thank you, too. It's been a pleasure. It looks like I've got some
work ahead of me when I get back to Greenwich."

"C'mon this way, I'll see you out." Stern leapt from his
chair.

"Thanks, I'd better run. Here's my card with my address
for the bill."

...g up lower Broadway toward the City Hall subway
..., Jake held his cell phone to one ear and one hand to the
... against the midday automotive din. Catherine answered
...er three rings.

"Jake! Glad it's you. Been missing you. How'd the
lawyer go?"

"Fascinating. Couple of surprises. I'll tell you more when
I'm back. I talked mainly to the son of Dad's attorney Morton
Stern. He's a real character, this Mickey, huge and loud and
hyper, but sharp as a straight razor."

"Just give me a summary."

"The fifteen-second version goes like this: Dad's finances
are painstakingly documented and kitchen-clean—no gaps, no
funny stuff, nothing—but somebody else has apparently been
showing interest in them, or in him. Some shady-sounding
organization with Russian lawyers tried to subpoena Dad's
files a few months ago on the pretext of litigation that strikes
both Mickey and me as a wild goose chase. Griffin, Stern gave
them basically nothing, appropriately, but the whole incident
looks . . . well, too pointless to be entirely meaningless, if that
makes sense. Sound like anybody we know?"

"I'm not entirely sure I follow you. It could be that's an
effect of the phones. Anyway, I can't wait to have you back. I
want to wrap my arms around you, pour you a glass of
Riesling, and tell you all about my morning in the OR, which
has no murderers or shady Russians in it and is bound to cheer
you up."

"Sounds like it will."

"And then I want to wrap all the rest of me around you.
And then I think I want to ask you to look at my computer."

"Your computer?"

"Yes, the one I use at the office. The damned thing's been acting up all day. It doesn't look like the routine Windows blue-screen condition. This is something the help screens don't seem to cover. . . ."

"They rarely do."

". . .and when I sent a trouble ticket to the hospital IT department around 10:30, they said I was number 33 in the queue."

"Also not an unprecedented situation. I'll see what I can do. If it takes system-administrator status to get access, though, I'm sure they won't let me work on it. I'd expect a hospital IT to be like every other institutional IT crew I've ever seen, turf conscious beyond all rationality. What were you trying to do when it crashed?"

Jake had just crossed Fulton Street—pausing for a high-speed, westbound bike messenger who would have sheared at least one of his limbs off had he kept moving—and was now veering right at Park Row past the city's best-known electronics discounter. He considered simply popping in to buy Catherine a new machine, a laptop he could carry home on the train and surprise her with. *Fast solution*, he reflected, *but obnoxiously extravagant, especially as a snap decision. Is component repair really a lost art?*

"It's not so much a crash as a scramble," continued Catherine. "The programs don't lock up; they just stop doing what they're supposed to do and do something utterly loony instead. I'll show you when you're here. My Web searches and bookmarked news sites are taking me to absolutely random places instead. Or else File Not Founds, lots of those, which isn't much help when I'm running a Medline search. For God's sake, patients depend on my staying up to speed, and I'd hate to have to go back to browsing twenty paper journals a day. Plus, now all my email looks like it's been translated into Martian."

"I've always wondered what conversational Martian sounds like, but Berlitz doesn't cover it."

"Not funny, Halsey. Seriously, translated isn't the word I want. It's more like transliterated. All the letters and numbers are wrong and some of the words have numerals in them, but things don't just look random—I can pick out recurring patterns. There's a three-character combination popping up from time to time, for example, 7i5. I'm looking at an email from a colleague and the '7i5' thing comes up about as often as you might see 'the' in normal English."

Seven, i, five. Jake tucked the phone under his chin and went through the motions of typing it with his idle hands. Fingers of both hands were required for this. Something felt familiar, like a reflex.

"Whoa, Cat, hold on. Let's think this out for a second. You're up on genetics, and you operate on patients and review their charts, and your sense of pattern recognition is strong. You give it a professional workout every day."

Jake had crossed Park Row and stepped into City Hall Park to get out of the flow of pedestrians and avoid coming any closer to his subway stop, where he'd catch the next 6 train but lose phone reception. He wanted to get home as quickly as he could, but he wasn't going down to that platform just yet. He averted his eyes from the faces of passersby to concentrate.

"If you see a pattern, I'm willing to say a pattern exists. If something's got your machine making patterns out of the alphabet, it's not only not random, it could be intentional. It seems trivial, but does it look like it might be a code? Not computer code, but code like in World War II, like the Germans' Enigma machine. Substitution ciphering. Don't rule out the possibility your machine's been hacked."

"Oh, lovely. Those nasty little kids. And I was beginning to think of this as a relatively pleasant day."

"I'm trying to visualize the keyboard. If what I'm seeing in my head makes sense, you may not have all that tricky a code. If 'the' becomes '7i5' every time, think of the shapes these sequences form. Or if you're near a keyboard, just look down at it. Kind of similar, aren't they?"

"Hmm . . . I see what you mean. From either T or 7: first key, down a row and over a little to the right, then back up and two left of where you started. It might correspond, or it might be random. I can't even look at this for long; it makes my head swim. I want to read English, not alphabet soup."

"Of course. Tell me this, though: Do you see any one letter or number appearing the most often?"

She paused for a few seconds. "Maybe fives. There are a lot of fives."

Jake almost leapt up off the pavement. "Excellent! You saw '7i5' a lot, too, and if that corresponds to 'the,' then 5 is E, which is the highest-frequency letter in English. Cracking a classic substitution cipher begins with the E's. If it's based on English, of course."

He started half-consciously forming questions he could ask of . . . somebody. Of Allen. Brian Allen wore the term "computer geek" like a badge of honor. This was Allen's kind of problem, all math and if-x-then-y logic. He would eat this stuff up like popcorn.

Catherine's voice chilled his enthusiasm.

"I'm starting to get the creeps about this. It's either accidental or a pattern. If it's a pattern, there's some regular machine failure or program failure, or there's a person playing a little game. If it's a person, it's either some foolish teenager with nothing better to do or—I don't want to think about this, but, well, does it sound like somebody we know?"

"You're right. I think caution is in order until we find somebody who's good with cryptography. Never really had the patience for it myself—I just know a basic principle or two. We need a cryptography honcho. Can you save or print any of the messages?"

"I think so. I know how to do it even if all the text is looking like garbage. It'll at least print, though God only knows what sort of file names it would save."

"Good. Good enough. I think I know one guy who can run this output through some algorithms and come up with either a message or a diagnosis of a problem. Try saving anything you can save, print as much of the garble-code garbage as you can. I should be at your office before the end of the afternoon. And if you can do without the Internet today, you might want to disconnect the net cable from that machine.

If something got on there from outside, it can spread. For the time being, treat your machine like it's quarantined.

"Thank you. I've got the Ethernet unhooked already. Hurry back, will you?"

"Absolutely. See you soon, soon as I can. Wish I were driving both of these trains myself."

Entering the City Hall station, Jake snapped his phone shut, then forced his caffeinated and over-stimulated eyes shut as well. He tried to imagine how he could describe this situation to Riley in ways that would justify conscripting Brian Allen—the one person he knew who would relish a cryptography problem enough to have a decent shot at solving it—for an apparently meaningless puzzle in the middle of a murder investigation.

All the way uptown on the 6, he tried not to think of Wine Killers and foreign lawyers in tough neighborhoods of Brooklyn, and Swiss financial criminals planting malicious executable files on the hard disk in the office of the woman he loved. Yes, he'd use that word now. Maybe not to her just yet, not until the right circumstance appeared. But privately, he'd use it.

For now, he needed a clear head. He sensed his morning caffeine rush subsiding and grabbed one more cup at Grand Central, a maintenance dose.

He took a seat on the New Haven Line, stuffed the Greenwich ticket into his breast pocket, closed his eyes again, and visualized a computer keyboard. 7-i-5 to T-H-E. Simplest word in English. Good thing it's the one she spotted first.

T-H-E to 7-i-5.

T to 7. H to I. E to 5.

Each move was identical: one key to the right, one key up at an angle.

A knight. Not a computer keyboard, but a chessboard. The jutting move made only by a knight.

A computer keyboard that was also a chessboard.

A battle, hand to hand, between balanced forces.

A lawsuit, or a duel, or a wrestling match, or a war.

A knight, moving to the right.

You had to have the right knight. You had to know the right knight. You had to hire the right knight.

You had to be the right knight.

CHAPTER THIRTY-THREE

Catherine wasn't ordinarily a light sleeper, but these weren't ordinary days.

Some elements of her existence, like her demanding surgical schedule and her placid garden, had been steady and predictable for a long time. She had challenges, but she also had routines that helped her stay on top of them. Joining her world with Jake's seemed more natural than she would ever have expected. She was spending most nights at his house lately and it somehow felt like they'd known each other for years. The longer morning drive to Greenwich Hospital had been very easy to get used to. So had Jake's cooking, though she had noticed her favorite jeans fitting a little more snuggly than before as a result of his culinary skills.

What she knew now about his DNA, on the other hand, was different from any other burden she had carried. She understood they both had to approach the situation logically, as if puzzling out a diagnosis: what do the symptoms, signs, and tests rule in, and what do they rule out? The implications of the two lab reports boiled down to two main possibilities, both of which were inconsistent with everything she knew about Jake.

Barring an unimaginable coincidence, the hair and follicle that Jake had found in Bridgeport couldn't have come from anyone outside his immediate family. Neither could the skin samples, and he hadn't handled those. The odds that two random unrelated people would have the same DNA profile were roughly the same as the odds of winning the first prize in the Connecticut lottery a dozen times in a row.

Jake and Catherine had talked once about what it was like to grow up without brothers or sisters. They had spoken more than once about the losses of parents, his father four years ago and his mother three. Jake had no living relatives closer than a distant cousin in Maine.

Second cousins shouldn't have enough in common genetically, Catherine knew, to yield DNA fingerprints as close as those she'd seen in the lab reports. Either there was some grievous mistake, one that could put Jake under a terrible, preposterous suspicion, or . . . but no. Some hypotheses were not worth entertaining—even if the effort to find alternatives to them keeps you up half the night.

The idea of Jake having anything to do with murders—aside from helping Dave figure them out—struck her as absurd, even obscene. She had known him only for a few months, but she already knew him better than that. She knew her judgment in men, in human beings, could never be that wrong.

But she also knew that telling him what she'd observed had multiplied his burdens far beyond what he was already handling right now. She would have to find some way to make sense of this. She knew that a bombshell like "the DNA marked Wine Killer looks a lot like yours" was not something you dropped on someone you cared about. There was a mistake somewhere, and they would do what it took to find it.

After she had sent Jake's swab sample to a familiar genetics laboratory for analysis and the similarities to the report from the state lab had caught her attention, she had called in a favor from Charlie Chatterjee, a technician at the local lab. She'd known Charlie long enough to trust him about matters that might be confidential. She had sent him edited copies of pages from the state report on the killer's sample and the one from Jake—raw data, no names—asking him to double-check the comparison. Just to be sure, she had sent him a second swab from Jake for a fresh blind report, saying nothing about its source. During a half hour lull between surgical procedures, she called the lab from her office and spoke with Charlie. She asked if there was any way material or data from one source would ever find their way into another procedure. No, Charlie said, at least not at his facility. The results were airtight. The lab had been handling a number of high-pressure tests in recent years—mainly criminal cases and paternity suits as well as medical studies—and they'd built plenty of redundancy and double checks into their operations. Running blank control samples to detect contaminants was standard procedure. They hadn't seen a cross-contamination since the late eighties. He couldn't speak for the state lab. The hair from the Wine Killer and the oral swab from Jake had been processed several days apart by different technicians at different locations.

Without specifying the context—even an old friend, she reflected, shouldn't be tempted to put this particular two and two together—she asked Charlie about isolated pieces of information from the reports. He knew both technicians named in the paperwork, one as an immediate colleague and one from technical meetings, and described them both as careful professionals, not the kind who'd ever mislabel a sample or misinterpret a pattern. If the gels from two samples looked similar, then the same DNA had to be in both of them. Case closed.

As for the new sample, the studies would be done in a matter of days and he'd let her know as soon as the analysis was ready. She thanked Charlie, asked for his discretion, and received a firm promise of it.

According to the printouts, the labs had run eight probes in each case: four to six were standard for most medical or paternity studies. Both samples were good quality material, not tiny bits of tissue degraded by time. Whatever implications might follow from these reports, attributing them to lax testing would be a real stretch.

Catherine picked up a notepad and started listing other conceivable explanations. It felt awkward to be doing this on paper. *Handwriting,* she thought. *We all used to do it constantly without thinking about it; now it's one step up from scrawling with coal on the wall of a cave. When was the last time I handwrote anything but a signature or a phone message?* Writing things down clarified her thinking. However, the instrument she usually wrote with, her office computer, was gone. With the approval of the hospital computer tech, Jake and a colleague were going through it for a few days to troubleshoot whatever had scrambled its output.

Unless Charlie was just covering for the lab—not impossible, strictly speaking, but not consistent with his character—a mistake before the sample ever reached the lab was the first serious option to consider. Jake could have handled the killer's hair less carefully than he thought he had, allowing a hair or other material from his own body into the container. Even Jake, an engineer with a strong sense of control, could have slipped up imperceptibly in handling evidence with tweezers. Beneath the pharmaceutical company logo at the top of the pad, Catherine wrote, "Sample impurities before sent to lab?"

It was that or something outlandish. Time to look at the outlandish possibilities, as well. When you hear hoof beats, she'd heard countless times in medical school and since, you want to think of horses, not zebras. But from time to time, you do run into the occasional zebra.

Lately her environment—that is, her and Jake's environment—had become a herd of them. She might have come across one in her office the other day, right in her own computer. Fiendish, whoever unleashed these little disasters on the world and, in this case, diabolically clever. The contents of her screen—the alphanumeric parts, at least—struck her as pure gibberish at first. Then, the more she looked at it while talking with Jake, the more it seemed to have a structure of sorts. She knew enough about the operating system to recognize that if this was intentional damage, the virus had reached down to a fundamental level of the machine, somewhere in its ability to display text, while leaving the windows, buttons, cursors, and graphics acting normally. That had to be rare: the digital equivalent of a medical zebra.

Was it connected to what was going on around Jake? Everything about this monster he and Dave were chasing seemed to breed more zebras. If someone was deranged enough to kill people, it was beyond her how he could be so indifferent to who his victims were. He seemed more like a carnivorous plant, trapping whatever came its way, than a conscious being. Purposeful murder in the course of revenge or robbery was a kind of madness within sanity, a horrible moral obtuseness in the service of aims that at least made sense. This was madness wrapped in more madness.

The idea of Jake letting a hair or a hangnail get into a Baggie was practically a zebra. Beyond that, she thought, the real zebras here would be scenarios where somebody planted evidence that would point to Jake. Could anybody in the Greenwich police have a problem with him? Not that she'd heard, and it was impossible to imagine from anyone under Dave Riley's command. Riley ran a tight ship. Jake might be a civilian, but he was fully integrated into Riley's team.

Still, not everyone who might have access to the GPD evidence room was under Riley's command. Catherine wrote one word on her list to keep that disturbing possibility in view. "Planted?"

If it came to that, she knew, they'd have to bring up the subject of the DNA reports with Riley immediately rather than wait until they had more information. A police chain of custody was going to be off limits to any civilian—even, she thought ruefully, a resourceful and well-connected surgeon who happened to be a blonde with a persuasive smile. "If planted," she wrote, drawing an arrow, "DNA info to Dave," and underlining the last word, "*confidentially*." She hoped Jake could count on Dave to be as much a friend as a cop.

Nothing she'd ever heard about the GPD supported that one, she thought. The only point in its favor was that if anything had been planted, it might explain the findings from the Hartford glove. That implication, she reflected, didn't make it any likelier. *Not a good idea in a differential diagnosis—reasoning backward from what you'd prefer to be the case, not forward from what you observe—and not good methodology here, either.*

The other major scenario would be a deep family secret, of the classic extramarital variety. Even respectable old New England families sometimes had an unofficial branch mentioned only in whispers, one that not everyone in the family knew about. As a physician with a strong interest in genetics, Catherine had pored through such genealogical diagrams countless times.

Catherine instinctively reproached herself for imagining such a thing about Jake's father. They'd considered the possibility—skeptically, aversively—but Jake had never mentioned his parents in terms implying anything but respect. His call from Manhattan, after he'd hunted with the lawyers through legal and financial records, had confirmed that everything was aboveboard in those departments. Still, straying and its consequences were possible in any family. She knew she had to entertain even the ugly options to make sense of the evidence at hand. This line of inquiry would only have to be explored within the same generation; an eight-marker DNA match wouldn't be further away than a sibling and even that was seriously pushing the odds. Catherine had little doubt it would prove to be a blind alley. She wrote "Illegit. half-brother?" on the pad. She'd already started hunting down whatever medical records might exist that could yield hints about the personal life of Frederick Halsey. She wanted to track down any surviving family doctors, too, but that was a task that had to fall to Jake. Any advantages from being a fellow physician would pale next to the claims of family.

At least it wouldn't matter that her computer was down for a few days. Records from that far back wouldn't be digitized. If they still existed, they were on paper in a musty storage room, presumably somewhere outside Greenwich. She'd already checked the hospital, finding only recent years' records. As far as Mary Halsey was concerned, the critical notation in medical shorthand divulged no secrets: *gravida 1, para 1-0-0-1*. One pregnancy, one term delivery, no premature deliveries or abortions, one living child. A whole maternal life, boiled down to the barest essentials.

There was no such thing as a comparable paternal record. The impossibility of compiling one didn't make this seem any fairer to Catherine, but there was nothing to gain from railing against that. Best to save energy and attention for things she could do something about. Her last note on the pad read "Fred: surviving confidants?" According to Jake, these were exceedingly few.

It would soon be time for her next scheduled procedure, an uncomplicated gall bladder removal. Today's surgical calendar had been tight and time with Jake scarce; he'd been tied up a lot since returning from New York. After leaving a message on his voice mail with an estimate of her schedule, she went down the hall to the operating suite and began scrubbing. She found it a relief to wash away sweat from her hands and disagreeable thoughts from her imagination. But there was one thought that couldn't be washed away . . . *could it possibly be Jake?*

CHAPTER THIRTY-FOUR

When Catherine emerged from the day's final procedure, Jake was in the OR waiting room among the patients' families. She could tell in one glance that he carried more news, probably troubling, but first things first. She had things to say to her last patient's husband.

They were reassuring things, luckily. A silent exchange of glances with Jake bought her as much time as she needed to put poor Mr. Mastroantonio's worst fears to rest. The man had been there all afternoon, silent and expressionless, betraying dread in his eyes. Those were the trickiest to deal with, the guys who bottled it up. When she met one, it was a rare joy to be able to deliver the words they needed to hear: *uncomplicated, routine.* Or the best one, the one she couldn't honestly say right away after a procedure, but loved being able to convey from the pathology department afterward: *benign.*

Jake's presence was as calming an influence on her as her words were for her patient's husband. *An actual gentleman,* she recognized; *I hope I've found one at last, after thinking the species might be hunted to extinction.* He wouldn't be sitting here if something weren't urgent, but he knew he wasn't the only person in town with trouble. His could wait.

That was one of her favorite things about him: He was as steady as an oak. Not inert—incredibly alive, really—but unshakable at his core, regardless of the things he had been through—and what he was about to go through, whatever that would be.

"I couldn't wait to see you," he said as soon as they'd left the waiting room. "It worked out well to have a couple of extra hours before you got out of there, though.

"I've been making more calls. No big breakthroughs, but at least a couple of blind leads are closed off. I tracked down the only docs who might have seen Mom or Dad around the years our hypothetical black sheep could have been born. Their old internist here gave me two names, both now deceased. I knew of one who retired to Arizona, but that was just my old pediatrician and he's gone, as well. The critical thing would have been obstetrical records, but it turns out they don't keep them from that far back."

"Nothing about this is just going to fall into place, is it?" Whatever vision Catherine had held of some explanation materializing from a musty storage room had just vanished. It would have been troubling, whatever it contained, but it would have brought a touch of logic to the situation.

"Doesn't look that way. I take it you're not finding anything from the labs."

"Not the one I have a friend in. The state lab is a different story."

"I'm not going to let myself get any hopes up. You know the old Groucho joke with the punch line 'What are you going to believe, me or your own two eyes?' At some point I think I'm going to have to start wearing a greasepaint mustache. But all this isn't what I need to talk to you about right now. There's something in the car I have to show you." They headed for the parking lot.

"Jake Halsey, if you've gone out and bought another elaborate gift when your mind, and your time, are supposed to be. . . ."

"No, Cat, it's nothing like that. Before we get out there, will you promise me one thing? I have to recommend something that might sound alarming. Trust me on this; I wouldn't do this lightly. What I have to do right now—what we have to do—isn't anything I'd bring up if there were any alternative." His tone was new to her: grave, full of pauses. He'd been weighing his words, she recognized, and each one weighed a ton.

They reached his Renault and got in. Jake took a briefcase out of the back seat, opened it, and showed Catherine a stack of documents in a manila folder. He didn't open the folder just yet.

"I've been working on your PC with the tech guy from Dave's department, Brian Allen. It's been rough sledding, because we're doing it after hours. Dave didn't want to spare Brian during the work day. Once he sees these, though, he'll be damned glad Brian can get by on so little sleep—the guy's a complete night owl. Anyway, this bears on the Wine Killer case, and on you and me. It's grim, and it's personal.

"Brian ran some advanced diagnostics on your machine. Something's been planted there, as we suspected. There's one piece of good news: It was actually harmless to the computer, once Brian uprooted it. It's not one of the common viruses that fouls up the operating system or erases the hard disk or makes infinite copies of itself. It's not from a garden variety hacker. It did get into your BIOS"—she noticed him gauging her expression, seeming relieved that she showed no sign of stumbling over the term—"and rearranged how it displays text. Just the display, as we saw, not the actual processing. There's a substitution code, as I was guessing, and actually a fairly easy one to crack. The nasty part is what we found after Brian cracked it.

"It's not like that famous code from the Nazis. That one was designed to keep messages secret. This one's designed to deliver them, after drawing our attention to them. It's based on that shape on the keyboard: over a key and up a key. Bone simple, once Brian applied the usual character frequency tables. After half a dozen letters, he could pretty much predict all the others. Cryptography 101. Whoever wrote this cipher wanted us to break it.

"We're going to run all this by Ellen in the morning, of course, but we're pretty sure it's the Wine Killer. Please don't let this rattle you too much, but he's starting to show an interest in me personally. And, most unfortunately, in you."

Catherine's breath caught in her throat.

Becoming involved with Jake, growing close to Jake, was never supposed to take this form. She was out of familiar territory here. *Implications; corollaries*. She was not about to trivialize it and say *downside*. She could not bring herself to say *risk*.

Jake opened the folder. "Most of the scrambled material, once Brian worked out an algorithm to rearrange it back into English, turned out to be just your regular mail and readings. We tried not to pry.

"What grabbed our attention was a couple of documents that this guy seems to have added to your computer, maybe through some sort of executable file. There were several new things on your desktop with nonsense file names. Once Brian put them through the substitutions, the first couple of unfamiliar files turned out to be READMEDOC.doc and DRTAYLORIPRESUME.doc.

"Get ready," Jake said, looking at Catherine. He handed her two double-sided and stapled printouts from the top of the stack. Brian had prepared facing-page versions, an unreadable one in the hacker's cipher on the left and an English text on the right.

To the Lovely and Talented CATHERINE TAYLOR, M.D.,

My, aren't we on top of the world these days! (Or should I say the world is on top of you.)

"Does this go where I think it's going? I'm not sure I want to read this." She felt muscles tightening up throughout her body, breath quickening. *Classic fight or flight. Autonomic nervous system. Goddammit! Knowing what it is doesn't mean it doesn't happen to me.*

"It's offensive, yes, but, curiously, not all that obscene in the usual sense. The other one is much worse. I'm sorry you have to see any of it. The mind behind it is a twisted one. You don't have to go on with the whole thing if you don't feel like it."

"No, actually, now I think I want to. This makes me mad enough that I absolutely refuse to let it intimidate me. The nerve of this vile little man. Let me see it." She continued reading.

Years of training at the best of Schools,
to slice and sew the Flesh of Fools.
Alas, the sparkling Queen of Ice
could find no Mate at any price.
Yet fate would brighten up your Journey,
by rolling toward you, on a Gurney,
Your Shining Knight, your Great Mistake,
The Worldly Wealthy Classy JAKE.
Inventor, Dabbler, Connoisseur,
With myriad Talents, and Heart so pure,
That he alone, of the Privileg'd Few,
Would get to operate on YOU.
But take my Counsel, CAT. Heed warnings.
Your Knight, and You, should count your mornings.

"This is the dirty joking of a hateful little schoolboy." She was shaking. "But Jake, it's also a death threat, isn't it?"

"Yes. I'd read it the same way. Veiled, but unmistakable, I'd say. The other one, DRTAYLORIPRESUME, is nastier, many pages longer, and more personal. Then there was an animated graphics file. Hideous things assembled with Photoshop. Wine bottles combined with war atrocity pictures and worse, just in case we had any doubts about the source. I really don't think you want to see that."

"Actually I do, if only to try to take the measure of this person's disgusting imagination. I'm a surgeon. Nothing he can show me is going to shock me, as much as this infuriates me. But not now. Jake, what do you think this calls for?"

Jake expected the challenge; he'd already begun thinking it through. "In no particular order: Getting it to Dave's team—Brian's already on his way there with another copy; finding out how the guy knows anything about either of us; and analyzing his material for clues about just what he knows. We also need to find out how he planted this crap on your machine and what it implies about new directions in his MO. Before any of that, though, we're going somewhere safe, somewhere we've never been in case our movements have been watched. We have to presume they have. I hope you don't mind some nights in hotels until we know for sure whether either your place or mine is compromised."

"Not a problem. As long as I'm within a reasonable drive of the hospital every day, I'll be as flexible as I have to be."

"Excellent. As much as I hate the metaphor, this puts us on a war footing now. The killer has escalated the competition and brought in an explicit psychological component. Everything Dave and the team are doing, they'll keep doing. We have a strategy we think may trap him soon, and this threat doesn't change it. But it does change the game. Among other things, it drives home the point that this bastard is teasing us personally, maybe that he lives mainly for that game. For better or worse, I think it's time we spill everything we've learned to Dave, including coming clean about my DNA. He's already been floating a theory that I'm a prime target, and that's without knowing about this little drama."

"Agreed." She touched his hand and was relieved to find it was dryer than hers.

Jake started the ignition. Leaving the hospital parking lot he fell unusually quiet. After a few minutes on the road, he turned to Catherine at a red light and spoke to her somberly. "I'm sorry. I really am. I don't know what this is, but I'm sorry I brought it anywhere close to your life."

"Think of what else you've brought to it. I don't regret anything about us, and I sure as hell wouldn't undo anything about us."

"You're sure of that."

She looked directly in his eyes. Her silent affirmation was all either of them needed.

But, she thought, *what will I do if it is Jake?*

The light changed, and they drove forward.

CHAPTER THIRTY-FIVE

Three weeks had passed, and May had arrived. It had been a classic warm New England spring. Forsythia had bloomed, and the leaves now were green. There had been lots of pink apple blossoms, but they, too, had passed. However, the dogwoods were in full bloom, and most of Connecticut was alive with their pink and white flowers. The blossoms would last for another week or so; then they, too, would be gone for another year.

Jake had seen a wider range of the spring foliage than usual this year. For about a week after the discovery of the killer's message, he and Catherine had "enjoyed" a nomadic existence, staying at a succession of hotels, inns, and motels around the region—not quite the peaceful vacation they'd spoken of before—until a GPD team completed a thorough sweep of both residences for surveillance devices. The technicians had found nothing at Catherine's house, but a wireless directional shotgun microphone was concealed in a tree near Jake's. A trace on its broadcast frequency was unproductive; its signal went out in the high UHF "junk band," where operation does not require a license. Whoever had rigged it up was sharing the air with toys, cordless phones, and home stereo gear, hopping frequencies and probably getting poor signals most of the time. Jake imagined his eavesdropper didn't care much about audio quality.

Riley had set up nightly stakeouts, several more strategically placed "Halsey Brand" cameras but without bottles, and frequent patrol car drive-bys at both homes. Jake's offer to defray extra departmental expenses for this protection had resulted in a friendly haggling session and, in the end, a decision that the costs were legitimate police costs. Catherine got in the habit of bringing extra coffee and pastries to the uniformed officers outside Jake's house on her way to the hospital every morning. She had never been on a first name basis with so many policemen.

The mood in the recently dubbed command center was considerably less bright than the weather outside. Jake had set up the principal review computer in a police conference room that had a DSL connection and plenty of phones. He had also hooked up two twenty-one-inch video screens so that all twelve video camera feeds from Ivoryton could be viewed simultaneously. A separate computer and monitor covered his residence and Catherine's—not as completely as Jake would have liked, but affording a view of critical spots, including his own shop and wine cellar. He added recorders to each set of cameras, creating an additional permanent record of any activity. Every day, he had Miller and Phillips test the alarms in Ivoryton, first by phone and then by entering the cellars. Both men were to call before anyone entered their cellars, except for meal times at the inn.

The video system worked flawlessly. But after three weeks of surveillance and a reduction of the testing activities when Miller and his family headed to Northern California on vacation, the men were getting antsy. Monitor duty was a numbing round-the-clock routine, a rotation most officers came to view with little enthusiasm. Entropy appeared in various inevitable forms: moments of inattention, scheduling errors, jumpy over-interpretations of onscreen data that proved to be minor power surges when reviewed more carefully. In real time or in an occasional review, all anyone saw happening before the cameras was a long parade of nothing.

Then, one Monday night, there was a change. Catherine was at Jake's house and had retired early since she had to be in the operating room at six the following morning. Jake was reading the paper and sampling a half-bottle of a recently released Sauternes sent over that day by his favorite wine retailer. When the phone rang about ten o'clock, he picked up the nearest cordless handset. It was Riley.

"We've got action! The system shows some movement on the Copper Beech Inn feed. Tony is our point man on duty until midnight tonight, and he immediately called Phillips at home."

"Is anybody at risk over there?"

"Not right now. The inn itself is open, but the restaurant is closed on Mondays. Since the restaurant is pretty much the draw for guests who stay overnight, there are no guests tonight. Apparently this is typical for a Monday.

"We asked for several lights to be left on in the wine cellar to help with illumination for the cameras. The video image is that of an adult moving around with one of those lights affixed to a headband, like a miner. But the light shines forward, so the face is in shadow and we can only see the outline of a tall figure.

"Phillips is headed over to the inn, but I told him to sit in his car in the parking lot and keep his cell phone handy. I don't want him to get hurt. I called the local cops and they're on the way."

"What was the guy doing?" Jake had walked over to his computer. "I've got the feed on my screen and I don't see any activity."

"He moved to one of the largest wine bins and seemed to be rubbing or maybe painting something on the bottles. By now, he may have already left. Before I called, I sent a squad car to pick you up. Be waiting outside."

Jake scribbled a note for Catherine, ran upstairs and left it in the bathroom where she'd see it, grabbed a windbreaker, and ran outside just as a police car squealed into the driveway.

Jake hopped into the front seat and said "Let's go" to the driver, whom he recognized as one of Dave's junior men, Kavanagh. He had Riley on the radio and they arranged a rendezvous. Flashing lights and the late hour on a weekday allowed them to meet Riley in just a few minutes, and they headed east on I-95 at top speed with the siren on and all lights flashing. Dave spent some time on the radio alerting his counterparts in Stamford, Norwalk, Bridgeport, and New Haven to his route and speed, and they made it to Ivoryton in under forty minutes. During the trip, Pezzi had reported that there had been no more activity in the cellar since the initial two or three minutes of movement.

Local police from several towns had surrounded the property, found a broken window in the rear cellar door, and confirmed that no one was inside. Other than a fruitless search of the neighborhood, they had made no further moves, awaiting Riley's arrival.

There was a large crowd assembled in the Copper Beech Inn parking lot: three police cars from nearby Essex, an evidence tech's SUV, Jake, Riley and Kavanagh, owner Ian Phillips, and a few curious neighbors at the perimeter. Ian spoke up without prompting.

"You guys have got me caught up in this cloak-and-dagger stuff," he said. "I thought you'd like to know that at the end of every evening I've been going to the basement and wiping off both sides of the doorknobs on each of the wine cellars. I hope that will be of help."

"Good man. Nobody even thought of it. We'll soon see how important it might be," said Jake.

Although most of the crowd had not met him, this was Riley's ball game, and they looked at him expectantly.

"Who's been inside?" he asked.

One of the cops spoke up, "I was, my partner, and the evidence tech. We all were wearing rubber gloves, and we were very careful to not disturb anything. The rear cellar door had a broken window. That's how he got in. The door at the top of the cellar stairs was locked on the upper side, so he only went into the cellar and not into the upper part of the building. We got here within five minutes of Officer Pezzi's phone call. The guy was in and out in less than that. We thoroughly checked the two wine cellars and the rest of the basement, but no one was there. Other guys checked the neighborhood, again with no luck."

The two cops, the technician, Riley, and Jake headed for the rear door. The door seemed to be as old as the inn itself and had seen better days. Decades of moving food and other supplies had left their marks in the form of dings, dents, badly made repairs, replaced hinges, and many coats of paint. One of the broken panes of glass still showed jagged edges.

"Please dust the door handle for prints," ordered Riley, adding, "You'll almost certainly find too many to be productive, but we've got to be sure."

"Let's cut to the chase and check the wine cellar where Tony spotted the movement," suggested Jake.

There was no lock on the door. The padlock, which had been there on the prior visit, was missing. Jake recalled that it had been there primarily for show and probably had a regular steel shank, not a hardened one. It would have been easy pickings for someone with a bolt cutter, intent upon entering.

The door to the wine cellar was ajar, and Jake, Riley, several officers, and the evidence tech went in. The knob that Phillips had assiduously wiped each evening was polished brass, and Riley bent down to inspect it. There, on the inside, at the nine-o'clock and the four-o'clock positions, were partial thumb and reasonably clear index finger fingerprints, almost certainly of a right hand.

"Our video showed him to only be inside for five minutes, and, man, he must have left in a hurry. I'm feeling very lucky. That's one of the best set of fingerprints I've ever seen," exulted Riley. "It's damned good news—the partial fingerprint from the glove left behind in West Hartford was too small and smeared to match against any of the fingerprint databases. If this is our guy, we may be able to match the partial Hartford print against this one."

While the tech went to work on the doorknob, the officers were checking the rest of the room.

"The camera that caught the motion was number three. Over here," suggested Jake.

"Don't touch anything," said the tech, over his shoulder. Jake made a face at him as if to say he knew exactly what he was doing. Checking the angle of the camera, he sighted down from its position and moved to a bin containing dozens of wine bottles.

"This is the 2001 Chassagne-Montrachet the inn uses as one of its better white wines by the glass, which explains the large capacity of the bin," commented Jake, after glancing at a label. "There are more than two dozen bottles in this pile, and the bin's less than half full."

Jake closely inspected the bottles on the top level. The labels appeared to be damp and there appeared to be a sticky substance on the bottles. Some of it had run down the sides and dripped onto the bottles below. Jake said to the tech, "When you get over here, I'd treat these bottles with respect, if I were you. Gloves only, and double check every finger for holes or rips before you handle these. From the look of these labels, you may find a chemical on them, and you should assume it's poisonous. This guy has some pretty nasty stuff in his arsenal."

Jake and the others, hands held behind them in protective maneuvers, inspected all the other bins within the camera range. No foreign substance was found, and nothing else seemed out of place.

Riley pulled a spool of ribbon and a package of push pins from his jacket pocket and said, "This may seem like grade school stuff, but I'm going to get Tony on the cell phone and run ribbons at the viewing limits for this one camera. He can tell us when we're about to extend a ribbon beyond the viewing angle. This way we can see on site exactly what the camera saw and recorded."

The two cops and Riley got busy with this project as the tech gingerly wrapped and packed up several bottles affected by whatever had been spilled on them.

Once the ribbons were strung, it was obvious why only one camera had picked up the moving figure. The camera view had just missed the wine cellar door, but the intruder had been able to enter the cellar, cut the lock, spill his product on the bottles, and exit without moving more than ten feet past the padlock. No wonder he had gotten in and out so fast.

"Give the analysis of what's on these bottles the highest priority," said Riley to the tech. "We believe this guy has killed six people that we know about, and he may have more killings planned. We need to know not only what he intended to use this time, but also what the fingerprints show."

"Got it," said the tech, as he packed up his kit.

"I'm really pissed off that we couldn't get here in time to

catch this SOB," Riley said to Jake as they headed up the stairs. "We're getting closer and closer, but close isn't good enough. At least we figured out where he was going to be. And, for what it's worth, we did stop him from killing anyone here."

Riley's mobile phone rang. "Chief!" It was Pezzi again, close to breathless. "Bottle cam activity at Harry Miller's, too. We didn't pick it up right away. The day shift at the monitors was shorthanded before I started duty at five, so they left me a few hours of video to do a little catching up on at high speed. I just reviewed the afternoon footage and saw an intruder at 4:40 p.m. Guy in a utility uniform of some kind. Not the electric company, AT&T, or cable—something else. In and out of the cellar pretty quickly, about 25 seconds, and he may have left something or taken something. Maybe nothing, but this is nothing we expected. Isn't Miller out of town?"

"Halfway into his vacation but reachable. We'll get a couple of local uniforms over there. You keep zooming through that tape. Brief Ellen and Brian, too. I'll call Miller. And, Pezzi, good work on this, but no more short shifts and playing catch-up. Get a budget request in for 24-7 coverage on those monitors, even if we have to deputize a couple of goddamn meter readers."

Riley hung up, quickly called the Essex PD with a request for mobile backup at Miller's Ivoryton address, and dialed Miller's cell number as he and Jake approached Riley's car.

"Harry? Dave Riley here. Listen, sorry to intrude on your vacation, but were you expecting any sort of service visit at your house today? Our guys picked up some movement on the bottle cam monitor."

"Nothing scheduled as far as I know. The only person with access while we're gone is our maid, and she's under instructions to do only minimal upkeep once a week, stuff like watering the plants. Definitely nothing in the cellar. I'd have to check with my wife to see what the maid's day is this week. She has keys. We've known her a long time, and she's never taken any liberties before."

"I trust she hasn't, but somebody's been in there. Has she got a cell phone?"

"Yes, I'll try her right away."

"Thanks. Tell her not to visit the house until she hears from you, and don't mention why. I'm on my way there now, so be ready for another call . . . if you can be," Riley added, remembering he was talking not to a subordinate, but to a civilian. "I know this is supposed to be down time for you."

"Don't be silly. Thanks for keeping on top of this. Hope it's nothing."

"Maybe so. Catch you soon." Riley ended the call, summoned Kavanagh to drive, and brought Jake up to date on the maid—a minor loose end he'd have preferred Miller hadn't left loose—as they crossed town toward Miller's house at high speed.

In Miller's driveway were two white-and-blue cruisers from the Connecticut State Police. Ivoryton had no police force of its own, but the Essex department had a resident-trooper arrangement with the CSP and coverage had been quick despite the flurry of activity at the Copper Beech Inn. A CSP officer hailed Riley as he pulled into Miller's driveway.

"When it rains it pours, eh, Detective?"

"Fill me in. Anybody in there, anybody down?"

"Extensive property damage, but the house appears unoccupied. This is the place you gave Essex the heads-up on for extra surveillance, right?"

"The same."

"Some form of non-incendiary explosive device has damaged large parts of the basement. Didn't go off too long ago—there's still smoke. No fire. Load-bearing structures are intact, but there's glass, splintered wood, and wine all over the place. Owner had an extensive wine collection, which appears almost totaled. Gotta tell you, apart from the smoke, it's the best-smelling crime scene I've ever been to."

Riley looked at Jake just long enough to pick up his friend's reflexive grimace. Both men knew Miller would have the collection insured, but both also remembered the 1847 Lafite, a bottle that would be irreplaceable.

Pezzi was back on Riley's line within twenty minutes. "Chief, brace yourself for trouble at Miller's. There's nobody else moving on the cams, but at 10:15 pm something blows up in the cellar and all six screens on the monitor go out. There's just enough time to see. . . ."

"Thanks, Tony, I'm already there. No casualties, that's the important part. Harry Miller's wine collection is pretty much toast. We're gonna need your detailed description of the intrusion."

"Check. The 4:40 intruder is a white male, over six feet, slim build, as far as we can tell. Body type is generally consistent with the suspect in the DiVito photo. The face wasn't visible, concealed by both long straight brown hair and the bill of a baseball cap with an unfamiliar logo. Whole uniform's blue. Doesn't match any local service personnel profile I'm aware of; it's too nondescript. It isn't clear what he's doing down there, but he blocks a couple of the cams with his body for a few seconds in the vicinity of the Lafite. If he planted a device, I'd guess he specifically targeted Miller's prize bottle."

"Reasonable to speculate, but for now let's stick with direct observations. Until we get more forensic data over here, what strikes me is the attack on an unoccupied space—and the close timing between this explosion and the intrusion at the Copper Beech. We'll proceed to analysis tomorrow with the full team."

Dave and Jake stayed at the Miller house for another two hours, supervising Kavanagh as he assisted the CSP troopers and forensics techs from Essex in the site investigation. The intruder had entered without force, leaving no fingerprints and only a few featureless footprints from a pair of size 11C flat-soled shoes. Along with the remains of a homemade chemical bomb, the only thing on the premises that hadn't been there during Riley and Halsey's previous visit—detected only days later, when Miller and his family returned from their vacation in California—was an unfamiliar business card surreptitiously added to the refrigerator door, among the cards, photos, children's drawings, and emergency numbers suspended by magnets:

MONTICELLO HOME SECURITY, INC.
James T. Callender, Service Technician
7426 Hemings Court
Greenwich, CT 06870
(203) 662-1776   jcallender@monticelloalarms.com
"Eternal Vigilance Is the Price of Liberty"

Miller called Riley during the drive back to Greenwich, having reached the family's maid on the third try. What he'd learned from her explained how the saboteur had entered the house. Shortly after she had arrived that afternoon, intending to stay for only a few minutes' essential tasks, she had answered the doorbell and admitted a uniformed man who represented himself as an employee of a firm that had recently acquired the company that built Miller's custom alarm system. A routine maintenance call, he had told her: just three to five minutes at each customer's home to confirm the remote system was still working after a central operating system upgrade. She knew that Miller took security seriously: she noticed the official-looking logo on the man's uniform, his cap, the ID badge clipped to his pocket, and the magnetic sign on the doors of his van. She had given the man a few minutes of access to the basement and thought nothing of it.

"When she realized what had happened," Miller told Riley, "she broke down in tears and offered to resign on the spot. You could have knocked me over with a feather. I wouldn't hear of it, of course, but she was shaken to the bones, as if it were her own home the guy had violated. Don't ever let anybody tell you the concept of personal accountability is extinct."

"I'm sorry to bring this up at such a time, but you'll probably want to talk with both your insurance agent and your attorney about whether your coverage includes damages from illegal entry combined with fraud. I hope you haven't lost the financial value of your prize Lafite along with the intrinsic historical value."

"As it happens, that's the least of our worries. Maybe I

had a financial loss already, regardless of the break-in. There's been some discussion in the wine press lately about early Lafite bottles possibly being counterfeit. I bought mine in good faith through a British distributor that most everybody in the business trusted, but who knows? Maybe I didn't lose anything as special as I thought. What matters is that nobody's hurt—your warning may have saved our lives. I can't thank you enough for that." They ended the call, and Riley spent several minutes in silence.

Thoughts of Miller's old bottles brought him back to an animated mood. "Hey, about the 1847 Lafite? Miller said he'd heard it might be a fake, anyway. Small consolation, I guess. Is that anything you've heard about in the wine world?"

"So far it's mostly scuttlebutt." Jake answered. "I understand some experts are trying to verify the rumors about fake bottles from the eighteenth and nineteenth centuries, and they'll probably call in specialists from the auction houses. Give it a couple of years and something reliable will probably emerge. In the meantime, if you're thinking of investing, I'd steer clear."

Dave shot him a pair of raised eyebrows in mock outrage and pointed at the bulge of his own wallet inside his jacket. They'd joked so often enough about the income differential between technology entrepreneurs and public servants that it wasn't even close to being a sore point. "OK. But seriously, if you absolutely had to guess—gun to head—would you say that bottle was genuine?"

Jake spoke with some deliberation. "On some level, even considering the damage, I *want* it to be true. I want the provenance to be clean. I like Harry Miller and don't want to see him cheated. I also want to think I was a couple of inches from some tangible reminder of Halley's Comet. Every era has its historical relics. Unfortunately, when it comes to old wine bottles, an awful lot of gaps seem to be opening up lately between what people want to be true and what they can verify. That's why I'd have to guess no and assume the bottle's bogus. Every time I find my own interests shaping the way I look at facts, I notice the facts have a tendency to turn around and bite me in the butt."

Riley agreed, then went quiet for another mile or two.

Kavanagh, in the driver's seat, struggled with his own curiosity, his desire to be part of the older men's conversation, and the junior officer's reflex to avoid speaking until spoken to. For a few minutes he nearly swallowed his own tongue. Curiosity won out.

"Chief, if you don't mind my asking, what do you figure is biting us in the butt about the Wine Killer? Is there something everybody wants to see happen, something that's keeping the whole force from seeing some big critical fact about this creep?"

"Kavanagh," Riley intoned, "that's a better question than you may be aware of." He reflected for a moment. "We all want to see him act cocky and slip up. So far all he does, along with killing people and trashing property, is act cocky and give himself reasons to be cockier."

"Don't underestimate the partial victory tonight," Jake interjected. "The timing suggests he was aiming for two strikes at once—blowing up one collection to get our attention and confuse a small town force, while across town he's setting up a lot of people to get poisoned. Big splash if it happens as planned. . .a big mind game at our expense. We didn't stop his whole performance, but we bitched up half of it for him, and it's the half that matters.

"If there's another silver lining here," Jake continued, "you've got two big fat prints now from the Copper Beech Inn. Think he got careless or purposely left us another calling card?"

"Everything we see from this guy implies he knows exactly what he's doing," replied Riley. "You nailed it before, talking to the tech: Expect the worst from him. I'd guess we're going to get another message.

"The other thing we've got to move on is to approach anybody in Jewett City who's involved with wine. No false alarm there this time, I'm willing to bet. At least there's only one J in the state. If this bastard gets as far as the Ms and Ns, we won't have that little advantage. Middletown, Middlebury,

Meriden, New Haven, New Preston, New This and New That. Christ, he could turn up anywhere."

"All the more reason we need to force him to make a mistake while he's in this bottlenecked part of the alphabet." Jake cracked a smile that was half a wince as he realized his wine-related reference. "He probably has something really perverse in mind for the Ks. I know of maybe three of those, and if it isn't Kent, you know where I bet he's headed?"

"Surprise me."

"Down toward the Sound to Killingworth or up in the northeast corner to Killingly."

"Absolutely hilarious."

CHAPTER THIRTY-SIX

From his hiding place high in a huge beech tree two doors away from the inn, the man in black had watched the police cars converge on the now well-lighted old building. He had barely had time to escape the wine cellar after he'd heard their sirens in the distance. Thank God small town cops, predictably hungering for a little excitement, weren't smart enough to think of rushing to a crime scene without the theatricality of that blaring noise.

How the hell had they known he was there? He would have to think about that one. It certainly added a bit of spice to the game, didn't it? So be it, he thought, and smiled. He'd never been one to duck a challenge. Taking care not to rustle the beech's thick blanket of new leaves, he nestled in a crotch formed by two large branches, making himself comfortable while he calmly awaited the police's departure. Too bad he hadn't brought the mug of coffee from the car he'd parked several blocks away. Ah well, *he thought,* settling back against the smooth old tree trunk, he'd waited in the dark before.

Keeping half an eye on the inn's parking lot, he let himself drift back to the first time he'd hidden from the police. It had been shortly after his fifteenth birthday. A few months earlier, well-muscled and already tall enough to pass as older, he had run away from his increasingly cruel adoptive parents, leaving the suburbs for downtown Boston. He remembered half hoping his parents might look for him and being glad when they hadn't.

Initially, he had lived in the shoddy, often-dangerous areas around Fenway Park. When he was hungry, he'd begged for money or stolen a sandwich from one of the many delis and convenience stores dotting the streets. There were other sources of income available in that neighborhood in the 1970s, too, from furtive men who viewed his lanky body in ways he found oddly comical. . .and who rarely viewed his damaged face at all.

Daniel—he still used that name, when he had to use a name at all—learned to live frugally enough that he could stretch out the earnings from one such experience every few weeks. He was sometimes violently sick afterward, and he did as little of this as possible; he'd far rather steal. Thefts of various kinds—and he was quickly learning how many kinds there were—offered an array of challenges, and challenges were the only things he truly enjoyed.

It had been on one of those occasions that he'd had his first experience of running from the law. He'd hidden in the cellar of a cockroach-infested apartment building, marveling, as he did now, at how stupid the police could be. He'd quickly realized that, without a scriptwriter to provide the clues, real cops were nothing like those on TV. Even a teenager could elude them, if he was quick and smart.

Shifting his position slowly and carefully, noting that the cadre at the inn seemed in no hurry to leave, he reflected back on those days. He had lived on the streets for a bit and in shelters and, often, despite the food he stole, was hungry and cold and envious of the handsome, wealthy Bostonians around him. Tired of being taunted by other teens and stared at, or worse, on the streets, he had often sought refuge in the old public library on Copley Square. Even now, he could see the reading room as clearly as he could see the police cars across the way. He had loved the old wood, the high ceilings, the silence, even the smell. That library had become a sanctuary for him, away from the filth of the alleys and the caterwauling music of people his own age. He had buried himself in books, both to escape the streets that always seemed too warm or too cold, and to escape the pitying looks his distorted face always inspired.

And then a miracle had happened. When he was seventeen, he was befriended by one of the librarians, a kind, elderly woman who had seemed to see past his ragged clothes and equally ragged features. They would sometimes find a quiet corner of the vast library and speak for hours of Thomas Edison or Leonardo da Vinci, of the legend of Si Ling-chi discovering silk or Wei Boyang describing the alchemists' work that led to the use of gunpowder. She spoke some Mandarin, and she was both surprised and impressed that he could as well. She had urged him to go back to school, to get a GED, and arranged for him to take the SATs, which he suspected she had paid for herself. He had done brilliantly on the test, securing a full scholarship to MIT, despite his unconventional background.

At college, he'd more than justified her faith, succeeding well and winning several science awards. He remained reclusive and sullen through those years, but he was far from the only student at the institute who preferred technical pursuits over cultivating friendships. MIT was perfect for Daniel; there, he could stand out while remaining in the shadows.

He'd not thought of the old librarian in a long time. She had been his friend, perhaps the only one he'd ever had. He half believed that it was in payment for the sin of caring for him that she had been mugged and killed in a random event just after he graduated from college. It had been a lesson. He'd let his guard down, and the world had turned on him as it had so many times before. His rage rekindled, he'd vowed he'd not let anyone make that mistake, the mistake of caring for him, ever again.

The sound of a car engine brought him back to the present. Good: The police and the others were leaving. There would be more for them to do on the other side of the town, of course. He wondered whether they'd yet discovered the rest of the operation, the Two, the sign that his imagination and his power would forever dance beyond their reach.

He saw a tall figure in jeans get into one of the police cars. Well, well, Jake Halsey, hot on the trail once again. He was getting to be something of an annoyance. Did this require an acceleration of his plan for Jake? That was something else he'd have to think about.

He allowed himself a slight, silent smile, reflecting on how he had flushed out information about Jake. Computers were very good at helping to secure information.

It had taken hardly any time at all to generate a strangely pleasant surprise: who Jake Halsey was and where he might be found. For the rest, he could use techniques and instruments of his own design, plus instruments that others had contrived. He sometimes marveled at the things that were nowadays placed right out in the open, where anyone who knew what they were really for could do what he wanted with them.

The man in black maintained his perch for another twenty minutes until the inn was in darkness and he was certain everyone had left or gone indoors to stay. The night was quiet as he climbed carefully to the ground and calmly strolled the five blocks to his waiting car.

CHAPTER THIRTY-SEVEN

Riley got about five hours of sleep and was in the office by eight the next morning. He got on the phone with the state lab.

"What do you mean the mass spectrometer is down?" he yelled.

"I'm sorry, Detective Riley, the computer that reads the output is working fine, but the machine itself quit last Tuesday. We've got a repairman coming sometime this week to look at it." The technician continued, "We don't use it too much in Connecticut, so repairing it's not been a first priority.

"As soon as the bottles were brought in last night, we tried to identify the substance on them with a chemical analysis, but had no luck. We really need the mass spectrometer. You know what it does, right? It scans and ionizes the particles in the substance and subjects them to electrical and magnetic fields, which deflect the particles in angles proportional to their mass. Then it's read by a computer. That's how we can ID a substance."

"Spare me the physics—we just need to know what that stuff is, *yesterday*."

"Fortunately, I've got better news on the fingerprints. They were both perfect images and we've got an exact match in the FBI fingerprint database."

Riley let out a yell. "Tell me, tell me!"

"I'm faxing the report to you now. It's in the machine or I'd read it to you, but you'll have it in a minute or so. The computer found more than twenty points of exact comparison, which is phenomenal. It will be perfect evidence when your case goes to trial."

The fax machine in Riley's office whirred to life.

"You guys really moved fast on those prints." Riley's tone had changed. "A lot of people down here and elsewhere

252

in the state appreciate your speed. Just let me know ASAP when your spectrometer's fixed."

Riley hung up and walked over to the fax.

Three sheets had come in from the lab. The first two were blow-ups of the two prints the lab tech had lifted from the wine cellar door knob. At that magnification, each image was about six inches high, and the impression of the entire print was textbook perfect.

The third page, however, caused him to sit down. The man they had been chasing for six months—their criminal, the man who had killed six wine lovers and damaged collections of wine and destroyed a man's livelihood and used an airplane to blow up a house, the man behind the fingerprint match—was named Daniel Lee.

Riley read the report. Lee had been arrested by the Cambridge, Massachusetts, police for a sit-in at MIT in 1982, while he was a junior at the institute. He and twenty-one other unruly students had been fingerprinted and spent the night in the Cambridge city jail. They all went before a judge the next morning where, in a gesture of good town-and-gown relations, each was fined only $50, an amount the judge figured was what their overnight stay had cost the city. The reason for the sit-in had not been recorded.

A local Massachusetts address was given for Lee, but Riley knew that Lee would be long gone from any address that was twenty-one years old.

He called out for Arlene, the department administrator.

"Please contact Tony, Ellen, Brian, and Jake. Call Jake last, because he may still be asleep—he was up late last night, with me. Ask—no, *tell* them to be here at one for a meeting. You can also say that I'm pretty sure we know the name of the killer. That'll get their attention!"

"Right away, Boss." Arlene went back to her desk to make the calls.

At 1:00 p.m. the team assembled in Riley's office. As Jake walked in, Riley asked if he'd gotten any sleep.

"To tell the truth, after I got to bed I tossed and turned until about five, thinking about how close we're coming to our killer, and just missing him. I'm getting weird dreams about this case lately. Last night it was enormous chessboards that kept turning into printed circuits. Can't say I enjoyed chasing somebody around one of those, with capacitors twenty feet high."

"Well, the news I've got should help your sleep *and* your nerves. There was a match in the database on the prints our guy left in the Ivoryton wine cellar. The name of our killer is Daniel Lee."

Everybody cheered.

"Twenty years ago, as a college kid, he spent a night in jail for participating in a campus sit-in. At the time, he had a Massachusetts driver's license and lived in Cambridge—we just checked and neither the license nor the address is valid now.

"Before you arrived, we checked DMV of Connecticut licenses and registrations for Lee. Here's the list. We got a lot of matches on the last name, and they're all over the state, so the list has to be narrowed down. Tony and Ellen, please check every name on the list. Based on his years at college, our guy is probably forty to forty-three years old, so you can eliminate everyone else for now.

"We also checked and Social Security has nothing, Social Services has nothing, and he's not a parent, at least not on the Board of Education list.

"Brian, I want you to check all phone numbers for the name Daniel Lee in the state and match them against the license and registration list. Let's see what we come up with, especially if there's a number and no car or license, or vice versa.

"Jake, can you fly up to Boston and check with Alumni Records at MIT to see what they've got? If there should happen to be a picture of him in the file, please get a copy. I'm asking you to go in person because they may balk at opening the records, and you can be more persuasive in person than if we tried to handle the inquiry on the phone. Also, I don't want to spend time contacting the Cambridge police. They'd need to hear the whole story and they'd want to get involved, and life is too short.

"In the meantime, now that we have a name, I'm going to see if we can dig something else up about this guy. For example, if he was personally involved with that plane which crashed into the Fairfield house, he may be licensed, and the FAA may have a record. Let's meet at 8:00 a.m. tomorrow to go over the details. I hope that will give you enough time."

The next morning Brian was the first to report. "Connecticut has about three-and-a-half million residents and twenty-eight of them are named Daniel Lee," he said. "That's the bad news. The good news is that I was able to either reach or get information about twenty-five of them and only two of those are in our age range. I asked for a visit by the local police to each of the three remaining residences. We should know the results by noon today. Unfortunately, if our Lee is in the bunch, he'll be alerted by our call or by the police visit, but there's nothing we can do about that. In case it *is* our perp, I suggested it might be wise to send at least two men on each visit and to have them ready for a chase if Lee runs."

"Good," Riley offered. "Tony, Ellen, what did you find out?"

"We've got a half-dozen possibles from the DMV. When Brian gets his answers, we can compare them with the phone information and see if we get any matches," said Tony.

"Okay. Jake?"

"I flew up to Cambridge. It's a bit unusual, even at MIT, but Lee didn't play any sports while in college or get involved with any extracurricular activities. At least his name doesn't appear in the Institute's records in those categories, and there are no team or group pictures that include his name. I did get a graduation photo, but it won't be of much help. The guy had long, stringy hair down onto his shoulders and covering part of his face, not unlike a male version of Veronica Lake."

Tony mouthed a silent "Who?"

Ellen quickly whispered, "Forties actress. Sex bomb." Tony still looked at sea. "Peek-a-boo long blond hair. *This*

Gun for Hire. Ask your mom. But first, *focus*."

Jake continued. "Unfortunately, the photo is about as generic as you can get and its quality isn't very good. We could give it to a digital artist and have him age the photo by twenty years, but my gut says that the result won't be much help. I also picked up a copy of his transcript, which carries the Cambridge address you already have from the police report, as we might have expected. Turns out he was an excellent student. Anyway, we really need something more recent."

"Thanks," said Riley. "As far as the FAA is concerned, there is no licensed pilot named Daniel Lee in New England and only one in New Jersey, who isn't our man. If Lee was the flier or otherwise directly involved in the crash in a way requiring a pilot's license, he could have changed his name or be licensed under an alias. I suppose he could have even been flying without a license, but if he was, we wouldn't be able to tell. Maybe we should check flight schools, too. I hope we'll have better luck with the phone numbers or car registrations."

"What's next?" asked Brian.

"We call in the digital artist anyway," said Riley, "and get this face in front of a lot more cops. It may be a long shot, but if due diligence didn't occasionally pay off, they'd call it undue diligence and nobody would do it. As for us, we wait, and see which ball we've got in the air comes down first."

CHAPTER THIRTY-EIGHT

The next day was a complete opposite of its predecessor, overcast and cold. New England was having a hard time letting spring turn into summer. On the second floor of the Greenwich police station, the mood was all business. Nothing had been cleaned up overnight, and Riley's office looked like the aftermath of a Christmas party: full ashtrays (against regulations), overflowing wastebaskets, empty paper cups with an occasional partially-finished coffee, its surface sprouting a patina of congealing milk. All that was missing were any bottles that had once held wine, beer, and liquor—and any lingering suggestion that anyone might have enjoyed themselves.

Most of the department's detectives had been there all night. Riley had dragged a cheap Army cot up from the holding cells downstairs to the interview room down the hall, allowing each of them to catch two or three hours of sleep in alternating shifts. He couldn't remember the last time there had been enough overflow occupancy downstairs for the cot to see any use; its canvas smelled unmistakably of mildew.

Jake had slept at his own home, briefly. When he came in he made a beeline for Riley's desk, and the two of them disappeared down the hall to confer behind closed doors. Riley's voice resonated in the hallway at one point, raised in a tone of incredulity, but the only word anyone back in Riley's office could make out was "What?" No one looked up from their phone calls or computer screens to voice a comment. They didn't lack interest, but they did lack time.

On one wall, a pair of black-and-white portraits now hung: the MIT graduation photo of Daniel Lee and its digitally aged version, a slightly unnatural-looking computer image. The forensic artist had shortened Lee's 1983 hairstyle to something less flamboyant and more symmetrical, moved back his hairline, replaced his graduation gown with a conservative sport shirt, added a few pounds and wrinkles, and taken her best shot at the facial bone structure. With nothing to work from but Lee's half-hidden expression in the MIT photo, augmented by Hannah DiVito's photo and comments from Miller's maid for a rough estimate of his physique, the artist had produced an image that, if not for certain uncanny distortions, might be mistaken for about half the tall, dour white men in New England. Regardless, Allen had spent a large part of the night faxing the pair of portraits to police stations throughout Connecticut and bordering states and had uploaded them to the VICAP system for national circulation. Lee was in the process of losing the advantage of anonymity.

Beside the portraits was a series of stills from the bottle cam at Miller's house. The afternoon intruder in the makeshift blue uniform was too vaguely detailed to be worth posting on VICAP, but every rendering of him was deemed useful. No one expected him to appear again wearing the Monticello Home Security baseball cap.

In mid-afternoon, Riley called the meeting to order. He stood motionless as the team took their places around the conference table. Ellen Green, long accustomed to taking readings of her colleagues' nonverbal cues, noted that the chief's eyes were aimed discreetly but steadily in Jake's direction. She couldn't read an expression on either man's face.

Riley began bluntly. "All right, guys, let's have it."

Brian, wearing a day's growth of beard, was the first to respond. "The phone numbers, including cell phones, and the car registrations were all checked. Nothing. Every possible candidate was checked out and not one fit the description. Either the age was wrong or something else was wrong. You know, we didn't consider it, but Lee is a common Chinese name and most of our Lees were Asian. Given the age difference, the picture of Lee picked up in Cambridge by Jake was hard to figure, but he sure didn't look Chinese. In sum, many were older, some were younger, but there was no

Caucasian anywhere near our age range." Brian added, as an afterthought, "I'm sorry."

"Not your fault," Riley said sympathetically. "It's good work. It's helped narrow our search.

"One new piece of information came in this morning from Harry Miller in Ivoryton. He scanned this and faxed it to me personally, then gave the original to the Essex PD in the unlikely event it carries any fingerprints. It's a business card that Lee apparently tucked into a blank spot on the family fridge." He circulated copies of the Monticello card. "Arlene informs me that there is no such entity as Monticello Home Security doing business in the United States, not even in Monticello, Minnesota. Because there is also clearly no such street in Greenwich as Hemings Court and because of other anomalies in this information, the sole value of this little document is presumably psychological, a highly annoying taunt-and-flaunt message.

"Monticello, of course, is Thomas Jefferson's estate in Charlottesville, Virginia. As for the rest of it, Miller is enough of a student of Jeffersoniana to have informed me that James T. Callender—yes, spelled this way—was the disgruntled office-seeker who originally published the story of Jefferson fathering children by his slave Sally Hemings. He also told me that 7/4/26, or July 4, 1826, is Jefferson's death date.

"The kicker, of course, is that Thomas Jefferson was a noted wine collector . . . imported bottles from France . . . the whole bit."

He paused. "But, this business card is more than another clever wine tie in. Using a Greenwich address on a card planted at an Ivoryton crime scene is a pretty clear statement that the perp is aware his actions are of interest here. In other words, friends, we should assume that either individually or collectively, we have been made."

Groans filled the room. Pezzi muttered imprecations in a Sicilian dialect.

"Jake?" Riley sat down at the end of the conference table and yielded the floor to Halsey, who rose from the seat beside him. Bleary eyes all around the table turned toward Jake.

"Let's summarize where we are right now," said Jake. He pulled over a white board and some markers, speaking aloud as he wrote.

"We've got a name, Daniel Lee. We assume he's Caucasian. We've got at least two of his fingerprints. We have his DNA. We assume he doesn't have a pilot's license, at least in his own name. He doesn't have a driver's license in his own name. He doesn't have a car registered in Connecticut in his own name. He doesn't have a telephone number in his own name. No cell phone. Here's what the list looks like, so far."

NAME: Daniel Lee.
RACE: Caucasian.
FINGERPRINTS? Yes, two.
OTHER CRIMINAL RECORD? Nothing in system.
DNA? Yes.
PILOT'S LICENSE? No.
DRIVER'S LICENSE? Not in Connecticut.
CAR REGISTRATION? Not in Connecticut
PHONE? No landline or cell
OTHER STATES: Not checked yet

"We do know that he's killing in Connecticut. Looking at this list, I think we can guess he's operating under an assumed name. Although we've got all this information about him, none of it helps us get any closer to him. On the contrary, from what Dave has just told us about his latest message and from observations I'll describe in a moment, we should assume he knows enough to try to get closer to one or more of us.

"There's one other thing that may or may not help and the responsibility for explaining it falls directly on me." The room grew quieter as everyone, even the restless Pezzi, unconsciously stopped moving in their chairs or rustling paper.

"A few weeks ago," Jake continued, "I underwent a routine genetic test with two purposes in mind. First, for medical screening, and second, to establish some records of my own DNA in case a crime scene contains any traces of it.

Around the same time, the state lab report on materials associated with the Wine Killer came through and Dave informed me that his blood type was AB negative. This type is relatively rare. As it happens, it's also my own."

He paused, leaving the buzz of the overhead lights as the only audible sound.

"I don't know whether to call it a whim or a hunch, but I thought it might be informative to have a knowledgeable person in the medical community look at the state lab's report on the killer's DNA. This, um, informal consultant also saw my own test results. There are similarities, too numerous and too close to be accidental. The consultant and I have put in quite a bit of time checking out the possibility of some accident or lab error. The chances of that are vanishingly small, we now know. Negligible.

"I wanted to avoid bringing this in until I was sure there was something to it. It's important to get you all on the same page from here through the duration of the investigation. I'm sure that Dave will agree—I briefed him earlier today on the basics—that what I'm about to tell you does not leave this room in any form."

Jake's bearing, perhaps for the first time since he had left the Air Force, could be described as military. "First: the DNA analysis neither confirms nor disconfirms any rumors you may have heard to the effect that I am actually the Wine Killer." The tension in the room, considerable after a collective all-nighter, broke in peals of laughter.

"Second, barring a spectacular and highly unlikely convergence of foul-ups, conspiracies, and lies, the analysis confirms that the Wine Killer is almost certainly a close relative of mine."

Even Pezzi choked off his horselaugh at this. All members of the team were now motionless and sharply awake.

"The existence of this person comes as an absolute surprise to me and to those who have known me for years." Jake and Riley locked eyes momentarily. "I have no brothers or sisters as far as I know. All relatives who might have relevant information are deceased. I've looked at all financial, legal, and medical records that might hold any clue to possible extramarital offspring of my parents, either one or both of them, and the possible inferences are exactly as Brian found with the phones and car registrations. Zero. Nothing."

Riley cut in momentarily. "Let me underscore what Jake said. You are not to share this information with *anyone* outside this room. The press would have a field day. That prohibition includes rumor, banter, scuttlebutt, scandal, dinnertime conversation with loved ones, barroom conversation with strangers, and professional conversation with each other within earshot of anyone not affiliated with this division of this department. It also includes—Tony, please pay particular attention to this—jokes of any form, anywhere, tasteful or otherwise." Pezzi covered his stricken expression with a forced smile.

"Last winter someone, perhaps Lee," Jake continued after a strained silence, "used a spurious legal dispute involving a foreign business to try to get a look at legal records about my family by means of a subpoena. He got very little info, but what little he got may have served his purposes. We don't know. Brian, a few days back when I asked you to check out a foreign-based law office? That was the firm that handled the subpoena."

Allen looked taken aback. "Konstantinov and Plotkin, right? Down in Brooklyn, a branch office in an immigrant neighborhood. I wondered what you wanted with that. There's almost nothing about them online, and their phone's been disconnected. Lost to follow-up, as the medics would say."

"I paid their office another visit and it's closed down," said Jake. "Abandoned like a boiler-room scam shop. The building is unprofessional and shabby, not just impoverished. Nevertheless, they remain persons of interest, if anything about them should turn up." He found an open section of the white board and wrote out the firm's name and the Brighton Beach address.

Then he added Transalpinia. "This other name is the business involved in the litigation. It's Swiss, at least officially, and I have to assume that any tracks leading back to

Lee would be extremely well covered. At least they've been successfully hidden from my inquiries. I'll be the first to admit that I'm not in my element searching through business records—but I'm running it up the flagpole in case anyone has an hour of spare time."

Everyone was too tired even to groan.

"Friends, we're in a logical *cul de sac*," he concluded. "DNA says I have a monster for a brother—or half-brother or cousin or whatever the hell he is. Family history and common sense say I don't, and nothing else says I do. Whatever the truth is, the owner of the fingerprints we call Daniel Lee has it in for the wine lovers of Connecticut. On top of that, someone appears to have it in for yours truly. I favor the inference that they are the same person.

"You may have heard that my home and the home of someone close to me are under GPD protection and surveillance because of threats. This is true. Ellen, you've been looking through that message. Do you have any. . .?"

Arlene Bianchini stuck her head in the door.

"Not now, Arlene," Riley said dismissively.

"I think you're going to want to see this, Boss," she persisted. "Remember yesterday afternoon when you left you asked me to check the lab's progress with the mass spectrometer? While they were waiting for it to be fixed, they worked on the chemical composition of that stuff on the wine bottle from the Copper Beech Inn. They identified one of the ingredients. It's *curare*. The only place to get your hands on the stuff legally, without visiting Peru or Brazil, is at a place called Ajax Laboratories in Hong Kong. So I got authorization and called the Hong Kong police and asked them to visit Ajax and see if it had any records of a shipment to Connecticut.

"Guess what?" She smiled a huge grin. "Four weeks ago Ajax shipped 750 milligrams of curare to the Mail Boxes, Etc. in Riverside. The *only* shipment to anywhere in New England—in the past ten years!"

The room erupted in smiles and whistles.

When the noise died down, Riley spoke. "That's the best news we've had since that case began. If we catch this guy,

I'll see to it you get a department citation. Way to go!"

Brian grabbed a networked laptop off the conference table, looked up a few figures online, and did some quick calculations. "The lethal dose is estimated at 0.1 milligrams per kilogram of body weight. Ten milligrams is more than enough to ice a guy who weighs 200 pounds. Looks like Lee bought enough of it for mass murder."

Tony let loose a long, low-pitched whistle of astonishment.

"Good thinking, Brian," Riley admitted. "Puts some things in perspective." He glanced at his watch. It was 4:00 p.m.

"Jake, let's you and me pay a visit to Mail Boxes and see if we can get the name and address of whoever picked up that package. The rest of you stay put—I'll call you with whatever we find. I'm willing to bet that things are going to get exciting real fast."

Since he knew she was out of the operating room for the day, Jake decided to call Cat to bring her up to date. Brian cleared his desk, and Ellen went out to pick up a very late lunch.

Riley took note of this. Ellen rarely ate alone, without Pezzi as her foil and sounding board, unless she was engrossed in developing a private theory about a suspect's mindset. When the team eventually heard about these speculations, some turned out to be dead ends and some were surprisingly insightful. Riley had not yet decided whether his profiler's penchant for solitary work was the way he wanted his department to operate, but in past cases, Ellen had been right often enough for him to cut her some slack.

When she returned carrying a sandwich, gripping a notebook in her other hand as if it were an animal about to escape, she asked Riley for a private moment. She closed the door behind her after entering his office.

"Good memory you've got there, under all this pressure," Riley began. "When Arlene told us about the curare, wasn't Jake about to ask you about the vandalism to Dr. Taylor's PC? Sorry you got cut off."

Ellen looked taken aback. "Actually, that wasn't it but . . . come to think of it," she said slowly, "the computer messages are consistent with what I've been thinking, in a strange way.

"What I was about to say in the meeting was this: The mind behind those messages is meticulous about details, immature, too clever by half, desperate for attention and praise, obsessed with wine—red in particular—and furious at women. All women, probably, not any one specifically. Judging from his Photoshop work, he seems to view the human body with more disgust than desire. He may loathe his own body as well—the classic Puritan/pervert two-sided coin. He was probably a virgin until well into adulthood, and he may still be. His resentments run too deep ever to stop boiling over into violence. He's the nerd from Hell."

"This doesn't surprise me, Ellen, but it helps. Thanks."

"But, Chief, there's something else, and it bothers me a lot more than the profile. I can't believe I can even entertain this thought, given what we know about everyone involved, but not voicing it would be unprofessional." *The Somewhat Darker Knight,* she thought. *Darker now.* There was no way this was going to be easy.

Riley was silent.

"Jake surprised us with the DNA."

"When he briefed me on it, I was absolutely floored. Imagine how much it surprised *him.*"

"Are we all a hundred and ten percent sure that it was a surprise?"

"Meaning what?"

"I don't like where this line of reasoning takes me, and I'm sure you'll like it a lot less. I know how far you and Jake go back. I've admired his work and liked him from the first time you brought him onboard. But from the DNA, with no known relative as the source, aren't we obligated. . ." She hesitated. "To try to rule Jake out, or in, as a potential suspect?"

"You've got to be pulling my leg! If Pezzi came in here with a routine like this, I'd not only have his badge, I'd run him out of town!" He stared laser beams at her. "You're serious," he said incredulously.

"I wish I could find some way not to be. Blocking out everything we know about him for a minute, taking him just as a person tied to some evidence—not, well, as Jake—and trying to think the worst just as an exercise, think about how this *looks*. If someone wanted to insulate himself from incriminating DNA, how better to do it than to get close to the investigation, joke about rumors that he's a suspect, concoct a story of a phantom relative? On top of that, he claims his own genetic test was done for the sake of forensic analysis."

Again, Riley was silent.

"And he knows wine, *and* he knows machinery. All the Wine Killer's showing off plays right to Jake's technical abilities. Plus, he had access to Taylor's computer. Don't forget that before he met her, he was practically as reclusive and solitary as. . . ."

"Stop. Ellen, just stop."

"I know." She looked pained.

"Among other things, he's ten feet behind you." Green instantly went ashen but did not turn around. Jake had returned from phoning Cat and was waiting in the hall outside Riley's office, reading a newspaper.

"Speaking strictly as a cop and a colleague," Riley said, "what I have to say about this is 'duly noted.' It's logical of you to lay this all out, even commendable. It does what any conjecture has to do, link known evidence with possible motives and actions in a story that's at least coherent. Speaking as a friend, *as me*, all I can do is ask if you're out of your mind."

"Believe me, I've been trying to find shorter distances to connect the dots. There just aren't any."

"Can you see Jake holding attitudes about women that your profile attributes to this guy?"

Ellen measured her words. "Not from anything I've ever observed."

"More likely, if anybody's been building any elaborate ruses here, it'd be the killer putting together a pattern that would draw suspicion toward Jake."

"That's plausible too, Chief."

"Are you going to have any trouble continuing to work with Jake on this investigation?"

She looked him square in the eye. "No, sir."

There was one consideration Riley knew would banish all doubt. Three words would probably do it. He had never divulged what he knew about Halsey's past to any of his personnel. He had never needed to make any explicit promises to Jake to know this was not a time to start. If any of the junior detectives even knew the names Melinda and Courtney, it was from some local grapevine, not from him. Rank, this time, would have to suffice, although he was not the sort of leader who relished such moments.

"Ellen, thanks for your honesty about this. You don't need to worry about Jake. Let's both get back to what we were doing." She nodded and left the office. As she passed Jake in the hall, he might not have noticed a bit of mist in her eyes, but if he did, he would probably have attributed it to allergies.

She may still have doubts, Riley thought. *They come with the job. They're an easier price to pay than the alternative.*

As they drove up the Post Road, Riley turned to Jake and thanked him for briefing the group. "Aside from not telling your buddy about your DNA, there's something else I have to add," he said gravely. "Do you know how close you skated to an obstruction of justice charge by sitting on those DNA reports?"

"I have some inkling," said Jake. "You've saved my bacon by being understanding. Thanks . . . I don't know if I can say thanks often enough. You understand I had to make sure the analysis was reliable as well as relevant, I hope."

"Yeah," grumbled Riley. "I've known you most of your life and that was the deciding factor. I don't know if I would have made the same call if it had been my genes, but I don't know that I wouldn't, either. Family stuff goes by different rules, I suppose. Anyway, what's it been like knowing you've got some, uh, *literal* skeletons in the family closet?"

Jake sensed how close Riley was to changing his mind, to letting the volatile mixture of cop and friend approach an ignition point. He took his time. "It's too unreal to spend a lot of time thinking about. One other thing we Halseys inherit is a fantastic capacity for the ol' British stiff upper lip." Riley chuckled at this. "Whoever he is, he's less than nobody to me. He's sure as hell not family in any sense that matters. There's more to being in my family than sharing some sequences of deoxyribo-goddamn nucleic acid."

"Hell, there's a lot of mysterious stuff, about being part of *anybody's* family" Riley replied,

The detective looked long and hard at Jake, half relieved to see his old friend's glare was as icy as his own, half curious at how that determination might translate into action if push ever came—as it easily might, and soon—to shove. As well as he knew Jake, he had to wonder how often push came to shove in *his* world.

Years ago, Riley recalled, he had admired his friend's decision to join the Air Force, then struggled to understand his decision to leave after three years. Men of their generation, too young for the Vietnam draft and too old for later engagements in the Middle East, had been spared certain risks and tests by the accidents of history. Riley had no doubts about what Halsey was made of; he'd seen the kinds of pain his friend could take, on sports fields and elsewhere, and take with grace and grit.

Still, only one of them, by profession and by nature, was a cop.

"Hombre," Jake said firmly, interrupting his train of thought, "please be sure about one thing. If I come into contact with Lee in any situation that calls for force, you can count on me. No special consideration of any kind. He's not a relative to me; he's murderous vermin. If he's menacing anyone or fleeing and peaceful arrest isn't an option? If I'm armed, I will not hesitate to take him down."

Riley acknowledged this with a somber thumbs-up, then said nothing until a few moments had passed. "Anyway, about this shipping joint up ahead. I know you probably would anyway, but let me do the talking. I don't intend to take any shit from the manager and I may have to lean on him or her a little bit. Maybe even a lot."

"You can count on me," Jake responded with a smile.

CHAPTER THIRTY-NINE

They walked into shipping and mailbox store, and Riley held out his badge to the clerk. "May we see the manager, please?"

The clerk beckoned to one of the other employees, who stepped up and said, "I'm Josh Maleski. How can I help you?"

Riley flashed his badge again.

"I'm Greenwich Chief of Detectives Dave Riley. We need the name and address of the person who rented your box 298."

"I'm sorry, detective, but it's company policy not to give out that information under any circumstances."

"We're investigating a serious crime and we've got a subpoena in the works. Unless I find out who rented that box within sixty seconds, we'll have ten Greenwich policemen, the state cops, and maybe an FBI agent or two breathing down your neck. Then, we'll probably throw your ass in jail for interfering with a police investigation. After that, we'll be back with a subpoena, making your noble little gesture an absolute waste of time." Riley's voice was low but full of steel.

"Hey, wait a minute! I'm only doing my job. But, as long as you put it that way, Detective," the manager said, "to hell with regulations. Come with me." Riley motioned for Jake to follow.

The office computer was already on and, with a few keystrokes, the manager brought up a page of information with box number 298 highlighted. Riley read from the screen.

"John Q. Doe? What is this shit?" he thundered.

"Hey, man, calm down. Maybe that was his idea of a joke, but that's all we've got. Here's his address, probably his real address, right here: 14 Hickory Lane, Riverside, Connecticut."

"In addition to everything else, we've got a comedian on our hands," Jake noted. "Gotta admit it's funnier than his poetry."

Riley pulled out his police radio. "Get me Brian Allen," he said abruptly.

"Allen here," Brian responded immediately.

"Call in the troops. We need two more cars with two men each and a couple of rifles. All radios should be on the new frequency we've been using, which might give us a small time advantage, particularly if this guy is monitoring the old frequency. Now, don't laugh—the assumed name of our perp is John Q. Doe. Yeah, I know. He gave an address of 14 Hickory Lane, in Riverside. Check it out in the phone records. Jake and I will be back in ten minutes for a preliminary meeting."

Both ran to the car. Riley laid down some rubber on the way out of the parking lot and turned on his siren. Within five minutes, they walked into the busy squad room, and Riley started barking orders.

"You heard it from Brian, but here it is again. Everyone, including Jake, wears vests. And everybody set your radios to the new frequency. It may not help if he has a scanner on, but the new frequency is on a different band, which makes his scanning much harder. Let's be ready to go in five."

Riley and the two unmarked cars eased to a halt in front of 14 Hickory Lane. Two of the six men crouched behind the cars, one with a rifle. Two other men headed down the sides of the property until a four-foot fence, surrounding a pool kept them from going further. One jumped the fence and continued to advance. Jake stayed in the car, monitoring the radio, while Riley and a uniformed officer approached the house.

At the front door, Riley rang the bell and drew his gun.

After a pause of about thirty seconds, the door opened to reveal a pretty young woman in shorts covered with an apron. She had her hair up, yellow rubber gloves on her hands, and a dishtowel clutched in one fist. Obviously frightened, she gingerly raised both hands. Riley spoke again.

"Please come out of the house, ma'am."

A two minute conversation confirmed that she was Mrs. Rebecca Adams, mother of two kids currently in school, wife of a husband currently at work. She went back into the house with the uniformed policemen and pulled a wallet out of her handbag. Opening it, she displayed a Connecticut driver's license with her photo, which showed that, indeed, Rebecca Adams was a resident of 14 Hickory Lane, Riverside. Riley radioed Brian, who confirmed the Adams name and address according to the reverse-lookup telephone directory. A call to Mr. Adams at his business established that he had been there all day, while Mrs. Adams confirmed that he never received packages at home.

"What the hell!" Riley was very upset.

"Anybody got a local street map?" asked Jake. One of the officers ran to his car and brought him one. Jake checked the Greenwich street listings, Riverside being a community within Greenwich. The atlas showed a Hickory Drive, a Hickory Lane, and a Hickory Street. Hickory Drive was on the western edge of the Greenwich border, while the other two were in Riverside. He said, "We've also got a Hickory Street a few blocks over. Maybe a mistake was made, maybe it was intentional. We'd better check the Hickory *Street*."

"Done," said Riley. "This time, Jake and I'll take an unmarked car while you guys park around the corner. Two of you get as near as you can to each side of the house. We'll soon see if we're on a wild goose chase." They drove a few streets east and stopped in front of 14 Hickory Street.

The house was a '60s split-level with the garage on the lower level. Although it appeared reasonably well maintained, in Riley's estimation it had an absentee-owner feel. Some of the foundation planting needed trimming, and there were a few dead limbs on one maple tree. All the window shades were pulled down. When the two officers had disappeared around the sides of the house, Riley walked up to the front door and pushed the bell, one hand on his gun. When there was no response after about thirty seconds, he pushed again. No response.

He walked back to the car and grabbed the radio

microphone. "Brian, get the judge out of the bar at the country club and get him to sign a warrant to enter 14 Hickory Street, Riverside, ASAP. He's familiar with the case. You'll have no difficulty convincing him to sign. In the meantime, we're going to check out the neighborhood. Call me when the warrant is ready and send it over in a squad car, not that we need the warrant to go in and grab somebody. Also check arrests, warrants, and neighbors. While you're at it, send over the entry team. With this guy's knowledge of explosives, we could be running into an ambush or booby trap."

Turning to Jake, Riley said, "You're going to hate this, but if there's trouble inside, don't get out of the car. I don't want anybody unarmed going in pursuit here."

Jake and Riley cruised through the neighborhood after units were posted where they could see the front and sides of the residence. Most of the houses were thirty to sixty years old, packed fairly densely at three or four per acre, with most showing the mature planting that would be expected given its growth over decades. They saw many instances of boxwoods or other planting untrimmed, encroaching on front doors so that a person could hardly pass through. The extensive underbrush, hedges, yews, forsythia, and other plantings served as a shield and a smorgasbord for the white-tailed deer throughout the area, but it also made it virtually impossible for any but a determined human to get through it without using the street or going around the end.

Riley's radio crackled to life.

"Chief, the judge was headed home when I reached him on his cell. He drove over to the station and signed the warrant. I'll have a patrol car bring it over."

As the sun was setting, Riley again walked up to the front door of the house, this time with two uniformed officers flanking him and all three in bullet-proof vests. He rang the bell and waited. Receiving no response, he tried it again. After a short interval, he nodded to the man on his right, Corelli, who carried a three-foot crowbar. The door popped open easily.

Riley called out, "Greenwich Police, anyone home?"

Corelli stood aside as his partner, Tsai, entered the house stealthily, followed by Riley. Jake stayed in the unmarked car, fighting down the urge to rush the door as well.

Riley and the two patrolmen found the interior of the house unnaturally dark for that time of the evening. They switched on flashlights and began an orderly procedure they had often rehearsed, but had seldom needed to put into practice. Corelli swept the front hall with light while Tsai cautiously aimed his beam into the living room. Finding no one and no visible tripwires, Tsai called out, "Living room clear!"

Seconds later, a loud crash came from upstairs, the sound of a heavy piece of furniture falling to the floor. Riley, Corelli, and Tsai all headed toward the source of the noise, taking the stairs two at a time. Riley radioed their movements to the three men outdoors, reminding Jake to stay in the car if the suspect emerged by the front door.

"Don't worry about it," Jake replied. "Anyway, there's nothing moving out here."

As the team headed down the second floor hall, cautiously approaching each doorway to clear the upstairs rooms, a door slammed in the rear of the house. *Dammit.* All that was in Riley's mind at that instant was whether, with all that dense growth, his men could see the entire scene clearly and had made it to the back yard. His radio crackled to life with an excited voice. It was Sam Petersen, one of the patrolmen outside the house.

"It's a forest back here. A white male must have come out of an upstairs dormer window and crossed the garage roof. We heard him drop to the ground, but he disappeared into the bushes before we saw him and headed into a neighbor's yard. I couldn't follow him. Harry took off where he thought the guy went, but got ensnared on some rosebushes and lost his trail. We'll keep going in the direction he was headed. He had to be going downhill, probably to the water. Big guy, dressed dark. That's all I could get a glimpse of."

Jake, in front of the house, heard the noises but saw nothing near the front entrance. *Stay in the car, hell,* he thought.

He moved quickly and quietly toward the end of the block, figuring that after a rear escape Lee would have to emerge from the foliage to reach a cross street. It was a 50-50 guess which street he'd take.

When a movement in the shadows caught Jake's attention, he sprinted toward it, half expecting to be shot at and half convinced he was reacting to a deer or a dog. He ran a block and a half, zigzagging between the street and several front yards, before realizing there was nothing in front of him.

Riley, seeing Jake re-enter the unmarked car, just shook his head.

When Corelli and Tsai returned to Lee's house later that evening for further examination and to cordon it off with crime-scene tape, they would check one of the upstairs rooms and find a large, cheap pine armoire face down on the floor, apparently pushed over by a mechanism mounted behind it on the wall. The device used a telescoping rotary steel arm driven by a small, powerful electric gear motor. It had, apparently, been triggered by the sound of Tsai's voice to expand quickly from six inches to two and a half feet, apply a thrust to the back of the armoire, and tip it over. Small wooden stops bolted into the floor in front of the armoire's feet ensured that it would go over smoothly and reliably.

Searching the yard, they would also find a mannequin lying in the bushes outside an open upstairs window. It had been ejected across the garage roof by a larger spring-loaded mechanism and fallen harmlessly into the foliage. It was over six feet tall and dressed in a cheap, dark suit. In an unhurried moment it looked obviously inanimate—but in the heat of the moment, by twilight, it had been lifelike enough to convince Petersen that it was a man running in panic and leaping from the roof of his garage.

In the inside pocket of the dummy's suit coat was a folded sheet of paper bearing a single line of laser-printed text:

Officers: Ever get the feeling you've been cheated?—J. Rotten, 1978

The man living here had invested considerable time in

engineering these simple and effective diversion-producing instruments, even though they would be used only once. He had expected hostile visitors and had been ready for them. There was no way to determine whether he had even been in the house that evening.

They had his den, but for a moment Riley feared that their quarry had outwitted them once again.

CHAPTER FORTY

"We may have just missed him, but we've taken away his base of operations and we're close!" Jake could hear intensity and excitement in Riley's voice. Nothing was rarer in Greenwich police work than the pursuit of a violent suspect and nothing energized his old friend quite as much. The team conducting the search had an experienced supervisor and would not let the excitement of the moment jeopardize their safety or the chain of custody of any evidence.

"I'm going to drive around the area and see if we can find anything. We still have to deal with the warrant. If our guys have any luck, they'll let us know."

Soon, the radio squawked. It was Petersen.

"Chief, while we were securing the house on Hickory, a report came in about activity on Cos Cob Harbor that might be our guy. A blue-and-white on the Cos Cob side picked up a speeder on radar, headed south on Strickland toward the docks, going maybe 60 or 70. Officer Alomar gave chase and got close to him near the junction of River Road, but the suspect beat him to the marina. When he got to the river, Alomar spotted the guy going to a dock right under Interstate 95. He jumped into a speedboat with twin Mercury outboards. That was too convenient not to have been prearranged. He was last seen going down the river through the harbor, out into the Sound."

Riley headed back to the station and had a few more words on the radio with Brian. He turned to Jake.

"You heard what he said. This is probably our suspect and we're going to chase him, but here's the problem. The Greenwich Police boat is hauled out for repairs and can't be put back in the water fast enough to chase this guy. The Coast Guard boat patrolling the Sound is way up at the other end in

Mystic—it'll take several hours to get here, even at top speed. The state got a mandate from the Coast Guard post-9/11 for each coastal town to have at least one boat on call at all times. Trouble is, many towns have not yet complied or have low-horsepower fishing boats good only for pulling somebody out of the water. That leaves the air, but there's no police surveillance plane or helicopter available, either.

"We're going to try to keep the boat in sight from the shore but we need to track him on the water or know when and where he goes ashore. Is there any chance you could follow him in the air?"

"Are you kidding? I'm on it!" said Jake.

"Take your cell phone," Riley suggested. He hesitated, the added, "And take your pistol, too. There's no telling where he'll go or what he'll do. All our officers are fully deployed, or I'd send someone with you."

They drove up to a squad car. Riley told the driver to take Jake home as quickly as possible, then told Kavanagh to guard the house and not let the excitement jeopardize the chain of evidence.

"I'll call you when I'm in the air," Jake said, jumping into the other car. "I can jack my cell phone into the plane's audio panel and hear it on my headset; otherwise there'd be too much noise."

In five minutes they were in his driveway.

After retrieving his gun, a .40-caliber Glock, and ammunition from a locked drawer in his study, Jake ran to the hangar, turned on the runway lights in the afternoon dusk, pulled *Shady Lady* outside, and closed the wide door. Abbreviating the normal pre-flight inspection, he fired up the engine, taxied to the runway, and took off to the north. Reversing direction and climbing to 1,500 feet, he quickly passed I-95, crossed over the shoreline, and called Riley.

"Where's he headed?" Jake asked when the connection was completed.

"He went out the channel and turned west toward the state line. We've contacted our Westchester colleagues and recommended an APB for Rye, Milton, and points west. The best we can do until you spot him is keep up surveillance with binoculars from onshore. From your vantage point, I'd expect you might cross paths with him around Little or Great Captain Island. Maybe Calf Island if he's hugging the shoreline. Stand by for anything else we can give you."

"Roger." Jake felt an odd rush of memories from his military days. He couldn't recall using the phrase "roger" with a straight face since he'd left the Air Force. Certainly not from a plane.

There was an undeniable joy to this. The controls felt like organic extensions of his hands, and the sensation of pursuit was exhilarating. Something rang in his ears that he'd heard an old throttle-jockey pal tell him dozens of times: Once you flew for the Air Force you were an Air Force pilot for life. Whatever else you might do later on, there was no such thing as an ex-pilot.

Let's see you outrun Shady Lady, *Lee,* he thought. *You may not be slowed down by anything as mundane as rationality or common decency, but you don't have an airplane.*

Then again, down on the water there were no Visual Flight Rules, no air-traffic controllers, and very few eyeballs at close range. For stealthy escapes by night, a powerful motorboat was hard to beat. *You picked the right vehicle for your purpose, Lee. There are many, many things wrong with you but stupidity is not one of them.*

Within a minute Riley was back on the line. "Cancel the earlier directions . . . it looks like Lee's taking evasive action. We got a report from one of our onshore officers that he made a left turn near the Captain Islands and is headed due south toward Long Island. It's hard to tell from shore in the dark, but he had his running lights on, and our guy caught a glimpse of the aft white light. It looked like he was moving fast, about 45 knots. If he's headed for a prearranged landing point, it could be anywhere on the Island's North Shore. We're alerting the local force accordingly."

Jake adjusted his bearing. "Got it. I'm cruising south, air speed 105 knots. Altitude lower now, around 1,000 for a better view."

"Excellent. There don't seem to be any other boats around, so you should pick him up easily, look for the wake. That's the good news. The bad is our spotter lost him around the Captain Islands . . . he seems to have used them as a blind."

"Clever bastard. I'm bound to catch up with him, but later rather than sooner if he keeps changing course. I'll yell the minute he's in view."

Jake reduced altitude again and scanned the water below. Nothing yet. As he approached the North Shore without spotting a boat landing, he veered left to make a 180 and begin sweeping the Sound in crisscross motions. It wasn't quite a coin toss whether Lee would go east or west, Jake figured: the odds favored the east, because Long Island's denser settlement closer to New York City would offer fewer places to stash a land vehicle. He guided *Shady Lady* back across the water toward Connecticut and called in his change of course to Dave.

As he scanned the water below, Jake noticed an onrush of adrenaline and silently reminded himself to keep his head on straight. *What was it Hemingway said about there being no hunting like the hunting of man?*

Crossing Long Island Sound by air takes only a few minutes, but each minute seemed agonizingly long. A few rough speed and mileage calculations told Jake that Lee probably hadn't gotten away. Still, as long as Lee's intended destination was unknown, the Helio's speed was only a theoretical advantage.

Suddenly, as the shoreline approached, a small craft came into view, bearing northeast off Greenwich Point, headed toward Shippan Point in Stamford. There was still no other marine traffic; it had to be him. Lee had reversed course after eluding the only observers he was aware of.

"Got him!" cried Jake. "This plane can fly as slowly as he's moving. As long as he doesn't slow down, I'll stay right over him and a bit behind. Altitude's back up around 2,000. His Mercs are pretty loud so there's an excellent chance he won't hear my engine. I'm just hoping he won't turn around and see me. I'll let you know if he goes ashore. I'm going to turn the cell down for a while so I can concentrate on my flying. The last thing I want is to get into trouble with another plane heading for La Guardia."

Jake followed the boat past Stamford Harbor toward the east, out Long Island Sound. It was a clear night with a rich array of stars and a nearly full moon. Even if the running lights weren't on, Jake could have followed the boat. The moon was very bright, and the boat cast a shadow that was easily seen. From Jake's altitude, even the bow-wave phosphorescence was visible as a glow in the water.

The boat followed an east-northeast course. Jake called Riley. "He's just gone past Long Neck Point in Darien, heading zero six one degrees ENE. The site is easy to spot because I can see the two remaining ends of a mansion sitting on two different lots."

Riley replied, "I know the place . . . it's where some crazy developer tore down the middle of a 50,000-square-foot home in the seventies."

"I can see it from the air," Jake confirmed. "Hold on, the boat's moving fast now. He's about to go outside Sheffield Island, off Norwalk."

Jake was able to maintain his speed at the same rate as the boat, but he couldn't tell from the air whether he had been noticed. The boat's course and speed hadn't changed, and Jake figured it was safe to assume he hadn't been heard.

In a few minutes, Jake spoke to Riley again. "We've gone by Westport's Sherwood Point. He got closer to land off Fairfield Beach, where I could make out the Johnson house under reconstruction, then went past Black Rock Lighthouse in Bridgeport.

"Wait a minute!" he said excitedly. "He's making a left turn and heading into Bridgeport Harbor. I'm going to descend to 1,000 feet to try and keep him in view if he pulls ashore. I'll keep the line open.

"Damn. Even though he's in the harbor, he's still at full speed and is kicking up a helluva wake. I can see the entire

Bridgeport harbor. It's shaped like a giant Y. He's headed for the west side of the left branch, near the electrical generation plant. You've seen it a hundred times from I-95; it's got the tall smokestack painted with concentric red circles. Okay, okay, he's slowing and turning in to the shore.

"Goddammit! He just looked up at me . . . his engine noise diminished, and he must have heard the plane." Jake paused.

"Now he's run the boat up on a small gravelly area that's exposed because the tide's halfway out. He's jumped out, climbed a ladder attached to the pier, and is running toward what looks to be an abandoned two-story brick industrial building. I'm going to circle to get lower and get the plane up on the same beach. Call you when I'm on shore."

"Okay," said Riley. "I'll alert the Bridgeport police, then head up the turnpike in that direction and wait for your call."

Jake turned in a tight circle to lose altitude, executed a well-controlled pontoon landing in the harbor to the northwest, and taxied in the direction of the boat. He ran the plane up on the gravel beside the boat and ground to a stop as the wheels sank into the mud beneath the stones. Jumping out, he grabbed a small anchor, clipped its line to an eye on the plane, and jammed it forcefully into the gravel. He used his foot to pack more gravel around it. With any luck, it would hold the plane when the tide came back in.

Riley rang back. "It looks like a nasty night in Bridgeport. I spoke to the chief over there and all available men are tied up with some trouble on I-95 South. An eighteen-wheeler lost control and jackknifed going about 75, spilling its cargo all over the road. Household products—thousands of ruptured containers of detergent and soap slicking up all three southbound lanes. Traffic's backed up about four miles. They're trying to get the Fire Department out there with hoses, but you know how well the PD and FD in some towns cooperate. They can get backup to you in maybe fifteen minutes, but the highway is the local priority. In the short run you're the closest man to Lee."

"Okay, I'm in pursuit. If he gets back in the boat, you'll

hear from me ASAP."

"Got it. Easy on the heroics until Bridgeport PD gets there or I do, okay? Don't forget you're a civilian."

"I've never felt more civilian in my life," Jake said and hit the End button.

He climbed the same ladder the killer had used. As he stepped off onto the pier, the side of the ladder knocked his cell phone out of its belt holster. The phone clattered to the ground at the bottom of the ladder, well out of reach. Jake sensed the urgency of moving quickly and continued without it, heading for the building.

He cautiously entered the wide overhead door where, for a moment, he was silhouetted in the moonlight. A bullet from within the warehouse ripped by and hit the ground ten feet to his rear. Startled, Jake jumped to his right and saw a muzzle flash as another bullet whizzed past his head. He crouched behind a rusty piece of machinery and reasoned that the bullet came from a catwalk running left to right through the cavernous space. His throat clenched up as he realized, a few seconds after the fact, what he had just seen and heard. For all the times he had seen gunfire, this was the first time it had been directed at him with intent.

As his eyes acclimated to the darker interior, Jake could make out other machinery in what had once been the boiler room of a three-story factory or warehouse. Steel drums and assorted castoff pieces of steel and pipe lay around the floor. There was a variety of machinery, including space heaters, hanging from the ceiling, and there were catwalks that had seen better days. Empty wine bottles were scattered around, and one corner held a pile of broken-up wooden Bordeaux cases. It occurred to Jake that the warehouse might have been used for wine and liquor distribution in an earlier life. Old furniture, beer bottles, discarded newspapers, and other detritus identified another, more recent, use of the building.

Jake pulled his Glock from its holster. Even in the dark, he knew the gun well enough to chamber a round and eject the Saf-T-Blok from the trigger in nearly complete silence. Sliding the small plastic guard into his pocket, he felt a bit better, knowing that the fight would be more balanced. *Closer to balanced, at least; who knows what Lee is armed with? Assume the worst.* He searched for a spot that would offer some sort of protection.

Suddenly, a three-foot piece of rusty pipe flew through the air, bounced off the machinery in front of him like an errant oversized boomerang, banged on the floor, and skidded out of sight. Jake aimed and fired at the space where he thought the pipe had originated, then immediately moved further right to a spot behind a massive column that supported several catwalks and the roof.

He stopped and strained to listen. Although the distant rumble of traffic on busy I-95 northbound and lots of impatient horns on the southbound side could be heard, mixed with the scratching of a rodent or two, there was no other sound in the building. Jake guessed that his opponent, not knowing he would be facing a gun, had been surprised by the shot and had not yet reacted. Either that or he was moving about silently.

Jake looked around carefully for any loose equipment on the floor that he could use to his advantage. He bent over, picked up a six-inch bolt, and threw it in the direction of the killer. It bounced off the catwalk and fell, hitting other metal and concrete surfaces on the way down. The killer got off two more shots aimed in Jake's direction in quick succession, but neither came close. Jake responded with two skillfully spaced rounds aimed toward the flashes from the killer's weapon. These missed as well.

Neither of us can see the other. This could be a matter of pure chance.

In the lull that followed, Jake searched for a better hiding place and moved deeper into the building. To his right, he spied a flight of steps with diamond wire steel treads leading up to one of the catwalks. He bent over to offer a smaller target while moving and ran for the third step, which was protected by another massive column and would shield him from the killer. This time his movement brought no response from the catwalk above.

He's holding still up there. Reloading? Rethinking his options?

Jake's heart was racing and not in a familiar way. He was accustomed to feeling his pulse quickened and his perceptions heightened from flying or a good hard workout, but this was a foreign, disagreeable experience. Some of his thoughts seemed to be running on autopilot. He wanted not just to survive and prevail, but to damage his opponent. Assuming the man on the catwalk was in fact the suspect, Lee, Jake wanted to see him flushed out, knocked down, broken in spirit and body, and either frog-marched out of the building or hauled out dead.

Recognizing this state of mind as a classic, hard-wired fight-or-flight adrenaline response did not reduce it a bit. His task was to make it useful.

"Who the hell are you?" Jake barked. *Distract him. Confuse him. Get his attention and wreck his head.*

"Why, Jake," said the man above, "That's rather impolite. I know *you*. I have gone out of my way to learn everything about you. To know you . . . intimately. Haven't you the good breeding to show your curiosity about me in more respectful terms?"

He paused theatrically, took a deep breath, and said in a voice of steel, "My name is Daniel Lee. I am your brother."

CHAPTER FORTY-ONE

As he sped east toward Bridgeport through Norwalk, Westport, and Fairfield at eighty miles an hour, Riley's thoughts were also speeding, second-guessing involving Jake in the Wine Killer case.

I'm a get-the-job-done kind of guy, he thought. *Pragmatic, decisive, usually correct. But this time, I'm not so sure. Jake is a civilian, after all, untrained for police work. Maybe he's been pulled too far in. His involvement in this chase sure as hell goes way beyond what wise decision-making should allow. I'm at fault for letting this happen.*

We've done a remarkable job with this case and its complexities, but has it gone beyond our abilities and our available manpower?

That wasn't his real concern, though, he realized. The skill of his team wasn't at issue; his true fear lay somewhere else. *If Jake is hurt or killed while helping solve this case,* he admitted, *I'll never forgive myself.*

There were more thoughts, but Riley had reached the outskirts of Bridgeport and had to focus on his driving.

CHAPTER FORTY-TWO

Brother?

Jake stared at the point from which the voice came, his situation forgotten until Lee started to move. Then he quickly studied the room for alternative positions as his vision adapted and more details of the vast space came into view. As long as Lee stayed in the corner of the catwalk, using an internal wall as a blind, Jake would have to risk a moment of visibility to get a decent angle for a shot. If this was high stakes chess, it was all about positioning, minus one key assumption: a chess player doesn't customarily wonder whether his opponent is rational.

"I don't know what your game is or who the hell you are," he managed to get out. "But you sure as hell aren't my brother."

"Oh, I beg to differ," Lee said, with unnatural calm. "I am indeed your brother . . . and not *just* your brother. I am, my dear Jake, your twin."

Jake sat still, momentarily stunned by the seemingly fantastical claim. He heard no movement above, just the voice.

"In 1961, our mother bore you, but exhibiting an ignorance that continues to mystify me, the cow apparently didn't know she was still pregnant with another child. Fortunately, we're not identical twins. Nevertheless, to my everlasting and great regret, I am your fraternal twin, your closest blood relative. As a matter of fact, in a rather fitting twist of fate—" Jake heard a sound that might have been a laugh. "—I am now your only blood relative.

"Did you know, my clever brother," the voice continued, "that although twins are almost always born on the same day, there are occasional exceptions?"

"What are you talking about?" Jake asked, with an

increasing sense of unease. "I. . . ."

"Interrupt me again and you won't live to hear the rest of my story," Lee said, emphasizing his words with another shot from his pistol. The bullet ricocheted off a concrete column and struck the wall some twelve feet behind Jake.

Does he know where I am? Was that a wild guess or a bank shot?

"That would be a shame, as it's a story I have waited a very long time to tell. It is," he continued with a flourish, "an exceptional story. You and I are one of those biological exceptions. We are each, in our own way, *exceptional*."

Jake eyed the column. If Lee could hit it, he could hit Lee from behind it. If he could get to it unscathed, that is, and if Lee didn't move. On the other hand, maybe the killer was trying to draw him there.

He's been rehearsing this for years, Jake thought as Lee's revelation continued.

"Some weeks after your birth, our mother and father wrapped up their precious newborn in swaddling clothes and embarked on a trip to Hong Kong. Our mother, still pregnant and not knowing it, popped me out in the filthy, second floor office of a Chinese doctor in Kowloon. Alas, it seems she never realized the miracle she had accomplished.

"In those days, Caucasian babies were much in demand for adoption in the Orient. So, you see, when the doctor discovered the stupid woman didn't know about me—thinking I was nothing more than weight gained during her pregnancy or perhaps dreading I might be a tumor—he drugged her and delivered the baby."

Try rattling him. "A tumor is a pretty fair description of what you are, Lee," Jake called out. "What you've become. You got anything to be proud of, dirt bag? Ever think about the people in seven towns who are dead because you thought a little game with the alphabet would show everybody your towering intellect?"

The response was a spray of bullets. The muzzle of a weapon emerged from behind the wall; Lee himself did not. His aim was indiscriminate. Small puffs of dust and debris rose in a punctuated line across the warehouse floor.

That was an automatic. Hell of a way to handle hecklers.

Jake did his best to keep his breathing both regular and quiet. *Two guns? At least two. If he'd only had the automatic, he'd have started with it. Why didn't he, anyway? Frugal with his ammunition, presumably.*

The right tool for each part of a job. Certain things about Lee are not insane.

Lee continued speaking. "Not being particularly skilled in what was, after all, a rather basic medical procedure and, of course, having no assistance from an unconscious patient, that quack of a doctor damaged my facial nerve using the wrong forceps to drag me from the womb. I've had to live with the unhappy result ever since." He touched his face in the darkness. "As your twin, I am like you, my handsome brother, but, alas, as you'll see soon enough, an extremely distorted reflection of you."

Not waiting for a response from Jake, he continued. "Doctor Quack sent our mother away after a few hours with a diagnosis of food poisoning, or something to that effect, to explain her cramps. He didn't tell her she'd had another child, and she was too groggy, sore, and confused to guess.

"Soon after, the old bastard sold me to a wealthy Chinese family, and I was raised in Hong Kong as their son. But I hadn't been born to them, and they didn't love me. In public, I was a status symbol, despite my disfigurement—in private, little more than their slave. When I displeased them, which I managed to do with some frequency, they hit me, always where it wouldn't show. You can't imagine how I longed for the day when I'd be old enough to hit back."

Gonna take that sentimental journey home, Jake thought. *Now's the time.*

He broke for the column, running in a zigzag pattern among the trash and rusted machinery. Lee fired the automatic again and missed; one round struck a steel drum with a clang that filled the room. Jake took advantage of the noise, spinning to fire twice at the catwalk, drive Lee back to his safe niche, and buy himself enough seconds to reach the space behind the column.

"You are becoming rather unfraternal," Lee called out. "Did being an only child make you this defensive? Do you have no regard for your own blood?"

The column was roughly three feet wide. Above his head on the right side, Jake saw where Lee's earlier bullet had struck it, dislodging concrete and exposing rebar. A clump of concrete lay on the floor behind him. Estimating angles as if he were shooting pool, Jake realized he could reach it without entering Lee's line of fire. Silently and carefully he picked up the clump, gauged its shape in his hand, decided it would fly almost straight, and then threw it hard into a sheet of steel ductwork across the room.

Growing up in Hong Kong, you blood-crazed freak, I bet you never saw anything like my split-fingered fastball.

Jake leapt quickly to his right from behind the column as the ductwork boomed sixty feet away. Lee emerged long enough for a quick burst of fire toward the sound. Jake fired twice toward the catwalk and darted back behind the column. Lee's voice leapt an octave as he emitted a yelp of pain, stifling it just as abruptly.

Got him!

Once, probably. Somewhere.

"Don't delude yourself that anything you do is going to save you," Lee called out, his voice showing strain. "If you've been living by the myth of Virtue Rewarded, it's well past time you grew out of that illusion. Your story ends tonight, Jake, but not before you've heard the rest of mine."

This guy would rather bleed to death than shut up, Jake thought. *Should have sought a career haranguing crowds. Politics, maybe. Or the televised pulpit.*

But Jake could not ignore what Lee was saying.

"When I was twelve," Lee continued, "I was searching for money in my so-called father's desk and found the papers the doctor had given him when I was sold. I set out to find that doctor . . . for what reason, I'm not sure. Perhaps to get a scrap of evidence about my real family. Perhaps to punish him. Maybe even to kill him. By the time I did find him, he was an old man and sick. Wanting to clear his conscience before he died, the old fool told me what had happened and asked my forgiveness. I thanked him by helping myself to the few valuable trinkets he had in his rooms. It didn't matter, though." He smiled coldly. "I had what I wanted. Information. Fortuitously, my Chinese parents brought me to America, and I was able to trace my real parents—our parents—back here."

Jake remained silent, awestruck even while calculating angles and timing, digesting the news. It was true that his family had taken such a trip to Hong Kong. He had been far too young to have a memory of the voyage abroad, but he had heard the story, seen the photos, regaled first Melinda and later Cat with the family legends that had conferred on him the title of Youngest Globetrotter. As he was growing up, his mother had even made jokes about how heavy she was at that time and about the illness that finally helped her to lose weight. But could the rest of this story be true?

He saw several drops of blood fall from the catwalk, reflect moonlight from an upper window, and spatter in the dust below.

"How could a woman have twins so far apart? That's more than two months, for God's sake," Jake challenged.

"It happens very infrequently. But as I've discovered, sometimes there are as much as two-and-a-half months between deliveries of twins. The medical profession calls it an interval delivery. Too bad you won't get the chance to discuss the phenomenon with your pretty physician friend."

"I don't understand," Jake said, stalling for time, his mind churning. "Even if what you say is true . . . ."

"*Don't call me a liar!*" Lee shouted. He accompanied his outburst with two seconds of automatic fire. This time the bullets struck closer.

No more uncertainty about this: he knows I'm behind this column.

"Assuming what you say is true," Jake corrected himself calmly, "what is it you want? Why go after wine lovers?"

Lee's mood turned darker. With a voice of steel he said, "Good old Frederick Jackson Halsey, our dear father, never knew he had another son. As a result, I grew up despised by my Chinese *parents*, while you had *everything*." He spat the words out and stopped, trembling.

Jake looked cautiously around the column to see whether Lee had returned to vulnerable space. As he was changing position, another shot rang out. This time the bullet struck a piece of machinery, ricocheted, and drove into the fleshy part of his left thigh.

Dropping his gun and grasping the thigh with both hands, Jake fell, crumpling to the floor in extreme pain.

The bullet had passed almost through the muscles of his thigh. The entire lower left quadrant of his body was an inferno.

He was dimly aware of footsteps slowly coming down the catwalk stairs in the background, but he couldn't move. Standing and hopping on his right leg was out of the question. He was too concerned with his injury to pay full attention to the steps. He pulled out his handkerchief and tied it tightly above the wound in his leg, hoping to slow the flow of blood.

"Well, fee fie foe fum, I smell the blood of New England scum! Now *you* get to do some of the bleeding. Good clean blood, Jake. So blue. Connecticut's finest. I confess it's good clean fun to watch some of it flow."

Jake heard the voice from across the room. A new tone had entered it, playful and menacing, in love with its own sound in the cavernous room.

"At last, Big Brother," Lee exulted, "a modicum of fairness enters this family."

The steps progressed across the floor, coming closer, until Jake was aware of a tall man standing above him. Lee kicked Jake's Glock into the distance, then backed up and stood about five feet away, pointing his gun at the prone figure. A second gun, larger, was holstered at his side.

In the odd lighting Jake could see that his opponent was roughly his own height, slightly heavier, and dressed head to toe in black. Lee was bleeding from the left shoulder, but not enough to incapacitate him. His face, suddenly and eerily illuminated from beneath by a flashlight gripped in his left hand, seemed to sag on the right side. An asymmetrical haircut hid most of the disfigurement behind a long shock of greasy, light-brown hair.

"Look carefully at me," Lee said. "Don't you see anything you recognize in my features? Is my face not somewhat familiar to you?" He began laughing in maniacal triumph—then went stock still, aimed just to the right of Jake's face, and fired another bullet, which whizzed past inches from his target's ear. Jake felt the breeze and held his breath.

"But allow me to finish my story," Lee said, regaining self-control.

"The family that adopted me emigrated to Boston in response to a promise of work and wealth. Instead they found failure, which only worsened my relationship with them. When I was fifteen, I took a baseball bat to my adopted father—so very American, don't you think? I never did find out whether he lived or died. Not that it really mattered to me. There's one thing I discovered long ago that you never will. Take my word for it: when you have to hurt people, the idea that it hurts you too is *extremely* overrated.

"Killing is much easier than common people assume. Too bad you'll never get to try it. I suspect you'd have developed a taste for it. I've noticed you respond avidly to certain pleasures, and the pleasure of utterly vanquishing another human being is far more exquisite than anything you've known from your wretchedly overpriced fermented fruit juices. It's been *delicious* developing new ways to take others down. Sometimes watching them die right away, sometimes just relishing the knowledge that they're to die at some unknown time, farther enough along that your little cleanup crew wouldn't have much chance of seeing my pattern. I suppose, to be fair, I should compliment you on finally catching on. I would have expected no less.

"But I am rambling, dear Jake. You deserve to know at least a few more things about the man who is about to kill you, the man who has the pleasure of mastering you," Lee continued. "After I homered my way out of Boston's lovely, leafy suburbs, I moved to the city and lived on the street for a while. You would have loved it there, my Yalie brother. While you were playing lacrosse, chasing debutantes, and hobnobbing with future diplomats in New Haven, I was among people who could have eaten you alive and picked their teeth with your bones. Surviving among them had its occasional compensations. But, somehow, repaying the old Chinaman for all those beatings and winning my freedom, such as it was, didn't make me feel any better. I was motivated by a desire to get back at my *real* parents—*your* parents—*our* parents—for leaving me in China and condemning me to a life that wasn't worth living.

"I won myself a scholarship to MIT. Oh yes, I share the family brains and talents. When I graduated, I got a succession of good jobs and made some money. There is always a call for a man who can do what I do with numbers. But it meant nothing. I was still the freak, still the outcast. My parents, who should have raised me and protected me, had ruined my life, and I decided to dedicate that life to ruining the parents who abandoned me. More than that: putting my mark on the *world* that abandoned me. Whatever happens after tonight, you cannot deny that this vile world now bears my mark."

So far over the top, Jake decided, *he couldn't find the top if he used radar. Missed a hell of a career in B movies.*

And what career have I missed?

"But you see, fate has never been my friend," Lee said and smiled crookedly. "By the time I had amassed sufficient skills and money to actually do something about the situation, the family wine business had been sold, and both our parents had died. So I vowed to correct their wrong by destroying, among other things, the one thing that paid for their lifestyle—wine. It's been an unimaginable joy killing wine lovers and destroying wine collections. Alongside all the oenophilic swells, I particularly relished the truck driver, because all he did with the stuff was haul it around; he probably drank Budweiser on his own time, don't you think? Sending him on his little voyage, you might say, demonstrated my range. The unfortunate Mr. Cox was far enough outside the range your public payroll friends could imagine that he undoubtedly bought me at least a few more months to work.

"And then, when I was done, dear brother, I was going to come after you, you and your delectable new doctor friend in the bargain. I trust that you and she have read the warning shot I recently fired across the bow of her computer."

"Why involve her in this?"

"That is no longer your question to ask. Trust in this, though: your blood is valuable to me, perhaps supremely so, but it will not be the last I spill. Mastery, to be pure, cannot be anything less than total and arbitrary. We started with the same exceptional blood, but yours is polluted by pleasure. Trivial hobbies. Wenching. *Wine*.

"Have you ever purified your blood through pain? Have you ever shed enough of it to know true blood from false? I have. My life hasn't been a mockery, Jake. I've contended with things that would have destroyed you, and I've mastered them. Your life has been one sport after another; nothing you've mastered has been worth the effort. You have your pathetic inventions, but not one has brought you any interesting form of power. The airplanes you toyed with out West, as if preparing for war—your pardon—as if *serving your country*—were just another graduate degree. The witty little giddy little bitch you married. The great adventure of yuppie parenthood. And then your big tragedy, your noble pose. The scarred, bereaved reclusive hero, the mysterious public benefactor with a police puppy for a best pal. Christ, you make me sick. Cry me a river, for your pretty little dead little darlings. From what I've learned about you, I could vomit you an ocean."

Lee's voice was becoming a shriek. Jake watched a frightened rat run along a wall and recalled what a coach at Greenwich High had once said about injuries: a man in serious pain might stay silent or he might roar, but a man doesn't shriek. If you hear a man shrieking, either the pain isn't real or the man isn't. Shrieking is theatrics, nothing to be trusted.

He's giving a command performance. This is material he's been writing for decades, for an audience of one. He's never heard applause. Would it distract him?

"So what does it mean, Lee? Everything you've done. If my life adds up to trivia, what's your score?"

"The simple, unescapable, unceasing, and irrefutable demonstration of what is real and what is not real. I am as real as death, brother. Real in all the ways a jumped-up boomer bastard like you is unreal, no matter how hard the world has tried to convince me otherwise. I wasn't even left for dead— Fred and Mary left me for *nothing*. I am not quite so random, you know by now. *I am the master of liquids and numbers!*" Lee shouted at the top of his voice, waving his pistol at the catwalk, then he dropped back down to an icy whisper.

"And I am the master of you."

Jake held his tongue. One word in opposition, he sensed, and Lee would snap. And shoot.

A fighting man needs the taste of blood.

Lee walked a few paces to the right without shifting his gaze, rubbed his wounded shoulder, then pivoted dramatically and pointed the automatic directly at Jake. "You grew up surrounded by reminders that your existence mattered. Imagine spending every minute of your life surrounded by the opposite message and forced to prove it wrong. Perhaps you would have become highly skilled at these proofs, as I have. Or perhaps you don't have the gumption to rise through muck and make order out of the viscosity of chaos. Perhaps you would have sunk back down and dissolved into the puddle of low and common beings, the world of snot and vomit and jissom and tissue and all manner of organic foulness. Perhaps only the man who shouts his 'I am' in blood, *because he has to*, deserves to taste the joys I've come to know.

"It boils down purely to this, Jake: I am real, and you are not."

Jake offered no answer for this.

Not that I don't have one.

"It's so ironic, don't you think? Our father made his fortune in the wine and liquor business, yet I was left with a birth defect that compromised my ability to taste. I never did see the appeal of the nasty stuff."

With all due respect for what he's suffered, this is the most self-absorbed, pity-hungry SOB I've ever heard in my life. The longer he stands there explaining, the better my chances. Let him rant.

"Surely something could have been done," Jake said, scanning the area for anything he could use as a weapon. "Could still be done . . . ."

Lee continued as if in a trance, apparently unaware that Jake had spoken. "In the beginning, I bought wine—or shoplifted it—and used the full bottles for target practice. One for you, Pop. And one for you, dear Mother. As the bottles shattered and the wine flew out, I imagined it was their blood, their blood gushing into the air and staining the ground. Wine and blood . . . blood and wine. So red, so perfect. Dripping from the bottles . . . staining the ground . . . .

"You can't imagine how satisfying that was. I did it over and over." Lee was rocking back and forth now, repeating "over and over" as if reliving the pulling of the trigger, the gushing of the wine. Jake contemplated making a move, wondering whether his damaged leg would support a sudden lunge.

As if reading Jake's mind, Lee suddenly focused on him once more. "If we weren't about to permanently part company," he purred, "I could take you to where I lived then. I could show you the stained ground." He paused. "Why, we could see whether your blood would match the wine. Is that what flows in your veins, Jake? A vintage Bordeaux? A Grand Cru Burgundy? Surely, if you had any real imagination, you might have deduced a few things about me from that lovely coed with the wine in her veins."

Lee's face, with exaggerated effort, slowly constructed his best approximation of a smile. "But I have always been ahead of you. Ahead of all of you."

Have you ever tasted blood, Halsey? The unfit never survive.

Lee abruptly returned to reality. "Our parents may not have known what really happened, but I blame them both for being stupid enough not to know that our mother was still pregnant with me. So wealthy, so sophisticated, and so very stupid.

"And yet, their mistake was one of time and circumstance, so random, so *unnecessary*. If only fetal heart monitors had been available at the time. If only sonograms had become standard before the 1980s. Today, they tell me, the interval deliveries that do occur tend to be deliberately induced. *They don't result in accidents like me.*

"But these are all rather feeble rationalizations, don't you think? Even though it was night and he apparently didn't examine our mother, the Connecticut doctor was an imbecile not to know there was a second baby. By not knowing, he allowed our mother to take her trip. He allowed her to deliver me in that filthy office, to let that Chinese bastard hurt me, *to force me to live in hell.* Luckily for him, the stupid man died of old age, died in his Greenwich mansion, before I could get to him, died before I could make him suffer prolonged agony for his unforgivable mistake."

Lee's voice was becoming raspier, Jake noticed, and just perceptibly quieter. *How much of him is in the present and how much in the past? If he's drifting, if his wound is blurring his concentration, he may not have the drop for long.*

"You, on the other hand," Lee resumed, "have been on my radar for a long time. I was saving the pleasure of dealing with you for last, but you seem to insist that I deviate from my timetable. You know, for a while, I didn't even consider you a target, since you had nothing directly to do with my principal complaints.

"But you began to spoil my fun, brother dear, and must therefore be eliminated. A pity it's to happen here and prematurely; I've had some unusual delights prepared for you for quite some time now. I'll just have to savor those as fantasies. Certainly, you must have some dim awareness how someone like me relies on the imagination, and only on the imagination, for the kind of recreation that seems to come rather easily to you? Or perhaps one day I'll run across someone else who deserves those particular delights as richly as you do, Big Brother. Some of them, come to think of it, might be exquisitely well-suited to that brightly plumed bird of paradise Dr. Taylor."

"You have no quarrel with her. Leave her out of this."

Ignoring Jake, Lee continued, "You have to admit there is a certain justice in the fact that once again there will be only one Halsey son.

"But *my* inventions, *my* choices, will reach people. I will create change. We know how the press responds when a masterful mind appears . . . how the *world* responds. Wine will never mean the same thing once all these lovely little stories are public knowledge. Some team of tabloid hacks will smell their Pulitzer in the Halsey family's ashes. They will share my exploits, celebrate my genius. And when that happens, all of those dilettantes, all of those privileged nobodies sipping Bordeaux at their fancy tables, all of them will remember my name—*our* names, Big Brother. When that happens, wine will no longer mean pleasure. Wine will be inseparable from death.

"Do you have any other questions? Is there anything else you are *dying* to know," he smiled at the irony, "before I put another few bullets in your body?" He raised his gun again. "Say hello to Mom and Dad for me."

Jake moved then, throwing himself across the floor as abruptly and as far as he could, wincing as he endured another silent shriek of pain from his left leg. Even as he did, a shot rang out. A red hole spurting blood appeared in Lee's left chest. The man's eyes widened; he dropped his gun and fell over, dead before he hit the concrete floor, the good side of his face smashed to a pulp.

Jake turned to look at the open door, and there, backlit in the moonlight, stood Dave Riley, still in the slight crouch of his wide shooting stance, still holding his gun in a professional double-handed grasp. After a moment, Riley lowered his hands, straightened, and walked forward, his eyes on the figure on the floor. He kicked the man's gun aside and examined Lee's body for any sign of life. Finding none, he turned to his friend, noting the bloodied leg, the ashen face.

"Buddy boy," he said crossing to Jake, "that was a close one. I homed in on the red and white smokestack and arrived here just in time to hear a big chunk of the story. I couldn't shoot the son of a bitch until I was sure I wouldn't miss and provoke him to fire at you, but I got him. I got him," Riley repeated the words, as if he had to convince himself they were true. "That was one guy I think our species can probably get along without."

"You know, you didn't have to wait until he was finished," said Jake, smiling weakly.

Riley studied the body on the floor as he radioed for an ambulance and helped Jake to a more comfortable position. He couldn't help but look for the resemblance Lee had claimed.

"Was his story true?" he asked, quietly, while they were waiting for help to arrive.

Jake started to answer as he attempted to arise to a standing position, but was suddenly overcome by a wave of nausea and pain.

Riley put an arm around his shoulder to support him. "I think we'd better move you to a hospital," he said. "I know a pretty lady doc just down the highway who might be available to look at that leg."

Jake chose that moment to pass out.

CHAPTER FORTY-THREE

Jake was initially treated at the emergency department of Bridgeport's St. Vincent's Hospital, then spent two days in Greenwich Hospital until Catherine pronounced him recovered enough to go home. Reaching Greenwich Hospital at dawn, he'd slept most of the first day, groggy from the painkillers he'd been given after they'd removed the bullet and cleaned and sutured his wound. Late the second morning, as soon as he was awake enough to think coherently, he reached for the phone and dialed Riley's private number at the GPD.

"So?" he said as soon as he heard Riley's voice.

"Well, Sleeping Beauty is awake," the detective replied. "How's the leg?"

"Still there, apparently," Jake countered. "Feels like barbed wire got dragged through the middle of it, but so far they say there's no sign of infection. Are you going to tell me what's been going on or do I have to break out of here and come pound it out of you?"

"As it happens, I'm just heading out to an appointment. How about I drop by in, say, an hour and bring you up to speed."

"How about if you're late for the appointment and talk to me now?"

"Can't do, pal. Think happy thoughts and I'll be there before you know it."

Riley hung up, leaving Jake with no choice but to wait. As he lay there, he thought about the story Daniel Lee had told him. As improbable as it seemed, the relationship the man had described rang true. His family's Hong Kong trip was real, as was his mother's illness and her treatment by a Chinese doctor. And there was the DNA; maybe Lee's tale was the only way to make sense of that.

Jake struggled to recall the man's face from their encounter in the dimly lit warehouse. As much as he hated to admit it, he had indeed seen a distorted image of himself in Lee's features. The ones on the left side, at least. Even their physiques were roughly similar. *My God*, he thought. *I was related to the Devil.*

His thoughts were interrupted by the arrival of a nurse who examined his wound, checked his temperature, and handed him a selection of pills of various colors, standing over him as he swallowed them one by one. By the time she had completed her ministrations and Jake had eaten a little of a bland hospital lunch, he found himself yearning to doze off once more.

As he slept, he dreamed that he and Melinda and Courtney were running through narrow streets in a foreign city, pursued by an army of torch-bearing men. Every one of the men looked exactly like him, except that their faces were all the colors of the rainbow and everything in between.

"Stop, brother! Stop!" they yelled in chorus, as they ran. But Jake knew he couldn't stop or they would take everything he had, everything that was running alongside him. He had to protect Melinda, had to protect Courtney. He gathered the baby in his arms as he and Melinda ran as hard as they could. While the men never got closer, they matched the Halseys' pace step for step, chasing them furiously, shouting as they thundered along behind.

A hand on Jake's shoulder jolted him awake, ending the bizarre dream.

"I got away a little early," Riley said, looking down at him. "You okay?"

"Yeah," said Jake pulling himself up to a sitting position. The leg still hurt like hell when he moved it against the sheets. "Tell me what you found."

Riley pulled up a chair and planted himself next to Jake's bed.

"First, I thought you'd like to know that we secured the *Shady Lady* so she was protected the other night. Yesterday, I drove one of my guys up to Bridgeport to bring her home. The plane is in perfect shape, and it's in your hangar." Jake nodded and raised a hand appreciatively. "We even picked up your cell phone," Riley added, putting it on a side table, "though I'm afraid the tide may have done it a bit of damage.

"Now, as to the case. To start with, the state lab got its mass spectrometer repaired and calibrated. You were right about the wine cellar in Ivoryton. Lee had painted some pretty nasty stuff on those bottles. The lab has identified two of its three components."

"Go on," Jake urged, his attention now completely focused on the man beside him.

"The first ingredient was DMSO, dimethyl sulfoxide, a commercial solvent that's a byproduct of the paper industry. The tech told me it was identified in 1953 and is still one of the most studied, but least understood pharmaceuticals.

"I don't know where he got the idea, but the lab guys think the reason Lee used it is that it can pass through membranes and carry other drugs with it. Medicines dissolved in DMSO retain their properties a long time and are easily absorbed by the skin."

"So he was using it to carry something else?" Jake interrupted.

"Oh yes, indeed," Riley answered. "He was using it to carry the curare Arlene told us about.

"Besides being a deadly poison that was once used as on arrowheads by Amazon headhunters, curare is used medically to relax and then paralyze breathing muscles or to stop convulsions. It's also been used to halt eye movement during corneal transplants. Real curare is pretty damn rare in the United States because it's been superseded by other products or by synthetic versions carrying fewer side effects.

"The horror of curare poisoning is that the victim is awake and aware, but can't move or speak until he loses consciousness. I remember reading somewhere that South American Indians measured the potency of their curare by pricking the skin of a frog with a drop of it on a needle. The number of leaps the frog took before stopping and dying became an index of the poison's effectiveness."

"Son of a bitch!" Jake said. "So Lee intended to asphyxiate his Ivoryton victims. The curare would be absorbed through handling, and the DMSO would be the agent to get it into the bloodstream. Several people could have been killed: whoever went to the cellar to get the bottle, the waiter, and maybe customers. Depending on how many frog-leaps strong the batch was would determine how fast people started dropping. Anybody who handled the bottles would have stopped breathing."

"That's right," said Riley, "There was also a third ingredient in the mix, an unidentified substance they think was used as a protection to keep the solution from denaturing, losing its potency, or breaking down. The lab didn't feel that its identification was an issue, since the active ingredient and the poison were identified."

"So he used poisoning twice," Jake observed. "Mitchell Livingston, then a group at the Copper Beech Inn. Only slight differences in the MO: poison *on* a bottle instead of in one. Looks like Lee was running out of imagination."

Riley glanced at his watch. "I'm sure you want to know what's in the Riverside house, but I haven't made a thorough search of the place yet. Right now, I'm afraid I've gotta run. Catherine told me you're getting out of here tomorrow morning. We've got the house sealed off and guarded, and the landlord's flying in from Chicago for questioning later this afternoon. There's no rush with Lee dead, but I'm giving the place a look tonight before we let the forensics team in, then again with them tomorrow by daylight. How about if I drop by the house after dinner tomorrow night and fill you in on the rest?"

It was not at all what Jake had in mind, but he curbed his impatience. The Wine Killer case had not been the only thing on Riley's plate, and there was certainly a great deal of work demanding attention.

"Sounds good," he answered. "I appreciate your taking the time to come over here at all."

Riley smiled. "I fear I'm hearing drug-induced diplomacy, but I'll take it." Rising, he looked at Jake. "Take care of yourself."

Jake nodded. It would take a lot more drugs to keep him from staying awake most of the night speculating about Lee's house and the strange story of the man. His brother. Even silently, he could barely pronounce those words.

It was 8:00 p.m. and Riley's feet were killing him. He had been standing at the one-way glass for nearly two hours watching the Green-Pezzi tag team grill Daniel Lee's absentee landlord. Jerry DeWinter was an investment banker who had followed his job to Chicago in a corporate restructuring five years earlier. He had paid little attention to his Connecticut property, screening applicants' financial qualifications and nothing else. Lee was only the second of two tenants to occupy the split-level since DeWinter had vacated it himself and opted to use it for steady income rather than put it on the market.

All DeWinter knew of Lee was that his massive cash payment—four years' rent up front—had eliminated any other questions about his background and activites. He didn't even know him as Daniel Lee; to DeWinter his tenant was J.A. Bosch. They had found each other through Craigslist on the Internet and had never met face to face.

Riley didn't think he'd ever admit it out loud, but he found Pezzi and Green's interrogation technique impressive. At least in this case. Pezzi played the classic short-leashed, snarling, bulldog, using fear as a weapon. Green was the sober, calming, maternal confidante once her hotheaded colleague had stormed out of the room. In contrast to his real-life personality around the office and in the field, Pezzi came on to DeWinter as cynical, dangerous, and absolutely humorless. Green had been the one to break the tension with occasional jokes. *The Oscar for best supporting role this year*, thought Riley, *goes to Officer Anthony Pezzi.*

The important thing was that DeWinter's statements to each detective alone and to the pair together were consistent and plausible, if embarrassing. He had managed his property naively and unwisely, never visiting in person or communicating with Mr. Bosch in any form after the cashier's check had gone through. By all estimates, he had no knowledge of what was going on in the basement. His surprise and horror were believable. As the conversation progressed, its tone became steadily less adversarial. Green and Pezzi grew satisfied that the owner was not complicit, and Riley, debriefing them before the witness was discharged, agreed.

It was now nearly sundown, and time to visit 14 Hickory Street.

Riley parked on the street, walked up, acknowledged the patrolman guarding the front door, and ducked under the yellow crime-scene tape. The foyer, like the rest of the house, was forbiddingly dark. He donned rubber gloves before turning on the lights.

Every ground-floor window was covered with cheap, garish faux-damask curtains made of synthetic materials that looked heavier than they were, but still effectively blocked light and vision. Natural light had not penetrated this house for some time. The walls of the living room were mostly bare, wallpapered with fuzzy maroon felt, uneven rectangular patterns showing the places where sunlight had once faded the paper around large picture frames, now removed. A two-step descent separated a large conversation pit and fireplace from the rest of the living room, but the lower segment held only one item of furniture, a Naugahyde easy chair with an adjustable footrest and hard plastic lever. Large heaps of ash indicated that the fireplace was more than decorative.

A few photographs adorned the front foyer, isolated spots in the living room, and the fireplace mantle. Prominent in the latter location was a bamboo-framed shot of a handsome Chinese couple in front of their house, with a long-haired, Anglo-looking toddler lurking in the background. Riley understood readily where this image fit in the story Daniel Lee had told Jake.

The kitchen was in abominable condition. Rust stains marred the porcelain sink, ancient clumps of hardened and unidentifiable food decorated the floor around the trash can, and no fewer than nine roach trap disks were strewn around the linoleum floor. Appliances included a trash compactor and an encrusted toaster oven, but no dishwasher. Riley had to suppress his urge to turn away as he neared the sink and caught a whiff from the garbage disposal.

He checked the refrigerator, opening it carefully by a corner of the handle to reduce the chance that his gloves would smear anything that might be of interest to tomorrow's prints, hairs, and fibers crew. Inside were the sort of groceries he had seen in too many solitary men's homes: cold cuts, a half-consumed package of ground beef, nearly a case of Coors Light, processed cheese in individual slices, a carton of milk that had turned, and another that was about to. A few mysterious liquids in vials labeled with Chinese characters appeared among condiments on the refrigerator door. *More fodder for the state lab's mass spectrometer*, Riley thought.

The freezer held something unspeakable divided into several small, tightly sealed plastic bags. Whether the parts had all come from the same animal, Riley couldn't determine and didn't want to. There was nothing he could recall seeing at any butcher shop. He presumed, or perhaps hoped, that nothing here was edible; he shivered at the likely alternative of experimentation. The contents of two of the bags were still furry. *Rat*, Riley hoped, but he found it hard to avoid thinking *small dog*.

He decided he had better get the worst out of the way, if there were worse sights ahead, and look through the basement. Noting that the cellar windows were tightly sealed he expected a dim and ghoulish scene, but what he came upon instead reminded him of hospitals and laboratories: brightly lit, meticulously organized, all instruments and supplies clearly labeled. The working areas were crowded, but not messy. Several orderly cabinets and a half-height refrigerator held the various chemicals, including the expected poisons.

This was where Lee really lived, Riley thought. *If lived is the word*.

One workbench had so many electronic components, circuit boards, black boxes, and stray unidentifiable parts that

Riley figured the forensics team might take a month to determine all of their functions. Some of the makeshift devices were connected to a state-of-the-art computer; several open manuals on programming, robotics, and hardware interface design hinted at some of the operations under way here. An entire side room held a vast range of machine tools, chem-lab glassware, and a Shop Vac whose nozzle had gathered both metal and wood shavings since the last time it was cleaned. None of the tools mounted on the walls or stored in toolboxes seemed gratuitous; the entire area had the purposeful look of a place where substantial things were accomplished.

Riley had only seen one personal workroom with more extensive equipment. *Jake might have envied some parts of this lab.*

One long, narrow section of the basement had been partitioned off with two-by-fours and sheetrock, with stained mattresses and egg crates attached to the walls and ceiling to provide acoustic insulation. A Walther PPK semi-automatic pistol and a box of ammunition lay on a TV table. The opposite end of the room was ankle deep in broken glass, mostly green. The mattresses affixed to that far wall, three thick, were shredded and stained mostly red. Further examination would turn up no unbroken wine bottles anywhere on the property.

Upstairs, Riley noted, there was little sign that Lee had had any personal life outside the world of his contrivances and computers. Of the house's three bedrooms, only one showed signs of occupancy; another room held workout equipment, and the third stored empty cardboard boxes, plus the empty armoire that the telescoping device had loudly toppled over when police had entered the house. Lee had kept a second, equally powerful PC in his bedroom, with the case removed and assorted tools and expansion-slot boards lying on a table nearby; frequent tinkering with his hardware seemed to be one of his most intimate habits.

Riley steeled himself for discoveries of other intimate habits. The machine was still on, and Riley pulled up the browser to examine Lee's history file. He would have been amazed not to find pornography and, amid arcane financial and research sites he found plenty of it, but what he saw was unlike anything he had seen before. Lee's machine apparently had accounts granting rapid access to the sorts of material that was usually hidden, at least in Riley's previous examinations of perps' computers, behind formidable walls of authentication and security. It took only a few screens of this for Riley to realize that Ellen Green, when the time came for her to add the Lee case to her extensive profiling records, would have to have a heroically strong stomach. Lee's fantasy life—at least Dave hoped it was confined to fantasy—apparently involved children, animals, women who might not be entirely conscious, and assorted implements blunt and sharp.

Riley returned the browser to its homepage and backed away from the computer gingerly, as if from a large rabid animal. He looked elsewhere around the bedroom. Shelving along one wall held a television and assorted audio equipment, but there were no CDs, vinyl records, or cassettes in the room, no prerecorded music in any format, no musical instruments anywhere in the house. The computer and audio amplifier were not wired together, so Riley didn't bother checking the computer for digital audio files. An old-fashioned Teac quarter-inch reel-to-reel tape recorder, with one partially loaded reel and one take-up reel, provided the only apparent source material Lee had been in the habit of listening to. A matching recorder sat nearby, its reels empty. Riley had seen similar rigs in the home studios of musician friends. Two tape decks allowed for primitive multi-tracking.

Riley powered up the amplifier and the first tape machine, making sure the recording function was disarmed. Pressing Play and watching several inches of transparent leader tape move across the heads, followed by the brown recording tape itself, he noticed that the tape bore multiple razor splices at irregular intervals. It had been pieced together by hand. He noticed a single-edged blade and an old Radio Shack tape editing guide on a lower shelf.

The signal began to emerge from the speakers, first a

simple white noise track gradually increasing in volume, from barely perceptible to deafening. Riley turned down the amplifier. The white noise was followed by random radio and television excerpts, shards of commercials and news reports and canned laugh tracks distorted by a range of signal processing devices, soon joined by piercing howls and electronic effects.

"Tonight after the game: is your child's diet providing enough. . . ."

"Investigators were puzzled and shocked today at the horrific discovery of a crude mass grave outside Sheboygan, Wisconsin, in the backyard of a 54-year-old man wanted in connection with the disappearance of . . . ."

"Meow, meow, meow, meow / meow, meow, meow, meow / meow, meow, meow, meow, meowmeowmeowmeow . . . (Tastes so good, your cat will ask for it by name!)"

"Stay tuned for more of the All-New . . . You've Got Your Price!"

Each element in the sound collage would begin, repeat, stutter, change speed and pitch, end abruptly before its message or context made sense, blend into others, and leap unexpectedly into higher or lower registers. Soon, a cacophony of twenty or thirty shifting, bubbling voices competed for the listener's attention. It was madness to hear. It must have taken madness to create.

Two of the repeating voices began to predominate, crowding out the others. Amid resonant newscasters, wailing sirens and children, intolerably perky voiceovers hawking household cleaning products, and studio audiences collectively reacting on cue, Riley thought he recognized certain voices. The ones he recognized eventually rose to the foreground.

"It's been a long time since I've felt this way about anyone. A long time since I've let myself feel anything." A man's voice, a calm and confident baritone, until artificial pitch shifts and warbles turned its repetitions into cackling parodies of itself. Howls of pain, perhaps taken from the soundtrack to a horror film, rose up to surround it.

A woman answered, also in repeating loop patterns. Her

voice was soothing and unimaginably arousing the first dozen or so times Riley heard it.

"Build it. Build me a carousel."

It was Catherine Taylor. Riley had never heard her speak in such low, breathy, inviting tones, and never would. Few had, he was certain. Perhaps only one.

But the couple had not been speaking to each other in the privacy they undoubtedly thought they were enjoying.

Her silken voice did not remain silken here for long. In creating this symphony of vocal shrapnel, Lee had manipulated the tape transport motors, speeding and slowing the recorder so that Catherine's voice accelerated into a hiccuppy helium cartoon, then dropped into a drugged masculine rasp. A chorus of mutant Catherines, soon joined by a battalion of Jakes, surrounded and fragmented her original solitary voice, replacing its beauty with something Riley found deeply unsettling.

Build me a caaaaarrrroooouuuussssssseeeeeellllllll, J-J-J-Jake. Build me – build me anyone anything! – BUILD ME A CAROUbuillllllld me buildme buildme buildme b-b-b-b I'VE NEVER FELT THIS WAY Build me a – long time since – I'veneverfeelanythingCarousel! Jake, build me a CAROUSEL.

With a shudder Riley switched it off. He pictured Daniel Lee lying in this room listening to his handiwork, his repetitive obsessive obscene little tape, focusing on his brother—on Riley's old teammate and lifelong friend—and stewing in a vat of the venom he gave off as naturally as most men sweated or bled. Riley imagined him enjoying his ability to capture something of Jake and Catherine and embed it, embed them, in the degradation that was his natural element. Though it violated all procedure, Riley found himself pocketing the tape, determined to preserve Jake and Catherine's privacy.

The detective made a note to himself to follow up with Jerry DeWinter, the property owner, after all forensic studies at 14 Hickory Street were complete. Whatever DeWinter had done or failed to do from Chicago, Riley knew how information tended to travel in town, how facts became stories, and stories in turn became facts in the marketplace. This house would never be salable. This was a teardown.

CHAPTER FORTY-FOUR

Jake arrived home from the hospital the next morning, armed with a rehab schedule, a pair of crutches, and a handful of prescriptions. Warning him to keep his hobbling around the house to a minimum and to stay out of the workshop, Catherine got him settled in his favorite chair and left for the supermarket.

That evening, she took over the kitchen, cooking him a filling meal, the first he'd had in days. Lighting the Weber on the patio, she prepared a thick New York strip sirloin, grilled medium-rare as Jake liked. The homemade fries that accompanied the steak were twice-cooked at exactly the right oil temperature, and the meal was completed by a salad and Pepperidge Farm Ginger Man cookies. She had previously chosen a bottle of 1985 Heitz Martha's Vineyard Cabernet Sauvignon from Jake's cellar, after assuring herself that the alcohol in the wine would not conflict with his medicine. Jake wondered whether she had any idea of the wine's $300 value. However, at this moment, value was not an issue. They had much to celebrate, after all. Besides, the wine was perfect with the steak. Those facts notwithstanding, Jake made a mental note to commence her wine education. Soon.

After dinner, waiting for Riley to arrive, Catherine poured two glasses of Fonseca 1977 Vintage Port, and they each sipped.

"What time did Riley say he was coming?" Jake asked her impatiently. "Boy, I wish I'd been there to see what they discovered in Lee's house."

Catherine took his hand. "You know, even though I saw the DNA reports with my own eyes, I still can't accept that this man could have been your twin. Do you believe what he said?"

"I do," Jake said slowly. "I think I do. It's not physically impossible, and it's consistent with the facts we know. As much as I don't like it, I have to believe it." He measured his words as if each one cost him something he wasn't sure he could afford. "Do you?"

"Medically, I can accept it," Catherine said. "There aren't a lot of cases of interval delivery, but there are a few. More now that more hospitals have neonatal ICUs. Obstetricians induce it sometimes in difficult multiple pregnancies. A high-risk preemie goes into intensive care, and the healthier fetus is retained for the full term. It's one of those subjects they don't spend much time on in med school. If you aren't going into that specialty, you usually file it away, figuring you'll never see one. As a general surgeon, I have pretty low odds of encountering it.

"But it wasn't really news to me; I'd first run across it in an old book of my father's." Catherine smiled at the recollection. "*Anomalies and Curiosities of Medicine*, by the good, ghoulish Doctors Gould and Pyle. It was something from the late Victorian days, full of things a lot stranger than multiple births a few weeks or months apart. Monsters, real ones, dating way back before thalidomide. And there were pictures. Strictly off limits to minors in Dr. Taylor's respectable household, so naturally when I was about twelve I practically memorized the thing. I'd sneak into Dad's study to read it when he was at work, and I had the bad dreams to show for it. What Lee told you is freaky, but plausible.

"As far as believing his story on the human level, though . . . believing he could be your brother . . . ." At this Catherine shuddered, and her voice trailed off. Jake wasn't surprised that she left the sentence unfinished.

"I keep wondering what would have happened if my parents hadn't gone on that trip," he said. "What if he'd been born here? What if he'd not been injured? Or, even if he were born there, what if he'd been adopted legally, not sold like livestock? God, flip a switch at any point and his life, my life, everything would have been entirely different."

"It's not likely, and it's definitely not your fault,"

Catherine said.

"I know. Guilt of any sort is not going to do any good." He paused. "The funny thing is, I always wanted a brother," he added softly.

Catherine waited, sipping her Port.

"Obviously, though, what matters is that his killing has stopped." He took a slow drink and stared outside for a moment, lost in reflection. He was looking northeast. "If one of us had to die in that warehouse, I'm glad it was him."

"Not much objection here," Catherine said.

"You may think this pretty cold, but I guess, at the end of the day, he's not a real brother to me. More of an oddity, something from your dad's book.

At that moment, Dave Riley opened the door without ringing the bell and walked into the room. "Ready for a little company?" he asked with a smile. Catherine poured him a glass of the Port, and Riley eased into a chair.

Taking in the crutches leaning against the table, he asked, "How long will you be out of action?"

"Dave, sorry to be crashing through the starting gate here, but let's skip the pleasantries if we can," Jake begged. "What did you find in Riverside?"

Riley didn't take long switching hats from old pal to chief of detectives. "Right. We took that house apart room by room. Lee had apparently been living there for several years, unseen by anybody including the landlord, and he'd built his own private world in there. Some of it you might not want to know much about.

"First the practical findings, though. We found maps, notes, lots of leads, and lists of wine lovers on his computer, as well as documents that link him to some pretty dodgy sources of supplies and even dodgier sources of income. He had a well-equipped workshop and mini-laboratory in the cellar. Chemistry, electronic gizmos, programming, the whole nine yards. He'd prepared himself in auxiliary fields, too: for example, we found a set of professional-grade locksmith's tools, and he clearly had the skills to put them to use. The crazy thing is that the shop and lab kinda reminded me of yours, though much smaller, of course.

"He was paying for all of it with his MIT mathematical skills, basically some statistical analytic work for marketing organizations of varying levels of legitimacy and, more recently some consulting for outfits based overseas that don't look legit at all. All freelance, all online, all off the books. Very little contact with anybody who might compromise his cover.

"In some respects it looks like he was operating as a one man university for parts of the Russian mob—showing them how to cook up bogus earnings for their investors, shuffle funds around through phantom companies to hide the tracks, and leave a lot of gullible investors in the dust. We don't know much about that world yet except that it's pretty close to lawless. The amounts of money circulating there are staggering, and the whole country has damn few people with much experience in legal and honest investment. It's the perfect atmosphere for a guy like Lee with big skills and zero scruples.

"There was even a diary. He seemed pretty cocky about not being found out, at least while he was still pulling this stuff off. Our guess is that he intended to reveal it all once the whole thing ended. He didn't want to be stopped, of course, but he definitely wanted us to know. He was here, right under our noses, the whole time."

"I'd like to see the house and shop when I can get around a little better," responded Jake. "Sort of a final chapter on the life of a brother I never knew about." He poured a refill for Catherine.

"We can arrange that. Whenever you're ready. But brace yourself for some grim sights. Among the things discovered in Lee's house were his city-by-city plans for more killings." Riley continued, "Destruction literally all the way to the end of the alphabet. There's no Connecticut town beginning with X, so his plans included twenty-five towns. Then, as he intimated, he was coming after you, his twenty-sixth candidate, with some real grand ideas for a bang-up finale.

"I don't mean to alarm either of you, but, Jake, his

fixation on you had reached the point of clinical obsession. Among other things, he'd recorded your voices in private moments, and I'm not at all sure the equipment we found in the tree could have done that at a distance. What he did with the tapes is a sound I never want to hear again, and I don't recommend it to you, either.

Catherine shook her head in disbelief. "Toying with us. Ugh—it seems like such a violation." She looked at Jake. "I might have lost you."

"Never" Jake smiled and then said to Riley, "It sounds as if he planned this spree pretty meticulously."

"Even the names of potential victims were there," Riley went on. "When you locate each of his designated towns or cities on a map, they're dozens of miles apart. We're guessing that Lee must have anticipated the spread-out nature of his targets would mean his individual actions would be less likely to be linked."

Catherine threw another idea up for consideration. "That may even explain why he picked something as obvious as the alphabet as his organizing principle: it's instant randomization, as in the design of a clinical trial, on a statewide level. No time wasted making complicated decisions."

"We were very lucky to discover the wine connection early on," Riley said. "In hindsight, that was a major shortcut to locating him, although it sure didn't seem so at the time. Otherwise, he might have continued killing people and destroying wine for years."

"I told Cat about the makeup of the poison," Jake offered.

Riley turned to Catherine. "Do you have any thoughts about Lee's psychological profile? Ellen is going to have a field day with all the material he left behind, but I'd be interested in your take, as well. His story is fodder for a real thriller. Hannibal Lecter, step aside." He waited for Catherine to respond.

"You're joking, but I can tell you this. I spent several months in a psych rotation in med school. That wasn't a lot of time, and it was a good number of years ago, but I was especially interested in learning about psychopaths who seemed to be quite normal. The out-and-out bloodthirsty animals just repel me, but the others are oddly fascinating, and, of course, much more dangerous. Considering what little I know about him, that certainly includes Lee.

"Did you ever hear of a book published back in 1941 called *The Mask of Sanity* by Hervey Cleckley, MD? Psychopaths are almost always, by definition, mentally ill, but Cleckley focused on those who outwardly appeared to be sane, exactly like Lee. He was skilled at using his talents in horrible ways, but from what you told me, there seems to have been the emotional hollowness of the true psychopath in all his actions.

"He also exactly met the definition of a serial killer— time between assaults and more than three of them, although there didn't seem to be obvious sexual overtones, at least that have been discovered. Rachel Charleson might be considered an exception. But leaving her naked may have just been a vehicle to aid an easy police diagnosis, with the real reason for her death being the horrible embalming. He beat her brutally, suffocated her, and filled her with cabernet, but he didn't rape her."

She paused. Jake thought he noticed her holding her breath.

"Was he crazy?" asked Riley.

"Crazy is an imprecise word," responded Cat. "He was a psychopath. He was mentally ill, unstable in his reasoning and utterly uncivilized in both his goals and his methods. There were deficits in his functioning. To him, the only purpose in his life was to get back at everything and everyone that shaped it, and the only way to get back at his family and his birth parents was symbolic."

She paused, looked at Riley, and then added, in a somber voice, "I can't get what happened in that warehouse out of my mind. I just keep thinking that, if it weren't for your getting there when you did, Jake wouldn't be here now."

"All in the line of duty, ma'am," Riley replied, looking away.